Veteran & Elder Stories

Uncharted Times and Unfamiliar Places
(1971-2020)

by

Hanna A. Saadah

Gratitude

My gratitude to my chief editor and wife, Judith Saadah, who encouraged and inspired me, designed and painted the book cover, gave me the space-time I needed to write and revise, and patiently waited until I was ready to share each story with her.

My sincere thanks to my editorial group—Angela (Angle) and Gregory Peck, Mari and Arnold Fagin, Terry Flaugher, and Joe Baughn—who have spent weeks picking typos and critiquing my work.

My thanks also to our photographer, Mackenzie Ford, who after numerous photo efforts, was able to produce the final cover picture, which met with everyone's approval.

And above all, my life-long gratitude to all the Veterans and elders who trusted me as captain of their health and chanter of their unsung lives.

Book Reviews

Veteran and Elder Stories is a riveting book replete with happiness, tragedy, pathos, and humor. These stories, which reflect the soaring human spirit, are desperately needed at this time of national turmoil. They fill an echoing vacuum with inspiring tales that celebrate the collective sacrifices of our individual Veterans and elders.

Dr. Saadah, a brilliant wordsmith, writes with high feelings, empathy, and clarity, making it hard to close the book before it is finished.

Arnold Fagin, Veteran and Attorney at Law.

Dr. Saadah's collection, *Veteran & Elder Stories*, celebrates the trying travails of our Veterans and Elders. Each story is unique in its cast of characters and events but one constant thread throughout is that wars do not end when peace treaties are signed.

Growing up in war-torn Lebanon has sensitized Saadah to the personal struggles and sacrifices of Veterans, inspiring him to commemorate their experiences in this fascinating collection.

Saadah's river-flowing sentences, startling poetic splashes, and spiritual explorations caused me to devour the entire book in just two days. It was, indeed, an epiphanic read.

Terry Flaugher, Vietnam Veteran and Attorney at Law.

The author has done it again. An excellent collection of short stories connecting the life of the author as a highly respected medical professional with the lives of Veterans and their families. Unveiling the devastating effects of war on Veterans, both young and old, this book is a must read.

J. G. Baughn, U.S. Navy, Vietnam Combat Veteran.

Dedication

For all the Veterans and elders

Past and present, living and dead

This high, red-white-and-blue opus

Will remain a flying squadron

Of our collective gratitude.

Table of Contents

II. Community (1977 – 2019)

III. Lebanon (1951 – 1996)

Prologue

I began my medical career as an internal medicine resident at the Muskogee VA Hospital in 1971. I am continuing my career—at the Department of Geriatrics, Oklahoma City VA Hospital and the Oklahoma University Health Sciences Center—as Emeritus Clinical Professor of Medicine. During the past half century, I have encountered numerous Veterans and elders, and have chronicled their life-inspiring stories.

"A teacher affects eternity; he can never tell where his influence stops," said Henry Adams.[1] The same can be said of Veterans and elders who also affect eternity and can never tell where their influence stops.

To immortalize these life-changing experiences vouchsafed to us by our Veterans and elders, I have turned their individual stories into high literature, because written words outlive us all, as was so well expressed by Lord Byron in his epic poem, *Don Juan.*[2]

> *But words are things, and a small drop of ink,*
> *Falling like dew, upon a thought, produces*
> *That which makes thousands, perhaps millions, think;*
> *'Tis strange, the shortest letter which man uses*
> *Instead of speech, may form a lasting link*
> *Of ages; to what straits old Time reduces*
> *Frail man, when paper - even a rag like this -*
> *Survives himself, his tomb, and all that's his.*

The subtitle of this book, *Uncharted Times and Unfamiliar Places*, comes from *Familiar Faces*, a love poem I

---

[1] Henry Adams (1838-1918), American Historian.
[2] Lord Gorge Gordon Byron (1788-1824), British poet.

had written in youth and published in a book of verse also called *Familiar Faces*.

> *Familiar faces*
> *Let us not pretend*
> *Though life may decimate and send*
> *Our unsuspecting souls across*
> *Uncharted times and unfamiliar places*
> *Wherever we are loved we end.*

This book holds a total of 38 stories, divided into three sections:

I. Twenty-one stories took place at Oklahoma Veterans Affairs Hospitals between 1971 and 2020.

II. Thirteen stories took place in the community between 1977 and 2019.

III. Four stories took place in Lebanon between 1951 and 1996.

All 38 stories were inspired by realities but have been fictionalized, embellished, and camouflaged beyond recognition to protect identities.

Any resemblance to any reality should be seen as the reader's perception rather than the writer's intention.

I Am A Veteran[3]
Sonnet 110

I joined, I served, I fell, I bled, I cried
So runs a soldier's journey on the roam
Homeless but lives in flashbacks of the mind
To strive, to seek, but oft to find no home.

Explosions violate souls-sanctified
Cohabit, uninvited, with the heart
Erupt long after dynamite had died
And sunder faith-filled families apart.

Time takes away the pleasure not the pain
Pain grows like flames until the fire ends
When death, more merciful than living rain
Comes home to summon heroes to their friends.

I'm a Veteran who gave and yet still gives
So long as love forgives, and conscience lives.

Hanna Saadah

---

[3] I composed this sonnet specifically for this book.

The Doctor Harrison[4]
Muskogee VAH, 1971

No matter how meticulously we plan and plot our lives, if we survive long enough, we will come to realize that our precious lives have been almost entirely shaped and reshaped by the wild winds of coincidence. We are the products of our times, places, genes, and happenstances—all of which are naught but coincidences beyond our control. However, forging opportunities out of happenstances is within our power, and those forged opportunities might grant us novel means to reshape our otherwise immutable destinies.

"While we speak, envious time will have already fled: carpe diem, seize the day, trusting as little as possible in the next day," urges Ovid in his *Odes*. Balance that with Louis Pasteur's adage, *"In the fields of observation, coincidence favors not but the prepared minds,"* and one can begin to apprehend the intricate clockworks of destiny.

At the medical school of The American University of Beirut, four *bibles* were, and continue to be, in perpetual circulation. I use the word, *bible*, un-capitalized, to mean tome, and to point out its root, Byblos, the Phoenician-Lebanese city from whose shore papyrus was exported, and which gave its name to the Greek nouns: *biblion*-book, and *byblos*-books.

The four *bibles* that shaped our lives as medical students were the Old & New Testaments, the Koran, and Harrison's Principles of Internal Medicine.

*

---

[4] Pre-published, *Journal of the Oklahoma State Medical Association*, January 2016.

When, in 1971, I came to Oklahoma, my Arabic Bible and Harrison's Principles of Internal Medicine accompanied me all the way from Beirut to Muskogee (circa 11,000 kilometers) for it was at the Muskogee VAH that I was to begin my internal medicine residency. During those B-C years, meaning those *Before-Computer years*, Harrison's tome was my life, especially during the first few months of residency when my medical confidence was thinner than rain.

I still remember the conversation I had with our Chief of Medicine, Dr. Phipps, in September of that year. We had just finished rounds when he said, "This patient would be interesting to present at our upcoming Grand Rounds."

"He had an uneventful myocardial infarction," I protested. "What makes him so special?"

"Because Dr. Harrison will be our speaker, and his main interest is cardiovascular disease."

"Dr. Harrison?" I inquired. "Have you recruited a new cardiologist?"

"No," he smirked. "I'm talking about Dr. Tinsley Randolph Harrison. Does the name ring a bell?"

"Am I supposed to know him?" I asked with a sheepish voice.

"He's the founder and editor of *Harrison's Principles of Internal Medicine*, the book which never leaves your side."

"Oh," I gasped, with awe-stricken face.

"Start working on your case presentation for next week's Grand Rounds. You will have ten minutes to present."

I spent that evening in our two-bed intensive care unit reviewing Mr. Morgan's chart. He came in the night before with a small inferior myocardial infarction but had good vital signs. Sublingual Nitroglycerine and intravenous Lidocaine took care of his chest pain and arrhythmias, and he quickly stabilized. Dr. Phipps favored keeping him monitored in the ICU for two more days before moving him to a regular room.

We planned his discharge for the day after Grand Rounds, just in case Dr. Harrison would want to visit him.

During that apprehension-riddled week, I lost my appetite, and my hyperbolic anxiety deprived me of restorative sleep. I spent my nights rehearsing Mr. Morgan's medical details, re-editing my ten-minute presentation, reading about arteriosclerosis, and preparing my mind to respond with confidence to questions, which Dr. Harrison might hurl at me.

*

At Grand Rounds, Dr. Morley and I were the only two medicine residents present. There were no other residents, no interns, and no students during those *lean years* because the Muskogee VAH had just started functioning as a teaching hospital. The rest of the meager audience in the conference room was made up of staff physicians, physician assistants, nurses, and the librarian.

Dr. Harrison—lean, cheerful, unassuming, and simply dressed—sat with Dr. Phipps in the front row. Dr. Phipps opened with a brief extolment of Dr. Tinsley Randolph Harrison's legacy: his birth in Alabama in 1900, his medical education at Johns Hopkins, his chief residency at Vanderbilt, his consummate interest in cardiovascular disease, and his innumerable research and teaching activities. He then ended with this panegyric: "Professor, Dean, Chairman, Distinguished Physician of the United States Veterans Administration, holder of the torch of Osler, founding editor of the most influential, most international, best-selling textbook of medicine in history—he has and continues to spend his life in the insatiable pursuit of knowledge, excellence, and patient care." Then, before our gaping eyes, he held up for all to see, the first edition of *Harrison's Principles of Internal Medicine* published in 1950, and he then read the first paragraph from the first page:

No greater opportunity, responsibility, or obligation can fall to the lot of a human being than to become a physician. In the care of the suffering he needs technical skill, scientific knowledge, and human understanding. He who uses these with courage, with humility, and with wisdom will provide a unique service for his fellow men and will build an enduring edifice of character within himself. The physician should ask of his destiny no more than this: he should be content with no less.

As I stood up, after this awe-inspiring tribute, to present my case, Dr. Harrison smiled at me and lit a cigarette. Dr. Phipps followed suit and so did others in the audience. In 1971, smoking was fashionable at medical and intellectual gatherings.

When my presentation ended, leaving me with wet palms and a thudding chest, Dr. Harrison stood up and, with a shimmering Georgian accent, asked, "Did you do a rectal examination on this 60-year-old Veteran with an inferior myocardial infarction?"

"No, Sir," I replied with confidence.

"Why not?" He grinned. "It is a necessary part of the complete physical examination."

"It is contraindicated during acute myocardial infarction, Sir, because it can trigger brady-arrhythmias."

"Good answer." He grinned again. "But, don't forget to do it before discharge," he forewarned.

Then, with utter humility, this great doctor, author, researcher, and mentor, began his discussion about the risk factors of arteriosclerosis. He discoursed on hypertension, diabetes, obesity, hyperlipidemia, sedentariness, stress, and— as he lit one more cigarette—smoking. When, after an erudite presentation, he opened the floor for discussion, my hand went up first.

"Yes, young man," he grinned, looking at me with questing eyebrows, as he blew smoke into the air.

"Sir," I began with a scattered voice. "If smoking causes arteriosclerosis, why are you still smoking?"

"Young man," he grinned again, looking at the cigarette, pluming in his hand. "How old are you?"

"I'm 25 Sir," I answered with a blush.

"Well, I'm 71 and the best thing that can happen to a Veteran like me, at this point of life, would be a heart attack. I have little to lose and much to gain by dying with unscathed dignity. He followed his rationale with a quote from Shakespeare's *As You Like It:*

> *Last scene of all*
> *That ends this strange eventful history*
> *Is second childishness and mere oblivion*
> *Sans teeth, sans eyes, sans taste, sans everything.*[5]

Then, looking intently into my eyes, he admonished with fatherly kindness. "You, on the other hand, have a whole life to lose. Don't start because, once you begin smoking, you'll find it very difficult to quit."

I did not know if I should smile or frown. The smokers in the room chuckled and nodded their approval. Dr. Phipps saved the moment when he stood up, thanked Dr. Harrison, and concluded the conference with this question:

"Dr. Harrison. What is the single, most valuable advice you can give to our doctors in training?"

Without a hint of hesitation, Dr. Harrison replied, "Be thorough. Be thorough at any cost. Never resort to shortcuts

---

[5] *As You Like It*, Jaques, *All the world's a stage*, William Shakespeare.

to save time. Saving time, at the expense of quality, can prove deadly to your patients and to your reputation."

*

Before I discharged Mr. Morgan, I told him that I needed to do a rectal exam to complete his admission medical examination. He refused. I insisted and informed him that if he did not allow me to complete my medical examination, I would have to discharge him against medical advice, which could have dire health consequences. After a tense debate, he acquiesced, and upon preforming the examination, I discovered a rectal mass, which surprised both him and me, and radically changed our contentious views. We both felt like we had just dodged a sniper's bullet. A sudden friendship erupted in our eyes, the friendship that binds strangers when, together, they narrowly escape death.

His rectal cancer was successfully resected at a later date, and at discharge, he thanked me for being more stubborn than he was.

"Your stubbornness has saved my life, Doc," he intoned as he shook my hand.

"You can thank Dr. Harrison for that," I teased.

"Who's Doctor Harrison?" He asked with a confused aspect.

"He is the author of our medical textbook."

"And what does he teach y'all in this book of his?"

"He teaches that a doctor should be thorough, thorough at any cost, and should never resort to shortcuts to save time because saving time at the expense of quality can prove deadly."

*

Dr. Harrison's wish of dying, with dignity unscathed, was granted and he eluded that last scene of *second childishness and mere oblivion.*

Fearless, he rejected hospitalization and died peacefully at home, in 1978, from a massive anterior myocardial infarction. [6] His influence, however, continues to live on through those who had the fortune of knowing him, and through all the future generations that will continue to be educated by his phoenix book.

"The chief event of life is the day in which we have encountered a mind that startled us," said Ralph Waldo Emerson. I am a living example of this adage.

Dr. Harrison's textbook still ranks, uncontested, among today's medical tomes and continues to instruct doctors all over the world. As Henry Adams[7] said, *"A teacher affects eternity; he can never tell where his influence stops."*

---

[6] *Tinsley Harrison, M.D., Teacher of Medicine,* Biography by James A. Pittman Jr., M.D., 2015.

[7] Henry Brooks Adams, American historian and member of the Adams political family.

8

Shooing Hallucinations[8]
Oklahoma City VAH, 1972

It happened unexpectedly, like a lightning bolt in fair weather. But 1972 was that kind of year—the Vietnam War was raging, I was new to America, and I had never heard of DTs.

In Lebanon, we watched the Vietnam War explode on the black-and-white screens, but the war remained distant from our hearts and misunderstood by our minds. We had our own social problems then, our own wars to comprehend, and our own defeats to accept. America, on the other hand, was our El Dorado, the open-armed land from whose bosom all knowledge flowed, and from whose breasts all humanity fed. It was the mighty beacon of science to which we all flocked to specialize after finishing our medical training at the American University of Beirut.

Alcoholism in Lebanon was socially contained. Every town had its few *drinkers* who were contained by their families and friends. Moreover, it was legal for families to make their own *arak* (a distilled alcohol made from grapes) and there was plenty of it. It was also sold everywhere, even in the minutest grocery stores, and there was no age limit for buying it. Kids were allowed to drink it and often did so on festive occasions. Because it was so widely available, alcoholics never ran out of drinks, DTs were unheard of, and the term was unfamiliar to my ears.

As a first-year resident in medicine, I was re-assigned to the Oklahoma City VA Hospital in 1972, and my first day on the service was also my first night on call. I was busy admitting two new patients when my pager screamed, "Doctor, you're

---

[8] Pre-published, *The Bulletin*, Oklahoma County Medical Society, November-December 2014.

needed on 5-North. Immediately." I darted out of the emergency department, ran up the stairs, and, when I reached 5-North, I found Head-Nurse Stalwart pacing in front of the elevators, waiting for me.

"Oh, you used the stairs."
"It sounded urgent."
"You're the resident on call?"
"Yes, ma'am."
"I hope you can handle this situation because we can't."

On the way to Room 505, Nurse Stalwart went over the details and handed me Mr. Bowser's chart.

"He's a Vietnam Veteran who took to heavy drinking after he returned and has been at it for several months. His wife and two daughters finally gave him the ultimatum and told him that if he did not quit, they were going to leave him. He stopped drinking five days ago and started to go crazy on them the day before yesterday. He was admitted at four o'clock today and has all the right PRN orders, but we can't get to him to start an IV or to administer his Valium and Thorazine."

"And why can't you get to him?"

"He's in pretty bad DTs and thinks that a pack of dogs is after him."

"DTs?"

"Yes!"

"What are DTs?"

Nurse Stalwart rolled back her eyes as she exclaimed, "Oh God, don't tell me…"

"No need for alarm, Ma'am." I interrupted. "I can handle it if you will just tell me what the initials stand for."

"Delirium Tremens."

"What's that?"

Nurse Stalwart lowered her eyeglasses down her nose, took one piercing look at me, and with a [*sic*] matronizing tone inquired, "How old are you, Son?"

"Twenty-five," I mumbled, feeling a bit intimidated.

"And you've never heard of DTs?"

"We must not have them in Lebanon," I sheepishly answered.

"Lebanon? You've no alcoholics over there?"

"Oh, we have some, of course."

"And what happens to them when they stop drinking?"

"They don't stop drinking. In my hometown, Amioun, there are three *drinkers*—for that's what we call them over there—and they're always drunk. I've never known any of them to stop drinking."

My innocent answer must have touched a motherly nerve in Nurse Stalwart's heart. Slowly, her frowns gave way to a faint gleam that glowed underneath her concerned aspect. I could almost hear her heart whisper, *"What's this poor little man from Lebanon going to do when he sees what awaits him in Room 505?"*

Walking toward 505, she took my arm and began educating me.

"When heavy drinkers stop drinking suddenly, they develop an alcohol-withdrawal syndrome with agitation, confusion, hallucinations, body shakes, rapid pulse, high blood pressure, etc. They basically go temporarily mad, but after we hydrate them and sedate them for a few days, they come out of it and go back home."

"What do you sedate them with?"

"His admitting doctor's orders say to give him IV fluids, IV Valium, and IM Thorazine[9] but, in case you didn't hear me say it, we're unable to get close enough to him to treat him."

---

[9] An antipsychotic.

"And why's that?"

"Because he's combative and thinks that the dogs are after him. That's why I paged you, Doctor."

That was the last thing she said to me before we entered Room 505. In spite of feeling profoundly ignorant, my state of mind when I walked in and surveyed the scene was inappropriately comfortable. It was merciful that youth had endowed me with an exaggerated sense of aptitude. Consequently, I took immediate charge of Operation Dogs without having the necessary knowledge to guide me. All that propelled me at that most strained moment were sheer confidence and blind faith.

During my last year in Beirut, I had amputated limbs, injected adrenalin into arrested hearts, intubated lungs, and gone without sleep for 48 hours at a time. Casualties arrived in droves, it seemed, when I was on emergency call. So, what could be worse, I thought.

But here in America people are giants. The man stood like a colossus, twice my size, holding the room's corner with his back, thrashing like a cornered lion at anyone who dared come close to him. His eyes were bulging, red, and paranoid. He was drooling at the mouth and roaring at the top of his lungs, "Get away from me you bastards. Go away. Go on. Shoo. Shoo."

I had never seen a more massive man in my life. He looked like he could bite a tree in half and use it for toothpicks. Several orderlies and nurses hugged the walls, wearing frightened aspects and serrated lips. Chaos flickered everywhere like the lights of a police car in a crowd.

When I walked in, for some reason, everyone stood still. I must have looked ridiculously minute before that mad giant. Nevertheless, even *he* stood still, as if at attention, and waited for me to say something. At that eerie instant, the last words of my mother echoed in my ears: *"Go on to America, Son. I have prayed for you and know that God will take good care of you. Just listen to him when you are in trouble and he will guide you."*

"God's on my side," I thought, as I approached *Goliath* with not even a sling in my hand. When our eyes met, I could see dread in his eyes, and he must have seen kindness in mine because he did not seem to mind the fact that I had gotten too close to him. Stopping at about five feet away, I asked, "What's bothering you, Sir?"

"These damn hounds," he roared, pointing at the empty corner to the left of the door. "They're rabid and aim to bite me. Just don't let them get any closer. Shoo them away. They're mad. Mad dogs. All seven of them."

I surveyed the room. There was an IV pole with a liter of intravenous fluid hanging from it. I looked at all the stunned faces for a hint, a tacit suggestion, but all I saw were the blank looks of astonishment and awe. I was a little man, alone, unarmed, in the middle of an arena, with seven rabid dogs and a mad giant glaring at me. The only thought that came to my mind at that most strained moment was Dr. William Osler's adage, *"Listen to your patient; he's telling you the diagnosis."*[10] All of a sudden, the giant's words came back to me like an epiphany: *"These damn hounds. They're rabid and aim to bite me. Just don't let them get any closer. Shoo them away. They're mad. Mad dogs. All seven of them."*

My external calm and small stature belied the aggression that I was about to evince. With sudden, ostentatious might, I grabbed the tall IV pole, shook off the dangling liter of IV fluid, and charged the rabid pack of dogs

---

[10] Sir William Osler (1849-1919) doctor, professor, author, teacher, humanitarian, and researcher.

like a Roman gladiator with a long spear. I thrashed and darted, parried and lunged, emitting fierce battle cries, scoring one fatal stab after another. "One out of seven, two out of seven, three out of seven," I shouted as I battled the rabid pack single handedly, until I had exterminated all seven of them. When I said, "Seven out of seven," I threw the IV pole onto the floor as if it were a bloody spear, and, dripping with sweat, looked to the giant for approval.

He began screaming again, "Doc. Doc. There's one more behind you. One more. Get him. Get him. Get him before he gets you and me."

I quickly picked up the IV pole and darted again and again at where he was pointing until his screams died down. Then, still holding the IV pole in my hand, I looked to him again for approval. This time, his red eyes were no longer bulging, and he had the hint of a smile on his exhausted face. I approached him with an extended hand, which he shook with gratitude. Then, leading him to his bed, I said, "The nurses need to start your IV treatment, Sir, so that you can get well and go home."

The next morning, as my team and I were making rounds with our attending physician, Mr. Bowser actually waved at me as we passed Room 505. He looked calm, was eating breakfast, and his eyes were no longer red. Nurses in the halls giggled as we passed them. Our attending, Dr. Neighbor, seemed a bit annoyed and asked, "What's going on? Did something happen that I don't know about?"

"Nothing of significance, Sir," I reassured. "Last night I had to shoo away a hallucination and Head-Nurse Stalwart must have reported the incident in her nurse's notes."

"How interesting?" he smirked. "Shoo away a hallucination? What on earth do you mean by that?"

"It's nothing but silliness, Sir. Mr. Bowser had DTs last night and believed that rabid dogs were after him."

"And, what did you do?"

"I shooed them away."

"And how did you do that?"

"With an IV pole."

"Shooed them away with an IV pole?" He repeated as he shook his head with disbelief. "Is that what you normally do in Lebanon?"

"No, Sir. In Lebanon our *drinkers* don't have DTs because they never stop drinking."

"Perhaps you could enlighten your team and me as to why the Lebanese drunks don't ever stop drinking."

"Could I do that some other time, Sir?" I pleaded with a blush, while glancing at my watch. "I have six new patients to present to you before the ten o'clock Residents' Conference begins."

*

The next time I was on call, Head-Nurse Stalwart approached me with a grin and said, "I don't quite understand how you knew what to do when you had never seen DTs before? So many of those who were present are wondering the same thing."

"I really didn't know what to do when I walked into that room. Mr. Bowser was the one who gave me the clue."

"I was there, remember? I heard everything he said, and he never said anything sensible."

"Oh, yes he did, but you must have failed to comprehend it."

"And what was it that *'I failed to comprehend'*, Doctor?"

"He said, *'Shoo them away.'* and so I did exactly as he asked."

Search Behind the Disease[11]
Oklahoma City VAH, 1973

"No matter how bright the physician, illness is always smarter. Like an onion, under every layer lurks yet another and another mystery... We peel and peel but seldom get to the core."

These were Dr. Muchhammer's humbling remarks to us, his internal medicine team at the VA Hospital. On that day in 1973, upon hearing his declaration, we all froze with awe before our attending physician—as if he were the Oracle of Delphi, pontificating from the southern slopes of Mount Parnassus.

"To become good doctors, you have but to know two things, he declared:
"First, you have to know the patient, who will always remain a half-solved mystery, no matter how much he reveals to you because no patient ever tells everything.
"Second, you must know the disease otherwise you would not be able to ask the key, unlocking questions. And disease will also remain a half-solved mystery, because it continues to change with theory and discovery."

With these precepts, Dr. Muchhammer led us on rounds, stroked patients' brows, asked infrared questions, peeled layer after layer, and then helped us deepen our shallow analyses. We yearned to learn how did he know to ask the one question that we never thought to ask, and how did he manage to unveil for us to see—*"And see, no longer blinded by our eyes"*[12]—the inscrutable diagnoses with hardly a test or an x-ray in hand.

---

[11] Pre-published, *The Bulletin*, Oklahoma County Medical Society, September-October 2015.

[12] From the *South Seas* Sonnet by Rupert Brooke (1887-1915) British Poet.

One dark winter morning, abuzz with admissions, we presented our cases with sleep-deprived eyes and yawning jaws, for we had admitted ten patients during our night shift. Presenting our last elderly patient, I happened to mention that he was a perennial seeker of emergency care.

"Perennial?" He asked with raised eyebrows.

"Yes, Sir. He is admitted through our emergency department about once a month, always with the same complaint, shortness of breath. His blood gases from admission till discharge stay about the same, with no measurable improvement, but he always feels better when he leaves. His emphysema has been rather stable even though he continues to smoke."

"Why, then, does he seek monthly admissions?"

"I don't know, Sir," I sheepishly replied. "I've reviewed his entire chart of five volumes but could find no clues. He seems ever the same, admission after admission, and his blood gases have never been alarming."

Dr. Muchhammer stood up, placed his palm onto the patient's piled, five-volume chart, scrutinized our listless aspects with his glittering eyes, and asked, "Did you search behind the disease?"

"Behind the disease, Sir? I'm not sure I understand what you mean."

"Search behind the disease," he muttered, and walked away.

At the dragging tail of that laborious day, my team and I went over the patient's details, re-examined and re-questioned him, but unearthed nothing of value. My intern suggested that we visit his home to look for dust, mold, sick house syndrome, and whatever else might be hiding behind his disease. The patient granted us permission. We called his wife from his room and set our visit for the coming Saturday.

Mrs. Poumon was delightfully hospitable. She gave us a tour of her very clean house and of Mr. Poumon's equally clean woodcarving shop. "That's where he spends all of his time," she announced, pointing to his stool, table, and tidy tools. "Ever since he returned from the war, that's all he wants to do. He was much more sociable before."

Sipping coffee and munching on doughnuts, we asked Mrs. Poumon various questions but uncovered no clues. On our way out, my intern asked her that one last question, which none of us thought to ask.

"Mrs. Poumon. Does the wood dust bother you, and do you cough or wheeze or suffer from any lung problems?"

"No, I feel mighty fine and Harry hardly makes any dust. I just wish he would spend more time with me and less time in his shop," she smiled, holding the doorknob in her hand. "We hardly go anywhere anymore."

Crestfallen, we thanked her and dispersed, with the impending Monday-morning rounds, nagging at our brains.

When Dr. Muchhammer walked in that Monday morning, he must have seen capitulation in our eyes because he asked no questions. He half-smiled and said, "Let's start with Mr. Poumon."

Sitting on Mr. Poumon's bed, Dr. Muchhammer greeted, said few words of encouragement, and then abruptly asked, "What war were you in?"

"Pearl Harbor, Sir. We didn't know we were at war when the Japs hailed their bombs on us."

"What was your position?"

"We were Antiaircraft Gunners on the USS Nevada, Sir."

"We?"

"Me and my buddy. James Lovelorn was his name."

"Was?"

"Under the orders of Ensign Joe Taussig Jr., we were returning fire against bombers that were targeting us when we sustained a direct hit from a torpedo. Parts of the ship started to burn, smoke was everywhere, and..."

At this point, Mr. Poumon choked, gulped, and his lips began to quiver. We stood in silence and watched Dr. Muchhammer grasp Mr. Poumon's hand, bow his head as if in prayer, and whisper, "And what happened to James?"

Mr. Poumon collected himself, cleared his throat, adjusted his oxygen nasal prongs, and whispered back, "Shrapnel beheaded him while he sat right next to me, Doc. There he was, sitting without a head, his body twitching, with blood spewing from his neck like a geyser..."

Another moment of silence.

Dr. Muchhammer handed a tissue to Mr. Poumon and waited.

Mr. Poumon, after a stuttering pause, continued.

"I began to choke on the bellowing smoke but continued to return fire until I was blown into the harbor and began to drown. I held on to a floating body, which happened to have its life vest on. *Underwater I would drown. Overwater I would choke and burn with the burning oil.* That's all I could think about while I clung to that dead man's life vest."

Another moment of silence.

"And who rescued you?"
"I have no idea, Doc. I woke up on a hospital ship with burns all over my body and a horrible heat in my lungs."
"May I see your burns?" Asked Dr. Muchhammer.
Mr. Poumon pulled up his sleeves and uncovered his legs for us to see.

"The burns were superficial, Sir, but what got me was the smoke. I coughed for years and I'm still coughing, but not nearly as bad as before. About once a month, though, when I get into a bad coughing spell, it sends me back to Pearl Harbor and I truly believe that I am choking to death. That's what scares me so bad and makes me rush to the emergency room."

Sweat began to accumulate on our sallow faces, not the sweat of awe or embarrassment, but rather that of epiphany. Dr. Muchhammer was revealing to us, layer by layer, the scorched landscape behind Mr. Poumon's frightful disease.

"So, do you think that re-living your fear is what sends you to the emergency room each month?"

"Yes, Sir. You just hit the nail on the head. I flat out panic and think that I'm choking and dying."

"If we were to take care of your sudden fear, you wouldn't panic, would you?"

"I didn't know there was a treatment for fear, Sir, which is why I've never told a soul..."

*

In the early seventies, even though the Vietnam War was still raging, the Post Traumatic Stress Disorder Syndrome, though partially remediable, was not yet a fashionable diagnosis. Nevertheless, under good psychiatric care, Mr. Poumon's *panic* admissions ceased and, in time, he was able to stop smoking. However, his incessant woodcarving, which was his self-discovered occupational therapy, continued unabated. For a while, I kept in touch with him by phone, calling him occasionally for a friendly chat.

At the end of that year, Dr. Muchhammer received a wood-carved *USS Nevada* from Mr. Poumon. On the hull, the following words were inscribed: *To Dr. Muchhammer, with gratitude. Harry Poumon.*

When Dr. Muchhammer's rotation ended, we grieved, but his indelible impact never left our medical minds. We spent the rest of our medical careers investigating the triad of patient, disease, and that undiscovered landscape, which always lurks behind the disease.

*

Learn all we lacked before; hear, know, and say
And feel, who have laid our groping hands away;
What this tumultuous body now denies;
And see, no longer blinded by our eyes.[13]

---

[13] From the *South Seas* Sonnet by Rupert Brooke (1887-1915), British poet.

Urine Fire[14]
Oklahoma City VA Hospital, 1974

Veterans are challenged by life as much as by their military service. To many, military life was relatively easy compared to civilian life, and death was often preferable to loss of love and family.

"You should have let me die," mumbled Mr. Kaz as he awakened from his coma and saw me standing by his bed. Then after a sighing pause, he added, "Death solves all our problems and life keeps piling them on."

*

1974 was a harsh year for Mr. Kaz, not because he had just returned from Vietnam, but because he found out that his wife no longer loved him.

"How do you know that she no longer loves you?" I asked. "Did she tell you so or you're just assuming?"

"No, Doc. She actually told me that she still loved me, but her eyes were the ones that said that she didn't."

"Are you sure?" Mr. Kaz. "Wives suffer when their husbands are in combat. They live with the daily fear of loss as long as their husbands are away, and it takes them time to adjust when their husbands return."

"I wish I had returned in a body bag, Doc," said Mr. Kaz as he turned his head away and closed his eyes.

*

---

[14] Pre-published, *The Bulletin*, Oklahoma County Medical Society, July/August 2019.

I left him alone for the rest of that day and busied myself with his medical issues. He was admitted last night, comatose with seizures. Eighteen hours later, his seizures stopped, and he awakened, disappointed that we did not let him die. Our studies did not reveal the cause of his seizures or coma. His exam showed an inflamed mouth and throat but was normal otherwise with good vital signs and no fever.

He refused to eat because his mouth and throat were too sore. When he tried to drink water, horrible pain traveled from his throat, down his chest, and all the way to his stomach. After a few, small swallows, he also refused to drink.

We suspected a suicide attempt, but he would not admit it, nor would he tell us what he swallowed that set his mouth, throat, esophagus, and stomach on fire. "You should have let me die," was his one response to all our questions. He kept his eyes closed as if not seeing the world protected him from what the world had in store for him.

Before I left that night, I tried to have a conversation with him, but again, he closed his eyes and turned his head away. His attitude was a hot pot of disillusionment and anger.

"You should have let me die," he growled. "No one has the right to keep a man alive if the man wants to die."

Standing by his bed, preparing to counter his right-to-die ethos, I noticed a shiny, blue-gray film floating over his urine in the Foley bag. It reminded me of fuel spills that, as a child in Lebanon, I used to see on rainy days at old gas stations. To drain the floating film, the nurse and I had to drain the urine bag from the bottom spout until a trace of urine remained with the film over it. That part, we drained into a kidney basin and took it away.

"Can you smell it?" I asked Nurse Spinosa.
"It smells like fuel," she replied with suspicious eyes.

"Let's put a match to it and see if it burns," I suggested.

"It's a fire hazard," she warned.

"Can we take it to the lab and ask them to light it?" I asked.

"It still would be a fire hazard. You're not allowed to light fires in the VA Hospital."

"I could take it home and see if it burns."

"You can't take lab samples home; it's against the rules."

"Knowing what this blue-gray film is could unlock Mr. Kaz's silence."

"If you're going to light it, light it in the kitchen, and don't let me see it burn."

"Why don't you want to see it burn?"

"Because if do, I would have to report you."

In the kitchen, with Nurse Spinosa peering at me from the corner of her eye, I dipped a cotton ball into the floating film, placed it in a clean kidney basin, and gave it a light. It burned with a bright, red-blue flame, which I immediately put out for fear that it might trigger the fire alarm. Then, abiding by the rules, I sent the urine sample to the lab and went home.

*

The next morning, I greeted Mr. Kaz and, holding his hand, I asked. "Did you try to kill yourself by drinking kerosene?"

This time, he opened his eyes, glared at me, and barked, "How did you find out?"

"I saw a blue-gray film, floating over your urine. It smelled like kerosene and when I gave it a light, it burned."

"How did you know it was kerosene and not some other fuel?"

"Because, in Lebanon, we cooked on Kerosene burners when I was growing up."

"Do you still do that over there?" he asked, looking bemused.

"Not anymore. We now use gas burners."

*

Having uncovered Mr. Kaz's kerosene ploy, he began to trust me, and his trust grew into fondness when, after some discussion, he realized that I knew a lot more about kerosene than he did.

When I shared with him that the lab had tested his urine and reported it as normal, he giggled. "If you hadn't set my urine on fire, no one would have known. You sure blew my secret, Doc," he said with a wry smile.

Mr. Kaz spent three days in the ICU. He and I, having become kerosene friends, had long discussions before he was transferred to the Psych Ward. I wanted him to tell me what was it that drove him to attempt suicide, but he wouldn't. However, during his last ICU afternoon, he opened up because he knew that we might not see each other again.

"I came back from Nam, Doc, to find my wife pregnant. She wants a divorce. We have two young boys, six and eight. My life is a mess. That's what I came back to after risking my life for two years as a combat soldier."

"Where will the boys go?"

"She [sic] don't want them and they want to stay with me. She paid more attention to her boyfriend than to the boys while I was gone," he croaked.

"What made you choose kerosene? It is most unusual for a soldier not to use a deadlier method."

"You mean a firearm?"

"Yes. Kerosene is not usually deadly unless you develop an inhalation pneumonia, which you did not because you did not vomit and aspirate."

"I had read enough about kerosene, enough to know that it isn't very deadly, but I did drink a large amount though. I drank as much as I could stomach, excuse the pun, thinking that it would be enough."

"It put you into coma, gave your seizures, and caused your mouth, throat, esophagus, and stomach to slough, but you survived it much like a good soldier survives a deadly battle."

Mr. Kaz sneered at me for the longest time, asked if I were a psychiatrist, and then asked, as if to test my abilities, if I really knew why he chose kerosene.

"We're all baffled about your choice, Sir. Did you choose it because it was not very deadly?"

"Nope. Try again, Doc," he whispered with a smug smile.

"I've read all there is to read about kerosene and I'm still flabbergasted about your choice. Did you do it for retribution?"

"Nope. You're wrong again," he frowned. Then after a deep, stuttering sigh, he added, "If you really want to know the truth, I did it for the boys."

"The boys?"

"I had read that kerosene is hard to detect by lab studies so I figured that my boys would never know that I had intentionally abandoned them. It would have been bad enough for them to go live with their mother, her boyfriend, and their soon-to-be-born half sibling. But, on top of that, to go because I had killed myself would have devastated them for the rest of their lives."

I paused, giving Mr. Kaz more time to explain, but he didn't. He just wiped a tear and fell silent.

"Mr. Kaz," I asked. "If you have your boys to live for, then you cannot have a good reason to commit suicide. Perhaps that is why you chose the not-so-deadly kerosene."

Mr. Kaz did not answer, but his face grayed with remorse. Then, after a long, reflective pause, he nodded a tearful yes and said, "Perhaps unconsciously, I chose the not-so-deadly kerosene because I love my boys."

Silence, like a cold, stone, wall stood between us, hindering further interaction. I could see the pain on Mr. Kaz's face, the pain that tasted of death, the pain of Lazarus, the pain of resurrection. I bowed my head to the solemnity of the moment and then, after a silent space, I resumed.

"Mr. Kaz. Have you heard of Albert Camus?"[15]

"I majored in Philosophy before I got my petroleum engineering degree."

"So, you must remember *The Myth of Sisyphus*, that famous philosophical essay, which Albert Camus wrote."

"It has been a long time since I've read any philosophy."

"Well, allow me then to refresh your memory. Camus says in that essay that the greatest philosophical question that we should ask ourselves is, *'Shall I commit suicide?'* If the answer is no, then it is because we have a reason to live. Did you ask yourself this question, Mr. Kaz?"

"I was blinded by anger and depression when I drank the kerosene, Doc. Depression makes us do things that are not reasonable. I know better now but I didn't then."

"What will you tell your boys when you return home?"

"I'll tell them that it took a little Lebanese doctor who was raised with kerosene to make the diagnosis of kerosene ingestion. I'll tell them that I am the only Veteran in the history of the VA Hospital whose urine was set on fire in the ICU. I'll tell them that I will be their forever father. I'll tell

---

[15] Albert Camus (2013-2060) French philosopher, author, and reporter.

them that I was so mad and angry that I couldn't think. I'll tell them that I love them. Then, I will gather them into my arms and beg their forgiveness."

After that declaration, as if Mr. Kaz's mind had been rekindled by our philosophical interlude, he smiled and teased, "What else did Albert Camus say?"

"I don't know," I confessed. "What else did he say?"

"He said that *'An intellectual is someone whose mind watches itself.'* When I was angry and depressed, my mind was off watch, Doc."

"That's a wise and sobering thought, Sir."

"He also said something else that now comes to mind."

"You know a lot about Camus, it seems."

"I've read most of his books."

"What else did he say that now comes to your mind?"

"He said, *'I shall tell you a great secret, my friend. Do not wait for the last judgment; it takes place every day.'*"

*

Mr. Kaz spent one week on the Psych Ward before he went back home to his boys. On his way out, he stopped to say good-bye. He couldn't remember my name, so he asked Nurse Spinosa if the little Lebanese doctor was there.

"He's in a meeting with his attending," she replied. "Would you like to leave him a message?"

"Yes, I would."

When, after the residents' conference, I returned to the ICU, Nurse Spinosa handed me a folded sheet of paper and said, "The man who ingested the kerosene came looking for you and left you this message."

I felt an urge to read his note alone, away from watchful eyes. Putting the note in my pocket, I walked toward the door.

"Aren't you going to read it to us?" Asked Nurse Spinosa with a curious expression.

"It might be personal. Let me read it alone first and then decide if I may share it," I replied, and headed to the cafeteria for my midmorning cup of coffee. There, in a quiet corner, I sat down and read his note.

*

Dear Doc,

Among the novels in the psych-ward library, I found a copy of *The Plague*[16], which I read during my week there. Do you know what else Albert Camus said in *The Plague*?

He said: *"The evil that is in the world always comes of ignorance, and good intentions may do as much harm as malevolence, if they lack understanding. The most incorrigible vice is that of an ignorance that fancies it knows everything and therefore claims for itself the right to kill."*

It is a most frightening realization that every one of us, no matter how educated and enlightened, could become temporarily ignorant when emotions overcome reason. This is my last contribution to our kerosene philosophy.

Thank you for befriending me when I needed a friend.

Babboor Kaz

---

[16] A novel by Albert Camus (1913-1960) philosophizing about absurdism.

East to West[17]
Oklahoma City VA Hospital, 2018

Tall, lean, handsome, but frail and forgetful, eighty-three-year-old Harold Pennmaster was brought to the V. A. Hospital by his wife of 45 years because he had fainted and was short of breath. We treated the blood clots in his legs and lungs and discovered that the cause was inoperable pancreatic cancer. After a few days of bed rest, we asked physical therapy to begin walking him. The next morning, I received a frustrated call.

"Doctor," she muttered. "I can't get him to walk."
"Why not?"
"I think he's afraid."
"But he walked into the emergency room. Did anything happen to make him afraid?"
"Not that I can tell. I've talked to his wife and she's baffled too because he used to love to walk."

I marched to Mr. Pennmaster's room with the simplest of ideas vying for an answer. But his exam was unremarkable except for his frail, frightened aspect. He talked with stuttered apprehension and could not stay in the moment.

"Mr. Pennmaster. Why are you afraid to walk?" I asked, holding his hand.
"The snakes are everywhere. They're out to bite me. They killed Jimmy. One little bite and he was gone."
"We have no snakes here. You're in the V. A. Hospital," I reassured.
"Oh, no, they're everywhere, everywhere, and I don't have my boots on."

---

[17] Pre-published, *The Bulletin*, Oklahoma County Medical Society, September-October 2018.

I walked out with his wife, who seemed equally frightened. "He's talking about Panama," she whispered. "We were stationed there in September of 1975 when the students stormed the American Embassy."

"Does he talk about Panama often?"

"He goes there many times a day."

"And how did the snakes come into the picture?"

"He was a drill sergeant when he sent his buddy, Jimmy, on a scouting mission and told him not to go into the bush. Jimmy never came back and no one could find him. He felt responsible and couldn't sleep. So, he went out looking for him the next day."

"Did he go alone?"

"No. The commander of the 39th Platoon ordered a search. They went in Jeeps up and down the canal. There were lots of squatters from Colombia but no Jimmy."

"How long did they search?"

"Not very long, according to Harold. They were more interested in evicting the squatters so as to please President Torrijos."

"What happened next?"

"They called off the search after three days and declared Jimmy missing in action."

"I was the one who found him," croaked Mr. Pennmaster from his bed, which stunned us because we were not aware that he could hear our whispers.

Back at the bedside, Mr. Pennmaster's eyes were gaping with apprehension. I did not have to ask. With remarkable fluency, as if he were still living in that 1975 moment, he told me the whole story:

"You see, when the students stormed the American Embassy because they were angry at Kissinger, we all thought that Jimmy was abducted by them. There were lots of anti-American protesters at that time, all angry because Kissinger

declared that the US has the right to defend the Canal whenever and forever. Our commander called off the search for Jimmy after three days because he was afraid that we could be ambushed by militants hiding in the bush.

"When things escalated and we could not tell how many militants were lurking in the bush, he asked for volunteers. I was the only one who raised his hand because I wanted to find Jimmy. He knew that I was a long-distance runner, so he ordered me to jog along the canal, as close to the bush as possible, and report back to him.

"Early Sunday morning, I jogged on the south side of the canal from east to west, twenty miles, without stopping for rest or water. I got to the end in about four hours, saw lots of folks squatting in the bush, but no sign of Jimmy.

"After I rested a while, I crossed over the Bridge of the Americas, and then walked back from west to east on the north side of the canal. No one bothered me because I was wearing shorts and jogging shoes. When I got close to the base on the east side, it was late in the afternoon. From the bush on my left side, I could smell something dead. I got closer and there was Jimmy in a ditch, lying on his back with eyes and mouth open, buzzing with flies. I ran to the base and told the commander.

"When we got him back, the doctor discovered that he was [sic] bit by a poisonous snake on his right leg. That's what killed him. I told Jimmy not to go into the bush, but he did anyway and died for it.

"The bush is very dangerous, full of snakes, spiders, sandflies, scorpions, poisonous insects, and all kinds of creatures that can kill a man in a few minutes."

At this point, Mr. Pennmaster stopped talking and his eyes assumed that frightened glare again. I paused a while before I intruded on his Panama mind.

"Could you outrun the rioters if you had your jogging shoes on?"

He grinned again and, knowingly, looked to his wife as if to ask where his jogging shoes were. Thinking of his jogging days must have rejuvenated him. I seized the moment and asked, "If Mrs. Pennmaster would bring your jogging shoes here, would you wear them?"

"Sure, I would. I've won many medals. You can ask my wife. I ran from east to west and walked back from west to east in one day."

I decided not to challenge his fear of walking lest I should unwittingly rekindle it. Instead, I left him in his Panama moment and stepped out with his wife.

"Do you still have his jogging shoes?" I hesitated.
"No way. He has not jogged for years."
"What did his shoes look like?"
"He always wore white shoes with thick heels."
"Can you buy him a pair?"
"I wouldn't know where to go."
"Target, Walmart, anywhere?"
"What if he refuses to wear them?"
"Buy the cheapest pair you can find."

The next day, Mr. Pennmaster was still refusing to walk. He was still seeing snakes and was afraid to step into the bush. He had been agitated all night, saw scorpions and spiders coming at him, and had to be calmed down with Haloperidol. His bewildered wife sat in the room with a shoebox in her lap. When she saw me approach, she came out into the hall and whispered in my ear.

"He sent the physical therapist and occupational therapist away. He will not step off his bed to go to the restroom. He's using a urinal and bedpan. He's still in Panama and thinks the floor is the jungle. Last night he went wild with fear. We left Panama forty-three years ago, but he's still there."

In the room, while Mr. Pennmaster's wife was helping him put his white, jogging shoes on, I asked him if jogging from east to west was exhausting.

"It's the walking back that was exhausting," he replied with mournful eyes.
"So why didn't you jog back, then?"
"Because I was tired."
"Are you still tired?"
"Not anymore," he grinned.
"How about a little jog then, just the two of us?"
"Where to?" he asked with roaming eyes.
"From east to west, of course. We don't have to walk back. We can return by Jeep."

Mr. Pennmaster's eyes lit up with fire. He was young again; his leg muscles twitched with excitement, his eyes quickened with youth, and his frightened face donned a sneer of resolve. I held out my hands. He grabbed them, swung his feet down the edge of the bed, examined the floor with scouting eyes, and looked to his wife for approval. She smiled and nodded. Cautiously, he stepped down, looked at his shoes, held on to my hand, and said, "Let's go."

"Please hurry his wheelchair to the end of the hall and leave it there," I whispered to Mrs. Pennmaster as we walked out of the room.

Then, hand in hand, we walked from east to west, past the gaping eyes of the nurses, reached the end of the hall, and stopped.

"Where's the Jeep?" he queried.

"Right there," I said, pointing to the wheelchair.

After I wheeled him back to his room, I asked if he felt tired. "No," he answered. "I didn't have to walk back on the north bank."

Mr. Pennmaster and I *jogged* from east to west every morning for several days, always returning by *Jeep* because walking back meant that he would find Jimmy dead in a ditch.

After discharge, his wife took him out for daily walks, always in his white jogging shoes, until he could walk no more. She always brought him back by *Jeep*, the car she had pre-parked at the end of the path. He died in his jogging shoes, which he never took off except when he showered or slept.

Furor in the VA Hospital[18]
Oklahoma VA Hospital, 2018

July 12, 2018

Commotion in the halls, frown-furrowed faces, alarm-riddled eyes, fright-hurried feet, and then the telephone rings.

"Nurse Timor?"
"Dr. Caput. I need to see you. We have a situation."

*

In Dr. Caput's office, Nurse Timor gasps her phrases. "Mr. Nocere is out of control, screaming suicide, shouting at the top of his voice, wants to leave against medical advice, and refuses to take his meds. Patients and nurses on the Community-Living-Center Ward are up in arms, and no one has been able to calm him down."

"Have you informed the VA police of his suicidal threat?"

"No. They'll incarcerate him on the Psych Ward. It'll kill him. Psychiatry was called instead to help evaluate his safety. He's a good man who has snapped for no real reason."

"What caused him to snap?" Asked Dr. Caput with his usual, calming voice.

"He was supposed to have his nephrostomy tube[19] changed at eleven today. They bumped him till three because they had an emergency. Then they bumped him again till tomorrow because they were jammed. That's when he lost it. Two patient advocates came to his room to explain; he called

---

[18] Pre-published, *The Bulletin*, Oklahoma County Medical Society, May-June 2019.

[19] A tube inserted through the back to drain kidney urine into an outside bag. It is used when the normal urine path is blocked.

them liars and chased them out. There's a crowd outside his door. No one dares go in. He's calling the TV channels."

"Let's take a look."

Dr. Caput stood up and motioned for me to follow. The phone rang. It was the hospital's Chief of Staff, Dr. Stabschef. A hurried conversation ensued, and all decisions were put on hold until after our visit.

*

Before we went into Mr. Nocere's room, we had to put on blue gloves and yellow isolation gowns, which concealed our professional white coats and stethoscopes. Looking like canaries instead of doctors, we cautiously ventured through the cracked door.

"Mr. Nocere, we are the CLC attendings; this is Dr. Hawi and I'm Dr. Caput, Chief of Geriatrics."

"I don't need no attendings and no chiefs," he roared. "Get out of my room."

"We're here to understand your side of the story, Sir."

"There's nothing to understand. They've [sic] done bumped me twice and I don't deserve that kind of treatment after giving forty-five years of my life to the Army. I'm leaving against medical advice."

"But you haven't finished your antibiotic course, which means you will still have your kidney infection."

"That [sic] don't matter to me now because I'm [sic] gonna kill myself as soon as I get home."

*

I looked into Dr. Caput's worried eyes. They were void of solutions but brimming with questions. Given that Mr.

Nocere had never flared up before, could this be his first anger burst from an unrecognized dementia or depression? We had all twenty years of his medical records in the VA computer. A thorough chart review was urgently needed.

Dr. Caput knew the VA computers' alleys very well and could surf them at supersonic speed. I was new to the system and could be of no use to him during this task. To release him from the bondage of Mr. Nocere's raging verbosities, I politely intimated that while he reviewed Mr. Nocere's records, I would stay in the room and babysit. It was a tacit agreement done with the eyes and approved without a whisper.

*

Violating the VA Hospital's isolation ordinance, I took off my canary gown and blue gloves, and with abject defiance to the establishment's rules and regulations, threw them into the trash. Mr. Nocere did notice my intimation and understood that I was moving over to his side of the conflict, but, nonetheless, he still continued with his loud barrage. Only this time, his eyes were peering at me with acceptance instead of at the crowd with defiance. Cautiously, I sat on the bed as close to him as I could, and with arms in lap, listened like a three-year-old child.

*

"You know, Doc., I left school in tenth grade. There were no jobs for a young black man, so I joined the Army at 15 and stayed till I retired five years ago. Here's my citation. I had my son bring it so people could see it."

I examined his citation and then read it aloud to him: *This is to certify that Sergeant Major (E9) Nocere, David, King, having served faithfully and honorably for forty-five years, eight months, and three days, was retired from the United States Army on the twenty-first day of January, 2013.*

"You know, Doc., I was the second black man in the history of the Army to achieve this high rank." A proud smile simmered in his eyes when he said that.

"Mr. Nocere, could you please tell me about your military experiences and the conflicts you have been in? It would help me understand you better."

*

Mr. Nocere talked for an hour-and-a-half without a break. He did not need prompts because my listening was his prompt. He was a lake that had been accumulating fear and anger for 45 years, and when the dam broke, it flooded the room, the halls, the wards, the hospital, and the entire city.

As a young soldier, he was ridiculed and castigated. His mother's words, *overcome and endure,* buoyed him throughout his entire career. Bypassed and bumped on numerous occasions deeply hurt his feelings, but he never expressed his anger while in uniform.

His time during the Iraq conflict, however, took a big toll on him. He was in charge of the Grave Registration, which picked up dead bodies, bagged them, and sent them back home. At times his unit had to use shovels to pry the bodies off the ground because they had been flattened by tanks that had run over them.

His unit was also assigned to roll Concertina Wires around the campsite and guard it. One Sunday, he was bumped from his day off to go on guard duty and was ordered to shoot anyone who tried to enter the camp without going through the main gate. During that harrowing month, they had lost twenty-one soldiers to knife attacks by unsuspected civilians.

Early that Sunday morning a little, blonde girl, who couldn't have been older than six, playfully approached wearing a white *djellaba*. He asked her to stop and go back, but because she knew no English, she did not heed his warning and continued her playful approach. His commander, who was watching from the tower, ordered him to shoot her. He called to her again and told her to go back. His commander again told him to shoot her. After three calls, with quivering fingers, he shot her in the chest. Instead of falling she exploded like an atomic bomb.

*

"If you had allowed her to get any closer, she would have been exploded by remote control and killed us all," barked his commander.

"If you hadn't bumped me from my day off to do guard duty, I wouldn't have had to shoot an innocent, little girl."

"She was doomed no matter how you look at it," retorted the commander.

"If you hadn't bumped me from my day off, someone less partial to little girls would have done the dirty work."

*

"The commander took it well and did not punish me. But, when I told him that I was through with death and killing, he reassigned me to a desk job."

"Is that why you got so violently angry when your procedure time was twice bumped?"

Mr. Nocere's tears streamed down his cheeks. I hugged him. He sobbed. "That little girl never leaves my mind, Doc. She's everywhere I look and, whenever I'm bumped, my heart is struck with fear that something just as horrible is liable to happen again. I'm sorry I exploded. But I exploded and I'm still alive. That little girl exploded and she's dead."

*

Back in Dr. Caput's office, having told him Mr. Nocere's story, I asked if his chart review had yielded any important information.

"I think he's suffering from suppressed PTSD," he replied. "He has never complained about it because he's stoic, but reading all his chart notes and understanding all that he had been through, indicate that he has suppressed PTSD"

"Being bumped, then, must be his most frightening cue because it portends something as horrific as an exploding little girl," I surmised.

"It does explain his horrifying anger burst, doesn't it? How little we know when we think we know, and how much more we stand to learn if we just search and listen."

The Fabric of Friendship[20]
Oklahoma City VA Hospital, 2018

A brief telephone conversation:

"You're sweating?"
"No, no. I'm swelling."
"Oh. Your feet are swelling?"
"Yes, Doc. You got it."

Mr. Édredon came to the VA Hospital, wearing soft, oversized shoes. As an infantryman of Vietnam-War vintage, he was especially proud of his feet. "With these feet, Doc., I jungle-marched for two years without any swelling," he smiled, looking at his feet. "Now, they swell even when I don't walk."

Mr. Édredon, a heavy smoker, did not only have swollen feet.   The swelling, which went up both thighs, portended obstruction to venous return[21]. Indeed, after he was admitted, imaging did reveal that his silent lung cancer had established colonies in his liver, bones, abdomen, and brain.

"Mr. Édredon, your cancer is widespread."
"Are you saying that it's hopeless?"
"There's always hope. We have new treatments that sometimes work miracles."
"Should I try them?"
"Let's ask the experts."

The VA Hospital experts, after staging the cancer and sequencing the tumor genomes, advised palliation[22] instead of aggressive treatment. Mr. Édredon was a widower who lived

---

[20] Pre-published, *The Bulletin*, Oklahoma County Medical Society, March-April 2019.

[21] The inferior vena cava returns blood from the legs to the heart. When it is blocked by cancer, the legs swell.

[22] Comfort care that only treats symptoms.

alone. His son and grandson lived in Germany and visited him only every few years. Ever since his honorable discharge in 1975, the VA Hospital has been his loving, medical home. It helped him through forty-three years of myriad illnesses and now it was going to help him die. That was his mindset when he was discharged from the medical floor to the hospital's Palliative Care Unit.

Our relationship grew because I happened to be attending during that month. In spite of radical measures, his swelling continued to worsen and did not respond to diuretics.

"I'm drowning in my own swelling, Doc." He told me one morning.

"Your swelling is below your waist," I reassured. "It cannot drown you."

"So, how will I die then?"

"Your heart will stop when it can no longer handle the advancing cancer."

"Will it be painful?"

"Palliative care is not only about controlling pain and discomfort. We have all kinds of medicines and tricks that help you stay as vital as possible for as long as you live, and help you make the best use of the time you have left."

After one week, Mr. Édredon suddenly sank into a deep depression. He took to his bed, hardly ate, and kept his eyes closed even when I visited him.

"Why do you keep your eyes closed?" I asked one morning. "Does light bother you?"

"It's not light that bothers me, Doc. It's reality."

"What do you mean?"

"A man has to have a reason to live, and I don't. I find comfort in darkness because it helps me see death."

"What does death look like?"

"It looks like a silent stretch of peace."

"So, you are spending your time, waiting for a silent stretch of peace?"

"What's wrong with that?"

"Is there something that is important that you could give your attention to during this time?"

"My son and grandson."

"Would you like to connect with them?"

Tears dripped from between Mr. Édredon's closed eyelids. I knew that his son had called to say that he wouldn't be able to come for a visit, which, I believe, is what hurled Mr. Édredon into depression. Before that call he was interacting with other patients, sharing Vietnam stories, and enjoying communal life.

"How old is your grandson?" I asked, hoping to revive his good feelings.

His eyes opened and gleamed. "He's sixteen and speaks perfect German," he declared with pride.

"Why don't you write him a long letter and tell him about your life's rich experiences, like an autobiography of sorts? I'm sure he would treasure it."

"I'm no writer and no reader, Doc. I've spent my life working with my hands, upholstering furniture, because it kept Vietnam out of my mind. My days in Vietnam were horrifying and I've spent my life trying to forget them. I certainly don't want to talk about them to my innocent grandson. I'm afraid it would ruin his love for me."

On the way back to my office, I met Dr. Nadel Kunst, the Palliative Care psychologist.

"Can you spare a minute, Doctor?"

"Sure?"

"It's about Mr. Édredon."

"How can I help?"

When I told her Mr. Édredon's story, her eyes gaped, not with surprise, but rather with expectation. "I think he needs to come to my Quilt-Therapy Class," she smiled. "My PhD thesis was on Quilt-Art Therapy."

I had never heard of Quilt-Art Therapy and my skepticism did not escape Dr. Nadel Kunst's keen, mind-reading scrutiny.

"You just told me that he's an upholsterer who does not like to read or write," she reminded me with a knowing smile. "Quilt-Art Therapy is ideally suited for Veterans who are unable to communicate their experiences with words. It would help them recall, re-enact and integrate traumatic experiences, and recover from emotional disorders associated with their psychological trauma."

What she said gave me immediate hope because it seemed to fit Mr. Édredon's needs better than any solution I could think of.

"I'll go back to Mr. Édredon's room, tell him that Quilt-Art Therapy can really help him, and suggest that he join your class."

"Oh, no." She gasped. "That's the wrong approach. He does not want help. He just wants to be left alone to die because he thinks that's his only way out of grief. Instead of offering him my help, tell him that I am the one who needs his help as an upholsterer. Helping others gives life new meanings and assuages despair and depression. And nobody can quilt with closed eyes," she said with a wry smile.

*

Mr. Édredon became Dr. Nadel Kunst's open-eyed *sous chef.* He helped alarmed PTSD Veterans relax and enjoy creating meaningful art. His mind became a beehive, teaming with little stories about what Dr. Kunst and his classmates said and did. Stopping by his room on rounds became my daily entertainment because he never ran out of stories.

As his health failed and he became short of breath, I gave him oxygen. As his heart failed and his lungs filled with fluid, I gave him morphine. As his brain tumors enlarged and his gait became unsteady, he went to class in a wheelchair. As his speech became slurred, he wrote notes on yellow sheets of paper that he tore from a notebook.

When he sank into coma, his nurses cried. "He cannot live long without food or fluids." Two days later, his nurse, Angela, called.

"Doctor. Mr. Édredon's breathing is agonal. He's leaving us."

I sat by his bed, held his hand, and watched him fade into dreamless sleep. Angela sat on his other side, held his other hand, prayed, cried, and kept whispering, "No Veteran should die alone."

*

The next morning, Angela came to my office. "Here's a package addressed to you," she said.
"From whom?"
"I don't know. One of the patients from the CLC delivered it."
She laid the package on my desk and waited.
"It's a colorful wrap," I commented as I stared at the large, rectangular, shape.
"Well. Are you going to open it?"

*

The package contained a beautiful quilt, stitched with professional care, with black-red-and-gold patches on one side and red-white-and-blue patches on the other. It took us a while to realize that one side represented Germany's flag, his ancestral country where his son and grandson live, and the other, America's flag, the country that he loved and served. Between the folds, there was a yellow sheet of paper.

*

Dear Doc,

When you get this note, I will be in my silent stretch of peace. Thanks to you, Dr. Kunst (who also helped me write this letter), and the palliative care nurses, I was able to enjoy and share my dying days in a meaningful way. I am very proud of this fabric of friendship, which I would like for you to forward to my grandson. I want him to remember me as a colorful, international, patch of time, forged by a well-lived, adventurous life, and escorted out by a peaceful, meaningful death.

Polstern Édredon

Mr. If[23]
Oklahoma City VA Hospital, 2018

Chapter One

I do not trust my mind
It tortures and it teases
And wanders where it pleases
Leaving me behind;
I do not trust my mind.[24]

There are microcosms within macrocosms, micro-cultures within macro-cultures, families within societies, and individuals within families. The infinite variety of nature defines our infinite universe with its infinite particles. And as variety defines nature, so does change define age.

The VA Hospitals (VAHs) are planets upon our planet with their own suns, moons, and atmospheres. The infinite variety of nature is replicated by the infinite varieties within the VAHs—where there is not a particle or an individual in the universe that is not represented, not a mood or emotion that is not exchanged, and not a law or order that is not promulgated. *Traveling* within the VAHs is equally entertaining and enlightening as is traveling upon planet earth, but it is far more affordable because instead of expense, VAH *travelers* are reliably reimbursed for their time. It is in this ever-changing, ever-bustling microcosm of humanity that I met Mr. If.

Tall, handsome, elegant, and lean, he walked into our Geri-PACT clinic with a straight spine that belied his age.

---

[23] Submitted, May 2020, *Journal of the Oklahoma State Medical Association*.

[24] *Loving of A Different Kind*, from the poetry book, *Loves and Lamentations of a Life Watcher*, by Hanna Saadah.

"Good morning, Mr. Dubitat," I greeted and then introduced him to the Geri-PACT providers: Psychologist Madison, Pharmacist Brenda, Social Worker Wilma, and Nurse Marissa.

"Call me Mr. If, please," he instructed with an irate gaze. "Mr. Daniel Dubitat died 23 years ago."

"Well then, good morning Mr. If," I re-greeted with half a smile.

"Do I make you uncomfortable, Doctor?" He challenged.

"A bit," I nodded.

"You're the first doctor to ever admit that," he sneered with triumphant eyes.

Instead of starting with an open-ended question, I held my tongue and hoped that he would be the one to re-kindle the conversation. When the stalemate lingered into awkwardness, interrupted by occasional glances, fidgets, and coughs, I resumed.

"How may we help you, Mr. If?"

"No one can help me," he retorted with an unfriendly voice.

"Would you at least give our team a chance, please?"

"It's a very long story," he sneered again. "You don't have the time?"

"We have 90 minutes, Sir, and I can add my 30-minute lunch break if we need more time."

His visage softened when I said that. He shifted in his seat, relaxed his fisted fingers, let out a deep, stuttering sigh that caused his white mustache to vibrate, and then began.

"For the past 23 years, I've been abandoned by every doctor I've seen. My wife left me. My daughter doesn't speak to me. No one can get along with me. I feel terribly isolated."

"What went wrong, Sir?"

"Everything changed after the explosion."

"What explosion?"

"9:02 am, April 19, 1995," he barked with a shrill voice.

"You mean the Murrah Building?"

"The Alfred P. Murrah Federal Building in downtown Oklahoma City," he croaked, as an ashen veil dropped over his face.

"Were you there?"

"No."

I was afraid to probe the solemn silence for fear of yet another explosion. Mr. If's face donned a blank stare as his mind traveled back in time, unveiling vivid, violent scenes. I watched his face quiver with frowns, his eyes, with held-back tears, and his lips, with unsaid words.

Silence droned like a bee, beating against the glass, vying for an exit. Then, out of this suspended, soundless state, a sad sunrise broke from behind his tenebrous[25] clouds and his story slowly dripped, one drop at a time, like water from a leaking faucet.

"That woeful morning, I drove my daughter and granddaughter to the Murrah building because her car wouldn't start. When I told them that I would be back to pick them up at 5, my daughter teased me with, *'If nothing happens.'*

"After dropping them off, I drove straight to the Court House. I was in trial when the deafening explosion quaked the building and shattered the glass. The shock froze us in our seats. No one knew what to do. Someone ran in and cried, *'It's a bomb.'* We all ran out into the dust and then the Sirens came.

"I called my daughter's office, over and over. Her line was dead. That was when the last thing she said started to

---

[25] Dark and shadowy.

haunt me. Her words, *if nothing happens,* took hold of my mind and pounded me while we waited for her and my granddaughter's bodies to be pulled out of the rubble. They pounded me during the double funeral. They pounded me when I tried to resume my legal work. They pounded me when my wife and daughter left me because they couldn't live with my grumpy madness. I hear the words, *if nothing happens,* day and night, like a tireless song that never stops playing, and it's driving me crazy."

"Has any doctor tried to treat your auditory hallucination?"

"Medicines don't work, which frustrates the doctors, so they give up and send me away. I've spent my years going from one renowned specialist to another, from one famous medical center to another, and I've even had ten sessions of electric shock therapy—all to no avail. I've finally accepted that my hallucination is incurable. I just need a doctor who is willing to tolerate me, a doctor who will not abandon me, a doctor who will not send me away."

I could feel Mr. If's pain, but I had no words with which to assuage it. Indeed, I felt as trapped as he was without a light in sight. His brain, like a record, had been permanently grooved by a horrific loss and the phrase, *if nothing happens,* had become an indelible idiom, playing over and over in his mind. Nevertheless, I felt that I had to do something meaningful, something helpful, something that would make his visit to our VAH worth his while.

"Mr. If," I asked. "Would you like to make the VAH your medical home?"

"I not only feel medically homeless, Doctor, I also feel socially homeless, homeless in my own home."

"Well then, if you're willing to work with us, our team will do its best to help you."

"But what if the team's best is not good enough?"

"We promise not to send you away, Sir, and never to stop trying."

"That's just what I wanted to hear," he smiled, got up, and prepared to leave.

"How about booking a standing, monthly appointment with us before you leave?"

"That would certainly preserve my sanity, which is ever teetering on the edge of madness."

"Well then, see you next month, Sir."

The team psychologist, pharmacist, social worker, nurse, and I huddled after Mr. If left. We reviewed the extensive records he brought and deliberated over strategies and treatments that had not been tried. We ended up feeling neutralized because no bright ideas came to us. Frustrated, we agreed to leave the matter until Mr. If returned in a month.

That night, I slept poorly. I ruminated over the many times a song had replayed itself over and over in my mind, came and left when it pleased, and I had no control over it. One time, to stop it, I started singing a different song, and it worked as long as I continued singing. But, when I would stop, the old song would resume.

Then I considered the content of the phrase, *if nothing happens.* How could nothing happen? If it happens, it is something. If it didn't happen then it didn't happen. *Nothing* cannot happen, nor can it not happen, because *nothing* is the absence of everything including the absence of change. For some reason, that idea pacified me, and I was able to fall asleep.

Night after night, I would put my mind to sleep thinking about Mr. If because I could not accept that he could not be helped. Some little, flickering light in the remote recesses of my mind kept telling me that there had to be a solution.

52

"It is what we aspire to be that colors our characters—and it is our trying, not just our succeeding, which ennobles them. But nothing happens without a lesson to offer, or without opening other routes into the future. The only true defeat lies in letting defeat win," said A. C. Grayling, and that quote became my motto, not just because of its indomitable determination, but also because it contained the phrase, *nothing happens,* used in a positive rather than a negative sense, to indicate that everything that happens has a lesson to offer.

I awaited Mr. If's return with trepidation because I had nothing to offer him but compassion, which was not enough. Mr. If had been incarcerated in his mind's torture chamber for the past 23 years and no one had been able to find the key to let him out. But now, that my geriatric team and I have accepted the challenge of helping a doomed Veteran, the heft of responsibility lay on my chest instead of on my shoulders, gasping with every breath and pounding with every heartbeat.

The month passed quickly and slowly. Sometimes, the days hardly moved and sometimes they sped as if they were seconds. *"For in a minute there are many days,"* [26] said Shakespeare in Romeo and Juliet. What great insight graced young Juliet's mind to so eloquently express her anxiety while awaiting her Romeo.

---

[26] Juliet, *Romeo and Juliet*, William Shakespeare.

Chapter Two

Mr. If honored his appointment and showed up on time. The team welcomed him with alacrity but, in return, he broke into discussion with an angry prologue.

"I've had a very bad month," he glared. "The fact that I now have a medical home that will not abandon me must have agitated my dormant emotions. Instead of feeling calmer, I now feel worse. I should have cancelled my appointment. I don't really know why I didn't. I don't think you're going to be able to help me."

"How about your auditory hallucination?" I quizzed, hoping to distract Mr. If's ill-begotten anger.

"It's worse too," he barked and clenched his fist.

I saw fear and sweat accumulate in tiny droplets over the brow of Nurse Marissa who had been abused once before by an angry Veteran, a Veteran suffering from the Post-Traumatic-Stress-Disorder Syndrome, i.e. PTSD

"Do you have any idea what made you feel worse?" I asked, hoping to draw out his speech.

"How can I possibly know? You're the doctor. Why don't you tell me why?" He challenged with an aggressive tone.

Hearing his crescendo voice, Nurse Marissa tearfully excused herself and left the room, which upset Mr. If even more.

"What? Did I offend her, or she doesn't like me anymore?"

"She must have felt uncomfortable," chimed in Dr. Madison, our psychologist.

"Are you saying that I was the one who made her feel uncomfortable?" He challenged again with a high-pitched voice.

"Mr. If. Your behavior is not acceptable. We're all trying to help you and you're returning our good will with provocative language," countered our psychologist with a kind but firm tone.

"You're threatening me and behaving more like a lawyer than a psychologist," he sneered.

"This response is again not acceptable, Mr. If," she admonished again. "I was reprimanding you, not threatening you."

"Well, well," he cried. "I did not come here to be reprimanded. I'd better leave you to your delicate manners and go back home."

Mr. If got up, shook his bushy white hair with remonstrative gestures, and charged the door. But, before he could reach it, Wilma, our social worker, sitting closest to the door, hugged the door handle with her back, looked him straight in the eyes, and whispered, "Sir, you need a dog."

"I don't need a dog," he shouted. "I don't even like dogs. I just need out."

"No, Sir," she insisted. "You're in dire need of a dog."

"I can't believe my ears. You're telling me that I need a dog when you don't even know me," he screamed at the top of his voice as he tried to reach for the door handle.

"You think that I don't know you, Sir, but in fact I do know you very well. You were the valedictorian of your law class, graduating with distinction. You taught criminal law for twenty odd years and were revered by your students. You stopped teaching and practicing law after the bombing. Your wife divorced you two years later and took your teen-aged daughter with her. You became a recluse, stopped seeing the few friends you had, and have been living all alone in your very big house by the lake. You have a boat that you don't even use, and you don't go fishing anymore."

The social worker blurted out this impromptu polemic without taking a breath, while continuing to hold the door's handle with her back. None of us expected this firm response from someone as meek as Social Worker Wilma, especially not Mr. If, who looked as stunned as one who had just taken a big blow to the head.

"You've been spying on me?" He barked, pointing his finger at her as if she were in the witness stand.

"No, Sir. I've not been spying on you. I've just diligently done my research. Your private life is posted all over Google and Facebook."

Mr. If's face suddenly softened under this firm, feminine confrontation and, for a spell, his tongue became tied and his posture, uncertain. The psychologist and I well understood the unpredictable anger eruptions that explode out of PTSD survivors, the lack of control they evince, and the ineffable fear and alarm they live with. Our social worker, a recovering PTSD victim herself, knew better than the rest of us how to handle such volatile, volcanic situations.

Her stare never broke, her stance never wavered, and it became clear to us that Mr. If was no longer in command. Trying to find a face-saving exit, he repeated, as if mumbling to himself, " 'You need a dog,' she says." She knows me so well to tell me that I need a dog when I know that I don't."

"Yes, Sir. You do need a dog," she affirmed.

"And why do I need a dog?" he asked with a cynical tone.

"Because you love to teach."

"You're talking way above my head, Ma'am. Why on earth would I need a dog if I love to teach?"

"Because you can't teach half-grown-up kids how to read if you don't have a dog," she replied, still holding him in suspense.

"I'm confused," he whispered, scratching his bushy white hair with all ten digits and, at the same time, surveying the smiles behind our gaping eyes.

"Sir," she affirmed. "Your church, which is also my church, has been advertising for volunteer teachers to teach illiterate teenagers to read. I've been with these teenagers when they were embarrassed to read for fear that they would make too many mistakes. One time, I brought my dog with me and asked them to read to the dog instead of to me, claiming that my dog loves to hear young voices read. When I positioned the dog in front of them and I sat behind them, they soon forgot that I was in the room and began reading, struggling, correcting each other, and laughing each time the dog moved or gestured. The reading hour passed in a flash and they were all back the next day, wanting to read to my dog again. Only then, after they had grown comfortable with me and my dog, did I start instructing them."

Mr. If, defeated by a meek woman, sat back in his chair, apologized, gazed into my eyes, and asked with a supplicating voice, "Do you often see volatile cases like mine, Doctor?"

"Has anyone explained to you that you suffer from the PTSD Syndrome?" I quizzed.

"PTSD Syndrome!" he exclaimed. "I've served in the armed forces, but I've never seen combat."

"Oh, yes you have, Mr. If. You've been in combat for 23 years, no different than any other armed-forces combat, heralded by an explosion as horrific as the one that took away your daughter and granddaughter."

Mr. If's eyes reddened with memory and remorse, his tears dripped down his quivering cheeks like a mountain stream from his snow-haired crest, and his hands trembled as he wiped his face, smudging his tears all over the place. Dr. Madison, our psychologist, handed him a tissue, which he accepted with gratitude.

After the storm, an intimate calm dropped down like a white, morning veil over our heads and hearts. Then, into this sad, solemn, silence, our social worker's voice flapped in like a white pigeon, returning home after a long, tiring trip.

"Mr. If," she whispered. "Would you like to borrow my dog? His name is Lexis. I'm sure you recognize the Greek root. It means *words*."

Chapter Three

Mr. If's church news traveled to us via Wilma, our team's social worker. The first time he taught, he borrowed her dog and the kids loved seeing a new face with an old dog. The second time, he borrowed his neighbor's dog. The third time he brought his own dog, a mutt, which his neighbor had rescued. All that happened during the first week, causing a sensation at church and among the kids.

On Sunday, he came to church services, which he had boycotted for years. Our social worker intercepted him when he was leaving, and they exchanged a long, somewhat friendly chat. By the time he showed up for his monthly appointment, he had increased his teaching schedule to five days a week, and his pupils were having as much fun reading to Lexicon (the name he had chosen for his mutt) as Lexicon was having, listening to them read. Having been neglected before he was rescued, Lexicon was especially appreciative of the attention and love he was now receiving.

Mr. If, being highly punctual, arrived for his ten o'clock appointment on time. The team received him with alacrity, especially since instead of a frown, his face wore an affable smile.

"Good morning, Mr. If," I began with knowing eyes. "I hope you've had a better month."

"Indeed, thanks to y'all, I've had the first decent month in 23 years."

"Wilma has been sharing with us your good progress."

"I owe my new life to Miss Wilma. I'll never forget how she told me that I needed a dog while blocking the door's handle with her back. I felt like an angry prisoner, but she sure was right. Lexicon, my mutt, which I named in reverence to Miss Wilma's reading dog, Lexis, has been a wonderful companion and loves to take long walks, which I direly need."

"So, you have a new friend then," interjected Dr. Madison, our psychologist, with a blushing smile.

"We share the same history."

"Oh?"

"Lexicon suffered from abject neglect and so did I. Only, he was neglected by his prior owners whereas I suffered from self-neglect."

Blushing, our psychologist grafted yet another twig into our, so far, friendly conversation tree.

"Isolation deforms our minds, Mr. If," she instructed. "We are social beings who thrive on interaction and decline in isolation."

"I had no idea I was suffering from solitary confinement, Ma'am, perhaps because it was self-inflicted."

"PTSD alarms, infuriates, isolates, and devastates," she instructed again. "You're no different than our shell-shocked Veterans. The first escape route from PTSD is to learn as much as you can about it. I have some reading materials for you that you will find enlightening."

Saying that, Dr. Madison handed Mr. If an orange folder full of PTSD pamphlets. He rejected it with a sudden head jerk and his pale face took on a frightened appearance. This sudden turn of events held us in its claws, and we all looked to our psychologist for an explanation.

Dr. Madison, unperturbed, smiled, cautiously repositioned her chair, looked straight into Mr. If's blinking eyes, and said, "Would you please tell us about orange folders?"

Mr. If mumbled unintelligibly, labored to breathe, and his breaths grew faster and louder under the incessant gaze of Dr. Madison.

"Would you please tell us about orange folders?" She repeated after grasping Mr. If's clenched fist with her hand.

"I had to identify my daughter and granddaughter," he sighed. "Then, I had to sign the papers," he sighed again, choking on his words.

"Were the papers in orange folders?"

He nodded a painful *yes* and burst into tears.

After Mr. If regained his composure, Dr. Madison explained that PTSD could be rekindled by the slightest cue.

"Years after a horrific trauma, certain triggers can push the brain's alarm buttons, causing stored memories to storm back into reality. Pop open a Champagne bottle in a hotel lobby and a combat Veteran, who was under fire during the Vietnam War, might hit the ground and cover his head with both arms. For similar reasons, combat Veterans avoid the July 4th fireworks, and combat pilots, visiting Paris during the July 14th celebrations, avoid watching the flying squadron formations overhead."

"Will I ever forget?" Asked Mr. If, having calmed down after Dr. Madison's explanation.

"I'm afraid not," replied Dr. Madison with a compassionate smile. "The brain does not forget pain but, with cognitive therapy, the impact of reminders can be lessened."

"Cognitive therapy?" Asked Mr. If with gaping eyes.

"Yes, and we can give you all the sessions you need here at the VAH."

"When can I begin?" He asked with visible impatience.

"We have already begun," smiled Dr. Madison as she took the PTSD pamphlets out of the orange folder, handed them to Mr. If, and with deliberate, slow motions tore the empty folder into small pieces, marched across the room, and defiantly threw the orange shreds into the trash bin.

Her symbolic action brought sighs of relief from all of us. Mr. If, witnessing the team's tension relax into soft smiles, stood up and announced, "I need to go feed Lexicon. He was starved when rescued, always acts as if he has not eaten for days, and if I'm ever late in feeding him, he makes heart-rending whines."

"Do you know why he behaves that way?" Asked Dr. Madison, hugging the door with her back.

"You don't think... You're not suggesting that he... Oh, surely you're not saying that he..."

"Indeed, I am," interrupted Dr. Madison, and, still holding the door with her back, waited for Mr. If to complete his unfinished sentences.

The symbolism, which was first enacted by our social worker, Wilma, did not escape us, nor did it escape Mr. If. Dr. Madison was intimating that she was not going to let Mr. If out of the room until he says the key word, which in itself is also a cue, a trigger, an alarm button, and an integral step in Mr. If's first Cognitive-Behavior-Therapy (CBT) session.

Mr. If surveyed our eyes, walked up to Dr. Madison with bowed head and a pain-riddled face, and blurted out his confessional.

"I guess both Lexicon and I are suffering from the PTSD Syndrome. Perhaps that's why we have bonded so strongly."

Dr. Madison smiled, shook Mr. If's hand, let go of the door's handle, and said, "Go feed Lexicon."

62

Chapter Four

Mr. If received weekly CBT sessions from Dr. Madison, and always came to his appointment with his dog because he felt very strongly that what was good for him was also good for Lexicon. Things changed, however, when he came in for his monthly appointment with our team.

Our nurse, Marissa, ushered him into the exam room and called in the team. He seemed in good spirits and was eager to tell us how much CBT is helping him and his dog. After some perfunctory conversation, peppered with pleasantries, I plunged into the heart of the matter with a simple question.

"Mr. If, are you still having your auditory hallucination?"

"What auditory hallucination?" He asked with a surprised face.

"The phrase, *if nothing happens,* that plays like a record in your mind."

"Oh, that phrase, yes, yes, it still plays, like background noise, all the time."

"Does it still bother you?"

"It bothers me less now, perhaps because I've finally gotten used to it," he smiled, without a hint of worry on his face.

The team, including Dr. Madison, froze with astonishment. How could he get accustomed that quickly to a hallucination, which had tormented him for twenty-three years, the very hallucination that had brought him in to us in the first place? It was obvious to me after scrutinizing the teams' faces that no one really understood what was going on. I held to the notion that CBT may have totally occupied his mind to the extent that it pushed the *If-nothing-happens* phrase into the background.

"Mr. If," I quizzed. "How's your sleep?"

"It used to be tortured by bad memories, but since Lexicon started sleeping with me, it has gotten better."

"What do you think about before you fall asleep?"

"Nothing really because I have no time to think."

"How's that?"

"Lexicon likes me to read to him before we sleep. He will not sleep nor will he let me sleep until I read him a bedtime story. I have *The Complete Short Stories of W. Somerset Maugham* and I read one story each night. Maugham's short stories are not exactly short, so by the time I finish reading one, we both feel exhausted and quickly fall asleep."

Mr. If's transformation was striking. He had climbed out of a self-destructive mood and taken charge of his own healing by applying his own creative methods. Moreover, he had succeeded in ignoring his haunting auditory hallucination by distracting his mind with matters of life instead of memories of death. After having been half dead for over 23 years, languishing under the grief of sudden incomprehensible loss, and surrendering to despair and inaction, he was now finding his way back to life, back to love, and back to meaningful existence. The powers of love are astonishing, I thought, even when they come from a little, rescued dog.

At that point, Nurse Marissa asked Mr. If to show her a picture of Lexicon. He reached into his wallet, pulled out a picture of his mutt, and handed it to her; and she in turn, passed it around for all of us to see. Mr. If's face glowed with pride as he listened to our admiring remarks. It was a moment of victory for us all.

When the picture was returned to Mr. If, he carefully put it back into his wallet, paused a while, and then pulled out another picture, wrapped in a browned, frayed piece of paper. Staring at the picture, his features changed, and his lips began to quiver as if he were saying something to himself, something deeply private, something he was not ready to share. Here, Nurse Marissa intruded on his trance with a question.

"Is that another picture of Lexicon?"

"No," he whimpered, staring at the picture without lifting his gaze.

"Whose is it then; I'm dying to know," she teased.

"It's a picture of my daughter and granddaughter taken just two weeks before the explosion."

Marissa got out of her chair, walked up to Mr. If's side, knelt down on both knees, and joined him in gazing at the picture.

"How old were they?" She asked.

"Mary was twenty-three and Hope was two," he whispered.

"They're beautiful."

"Mary would be forty-six now and Hope, 25 if they were still alive."

Marissa's eyes brimmed as she stood up, put her arm around Mr. If, and announced, as if addressing the 168 innocent souls who perished in the Federal Building's explosion, "Hope and Mary should never be allowed to die, Mr. If. By loving and teaching these illiterate children, you're keeping Hope and Mary alive."

Marissa's comment left us amazed and put a knowing smile on Mr. If's face. Carefully, he wrapped the picture with the frayed, browned paper and reiterated, " 'Hope should never be allowed to die.' Thank you, Marissa. I've never thought of it that way, but for twenty-three years, I was allowing hope to die and now I'm slowly bringing it back to life."

As Marissa walked back to her seat, we all noticed that after wrapping the picture in the browned, frayed paper, Mr. If did not put it back into his wallet. The symbolism, which escaped us, did not escape Wilma, our astute social worker. Cracking the hissing silence, she asked, "Mr. If, why do you have the picture wrapped in this old piece of paper?"

Mr. If's eyes, as if awakened from a deep sleep, peered at Wilma for the longest time then said, "It's the poem."

"What poem?"

"The poem that appeared in the paper a few days after the bombing."

"You've kept it all these years?"

"It spoke to me and I couldn't let go of it; that's why I kept it with their picture. I read it often because it brings me peace."

"Would you read it to us, please?"

"I've never read it to anyone else. I only read it when I'm alone."

"Perhaps the time has come to share it then. Would you please read it to us?"

With hesitant fingers, Mr. If unfolded the browned paper, stood up, and with a hoarse, whimpering voice recited...

*

It was an act of love
When the mushroom bloomed
Black upon blue
The Oklahoma skies
Cried their blue eyes
Until the smoke
Was washed away
With tears of sun.

Quiet pain is harsh
I heard the dusty dead whisper
Trapped in layers of suddenness
Not even one could scream.

It was an act of love
The way the dust was cleared
And not a drop was spilled
On other soil than ours;
Everyone made it out
Sooners and Laters
Now all together sleep
In Oklahoma.

Little feet couldn't run
Mothers' hands couldn't hold
When the deep noise drowned
Death surfaced high.

It was an act of love
All arms together
Armed with Christ
Undoing smoke
Undoing dust
Undoing death.

Memories are seeds
Grow into hopes
Free as butterflies
Free of hate.

It was an act of love
The way we raised our wounds
Up, up to the sky
And licked them high
Nor bowed our brows.

This pride, our cross
Borne with giant hearts
So Oklahoma
Would never heed
The Mighty Weight of Love.[27]

*

With moist faces, we watched Mr. If wrap the picture in the browned paper, put it back in his wallet, and slowly walk toward the door.

"I'll see y'all next month," he whispered without looking back.

---

[27] *The Mighty Weight of Love,* a poem from the book *Four & A Half Billion Years* by Hanna Saadah.

Chapter Five

When Mr. If returned for his monthly appointment, he was blushed with eagerness, as if he had something embarrassing to reveal. Instead of waiting for us to open the floodgates of discussion, he took charge of the meeting as if he were the defense counsel. Our psychologist, Dr. Madison, wore a knowing smile, which told me that her weekly CBT sessions had come to fruition.

"Doctor," he began. "I feel frightened of what's happening to me."
"Frightened?"
"Yes, like never before."
"Why?"
"My feelings are doing things that make me uncomfortable."
"You can tell the team," smiled Dr. Madison.

Mr. If, gulped, cleared his throat, hesitated, and then his words began to tread with caution, as if he were stepping into a dark room.

"I, think, I'm, in, love."
"How lovely," chimed Wilma, our social worker.
"But, she's a married woman," he stuttered.
"Oh, dear," mumbled Wilma, putting a hand over her lips.
"Does her husband know?" Inquired Nurse Marissa.
"No," he frowned, "and neither does she."

A sigh of relief wafted through the room when we all realized that it was only a matter of hidden feelings.

With painful embarrassment, Mr. If told us his story. The woman and her husband live in his neighborhood. She's in her fifties, has a perfect figure, and takes a fast walk every day, passing in front of Mr. If's house. For a long time, she passed unnoticed, but this last month, he has become obsessed with her, waits for her to walk by, follows her with his eyes, and cannot get her off his mind.

"When she walks by my house, the phrase, *if nothing happens*, begins to pace, one word with each step (*If* - step - *nothing* - step - *happens* – step) on and on and on… This cadence continues until she disappears from view, resumes when she reappears, and stops when she enters her house. Then, when she closes her door, the phrase, *if nothing happens*, resumes its baseline echoing in the background of my mind."

A coupling of an old hallucination with a new obsession had developed in Mr. If's mind this month, and none of us knew if that portended a healing or a relapse. Mr. If even changed his teaching schedule for the church kids, staying home to watch her pass by, and not leaving until she had returned.

"Mr. If," I ventured, when he had finished telling his story. "Does this new situation bother you or does it entertain you?"

"Both, Doctor. I'm thrilled to see her, but then I miss her and think about her all day long. I can no longer start my day without her and that bothers me to no end because it makes me feel like I'm her prisoner."

Mr. If's face quivered with pain as, unabashed, he delivered his confession. We could all feel his pains as well, his emerging-from-darkness pain, and his coming-back-to-life pain. We were thrilled that he was regaining his romantic feelings but saddened that he was enthralled by them. He was still grief stricken but his grief had taken on a new face, the face of Post-Traumatic Dyscontrol, the face of inappropriate love interest, and the face of love confusion.

"Since you are a literary man, why don't you turn her into literature?" I asked with a serious tone because I knew that obsessions can be very difficult to get rid of."

"Turn her into literature? I don't quite follow, Doctor."

"I learned that from Lawrence Durrell, the author of *The Alexandria Quartet*."

"What did Durrell say?"

The team's four women glared at me with incredulous eyes, waiting to hear what this Durrell, a name unfamiliar to them, said about them.

"He said," and I took in a deep breath under the gaze of ten expectant eyes. "He said, *'There are only three things to be done with a woman; you can love her, suffer for her, or turn her into literature.'* "[28]

"I see what you mean," sighed Mr. If with relief. "I have loved her and suffered for her all month long. The time has come to turn her into literature."

Dr. Madison seemed pleased with my suggestion. She waited for Mr. If to come out of his pensive trance and then added, "This is similar to the homework I give you after each CBT session. You have worked hard for me and now it's time to work hard for the doctor"

Mr. If got up, pulled out his wallet, retrieved a clean, folded, white sheet of paper, unfolded it, and stared at it without saying a word. Suspense grew as Mr. If's face blushed and quivered with tension. Dr. Madison's face darkened with concern and that worried us because we all knew about the explosiveness associated with the Episodic Behavior Dyscontrol Syndrome, which can be part of the PTSD. Silence fogged the room during this serious moment, which seemed to last and

---

[28] *The Alexandria Quartet*, a tetralogy of novels by British writer, Lawrence Durrell, published between 1957 and 1960.

last. Then, Mr. If coughed, cleared his throat, examined our strained faces, and mumbled,

"I've already turned her into literature."

"Oh," was the first word that escaped my surprised lips. Then I followed it with, "You must have read Durrell then."

"I knew nothing about Durrell or The Alexandria Quartet," he protested, "but I did turn her into literature, which is the only thing that saved my sanity. I used to write poetry, but I haven't written for years. Something in me is waking up, Doctor, and it's frightening me."

Mr. If stood up, shaking with stage fright. He wanted to read his poem but was awe stricken. It was Dr. Madison who came to his rescue. With a kind, warm voice, she whispered, "We'd love to hear your poem, Sir. Would you share it with us, please?"

Mr. If emitted a stuttering sigh and, with an uncertain voice, announced that he had a sonnet. He also announced that he had never written a sonnet before. His eyes, flickering with uncertainty, blinked repeatedly as if wondering how such a violent love could happen to him. Then, after a longsuffering pause, he gathered confidence from our smiling faces, lifted the paper to his eyes and read:

"Loving the imaginary is far more appealing and sustainable than loving the real. Whereas the imaginary gives us limitless freedom to create the ideal, the real sensors us to evidence. Nevertheless, because we do live in our minds, it is our minds that translate the hieroglyphics of life into meaningful messages, and it is also our minds that vouchsafe us our fifth dimension, our idealized imaginary world, which stretches beyond the realities of our time and space.

I Do Not Wish to Know You

I do not wish to know you; what I see
Is all I need to stitch a quilt of dreams
With whispering colors, faint, unreal and free
And disappointments tucked behind the seams.

In gardens I have fantasized your youth
And watered it with dew and drizzling rain
Sweeter than you could ever be in truth,
Which keeps my heart and mind immune to
          pain.

Not knowing is the harbinger of myth;
Imagination, child of the arcane,
Is freedom to create our own, our fifth
Dimension, which our knowing would disdain.

Not knowing keeps you perfect, keeps me free
To love and turn you into poetry."[29]

*

As we all applauded, Mr. If collapsed, exhausted, into his chair, his eyes gazing at a peaceful, starlit sky, far, far away from earth. Through poetry, he was transcending his painful reality and seeking refuge within the open arms of imagination. It was a sign of healing. The power of life within him had finally asserted itself against horrific tragedy.

---

[29] A sonnet by Hanna Saadah, specifically written for this chapter.

Chapter Six

The team huddled after Mr. If left to discuss future strategies. The goal was to rehabilitate Mr. If back to a meaningful life, which meant releasing him from his mental cage and freeing his wings to reach more friendships and more relationships. In spite of good healing, he was still a grief-stricken Veteran who was suffering from the abject lack of personal love.

Dr. Madison related that, although his weekly CBT sessions were still going well, they were now approaching a therapeutic plateau beyond which further improvement would not be forthcoming. She also interpreted his obsessive love for his neighbor to be a manifestation of his own starvation for love. Barring his dog, his church students, and us, Mr. If had no other love in his life. His sonnet was but an inner cry for a woman's love, a love that he once had, a love that had drowned, twenty-three years ago, into his profound ocean of grief.

Wilma, our social worker—who was the first to appreciate Mr. If's abject lack of love, the first to tell him that he needed a dog, and the first to suggest that he needed to start teaching illiterate students—declared that she was going to try to find his estranged daughter.

"She's probably married with children and grandchildren. She may not know it, but I'm sure that her need to reconnect with her dad is just as great as her dad's need to reconnect with her."

"How on earth are you going to find her after 21 years?" Asked Nurse Marissa.

"My husband is a private eye. He has connections. He'll find her for me. I already know her name and birthdate because I asked him in the church courtyard, and he told me. Finding her can't be that difficult."

"What if calling her and telling her about her father violates the privacy act?" Asked Dr. Madison.

"If I can help a Veteran by calling his daughter, nothing is going to stop me."

"But, don't you need to get his permission before you can share his medical information with his estranged daughter?"

Wilma paused, fidgeted, cleared her throat, and said, "Okay, okay, I'll get his permission first."

By the end of the huddle, we had all agreed that Mr. If's suffering was mainly caused by the lack of personal love, and that Wilma's effort to reconnect him with his only remaining daughter should feed his starved heart and pave the way back to his family.

Words of Edna St. Vincent Millay, from her sonnet, *Love Is Not All*, came to me as I walked back to my office:

> *"Yet many a man is making friends with death*
> *Even as I speak, for lack of love alone."*[30]

Wilma did not call Mr. If because she thought that her request would distress him. Instead, she waited till Sunday and had a conversation with him after church. He told her that his daughter has been angry with him since the explosion and has never returned his calls even though he had tried to call her on many occasions. He became tearful with hope when he gave Wilma her telephone number.

Wilma did get hold of forty-one-year-old Cynthia Dubitat. She lived with her sixty-seven-year-old mother in Herford, Texas, where they managed a consignment store. She had been married, divorced, and had a fourteen-year-old daughter, Joyce, named after grandmother Dubitat. When

---

[30] Edna St. Vincent Millay, from sonnet, *Love Is Not All*.

Wilma broached the topic of Mr. Dubitat's return to the family, Cynthia became irate and poured her heart out to Wilma.

"I don't ever want to see him or have anything to do with him again. I was eighteen when my sister Mary and her baby were killed in the explosion. She was divorced and living with us. That terrible morning, I woke up feeling heavyhearted. When Mary's car would not start, I begged her to call in sick and not to go to work. She had a lot of sick leave that she hadn't used. Of course, my father objected, telling her that it would be dishonest to call in sick when she was not. Instead of letting her spend the day with mother and me, he insisted on driving her to work. My mother begged him to let her have the day off so we could all go out to lunch, but he wouldn't hear of it. 'She'll be back at six and we can all go out to dinner,' he argued. What if something happens and you're not back at six? I asked. What if you had a long case and you couldn't bring her and the baby back till eight or nine? I challenged. 'Well then, they can wait in my office until I'm ready to bring them back,' he countered.

"Mary was a peacemaker. She went along with dad and as she left, she smiled at us and said, 'I'll be back at six, if nothing happens.' My heart stopped when she said that because I knew that something bad was going to happen to her and the baby. When I told mother about my bad feelings, she told me that she had the same premonition. We were both afraid that morning, prayed about it together, and wondered what made Mary say, 'If nothing happens.'

"After the explosion, my father became a bear. My mother and I held him responsible for the baby and Mary's death and he held us responsible for breaking up his marriage. We all fought continuously until life became unbearable. He stopped going to work, stayed home, and would have nothing to do with us. After two years of this hell, my mother and I left

and never looked back. He did give mother a good divorce settlement, though, and we didn't have to fight him in court.

"If he hadn't been so stubborn about taking Mary to work, she would still be alive, and her daughter would be twenty-five now. I don't think that my mother and I will ever forgive him for taking Mary and my niece to their deaths."

Wilma did not bother explaining Mr. Dubitat's condition to his daughter because Cynthia's anger was still too hot to be tempered. She did give Cynthia her telephone number and told her that Mr. Dubitat has never stopped loving her or her mother. Cynthia grew silent when she heard that declaration, and Wilma could hear her sniffle in the background. The last few words Wilma spoke into that sniffling silence were, "Because none of us can change fate, we would all have better lives if we would accept it."

Cynthia did not call the next day, as Wilma had hoped. It was Joyce, Cynthia's mother, who called. Her voice was more remorseful than angry, and she was eager to hear Mr. Dubitat's news. Wilma simply apprised her of the situation but did not plead with her to make amends. She merely asked her if she had found peace, to which Joyce answered, "I'm at peace because I'm far away from him, and I'm afraid we could lose our peace if we should come near him."

When Wilma related to us her two telephone conversations, it was Nurse Marissa who summed it up with a simple aphorism. "Some people would rather die than give up their anger."

Indeed, for 23 years, Cynthia and Joyce have held on to their anger as if it were their lifeboat. *"We hold on to our anger and increase it, as though its violence were proof of its justice,"* said Lucius Seneca[31] two thousand years before. He also said, *"Anger is often driven back by pity."* But, from what we had seen so far, pity was not capable of driving back Cynthia and Joyce's anger.

The day before Mr. If's monthly visit, Wilma charged into my office with a smile as wide as the horizon. For someone like Wilma, who is frugal with her smiles, showing me her face, aglow with unsuppressed joy, plucked me out of my seat. I stood at attention and before I could inquire about the source of her sudden cheer, she began.

"Guess who called me just now."
"Mr. Dubitat's wife?"
"No. Guess again."
"Mr. Dubitat's daughter?"
"No. Guess again."
"Mr. Dubitat's granddaughter?"
"We had the loveliest conversation."
"What did she say?"
"She said that she wants to talk to her grandfather."
"And?"
"I told her that we will call her tomorrow at noon. She gave me her cell phone number. Her last morning class ends at 11:55. She's going to find a quiet corner and wait for our call."
"What time is Mr. If's appointment?"
"It starts at 10:30 and ends at noon."
"Does he know?"
"No. We will need to prepare him for the shock. He does not even know that he has a granddaughter."

---

[31] Roman, stoic philosopher and dramatist, died in 65 A.D.

Chapter Seven

Mr. If, as usual, arrived on time, wearing a small smile over a worried face. I waited for Dr. Madison to start the interview because she had been seeing him weekly for his CBT sessions and monitoring his progress. When I saw from her downcast eyes that she had no intention to begin, I opened with, "Mr. If, we're all eager to hear about this past month. Could you please update your team?"

Mr. If lost his smile to a frown, his lips quivered with hushed words, and his eyes dropped to the floor and bounced aimlessly like little, rubber balls. Heeding the heaviness of the moment, I held my breath and waited for him to answer.

"Jimmy, my favorite student, was only fourteen."
"Was?"
"He was the brightest and was beginning to write."
"What happened?"
"He accidentally shot himself, playing with his stepfather's gun."
"How horrible," we all cried, except for Dr. Madison, who obviously knew.
"We held his services last Sunday."
"Was it well attended?"
"No. His family's life circle must have been very small."

I was afraid to disturb the shroud of silence that hovered over the room as Mr. If wiped his tears.

"I loved him like my own. He wanted to become a lawyer. Another senseless death. I'm not sure I want to go on teaching. Something bad always seems to happen when things are looking good. *'If nothing happens,'* the phrase, which my daughter left in my head, has after twenty-three years suddenly stopped playing. In its place, *'Something always happens,'* is playing nonstop now. I wish I were the one who had shot himself instead of Jimmy. Jimmy had a future. He was starting to write."

Mr. If was inconsolable. Nurse Marissa gave him gunlocks and asked him to lock his guns and put them away as soon as he got home. He reassured us that he was not suicidal but broke down repeatedly while we talked. Finally, Nurse Marissa changed the mood with an embarrassing question.

"How about your lady neighbor with the perfect figure? Is she still taking her walks?"
"I don't know?"
"You're not waiting to see her pass by your house?"
"Not anymore."
"What happened?"
"She slipped off my mind ever since the shooting. I don't seem to care about anything anymore."
"Yes, you do," interjected Wilma with a smile that lit up the gloom in the room.
"No, I don't," protested Mr. If.
"Yes, you do," insisted Wilma, looking Mr. If straight in the eyes.
"You always seem to know more about me than I know about myself," he retorted with an angry voice.
"Yes, I do," she calmly replied, still holding the same smile that lit up the room. Then, without giving him time to respond, she pulled a cellphone out of her pocket, handed it to him, and said, "Joyce Mirum wants you to give her a call."
"Who the hell is Joyce Mirum?" he croaked with a blank look.
"Joyce Mirum is your fourteen year old granddaughter."
"My granddaughter died twenty-three years ago."
"Wake up, Mr. If. Cynthia, your daughter, has a fourteen-year-old daughter who is dying to talk to her

grandfather. The Lord takes and the Lord gives. He took away Jimmy and now He's giving you Joyce."

Mr. If's face froze as he absorbed what Wilma had said. Then, as if his skin were made of old, dry wood, it burst into flame and his throat emitted inhuman howls that resembled the wild, nocturnal cries of wolves when they surround prey. He stood up, shook and swayed like a tree in a storm, held the cellphone to his ear, and screamed, "Hello."

Wilma took the phone out of Mr. If's clenched fist, found Joyce Mirum in the contact list, and dialed her number.

An excited, young voice answered, "Hello."
"Joyce?"
"Yes, that's me."
"This is Wilma, your grandpa's social worker. I have him here with me at the VA Hospital. I'm going to give him the phone and leave the room so you two can get to know each other."

Wilma handed the phone to trembling Mr. If, whose mouth was agape like a nestling about to be fed by his mother, and quietly left the room. We followed her in single file and closed the door.

We huddled in a nearby sitting area while Mr. If and his granddaughter had their first talk. Afraid to even whisper or stir, we sat in solemn silence and waited, everyone listening to what his own mind was saying. Time, like a long train, hummed endlessly in our ears, one wagon at a time, each wagon announcing the one behind it like a tireless, ticking clock. It was a deafening silence—a silence louder than fear, louder than pain, and louder than noise.

If time were measured with kilograms instead of hours, we would have collapsed under the tonnage of its heft. But, measuring it in hours was more merciful because it only took one hour for Mr. If to open the door.

When we walked back in, Mr. If had grown younger. His eyes, like an adolescent, scintillated with excitement. His face shone as if he were going on his first date. His stance was like an athlete about to start a long race. His motions were restless with anticipation and his words were a noisy waterfall.

"She wants us to Face Time every weekend.

"She wants to go to law school when she graduates.

"She has a four-point average.

"She wants to come see me as soon as she is allowed to drive.

"She wants me to come visit her as soon as I can.

"Her mother and grandmother are okay with that as long as it's not on a school day.

"She had to do a lot of begging to convince them to let me come visit her.

"I told her that I'd come see her the weekend after next.

"I can't believe I'm going to see my ex-wife, my daughter, and my granddaughter, all in one day, and all in one place, after all these years.

"I need to get a haircut and buy a new suit.

"I've not bought any clothes for twenty-three years.

"I used to be elegant.

"Oh, I'm sorry, I'm babbling, and I can't stop.

"I'd better go on home.

"I have so much to do now.

"I think I'll take Lexicon with me when I go to see her.

"She loves dogs.

"Oh, yes, thank you Wilma.

"Oh, thank you all.

"Oh, I'm beside myself.

"Oh, I'll see you all next month.

"Oh, I'd better go now.
"Oh, I'd better go."

Mr. If walked away a tall man, taller than he had ever been. We watched him fade into the crowd at the elevators and disappear into a new world, a world that came into being with a phone call, a world created by a sudden bolt of love.

Chapter Eight

Mr. If did all the talking when he returned for his monthly visit. His granddaughter was the most beautiful girl in the entire world. She hugged him when he walked into the house and screamed at the top of her voice, "Grandpa! Grandpa!" His daughter did not even smile but was courteous enough to shake his hand. His ex-wife did not even shake hands, but she did make tea before she and Cynthia retired to another room, leaving Little Joyce alone with her grandfather.

After visiting for a couple of hours, Mr. If asked Little Joyce if he could take her shopping. She ran to her mom to ask permission but returned with a disappointed face. He gave her a hundred-dollar bill instead and promised to come see her every month. They hugged for the longest time before he left. His ex-wife and daughter stayed out of sight even after he called to them, "Good-bye Joyce. Good-bye Cynthia. Thank you for letting me visit."

He and Little Joyce have been talking daily. He knows all about her friends, her teachers, her courses, and her activities. They have made grand plans. She's coming to OU when she graduates in two years. She's going to study law. She wants her grandpa to give her away when she gets married because her own father abandoned her and her mother, soon after she was born, and has not paid child support for years.

Mr. If was renovating his house. After twenty-three years of neglect, it needed a lot of work. He wanted to get it ready so that when Little Joyce comes to OU, she can come visit him with her friends and he can cook for them.

Each time he and Little Joyce talked, he asked to talk to her mother and grandmother, but they always refused, which disappointed Little Joyce. He was hopeful, however, that his repeated attempts to reestablish relationships would finally soften their anger. He had even written them a long letter, asking them to forgive him, explaining that Little Joyce would have a much better life if her family were reunited.

The metamorphosis we witnessed as a medical team was astounding. Mr. If had migrated from a life whose keynote was despair to a life whose keynote was hope, and this radical change had transpired through the mighty powers of love.

We did ask him, however, about his fast-walking neighbor and his *If nothing happens* auditory hallucination. They were both still there but no longer intruded on his life. He regarded them as peculiar annoyances and hardly noticed them because he was now busy with reconstructing his life, a life that had been neglected by hopelessness, a life that had been ruined by twenty-three years of confinement.

Mr. If never missed an appointment. He called the team his VA family, his only family, his true family, and he called his granddaughter, *The Rest of My Life*, explaining that just as our team takes care of him, he lived to take care of his Little Joyce.

The church school thrived under his mentorship. Every kid was his grandson, every girl, his granddaughter, and they all became his extended family. He was as proud of the kids' progress as much as he was of Little Joyce's achievements, and he loved them all with a heart as large as the church.

His ex-wife and daughter never relinquished their anger, never talked to him, and refused his invitation for a Thanksgiving dinner, which broke Little Joyce's heart. But as long as he had Little Joyce's love, he remained indomitable.

"In two years, Little Joyce will be at OU," he would say. "In two years, she and I will see each other at least once a week and I will be able to cook for her and her friends, take her shopping, and prepare her for law school."

Mr. If's string of aspirations was endless, alive with dreams, replete with ideas, and bustling with fantastic plans, all pertaining to Little Joyce and the illiterate church kids who were no longer illiterate. His life had acquired meaning, significance, and relevance. He pitied his ex-wife and daughter because they lived diminished lives, lives stunted by hate and sustained by anger, lives eclipsed by the sunny contrast of Little Joyce's magnanimous heart.

Chapter Nine

When Mr. If missed his appointment, we could not believe it. Dr. Madison said that he had made it to her CBT session two days earlier, and that he was excited about seeing our team because he had more news to share.

Wilma called Mr. If's cellphone repeatedly and when he did not answer, she called Little Joyce who said that they had talked the day before and that he sounded fine. He told her that he was planning on visiting her this coming Saturday, *if nothing happens,* which alarmed her a bit because it was not like him to say such nonsense. That's why she asked him if he felt okay and he reassured her that he felt fine.

What if he fell at home, we wondered? What if he's too sick to get to the phone? What if he had a car accident? Our *what-ifs* multiplied by the minute until they became innumerable.

Wilma brainstormed and she called the VA operator. "Did we admit a Mr. Daniel Dubitat last night?" She asked.
"Yes, ma'am. He's in the medical ICU."

We raced to the ICU. He lay comatose on a respirator with IVs running in both arms. The ICU doctor informed us that Mr. If had called 911 because he felt a sudden, heavy chest pain. They had to break in because the door was locked. He was in cardiac arrest with a flat line on the EKG. They resuscitated him and brought him to our ER because he had told the 911 operator that he wanted to be taken to the VA Hospital.

"Do we know how long he was out before they started resuscitation?" Was the first question I asked.
"We think that he had been out for at least fifteen minutes. His brain waves are flat. We're trying to contact his

family to see if anyone has a power of attorney or if he has a living will."

"Is it hopeless?" inquired Nurse Marissa.

"I'm afraid so," said the doctor with rueful eyes. "The EMSA team got to him a bit too late. He's seventy-three, and at that age, it's hard to bring them back."

Wilma called Little Joyce, who broke down at hearing the news. She then called Mr. If's ex-wife and daughter and asked them if they had a power of attorney. They didn't and they did not seem concerned.

When Wilma called Little Joyce again, she did remember that her grandfather had a living will because he had told her so in one of their conversations. He also told her that if something should happen to him, she would inherit all his estate.

"Did he tell you where he kept his will? Asked Wilma.

"Yes. He told me that all his wills are in the middle drawer of his desk. When I asked him why he was telling me all that, he giggled and said, '*If nothing happens* you won't have to worry, but if something should happen, you'll be the only one who knows where these important documents are.' "

Mr. If was pronounced dead after three days of ICU care. Wilma made all the funeral arrangements. His ex-wife and daughter did not attend, but Little Joyce did come. After the funeral, Mr. If's attorney handed Little Joyce a letter, which Mr. If had kept with his wills.

*

My Dearest Little Joyce,

Thank you for giving me back my love, sanity, dignity, relevance, hope, joy, life, and afterlife.

Upon my death, which I hope will not happen until I will have seen you graduate from law school, you will be well taken care of because everything I own will become yours.

Tell your mother and grandmother that I've always loved them and that I hope the rest of their lives would be filled with peace instead of anger. Anger suspends the soul, promotes hate, deforms love, and prevents joy from seasoning life. Anger is life's most vicious enemy.

Throughout your life, always insist on joy. Measure time, love, relationships, work, progress, success, and life with joy—for joy should be your measure of all things.

> *I love you more than all infinities*
> *More than all the fishes in all the seas*
> *More than the leaves and branches on the trees*
> *More than all the flowers that God's eye sees*
> *More than all the honey from all the bees*
> *More than the birdsongs that delight the breeze*
> *More than good sleep that puts our souls at*
> > *ease*
> *More than life's dreams and joyful memories*
> *More than every nascent minute that flees*
> *More than all life and its uncertainties*
> *And all its Ifs, which tantalize and tease...*

Grandpa Dubitat

Cold-Water Creek[32]
Oklahoma City VA Hospital, 2018

It was a day dipped in chilling history, which caused me to shiver in spite of my warm surroundings.

"The VA Hospital keeps us warm when it's cold outside," answered Mr. Vallo Pedites when I asked, "How do you feel, Sir?"

"Oh, yes," I agreed. "It's vicious outside."

"But it's warm inside," he reiterated.

"Indeed," I agreed again, "but how do you feel, Sir?"

"As I said, Doc, if it's warm, I feel good."

"And if it's cold?"

"That's when I feel terrible."

Of course, I was not visiting Mr. Pedites to chat about the weather. At 93, he was an old face with a young, articulate mind. He had been admitted because he had fallen and broken his hip. When they asked him if he favored surgery over waiting for natural healing, he chose surgery. When they indicated that they were hesitant to operate because he was a very-high risk, he quietly replied, "I'm rich in years and I want to get well so I can continue to enjoy my accumulated wealth."

Indeed, the surgery went well and, as anticipated, he needed rehabilitation on our CLC floor before returning home. That was the reason I was consulted and the reason why I had to ask him certain pointed questions. "Mr. Pedites," I resumed, hoping to avoid another weather chat. "Why did you fall? Did you trip? Did you faint? Did you lose your balance?"

"None of these, Doc. I know exactly why I fell. It was very cold, and I didn't put my warm socks on."

"You must have slipped, then," I volunteered.

---

[32] Pre-published, *Journal of the Oklahoma State Medical Association*, September 2019.

"No, Doc. I didn't slip. It was the sudden flashes of pain in my legs and feet that buckled me."

"Why the sudden flashes of pain?" I asked, for I had never heard that kind of a complaint before.

"As I said, Doc, I'm very sensitive to cold."

"So why didn't you put your warm socks on?"

"I never get up without putting my socks on."

I pondered Mr. Pedites's charming evasiveness and wondered why he was answering and yet not answering. Falls are deadly traumas for nonagenarians and knowing why he fell would help me prevent future falls. I had the subtle feeling, however, that he was not telling me something, something important, something he did not wish to share. Still, I had to know, and so I pressed on despite his manifest discomfort.

"Mr. Pedites, you told me that you fell because you had flashes of pain in your legs and feet."

"Yes, Doc. When these flashes come, they're so vicious they bring me down to my knees."

"So, you've had them before, I take it?"

"Oh, yes, but only when it's cold."

"Does anyone know why you have them?"

"I know, but the doctors don't quite understand when I tell them."

"Well, try telling me then. I am eager to hear your explanation."

"You're too young, Doc."

"I'm 73," I challenged.

"You weren't even born when it happened," he grinned.

I sat with bowed head and pondered what Mr. Pedites had said. I wasn't even born when his feet started flashing, which meant that they had been flashing for more than 73 years. As hard as that was to believe, I held on to my silence, hoping that he would eventually open up. He did not. He merely sneered and peered at me with knowing eyes.

"Mr. Pedites," I sighed. "Would you like for me to return at another time?"

"Perhaps that would be best," he affirmed, unapologetically.

"Would you like me to return this afternoon, after you've had lunch?"

"No, Doc. I've watched the news. It's going to get colder this afternoon."

"So, when would you like me to return, then?"

"Tomorrow afternoon would be best. The weatherman said that we're going to have a warm, sunny day after the morning fog clears," he affirmed and fell into silence.

We had one available bed at the CLC[33] and I could not hold it for Mr. Pedites if someone else needed it before tomorrow afternoon. I almost told him that he needed to make up his mind about coming to our rehab floor, but his melancholy gaze stopped me because his eyes were no longer in that moment. They had traveled back in time to when his feet had begun flashing, more than 73 years ago, sometime before I was born. I bowed to his wishes and took my leave without using words. For some intuitive reason, I merely saluted, turned, and slipped away, preserving the sanctity of his silence.

I felt bad when I had to fill the only available CLC bed that afternoon. Still, the next day, I went back to see Mr. Pedites at our appointed, post-meridiem time.

"You didn't forget," he greeted with a sad smile.
"I couldn't wait to return," I countered.

---

[33] Community Living Center, a rehab floor inside the VA Hospital.

"The sky looks as bad as yesterday," he frowned from behind his peering eyes. "The weatherman was wrong again," he sneered.

"You were going to tell me why your feet started flashing."

"I don't really feel like talking because the sky is still cold and dark, but I will anyway, because I promised. However, before I start, please take a look at my legs and feet."

Mr. Pedites's legs were red, warm, and swollen all the way up to his knees. The redness was most pronounced around the feet, tapered as it went up the shins, and abruptly stopped at about the same height on both legs. The contrast between Mr. Pedites's red, swollen legs and the bed's white sheets, made him look like he was wearing thick, red socks.

He was not surprised to see my surprised face. I reverently pulled back the covers over his crimson legs, which were genuflected as if in prayer, and stood lost in thought with dry words between my lips. Having never seen anything like that, despite of a half-century-long career, I slowly became aware that my feet were having trouble sustaining me. Mr. Pedites must have read my mind because he pointed to the recliner beside his bed and said, "Have a seat, Doc."

I did not sit. Instead, I collapsed into the recliner with a thud. Mr. Pedites smiled at my sudden collapse, which told me that he understood and that I need not ask him more questions. As promised, and in spite of the dark, cold sky, he had made up his mind to tell.

"Doc," he began. "As much as I hate to recall these memories because they come back smeared with fears and tears, I will tell you what happened because I think you're eager to understand. But, first, let me ask you some questions. Have you heard of the Battle of the Bulge?"

"Second World War's last major German offensive along the Western Front?"

"I'm glad to see that you know your history. What year were you born, Doc?"

"1946, Sir."

"Have you heard of the Malmedy Massacre?"

"No, Sir."

Mr. Pedites's face changed from pleased, because I knew my history, to forlorn, because I had not heard of the Malmedy Massacre. He looked out the window at the dark, sleeting clouds and muttered, as if talking to himself, "The sky looked just like this one on December 17, 1944."

Saying that, Mr. Pedites gazed at the angry Oklahoma clouds with trepidation, flew on the frantic, flapping wings of memory all the way back to Malmedy, and froze in a long, lonesome pause before he continued.

"I was a nineteen-year-old soldier in the 285th Field Artillery Observation Battalion of the 7th Armored Division. We were a small, lightly armed unit stationed between Malmedy and Ligneuville, in Belgium, dreaming of Christmas. All of a sudden, as if out of nowhere, a large German force led by Joachim Peiper surrounded us. We tried to resist but it was futile. We surrendered and all 150 of us were disarmed and taken to an open field. The sky was as dark as today's," he reiterated with brimming eyes.

"We huddled in the sleeting rain trying to stay warm, not paying attention to what the Germans were doing. Suddenly, they opened fire on us. Everyone panicked and started running. They massacred most of us because taking prisoners would delay their advance on Antwerp."

Mr. Pedites's throat, as if parched by the dry fire of memory, trapped his train of words and covered it with charred silence. His glazed eyes stared at the sleeting sky with disbelief as if wondering how could such an ominous sky return so blatantly after 75 years? I was afraid to move or make the slightest noise for fear that I might disturb the sanctity of that moment.

His hands trembled when he wiped his tears. And when he resumed telling, he talked to the bleak sky shrouding his window, which made me feel like an eavesdropper.

"I was one of the lucky ones. I ran without looking where I was going, left my dying friends behind, and landed in a creek below the bullet line. Although the freezing water came up to my knees, I decided that staying in the creek was safer than climbing out of it. I walked downstream until dark, evading the German military vehicles and soldiers, passing within earshot. I spent that night in the creek, shivering, without food, and lost all feelings in my immersed legs and feet.

"When the morning came, I resumed my walk but had to look to know where to place every step because my feet felt like they were not there. For three days, very slowly and very carefully, I walked down that creek and hid under the edge whenever I heard German vehicles approach. I did not dare climb out until the fourth day, when I heard American voices. 'Don't shoot,' I cried as I crawled out and collapsed.

"I was taken to a field hospital, given dry clothes and socks, fed, and kept warm. The doctors said that I had Trench Feet. It took me a long time to regain sensation and to be able to walk without looking to see where to place my steps. But the redness and pain flashes have stayed with me in spite of so many treatments. Some years ago, a neurologist finally told me that I had the Complex Regional Pain Syndrome and that it was not treatable.

"I've learned to live with the constant pain, but when [sic] them pain flashes hit, they still buckle me because they remind me of when the Germans opened fire on us, and we all panicked and ran. For seventy-five years, Doc, I've been walking with cold feet down that cold creek with German bullets flying over my head."

*

I admitted Mr. Pedites to our CLC rehab floor when a bed became available. When he completed his rehabilitation, I asked him if he was ready to return home or if we needed to make other arrangements.

"You must know from my chart that I live alone."

"Yes, Sir. I do."

"Is that why you're asking me, without asking me, if I prefer to go to a Vet's Home instead?"

"Yes," I confessed with a blush of shame.

"You're worried about me falling again, aren't you?"

"Well, as you said, when the pain flashes hit and you buckle, there's no way to protect you from falling."

"Yes, there is."

"Really?" I gasped with excitement.

"All I have to do before I get up is to put my electric socks on."

"So why did you fall and break your hip this time?"

"Because I didn't put my warm socks on."

"And why didn't you?"

"It was the 17th of December, the 74th anniversary of the Malmedy Massacre. All night, my dead friends kept calling me, saying, 'Run away Pedites. Run away. Run.' Before I realized what I was doing, I jumped out of bed and ran. That's when the pain flashes buckled me, and I fell."

"We carry our life's baggage on our backs wherever we go, don't we?" I asked with downcast gaze, avoiding Mr. Pedites's PTSD eyes.

"No, Doc. It's our feet that carry it all," he grinned as he put his warm socks on, pulled them all the way up to his knees, and readied himself for discharge.

Mr. Cauchemar
Oklahoma City VA Hospital, 2018

I happened to be in the ER when Mr. Cauchemar walked into the Oklahoma City VA Hospital agitated, incoherent, un-focused, and babbling unintelligibly about being shot. It took us quite a while to calm him down before we could understand what he was saying.

"They shot and mugged me; they did, I tell you; they did it in my own neighborhood."

With no bloodstains on Mr. Cauchemar's shirt, delirium was our initial diagnosis.

"Were you shot in Vietnam, Sir?" Inquired the ER provider.

"No, Sir, I was never wounded in Nam although I was shot at more times than you have hair on your head. But they did shoot me today, close to my home, and then they mugged me when I collapsed. They took all my money and left me for dead. The police picked me up and brought me here. Someone must have heard the shots and called them."

"We were in his neighborhood when we heard the shots, but we couldn't verify that he was shot. He was lying by the roadside, screaming, when we picked him up," said the police officer.

On removing Mr. Cauchemar's shirt, we found a small bullet-entry hole on the right side of his chest with a tiny amount of bleeding.

"It must have been a .22 caliber," said the officer, relieved that he had made the right decision to bring Mr. Cauchemar to the ER.

His chest exam was normal, and the chest x-ray did not show a bullet. We were baffled.

"Sir. Are you sure you were shot, not stabbed?" Asked our ER provider.

"I tell you, they shot me and mugged me and took all my money," barked Mr. Cauchemar, still wearing a frightened aspect.

"Let's take a look at your back, then. Please, sit up, Sir," said our ER provider as he helped Mr. Cauchemar sit.

"There [sic] ain't nothing wrong with my back, I tell you. They shot me right here," reiterated Mr. Cauchemar, pointing to the right side of his chest where the tiny, entry hole was.

Our trauma-experienced ER provider, finding a small exit hole on the right side of the spine, explained that the .22 caliber bullet must not have had enough power to penetrate the rib, but did have enough momentum to travel along the rib's arc and exit through the back.

"You mean you're not going to treat me?" Inquired Mr. Cauchemar with gaping eyes.

"There's nothing to treat, Sir. The bullet went in and out without causing any harm. You'd be better off at home."

"But, how about my money? How can I get home without money?"

"The police will handle that part, Sir, and they will be happy to drive you home. Who lives with you?"

"I live alone."

"Do you have family?"

"I have a son in Dallas."

"Would you like us to call him?"

"Yes, please. I'm afraid to be home alone anymore because that's where I was shot and mugged. I was walking in my own neighborhood when they attacked me," he reiterated. "There were three of them. I'm 77 and they were just a bunch of street kids."

Before Mr. Cauchemar was to be driven by the police to his home, we offered him sleeping pills and he was happy to receive them. We offered him psychiatric help, which he eagerly accepted. We also called his son who told him that he would leave right away and would be with him in about 3 hours.

"Would you come pick me up from the ER?" Pleaded Mr. Cauchemar with a supplicating voice.
When his son agreed, Mr. Cauchemar became suddenly calm and conversant.

*

"When I came back from Nam, I was equally frightened and it took me years to calm down," he explained. "For a long time, every noise or sudden sound startled me. This mugging may not be Nam, Doc, but it sure feels like it."
"Why don't you write it as a story," I suggested when I couldn't get him to smile.
"What would I do with a story like that?" He retorted.
"It may help you find closure."
"Closure? What does that mean?"
"When you finish writing your story, you'll be able to put the incident behind you and forget all about it."
"Sure enough?" He blurted with raised eyebrows. "You mean it won't linger in my mind for many years, like Nam did."
"That's what I mean by closure. It won't go away nor will it stay. It'll remain buried, deep in your memory, and won't bother you as much," I encouraged.
"Sure enough?" He quizzed with a skeptical smirk.
"Sure enough," I affirmed.

*

Time, like sea waves, ebbed and flowed between us as I resumed my work, hardly thinking of Mr. Cauchemar. It was several months later that he surfaced in our Geri-PACT clinic, wanting something for sleep, reported our nurse. His doctors had tried many treatments and so did his psychiatrists, but to no avail. He appeared frail, unkept, malnourished, frustrated, and cognitively impaired.

"Mr. Cauchemar," I jested, trying to diffuse his alarmed frowns. "Have you written your story yet?"

"I'm not sure it'll do any good, Doc. There's no closure to my insomnia. I had it for several years when I returned from Nam and now it's back with a vengeance."

"And the sleeping pills?"

"They do no good. It's like taking water."

"Do you have trouble falling asleep or staying asleep?"

"Both. I'm afraid to fall asleep because my nightmares are horribly frightening. And when they wake me up, I'm afraid to go back to sleep for fear of having them again."

"When did you start having these nightmares?" I asked, surprised.

"I had them for several years after I returned from Nam and now, they're back again."

"Do you still live alone?"

"No. My son and daughter-in-law sold their house in Texas and moved in with me. They take good care of me, but they can do nothing about my nightmares. I hate to wake them up every night, but I have to because they talk to me and calm me down. No one sleeps at my house anymore, Doc. No one, not even the dog."

*

Mr. Cauchemar had lost weight and muscle because the alarm of daily nightmares caused him to lose his appetite. He walked with fast, little steps like someone who is constantly falling forward. His frailty was doubly dangerous because it wrecked his energy and predisposed him to falls. One fall and his frail skeleton would crack. A broken hip would bring his end.

He ate well, walked well, and slept well before the shooting, hardly noticing his age or his loneliness, even though he lived alone. Now, in spite of the fact that he has live-in family and is never alone, his health has steadily declined. The shooting must have resurrected his Nam, which he had carried within him for the past fifty years. When his Nam demons re-awakened, they brought back with them vivid nightmares, which tortured Mr. Cauchemar's nights, and horrifying anxiety, which tormented his days.

My mind buzzed with sayings that I had collected over the years, sayings that I had only half understood until I witnessed what was happening to Mr. Cauchemar. Understanding him also made me understand what these sayings meant and how wise were the sages who said them:

"It is the future that decides whether the past is living or not," said Sartre[34].

"We know that memory requires forgetfulness—if we were to note down and store everything, we should have nothing at our disposal," said Simone de Beauvoir[35].

"I saw that pain itself was the only food for memory: for pleasure ends in itself," said Lawrence Durrell[36].

Indeed, Mr. Cauchemar's past was undermining his future. The way he had declined portended doom with

[34] John Paul Sartre (1905-1980) French existential philosopher.

[35] Simone de Beauvoir (1908-1986) French existential philosopher, partner of John Paul Sartre.

[36] Lawrence Durrell (1912-1990) expatriate British novelist.

worsening frailty, malnutrition, insomnia, anxiety, depression, fatal falls, and utter exhaustion.

*

"Is there nothing we can do about these nightmares?" Asked his son with a half-upset, half-desperate tone.

"There's one medicine that can work if we could give it," I replied, with my mind spinning the pros and the cons of *Prazosin,* which is a blood pressure medicine, a prostate medicine, and a nightmare medicine.

"And why can't we give it?" Retorted the son with glaring eyes.

"Because he's taking blood pressure and prostate medicines," replied the pharmacist, "and adding *Prazosin* is an absolute contraindication because it can cause a sudden drop in blood pressure with fainting and falls."

"And why can't we stop his blood pressure medicines?" Retorted the son.

"Because uncontrolled blood pressure causes strokes, especially at his age," affirmed the pharmacist.

"And why can't we stop the prostate medicine?"

"We could stop his prostate medicine," I replied after a pensive pause. "*Prazosin* will not be as good for his prostate, however, and he may end up with a swollen bladder and frequent urine infections, which could also be very dangerous at his age."

"So, what are we waiting for then?" Protested the son, still glaring at me with tired eyes. "His nightmares are killing us all. His bladder problems would surely be easier to fix."

"The VA computer has put a red flag on adding *Prazosin,*" said the pharmacist after checking her laptop, "and we're not allowed to go past it."

"Could I buy the medicine for him from an outside pharmacy?" Pleaded the son.

"That would violate the VA regulations, Sir," I said apologetically as I stood up and motioned to the pharmacist to follow me. "Let me please have a private moment with our pharmacist and we'll be back."

*

Huddling in the hall, the pharmacist and I had a sober discussion. If he were to take *Prazosin* and faint, he could surely break his hip and die from it. If he were to stop his blood pressure medicines, his pressure could go out of control and he would have a stroke and die from it. And if we were to do nothing, he could die of his malignant insomnia. The psychiatrists had tried all kinds of medicines, but nothing has assuaged his resurrected PTSD. We were his last and only hope and we did have an idea that was worth trying.

Silently, we walked down to the VA Pharmacy and asked to talk to the chief pharmacist. We presented our case and then suggested that we be allowed to replace Mr. Cauchemar's current prostate medicine, *Tamsulosin*, with the nightmare medicine, *Prazosin*, which also happens to be a fair prostate medicine. The Chief Pharmacist, seeing our dilemma, agreed to override the red flag and allow the even exchange to take place because it did not jeopardize Mr. Cauchemar's immediate safety.

*

Back in the examination room, we informed Mr. Cauchemar and his son of our collective decision to replace his prostate medicine with *Prazosin*, which we hoped would work for both his prostate and his nightmares. To be safe, I ordered the smallest possible dose and asked Mr. Cauchemar to start by taking one tablet at bedtime. He was to call me if he felt lightheaded upon standing up or if he had trouble passing urine.

"On your way out, please stop by the pharmacy and pick up your *Prazosin* so you can start it tonight," I said with an encouraging smile. "I shall call you daily to make sure you're tolerating the medicine and to increase your dose by half a tablet every few days until your nightmares stop."

"Are you sure this medicine will stop my nightmares, Doc?" Asked Mr. Cauchemar with a trembling voice.

"It's the best and the safest option we have," I reassured.

"But will it work?" He asked again, wanting absolute reassurance.

"No medicine works 100% of the time, Sir. To know, we have to try."

"So, what you're telling me is that it might not work," he retorted with a disappointed face.

"No, Mr. Cauchemar. I'm telling you that it usually works. Think of it as a car. It usually takes you where you want to go, but no one can guarantee that it always will because engines occasionally fail."

"But what if it doesn't work?" He asked for the third time, demanding absolute reassurance. "These nightmares are making me desperate, Doc. I don't think I have enough life in me to fight them any longer."

"If you can trust your car to take you home, you can trust this medicine to stop your nightmares."

"You have to think positive, Dad," added his son, looking both exhausted and exasperated.

"I'm telling you that I can't live like this anymore," snapped Mr. Cauchemar. "I can't and I won't. That's why I need to know for sure if the medicine is going to work."

"Are you having suicidal thoughts, Mr. Cauchemar?" I firmly asked.

"Suicidal thoughts? What on earth do you mean, Doc?"

"I mean are you thinking of killing yourself?"

"Killing myself?" He reiterated with an angry tone.

"Have you made a suicide plan, Sir?" I pressed on, seeing that he was getting more irate at my insistence.

"Oh, no, no, Sir. I would never do that. I have my son and his family to think about."

"That's all I needed to hear you say," I added, patting him on the back. "And, please don't forget to stop by the pharmacy and pick up your *Prazosin* so you can get started tonight."

*

The next day, Friday, I called Mr. Cauchemar's home several times, but no one answered the phone. They must have taken him out, I surmised. I was not worried because I knew that his son would have called me if anything had gone wrong. I called again on Monday and still no one answered. My mind began to wonder, but I was able to reassure myself that his son would have called me if things were not going well. On the next Friday afternoon, one long week after I had last seen Mr. Cauchemar, I was walking down the hall when I heard someone call my name.

"Mr. Cauchemar," I exclaimed excitedly, as he walked toward me, smiling and looking well.

"They're gone, Doc." he chortled. "My nightmares are gone. They went away after the first pill. This *Prazosin* is a miracle medicine."

"I'm thrilled to hear your great news," I said with a sigh of relief. Then, after shaking his steady hand, I asked, "What brings you here today? Do you have an appointment with one of your other doctors?"

"No. I just came to see you, Doc."

"How nice, but you could have called and saved yourself the two-hour drive."

"Oh, no. I couldn't do by phone what I came here to do. I have a delivery to make."

Saying that, Mr. Cauchemar pulled a handgun out of his satchel, and handing it to me, said, "I was going to kill myself, Doc, if your pill hadn't worked. I was that desperate. Here, please take my gun away. I never want to see it again."

"Let's go down together to the security office," I suggested, shoving the gun back into his satchel. "The security officers would be happy to take it from you."

On the way to the security office, I asked Mr. Cauchemar, "Why, when I asked you if you were thinking about killing yourself, you denied it and told me *'Oh, no, no, no. I would never do that. I have my son and his family to think about?'* "

Mr. Cauchemar suddenly stopped walking, looked me straight in the eyes, and replied, "I was desperate, Doc, and ready to blow Vietnam right out of my head. I also knew the rules. If I had told you that I was planning to kill myself, you would have admitted me to the Psych Ward and asked my son to hide my gun."

"Where are your son and daughter-in-law?" I asked after we had resumed walking.

"I sent them back to Texas to repurchase their home," he giggled. "I prefer my own company when I'm feeling good. Many of us who survived Nam became loners. Something about having seen so much jungle rot and jungle death forever separates us from the rest of unsuspecting humanity."

After Mr. Cauchemar surrendered his handgun to the security officers and signed the necessary papers, I walked with him to the outside door, shook his hand, and asked him to come see us in three months.

"Oh. I almost forgot," he cheered. Then, pulling a wad of papers from his back pocket, he handed it to me with a knowing smile and said, "Here's my story, Doc, and you were right, it did help with closure."

*

"Ideas come and go; stories stay."[37]

---

[37] Nassim Taleb (1960-) Lebanese American scholar. His 2007 book *The Black Swan* was described by *The Sunday Times* as one of the twelve most influential books since World War II.

A Worthless Death
Oklahoma City VA Hospital, 2019

"I don't know what to do with him," said the emergency-room physician. "He's not imminently dying and doesn't meet criteria for admission."

"We can admit him to our Palliative Care Unit (PCU) while we make arrangements for nursing-home hospice," I suggested.

"He doesn't want to go to a nursing home and doesn't want to die at home alone."

Mr. Sterben Leiden was an unmarried, childless, live-alone, 82-year-old Veteran, dying of Merkel Cell Carcinoma. When he could no longer care for his dog, home, and self, he gave his dog and belongings to his neighbor (who was not his friend) and came to the VA Hospital to die.

When I explained to him that he was not imminently dying, that we cannot keep him more than three weeks in our PCU, and that we will have to move him to a nursing home with hospice, he protested.

"Then help me get it over with while I'm here, Doc."
"What do you mean?"
"I know that I'm dying too slowly, but I don't want to die in a nursing home. Why don't you be merciful and help me die quickly instead?"
"I can't do that, Mr. Leiden."
"We euthanize dogs, for God's sake," he barked. "Treat me like a dog; that's all I ask."

*

At the PCU, Mr. Leiden and I had daily conversations. His mind, after an uneventful life, echoed with worthlessness.

He said that he had never had a girlfriend, never fallen in love, never married, never seen combat, never been to church, and never held an important position. After high school and thirty-four years in the Army, he worked as a security guard in sundry establishments. Having no friends, no hobbies, no passions, and no faith, he lived a reclusive life of platitudes, spending his free time reading magazines and watching television.

"Doc. I've nothing to live for and nothing to die for. Living is hard and few people do it well. Dying must be easy because everyone does it. Why don't you just help me do it so I can be done with it?"

Mr. Leiden lived, dreaming of death, not because death would lead to heaven or would end his suffering, but because it would end his feelings of worthlessness. I had trouble finding a counterargument to his worldview. Since he felt that he had led a "worthless life," hoping for a meaningful death never occurred to him. Happy at having terminal cancer, which provided him with the honorable discharge he needed, he now wanted to hurry up and get it over with.

His underdeveloped sense of worth mirrored by an equally underdeveloped ego offered him no alternatives. Thinking logically but from the wrong starting point caused him to arrive at the wrong conclusion, and there was nothing I could do to change his mindset. Dying was his ticket out of a "meaningless life" and that's what he wanted. The words of Simone Weil, a French philosopher-rebel, who died of tuberculosis in 1943 at the young age of 34, echoed in my ears:

"Death is the most precious thing which has been given to man. That is why the supreme impiety is to make bad use of it. To die amiss."

*

Laboring under the heft of Mr. Leiden's moral dilemma, I began to feel that I was the one who really needed help. My aching conscience could not countenance Mr. Leiden's wish to seal his "meaningless life" with an equally "meaningless death". Dr. Nadel Kunst, our PCU psychologist, came to my mind because on similar occasions she had helped me with ethical dilemmas that were equally vexing.

She was on the phone, having a death-and-dying discussion with a patient's daughter, when I walked into her office, wearing an anguished aspect. Scanning my face with circumspect eyes, she motioned for me to take a seat. When her conversation ended, she sighed and knowingly asked, "So, what's bothering you this time, Doctor?"

When I finished relating Mr. Leiden's story, she shook her head and said, "That's not possible."

"What's not possible?" I asked, a bit bewildered.

"Nature does not constitute such men."

"I'm lost, Dr. Kunst. What are you trying to tell me?"

"I'm telling you that Mr. Leiden is not telling the whole truth. Our ego defenses, which are mighty, are constituted to magnify self-worth, not to diminish it. Even when the entire world thinks that someone is worthless, that one person will continue to esteem himself as a misunderstood paragon of the highest worth."

"So, what you're telling me is that Mr. Leiden is concealing something?"

" 'The truth is rarely pure, and never simple,' said Oscar Wilde. Your patient is hiding behind convenient illusions and concealing many more things than you realize, Doctor. Hardly a man passes through youth without having sex and falling in love—and hardly a man grows old without friends, interests, desires, biases, and beliefs. Mr. Leiden has buried his secrets deep within his unconscious mind so that he would not have to deal with them. I don't think he's aware that he's hiding anything, though.   If he were, he would be in continuous emotional torment.   His mind is just like a dusty, old attic in which one puts away things that one no longer wishes to see but, nonetheless, things that one is unable or unwilling to discard.   Once they are tucked away into that dusty attic, they are soon forgotten, never to be again remembered unless one is forced to do an attic search.

'In the practical use of our intellect, forgetting is as important as remembering,' said William James.' "

"So, the reason he's seeking a quick death is because death insulates him from life and ensures absolute, irrevocable oblivion?"   I philosophized, trying to match her intimidating, psychoanalytical and literary wit.

Instead of answering me, Dr. Kunst simply stood up, smirked, and said, "Let us go and make our visit."   Then, in passing, she recited the first stanza from T. S. Eliot's Love Song of J. Alfred Prufrock:

> " 'Let us go then, you and I,
> When the evening is spread out against the sky
> ...
> Oh, do not ask, What is it?
> Let us go and make our visit.' "[38]

On the way to Mr. Leiden's room, I asked Dr. Kunst how I should introduce her, knowing that I had not prepared Mr. Leiden for the consult.   Rather than responding, she shrugged her shoulders and hastened her pace.

*

---

[38] T. S. Eliot (1888-1965) was an American poet who spent most of his life in England. The Love Song of J. Alfred Prufrock is one of his most famous poems.

"Mr. Leiden. I have with me Dr. Nadel Kunst, our CLC Professor of Psychology, who is here to help us make some important decisions about your care."

Mr. Leiden seemed astonished but not because of Dr. Kunst's comely, commanding stature, nor because of her almond-blossom smile. His aspect was that of a lost soul who has just had an epiphany.

While I shadowed in the background, Dr. Kunst gracefully sat at Mr. Leiden's bed, held his hand, smiled blue with her eyes, and whispered, "Are you having a good morning, Sir?"

"Oh, yes, yes, Doctor. Thank you for asking," he blurted out.

"May I ask you a few questions, then?"

"Sure, Doctor, sure," said Mr. Leiden, straightening his position in bed as if readying himself for a television interview.

"At what age did you join the Army?"

"I was eighteen, Ma'am."

"Um, that was 1954, wasn't it?"

"Yeah, one year before the Vietnam Conflict began."

"You had a high-school sweetheart when you joined, didn't you?"

Mr. Leiden's words froze between his pale-blue lips.

"Do you remember her name?"

After a long, solemn pause, tears welled in Mr. Leiden's vacuous eyes and, unwiped, dripped down his cheeks. Dr. Kunst handed him a tissue, which he received with tremulous fingers. Shadowing behind the scene, I eased myself into a corner chair and watched the magic of a seasoned interviewer scroll before my eyes.

"Do you remember her name?" Dr. Kunst asked again.

Mr. Leiden stuttered a long, lingering sigh. His lips quivered with unsaid words. Then, all of a sudden, he covered his eyes with both hands and burst into uncontrollable sobbing, which took a long time to die down.

Silence like a distant airplane droned, bespeaking the solemnity of the moment.

*

"What was her name?" whispered Dr. Kunst.

"Linda Marquez," he whispered back, then as an afterthought, he added, "and we shared the same birthdate."

"Linda means beautiful in Spanish. Was she Colombian?"

Mr. Leiden, seeming astonished that Linda's nationality was known to Dr. Kunst, nodded a meek yes.

"Would you like to tell me about her?"

"No," he replied, assertively shaking his head.

"In that case, would you like me to leave you to your thoughts and perhaps return later?"

"No," he assertively shook his head again, tightening his clasp on Dr. Kunst's hand.

"Did you love her?"

"Uh-huh," he nodded.

"Did you love her a lot?"

"Uh-huh," he nodded again, taking a deep, doleful breath.

"What happened to her?"

"I lost her."

"Why?"

An uncertain, pensive pause furrowed across Mr. Leiden's face, lingering for a long, long while. Then, his lips pursed, his eyes blinked, and his breaths became deep and rapid like a diver, preparing for a deep dive. Dr. Kunst patiently stroked his hand as a solemn smile shone from her kind, calming face. It was a shared moment of reflection with each of us having different thoughts about that very same *"Why?"*

"When I returned from my first tour in Vietnam," stuttered Mr. Leiden, "I got, I got, ah."
"Did you get drunk?"
A yes nod.
"Did you have a fight with Linda?"
Another yes nod.
"Did you hit her?"

In response, Mr. Leiden burst into loud, screeching sobs and could not stop. Dr. Kunst knelt her head down as if in prayer and let his avalanche of tears flow down his face, inundating his shirt, his sleeves, and his bed sheets. This cataclysmic catharsis continued unabated until he ran out of tears and his eyes, glazed with remorse, stared like a searchlight into his deep, dark, dusty attic.

"Mr. Leiden, you need to rest now," whispered Dr. Kunst, as she tried to withdraw her hand. "I'll return later to finish our conversation."
"No," he pleaded, tugging tighter on her holding hand. "I'm not finished yet."

*

Mr. Leiden's painful confession lasted a longsuffering hour. Back from his first tour in Vietnam, he went out with the boys and returned intoxicated to find Linda worried and extremely upset. They had a terrible argument and *"she started wailing like them Vietnamese women when we would overrun their little villages."* When he couldn't stop her *Vietnamese wailing*, he lost his temper, hit her, and then he collapsed into bed. When he awakened the next morning,

Linda was gone and so were her clothes and her few belongings. She left no note and he never could find her.

Heartbroken, he volunteered for five more tours in Vietnam, hoping he would get killed. Many of his friends were, but he escaped unscathed. When, after thirty-four years in the service he returned to civilian life, he felt like a released prisoner let out into a world that he no longer understood and no longer belonged to. His parents had died, he was an only child, his friends were all married and gone, and what was left of life had no meaning left in it.

He still carries a picture of Linda Marquez in his billfold, still thinks about her many times a day, and still hopes to find her to explain what Vietnam had done to him and to say how remorseful he had been ever since their fateful, sixty-year-old argument.

He became elated when he found out that he had cancer because it was a certain way out of his silent suffering, a suffering that had festered and sprawled all over his life, a suffering that was caused by not knowing his Linda's fate, a most bitter unknown that he no longer could endure.

Dr. Kunst's last words to him before he let go of her hand were, "Just give me some time to think about all this. I'll be back soon."

*

"What do you have in mind?" I asked Dr. Kunst as we walked back to her office.
"I have to find his Linda."
"If she's still alive, she would be eighty-two. She could be demented or sick or back in Colombia."

" 'Ultimately, literature is nothing but carpentry. With both, you are working with reality, a material just as hard as wood.' "

"What on earth does this mean?" I asked, feeling frustrated.

"It's a quote from Gabriel Garcia Marquez."

"Who on earth is Gabriel Garcia Marquez?"

"The Colombian author who was awarded the Nobel Prize for Literature for his masterpiece novel, *One Hundred Years of Solitude*. Mr. Leiden has had sixty years of solitude and the name of his Colombian girlfriend was Linda Marquez. Do you see the connection?"

"Was it the Marquez name that helped you surmise that Linda was Colombian?"

"It was a good guess, you must admit."

"For a while, you sure had me baffled."

*

Dr. Kunst sat down behind her desk and nervously scribbled on a yellow sheet of paper. She appeared to be in a pressured moment, perhaps reflecting on what Mr. Leiden had said and on what she could possibly do to help him.

After a few minutes of intense thinking, she raised her eyes, glanced at my baffled face, threw her paper and pencil into the trash, and announced:

"No Veteran should die alone, and no Veteran should die feeling worthless or unloved. I am going to find Linda Marquez because she holds the key to Mr. Leiden's self-worth."

"And how on earth are you going to find her after sixty years of solitude?"

"I have police connections inside and outside the VA. They'll do everything in their power to save a dying Veteran from loveless worthlessness."

*

I deferred the investigation of the life and whereabouts of 82-year-old Linda Marquez to Dr. Kunst and went about my work, doubtful that her efforts would prove worthwhile. That Mr. Leiden never had a girlfriend, never fell in love, and never saw combat—were the denials he needed to sustain his pacifying feelings of worthlessness. Feeling worthless protected him from guilt, from remorse, from responsibility, and from the painful processes of a civilian life, which he felt estranged from.

But now, with his mental attic explored and excavated, making rounds on him became a painful routine. Every morning he would ask me if Dr. Kunst had located Linda, the Linda he loved, the Linda he hurt because she wailed like a *Vietnamese-village-woman*, the Linda who was still as young and as beautiful as the day she left him. Rather than respond to his lamentations, I inquired about his symptoms and kept him comfortable. I treated his pain, nausea, swelling, headaches, weakness, muscle wasting, imbalance, shortness of breath, and double vision.

Like him, I wanted to know how Dr. Kunst's investigation was proceeding but was afraid to ask. Like him, I began thinking about Linda Marquez several times a day and could not get her off my mind. But, unlike him, I understood that the drama of their last night was a flash explosion of his Post-Traumatic-Stress-Disorder Syndrome. And unlike him, I understood that *wailing-like-a-Vietnamese-village-woman* was his alarm button, his call-for-action siren, and his combat-reflex trigger. And unlike him, I also understood his protective feelings of worthlessness, feelings that had sustained his sanity, feelings that had been pounded flat by a wood-hard reality.

*

My doubts became my demons. Did we save him from apathetic worthlessness to condemn him to agonizing guilt? Would he have been better off having a painless, "worthless death" than a painful, remorseful one? My conscience ached each time I visited him, empathized with his interminable pain, rolled over with his tumbling soul, and was scalded by his loveless inferno.

Words from Fyodor Dostoevsky's novel, *The Brothers Karamazov,* paraphrased themselves out of my memory:

Where is heaven, asked Alyosha, one of the Karamazov brothers? Heaven is in every one of us, waiting to be reached, answered Father Zossima. What is hell then, asked Alyosha? Hell is the suffering of being unable to love, answered Father Zossima.

*

The end of the third week in the PCU portended the transferring of Mr. Leiden to a nursing home with hospice. But I could not face him with the exigencies of this bureaucratic reality. My daily rounds and his dedicated nurses' kind attention provided him with emotional support that the nursing home environment could not emulate. We had become his hospital family, and estranging him from us would be a cruel, undeserved punishment. I pleaded my case with the Chief of Staff, Dr. Stabschef, and she was sympathetic.

"He doesn't have much longer to live. Let's continue to provide him with team compassion. For all that he had been through, we at least owe him a peaceful dying and a painless death."

I never bothered Mr. Leiden with these issues; the less he knew, the more at peace he seemed. Except for an occasional deep discussion, his life and ours had settled into equanimity with salutary routines, courteous conversations, and occasional laughs. Nevertheless, he still asked me about Linda Marquez every morning, and every morning I responded with the same answer: "Since you and she have the same birthdate, surely Dr. Kunst will be able to locate her." That answer not only appeased him, it also gave him hope, which sustained and supported him against his growing frailty.

*

One Sunday morning, lightning struck and the earth quaked.

"You need to meet us at the hospital."
"Dr. Kunst. I'm not on call this weekend."
"You may not know it, but for Mr. Leiden, you're always on call."
"You found Linda Marquez, didn't you?"
"No, she died in Bogota last year."
"So why do you need me in the hospital then?"
"Because Linda Marquez's grandson is flying in from Houston for the pinning ceremony [39] this afternoon. All arrangements have been made. We need you with us in Mr. Leiden's room at 4 p.m."

---

[39] An honoring ceremony attended by nurses, doctors, chaplain, family, and employees in which the chaplain offers a prayer of thanks for the Veteran's services, music is played, the soldier's creed is read aloud, an American-flag button is pinned to the Veteran's shirt, and a hand-made quilt is presented to the Veteran as a token of gratitude.

"What does Linda Marquez's grandson have to do with Mr. Leiden?"

"Mr. Leiden is his grandfather. Linda found out she was pregnant a few days after she left, but she never answered Mr. Leiden's calls and never told him that she was carrying his child. She did tell her son, though, who his father was, and her son, before he died, did in turn tell his son who his grandfather was. She was so angry with Mr. Leiden that she made both son and grandson promise never to contact him, and she clung to her bitter anger until the day she died. I had to do a lot of explaining before the grandson agreed to visit."

"What role would you like me to play in the pinning ceremony."

"Say something worthy of the occasion."

"Does Mr. Leiden know?"

"I've told him everything and he can't wait to spend time with his grandson. That's all he really cares about now. The other arrangements for the pinning ceremony were left to my discretion."

*

At 4 p.m. we walked in as a team into Mr. Leiden's room. His grandson, tall and handsome, bore a striking resemblance to his grandfather. Mr. Leiden's sunken eyes popped out of their sockets when he saw Juan, leading the team, wearing full military uniform, holding the American flag, and marching with regular, measured tread.

Struggling against unforgiving gravity, Mr. Leiden, clean-shaven, labored out of bed, steadied himself, stood at attention, and saluted.

*

The VA chaplain started the ceremony with a reading from Saint Paul, 1 Corinthians 13:4-8:

Love is patient, love is kind. It does not envy, it does not boast, it is not proud. It does not dishonor others, it is not self-seeking, it is not easily angered, it keeps no record of wrongs. Love does not delight in evil but rejoices with the truth. It always protects, always trusts, always hopes, always perseveres. Love never fails…

Next, CLC Nurse Angela sang with her opera voice, *O Fortuna* from Carl Orff's *Carmina Burana*:

"O Fortune, like the moon, you are changeable, ever waxing, ever waning…"

Next, Juan read the Soldier's Creed:

"I am an American Soldier.
I am a warrior and a member of a team.
I serve the people of the United States and live
*   the Army Values.*
I will always place the mission first.
I will never accept defeat.
I will never quit…"

Next Dr. Kunst pinned the American-Flag button on Mr. Leiden's pajama shirt, presented him with a quilt made by the VA Lady Volunteers, and proclaimed with a voice vibrant with awe:

"Only the deserving receive this quilt, only the honorable, only those who served our country and whose worth to us and the future generations is beyond verbal expression. A soldier lives in our collective consciousness unto infinity; he could never fathom the far-reaching influence of his actions."

Then Dr. Kunst motioned for me to say my few lines, which I had prepared that morning. I read them slowly to give Mr. Leiden enough time to absorb them:

> *"If we fill our souls with love*
> *We'd have no room for hate;*
> *If we fill our hearts with passion*
> *We'd have no room for apathy;*
> *If we fill our spirits with faith*
> *We'd have no room for despair;*
> *And if we fill our lives with God*
> *We'd have no room for fear."*[40]

*

When the pinning ceremony was concluded, we walked out in the same order we had entered, leaving Juan with his grandfather to fill in the gaps astride sixty years of solitude.

---

[40] A prayer by Hanna Saadah.

Raging Storm[41]
Oklahoma City VA Hospital, 2019

His face quivered. His eyes simmered. His wife hid behind dark glasses. The examination room was angular and sterile. I was pre-warned by the clinic nurse: "Beware, Doctor. He's a raging storm."

*

"Good morning, Mr. Tinnier," I began, cracking the stiff, dry silence.
"Where're you from?" He snapped.
"Lebanon."
"What brings you here?"
"I came fifty years ago to specialize."
"And why didn't you go back to your own country?"
"A civil war broke out and I couldn't return."
"Are you legal?"

*

Mr. Ira Tinnier's long, lean legs shook as he sat behind his bushy, white mustache and glared into my eyes. Cautiously, I inched my rolling stool closer and closer until his wife clasped his right arm and held it down. Then, with a tremulous voice, she whispered, "Honey. He's here to help you."
"No one can help me," he snapped back.
"We've come all this way for a second opinion. Might as well give the doctor a chance?"

---

[41] Published, *The Bulletin*, Oklahoma County Medical Society, July/August issue, 2020.

Then, while still clasping Mr. Tinnier's sinewy, right arm, she explained. "We drove three hours to this appointment because his doctor wanted to see if the VA had anything new to offer. He's 100% service connected for his PTSD"

"Mr. Tinnier," I said with a calming voice. "I can tell that you don't feel like talking. But, using just one, simple word could you please help me by telling me what bothers you the most."

"**Anger**."

His wife nodded approvingly and let go of his arm. Then, seeing my confused aspect, added, "He's angry all the time and snaps at everyone and everything at least once a day. He's never been able to keep a job. He's been fired more than thirty times because of his temper. He snaps at the dog, at the TV, at the weather, at the furniture, but mostly at me. I love him dearly, but I'm afraid of him. He gave me a black eye just the other day."

Mrs. Tinnier took off her dark glasses. It was her left eye. Mr. Tinnier seemed unconcerned as if this had nothing to do with him or her.

"He's a good man," added Mrs. Tinnier, putting her dark glasses back on. "It was his anger that did it, not him. He doesn't know what he's doing when he snaps."

Mr. Tinnier, as if uninvolved, somberly stared at his elaborately embroidered cowboy boots.

*

"Mr. Tinnier," I asked after a polite pause. "What makes you snap?"

"Questions, like what you're doing to me right now."

"Doctor," interjected his wife. "He hates to be questioned, but he also explodes for no reason. Scares the heck out of me."

"Mr. Tinnier. Do you have any warning signs before your anger snaps?"

"No. It just explodes like a dynamite stick."

"How long does it take you to get over it?"

"It lasts a minute, but then I stay shaken for twenty more minutes. Then a real mild headache follows and lasts about an hour or so."

"Where does the headache hurt?"

"All over but it isn't bad enough to take anything for it."

"Have they tried you on anti-seizure medicines?"

"I'm taking two. They do no good."

"How about antidepressants?"

"I've taken so many. Same thing. This last one helps me sleep, but it [sic] don't help the spells."

At this point, Mrs. Tinnier took over the conversation. "He was a wonderful man before he went to the service. I never gave up on him, though, because I love him. We've been married fifty years."

"Was he in combat?"

"I never saw combat," interjected, Mr. Tinnier. "I was trained in Morse Code and was a Morse Code operator on a ship in Vietnam's South China Sea from 1960 to 1964, 12 hours on, 12 hours off, seven days a week without breaks."

"He sometimes worked 18-hour shifts," added Mrs. Tinnier.

"Them headphones drove me crazy," he snapped again. "I can still hear that *dud-da-daa* in my head. Can you help me without giving me more medicines? I'm already taking nineteen."

His wife handed me his bulging bag of pills.

*

I examined Mr. Tinnier's medicines, moving them one-by-one out of the bag. He was taking pills for high blood pressure, atrial fibrillation, diabetes, anxiety, depression, insomnia, seizures, arthritis, osteoporosis, allergies, and cholesterol.

"I see that you're not taking any vitamins."

"He took bunches of vitamins for a long time, but then he got mad because they were expensive and did him no good," interjected Mrs. Tinnier.

"Nothing has ever done me any good except them weekly group sessions," affirmed Mr. Tinnier. "I'm seventy-seven. My ears ring constantly as if an endless train is passing through my head. I can't control my temper; it controls me. I've hurt everyone's feelings. I force myself to eat because I continue to lose weight. I am just waiting to die and am as ready for relief as is everyone else around me."

Having fumed out his frustration, Mr. Tinnier sighed and fell into a deep well of silence. His attitude, almost suicidal, worried me. He clearly disliked being questioned, but I felt compelled to further probe his desperate soul. After a cautious pause, I whispered, "Tell me about them weekly sessions."

"A psychologist holds group therapy for a bunch of us guys with PTSD. I've been going for twenty years and I never miss. I always feel calm when I leave. They're the only thing keeping me alive," he confessed, and then, after a moment's reflection, added, "that, and reading my Bible."

*

His last statement relieved my anguish. Men of faith do not commit suicide, I surmised. But, something about his anguished despair still worried me. As I composed my next question, Mr. Ira Tinnier stared at his boots and nervously shook his knees.

"Mr. Tinnier. Are you thinking of death as a solution?"

"What's wrong with death?" he retorted.

"You may think that death ends your problems, but it leaves all kinds of problems behind."

"No, it won't. No one will miss me. Everyone will be relieved when I die. My life has so much wrong with it. It can't be fixed." Then, with a softer tone, he pleaded, "I know you understand what I'm saying. Why can't you help me get it over with?"

When he said that, his wife seemed unconcerned, which surprised me. I needed her to hold his arm, to admonish him, to remind him of his daily Bible readings, but she behaved as if she were a spectator, watching a show.

"I do understand what you mean, Mr. Tinnier, but as a doctor, my mission is to save your life, not to help you end it."

"Save my life from what?"

"Save it from death."

"But, what's wrong with death?" He retorted again. "It solves all the wrongs of life and there's never anything wrong with it. Death cleans life's dung and makes room for others who need a place to live. I went to college on the GI Bill and majored in philosophy and religion. I know all about death. There's nothing wrong with death; there's everything wrong with life."

"But it is selfish to choose death, leaving those who love you with problems that have no solutions."

"We are born in bondage, Doctor. You are ruled by your profession, I am ruled by my infirmity, we are both ruled by life, and only death can free us from our captivity. All our so-called freedoms are illusions. No one is really free while alive."

"He reads philosophy every day," added his wife. "No one can win an argument against him."

*

"Do you believe in God, Mr. Tinnier?" I asked with a firm voice.

"Our beliefs are myths to others as the beliefs of others are myths to us. We don't only live on earth, Doctor. We live equally hard in our fantasies, which are just as real as the earth upon which we walk."

I knew at that point that I was dealing with a desperate man who still reads his Bible every day even though he had lost his faith in God. His wife and I exchanged knowing glances, which he noticed but did not seem to mind. Nevertheless, my options were limited. I could tell him that I had nothing to offer and apologize for wasting his long day of travel. Or I could keep the conversation alive, hoping that by verbalizing his thoughts he would feel improved, as he does after his group therapy sessions. Even though I was un-steeped in philosophy, my best idea was to challenge his notion that no one is free while alive.

"Surely, Mr. Tinnier, you must at least agree that our imagination is free."

"Imagination is not free," he sneered. "No one can imagine anything totally unknown to the mind. Imagination merely extrapolates from what we know, but all its images and scenes must remain tethered to our experiences. Try to imagine what God looks like and you will not be able to go beyond the collective images that are already in your brain."

"Mr. Tinnier. Can you imagine that I may be able to help you?"

A long pause followed without a response. Saying that he could not imagine that I can help him, would be hard to defend because my next question would challenge him with, *'Why did you bother to come to the VA then?'* As I waited for an answer, he sighed, fidgeted, roamed his eyes around the room, and then replied, "I have hope, and that's what keeps me going. But I don't want more medicines."

"Are you talking about prescription medicines?"

"Yes. No more prescriptions for me. I already feel overmedicated."

*

Despair conjures desperate ideas. The Tinniers and I were desperate. Mr. Tinnier was desperate for relief, Mrs. Tinnier was desperate for peace, and I was desperate for an alternative solution. I agonized under the gaze of Mr. and Mrs. Tinnier's expectant eyes. Silence hissed and grew louder and louder the longer I theorized: *"What if his 20-minute spells were violent migraine auras followed by very mild headaches? What if his PTSD anxieties were his migraine triggers?"*

*

"Mr. Tinnier. I have a theory."

I explained my idea to the Tinniers avoiding medical jargon.

"Vitamin B2 is a good migraine preventer. Fish oil is a good anxiety calmer. You can get them both without a prescription. Would you be willing to try them?"

"Sure. I've taken vitamins before. They don't bother me."

Diligently, I inscribed on a blank sheet of paper:

1) Riboflavin 400 mg daily at bedtime.
2) Fish Oil 900 (EPA 653 mg / DHA 247 mg) daily at bedtime.

*

When I called Mr. Tinnier a week later, he felt much improved and reported no anger spells. Two weeks later, his wife was happy with his progress and they were doing better as a couple. Three weeks later, he was taking care of his wife, going to the store, getting her medicines, and going with her to her doctors' appointments. Three months later, he still reported no anger spells, was eating better, and had gained much of his lost weight. After 54 years of turmoil, Mrs. Tinnier had her wonderful husband back.

*

I had always believed that complex problems couldn't have simple solutions. Mr. Tinnier proved me wrong. I was also a strong believer in traditional medicine and, were it not for Mr. Tinnier's refusal to take more prescription medications, I would not have stumbled on the ideas of Vitamin B2 and Fish Oil. This humbling experience served to remind me that, in comparison with what I think I know, what I do not know is as vast as the universe.

*

Alfred North Whitehead[42] put it best when he said:

"The Universe is vast. Nothing is more curious than the self-satisfied dogmatism with which mankind at each period of its history cherishes the delusion of the finality of its existing modes of knowledge. Skeptics and believers are all alike. At this moment scientists and skeptics are the leading dogmatists. Advance in detail is admitted; fundamental novelty is barred. This dogmatic common sense is the death of philosophical adventure. The Universe is vast."

---

[42] Alfred North Whitehead (1861-1947) was a British philosopher.

Mr. Oblitum[43]
Oklahoma City VA Hospital, 2019

"There's nothing wrong with me."

"But, Dad..."

"Shut up. I feel fine. You're the one who doesn't."

Walking in on this interfamilial interlocution, I introduced my Geri-PACT (Geriatric Patient Aligned Care Team) to the altercating pair. Then, one by one, social worker, psychologist, pharmacist, nurse, and I shook hands and took our seats, arranged in a semicircle, facing the father, an octogenarian, and the son, a sexagenarian.

After some awkward movements and seating rearrangements, I opened the conversation with a simple question directed at the octogenarian father.

"Mr. Oblitum, we are the VA Hospital team assigned to your care. Could you please share with us your complaints, concerns, worries, and issues that are most important to you?"

Mr. Oblitum, seated like a colossus—gray hair, draping his long neck, mustache, spiraling down both sides of his mouth, flat stomach, pressing against a custom-made buckle, and ornate cowboy boots, shining from beneath his pressed, navy-blue jeans—smiled with big blue eyes and a perfect set of dentures. Then, with nonchalant disregard to his son's contorted, blushing face answered my long, open-ended question with, "I feel fine, Doctor."

The son shook his head, dropped his gaze, and mumbled, "Why don't you tell the doctor about your memory."

---

43 Pre-published, *Journal of the Oklahoma State Medical Association*, February 2019.

"My memory is fine," smiled the father, crossing his lean legs as if to show off his expensive, hand-made boots.

"If your memory's fine, why don't you tell the doctor what I fixed you for breakfast this morning."

"Bacon and eggs."

"No, Dad. You had milk and cereal."

"No. You had the cereal and milk; I had the bacon and eggs."

At that point, I intruded on the father-son duel with a series of questions, all of which were answered correctly. The father knew, the day, month, year, city, hospital, governor, and president; he could add and subtract successive sevens from 100 and could draw a clock with the arms at ten past eleven. As I was documenting the father's impressive performance, the son, unexpectedly, chimed in with an accusation.

"Dad don't lie to the doctor. You had milk and cereal this morning."

"No, son. You had the cereal and milk and I had the bacon and eggs," insisted the father, a bit miffed at his son's inability to leave the breakfast issue alone.

I looked to my Geri-PACT providers, hoping that one of them would venture with a question that would discharge the moment's tension. It was the dementia-experienced psychologist, Dr. Madison, who came to my rescue.

"Mr. Oblitum. Would you repeat these three words after me, please? *Boots. Jeans. Buckle.* In a few minutes, I'm going to ask you to remember them.

"Boots, jeans, and buckle," repeated Mr. Oblitum with a wry smile.

"Would you say them one more time, please?"

"Boots, jeans, and buckle," reiterated Mr. Oblitum with a bored expression.

"This morning, did you have bacon and eggs or eggs and bacon," quizzed the psychologist.

"They're the same thing, of course, but common parlance prefers bacon and eggs."

"And did your son have milk and cereal or cereal and milk?"

"Again, they're the same thing, but common parlance prefers cereal and milk."

"And why's that, Sir?"

"I taught English for fifty years. Common parlance favors the easier flow. Bacon and eggs flow off the tongue easier than eggs and bacon. Similarly, cereal and milk flow easier than milk and cereal."

*

Many other questions crisscrossed between members of the team and Mr. Oblitum, all of which were answered correctly and with astonishing eloquence. All the while, however, the son shook his head disapprovingly and interrupted the interlocutors by reminding them that his father, like all English teachers, is a smooth talker, and that this morning, he had milk-and-cereal, not eggs-and-bacon.

It was at this point that I was seized with a wild idea. I looked to the psychologist, who was about to ask Mr. Oblitum to repeat the three words she had asked him to remember—boots, jeans, and buckle—and asked her to follow me out.

We excused ourselves, left the examination room, and huddled in the hall.

"What's on your mind?" She asked, bewildered.

"I want you to ask the son to repeat the three words, which you had given the father."

Her eyes glared at me with disbelief. I reminded her that it was the son who had used the expressions *milk-and-cereal* and *eggs-and-bacon.*

"So what?"

"What if the son is the one who's demented?"

"That's a wild idea," she gasped.

"But the father was the one who answered all the questions correctly," I reminded, "and the son was the one who exhibited disorderly behavior."

*

Back in the room, the psychologist coughed, cleared her throat, and looking at the son, inquired, "Can you tell us what kind of things your dad forgets?"

"Just about everything there's to forget. He forgets where he puts his keys, his phone, his eyeglasses, and so many other things."

Hearing that, Mr. Oblitum nodded disapprovingly and remarked, "He forgets a lot more things than I do."

"No, I don't," objected the son.

"What's your name, Sir?" asked the psychologist.

"My name is David."

"Do you mind if I call you by your first name instead of Mr. Oblitum, which is how I address your father, just to avoid confusion."

"Everyone calls me David."

"Well then, David, could you remember the three words, which I had asked your dad, Mr. Oblitum, to remember."

"What three words?"

"You know, words that had to do with how your dad was dressed."

"How he was dressed? I don't understand what you mean."

"You know, words that have to do with his shoes, pants, and belt.

"I don't recall anything like that."

"Who drove to this appointment, you or your dad?"

"My dad did."

"Why is that?"

"He won't let me drive anymore."

"Why is that?"

"Because he misses exits, gets us lost, and can't find his way back home," interjected Mr. Oblitum.

*

To huddle as a team, we excused ourselves, leaving son and dad alone in the examination room. It was the nurse who, upon reviewing the appointment records, declared that we had interviewed the wrong patient. It was the dad, Mr. Oblitum, who had made the appointment for his son because his son was the one who was getting more and more forgetful.

There was no way out for us, no way to cleanse our shame, and no way to expunge our mistake. We all fell into the same trap, suspecting dementia in the octogenarian father instead of the sexagenarian son.

With heads bowed, we went back into the examination room and completed our examination of David. His forgetfulness, according to his father, had started about 10 years earlier when David was in his fifties. It was subtle at first but became more obvious with time. The father denied it as long as he could, but when David was fired from his job because of incompetence, could not find his way back home on several occasions, became a dangerous driver, had difficulty expressing himself, and started to neglect his personal hygiene, Mr. Oblitum had to face the reality of his son's dementia.

*

David responded to the dementia medications we prescribed, but as often happens, his was a short-lived response followed by a rapid deterioration. When Mr. Oblitum could no longer provide adequate care for his son, we advised nursing-home placement, which Mr. Oblitum tearfully accepted. When David could no longer feed himself, we advised hospice. When David died, we went to his funeral as a team, which helped assuage Mr. Oblitum's grief.

*

A month later, we received the following letter from Mr. Oblitum:

Dear Geri-PACT Providers,

I will never forget our initial interview when you assumed that I was the one who was having memory problems. It took me a while to realize that you were making a mistake, but I played along because I did not want to hurt my son's feelings, and because I wanted to continue my denial and delay, as long as I could, facing my son's painful reality.

Dementia is a horrifying disease because it absconds with the soul, which we know and love, and leaves behind naught but a perfunctory corpse. It is the premature death of the mind before the timely demise of the body.

Lucky are those whose bodies and souls depart together at the point of death, because with our faith, we know that Heaven will be their souls' abode. But when the soul leaves the body before death, faith lends us no direction nor reveals to us where does the tortured soul wait while the body lives on.

I was relieved when David's body died because I knew that at the moment of death, his tormented soul would find peace in its heavenly abode. But, while he lived, I had no idea where his tortured soul lay waiting. I knew that it couldn't be at peace, having been evicted from his body by such a demeaning, diminishing, dehumanizing dementia.

He was a kind, caring, beautiful man when he was well. It is a most painful anachronism that sons should die before their fathers. I was tortured throughout most of my old age by witnessing my son's slow decline, which smoldered for more than ten years, until he became naught but a walking shadow of his former self. It would have been more merciful had I been the one with dementia and he, the one taking care of me.

These words of Macbeth will continue to haunt me until the day I die because they reiterate my strife with David's errant soul:

> Tomorrow, and tomorrow, and tomorrow,
> Creeps in this petty pace from day to day,
> To the last syllable of recorded time;
> And all our yesterdays have lighted fools
> The way to dusty death. Out, out, brief candle!
> Life's but a walking shadow, a poor player,
> That struts and frets his hour upon the stage,
> And then is heard no more. It is a tale
> Told by an idiot, full of sound and fury,
> Signifying nothing[44].

---

[44] *Macbeth*, a play by William Shakespeare.

Thank you for doing your best for my David. Your compassion inspired me, when I was on the brink of despair, and gave me the courage to struggle on.

As Harper Lee said in *To Kill A Mockingbird*, *"Courage is when you're licked before you begin but you begin anyway, and you see it through no matter what"*.

With gratitude,

James Oblitum, PhD

The Sound of Feet
Oklahoma City VA Hospital, 2019

I have stood still and stopped the sound of feet
When far away an interrupted cry
Came over houses from another street,
But not to call me back or say good-bye;[45]

My cellphone rings. I should have silenced it, but I forgot.

"You need to come see this," came Nurse Nora's pressured voice.
"I'm in a meeting," I whispered.
"I'll tell him you're on your way."

Some VA Hospital days start this way, hurried, forcing me to be partially present in two places at the same time. I withdrew from the meeting, drawing as little attention as possible, and took the stairs to the Community Living Center floor, better known as CLC

"Who, what, where?"   I asked, looking into Nurse Nora's gaping eyes.
"It's Mr. Iratus. He came back to us last night, after a six-hour surgery."
"So?"
"I was changing his dressing when he noticed his wound for the first time."
"So?"
"He started screaming at the top of his lungs."
"Did you hurt him?"
"No. He just was shocked when he found out that his wounds were not two inches long."

---

[45] *Acquainted with The Night,* a poem by Robert Frost.

"Well, how long are they?"

"About two feet long, starting at the knees and ending at the groins. His arteries were totally blocked, and they couldn't bypass them, so they replaced them with grafts."

"So, why's he upset then?"

"Because they did not get his written permission."

"What were they supposed to do?" I asked, a bit annoyed.

"Wake him up from anesthesia and ask his permission to save his feet," replied Nurse Nora with a cynical tone.

Mr. Iratus and I had a long, bedside conversation. He started smoking at 19 and has been smoking 4 packs a day for the past 35 years. Two years ago, he began having trouble walking and his feet changed color. He was not diabetic, had normal blood pressure, and normal cholesterol, which is why he could not believe that he had bad arteries. When his doctors told him that smoking was destroying the blood supply to his legs, he countered by saying that his feet were deep red and that had to mean good blood circulation.

He loved his cigarettes and would not consider giving them up. His ex-wife was an equally heavy smoker and smoking together was their favorite pastime.

"Mr. Iratus?" I asked with a hushed voice. "Do you drink?"

"I've never touched the stuff," he replied with pride.

"So, smoking is your only vice, then."

"Smoking is not a vice, Doc. It's a legal pleasure which makes me happy; and the pursuit of happiness is my God-given right."

Mr. Iratus smiled when he saw that he had won the argument, but his smile failed to erase his frowns. His un-tempered anger lurked behind his grin, ready to leap at the slightest provocation. I was not certain that I could diffuse it with reason because he was obviously using powerful reason to justify his own prejudices. *"A great many people think they are thinking when they are merely rearranging their prejudices,"* [46] said William James.

"Mr. Iratus," I ventured. "If you were the surgeon, would you have stopped the operation, closed the skin, waited for your patient to wake up, and then asked him, while he was still groggy, if he would give you permission to save his feet by putting in new arterial grafts?"

"That is not a fair question, Doc. A patient has the right to know if he's going to have major surgery instead of minor surgery. The surgeon should have warned me beforehand that the two-inch incisions might turn into twenty-four-inch incisions, and he didn't. If that had happened to you how would you feel, Doc?"

"I would feel grateful."

"Well, I don't. I feel betrayed."

"Is that why you're angry?"

"No. That's why I'm mad and that's why I'm [sic] gonna raise hell."

I left Mr. Iratus's room feeling defeated. His mind set was immutable, and I could not understand how he could feel so ungrateful for having his feet saved from impending gangrene. It must be his life's baggage, which travels with his mind and burdens him wherever he goes, I surmised. *"I am a part of all that I have met,"*[47] said Alfred, Lord Tennyson in *Ulysses.*

Whatever Mr. Iratus had met in life, changed him into what he is now. His brain's plasticity allowed his life's experiences to reformat his minds' software from a worldview whose keynote should have been gratitude to one whose

---

[46] William James (1842-1910), American philosopher and psychologist.

[47] *Ulysses*, a poem by Alfred Lord Tennyson (1809-1892), British Poet.

keynote is abject anger. The way Tennyson taught us that we are naught but our minds, which are continuously rewired by our experiences, was indeed a spark of poetic genius:

> *"I am a part of all that I have met;*
> *Yet all experience is an arch wherethro'*
> *Gleams that [sic] untravell'd world whose margin fades*
> *For ever and forever when I move."*[48]

In spite of all our efforts, Mr. Iratus's mind did not calm down. He complained to the VA Hospital's Chief of Staff, sent a letter to the medical board, consulted a malpractice lawyer, and asked to be interviewed by the television channels. Repeatedly, he counted the 102 sutures, numbered them with indelible ink, and posted pictures on Facebook with the caption, *"Look what the VA has done to me without my knowing."*

Of course, he refused to see the VA Hospital psychologists.

"There's nothing wrong with me," he declared. "Go interview the surgical team; they're the ones who need a shrink."

He also refused to let the nurses remove his 102 sutures when it was time.

"I'm keeping [sic] them stitches as souvenirs for the whole world to see what the VA has done to me."

When he was ready for discharge, he surprised the social worker with, "Because I've been out of my home for three weeks, the bank repossessed it. I'm suddenly homeless and so is my ex-wife. We have no place to go and you can't discharge me until you find us a place in some Vet Home. I was

---

[48] Ibidem.

a free man before I came to the VA; now, thanks to y'all, I'm a homeless prisoner."

The waiting list for a Vet Home is rather long and Veterans have to wait months to get in. We could not possibly keep Mr. Iratus in the hospital for that long a time. Moreover, Vet Homes do not allow live-in ex-wives, which complicates matters, especially that Mrs. Iratus is not a Veteran.

It was at that most inopportune time that Nurse Nora called to say that we needed Mr. Iratus's private room for a Veteran who has a methicillin-resistant *Staphylococcus aureus* infection (MRSA) and needs to be placed in isolation.

"What do we do with Mr. Iratus?" I asked, half puzzled, and half panicked.

"We'll have to move him to a room with two beds, which means he'll have to share a room with another Veteran."

"Oh, dear. What if he terrorizes his roommate as he has terrorized the rest of us?"

"The room has no roommate in it yet. He'll be alone for a while, which he might like because Mrs. Iratus can sleep in the vacant bed instead of on the recliner."

"I have a feeling things are going to get worse," I sighed.

"So, do I, Doctor, and so do all the floor's nurses, but we have no other choice."

"I better go prepare him, then."

I hurried to Mr. Iratus's room with a beehive mind, buzzing with phrases. Before I could even prepare my opening statement, I found myself already standing by his bedside. I was relieved when he was the one who started the conversation.

"What is it this time, Doc," he broke in with a sneer.

"We need your room for a Veteran who requires isolation. We'll have to move you to another room."

"It'll have to be another private room. I'm not shacking up with a sick vet."

"Except for yours, all our private rooms are occupied by Veterans who require isolation. We have a MRSA epidemic in the hospital, which we're trying to contain, and we cannot take chances."

"Find me a Vet Home, then."

"That will take at least three months."

"Then, I'll stay in my room for three months."

"You can't do that. What we can do is send you to a nursing home where you can wait until a room in a Vet Home becomes available."

"I'm not going to [sic] no dirty nursing home, full of old, demented folks. I'm only fifty-four, Doc."

"The room we're moving you to is private for now. It has two empty beds and Mrs. Iratus may use one of them for the time being."

It was Mrs. Iratus who jumped at the opportunity. "Sleeping in a recliner is killing my back," she declared. "A few days in a hospital bed will do me a lot of good."

For the first time, Mr. Iratus was at a loss for words. With a bowed head and downcast eyes, he mumbled, "I guess it'll be okay for now." Then, looking at Mrs. Iratus he added, "I'm doing this for you, Babe."

*

During our huddles, we all tried hard not to be distraught at Mr. Iratus. No matter how much we attempted to understand his anger, his mindset was impenetrable because he was unapproachable. There had to be a reason for his irrational belligerence, but he refused to share it. One day, running into Mrs. Iratus in the hall, I seized the moment.

"Good morning," I greeted. "I hope you're sleeping better in your double room."

"Oh, it sure beats sleeping in a recliner."

"Is Mr. Iratus still angry at us?"

"Oh, if only you knew what he had been through, you'd understand. He [sic] don't know how to lose his anger. He used to be better before the accident."

"What accident?"

"A speeding EMSA truck hit and killed our three sons. The oldest was driving his two younger brothers to school."

"Oh, how horrible. I'm so sorry."

"That's when he got angry at the medical profession, at me, and at the world. He divorced me because he blamed me for the accident."

"What did you have to do with it?"

"I was the one who usually drove them to school. Our oldest had graduated and was working. That morning, I had a hair appointment, so I asked Michael to take them..."

At my chest, Mrs. Iratus cried acid tears, which left me doleful. I knew that I could not broach the topic with Mr. Iratus because in his irrational, hyperbolical anger, he had lumped the entire medical profession into one culpable, high-speed EMSA truck, which had t-boned his three beautiful boys, reducing them to three bloody corpses.

Walking back to my office, pondering our options as a culpable profession, I heard my name called from a shuffled rush behind me. I turned back and there was Nurse Nora, scurrying toward me with hurried motions and worried words, dripping out of her eyes.

"Doctor. I'm glad I caught up with you. I was waiting for you to finish talking to Mrs. Iratus when my phone rang. Before I could hang up, you were gone."

"What is it now?" I gasped.

"Mr. Sine Pedibus is coming back to us. We'll have to put him in with Mr. Iratus."

"Oh, no," I cried.

"Oh, yes," she replied.

"When?"

"He's on his way."

*

Mr. Sine Pedibus was well known to us at CLC. He lost his right foot to diabetes two years before, and then he lost his left foot one year later. Both feet were ulcerated with infected bones and could not be saved in spite of powerful antibiotics. We had trouble healing his stumps because they got infected and had to be repeatedly debrided. He was readmitted last week for stump revision in preparation for prostheses, and now, with his stumps revised, he's coming back to the CLC for post-operative care.

This amputation scenario is not uncommon at the VA Hospital. Double amputees can be seen wielding their wheelchairs with proficient skill all over the place. But what was unusual about Mr. Sine Pedibus was that losing his feet did not cause him to lose his smile. His ruddy face glowed with hope and he was always grateful to be well cared for by his VA family.

"Why don't you visit us at the CLC when you come for your clinic appointments?" I asked him once when I chanced him in the hall—with stumps dangling from his wheelchair seat—on his way to Prosthetics.

"Because I would like to walk into the CLC with my prostheses rather than roll in with my wheelchair," he chortled.

I debated whether I should introduce Mr. Iratus to his new roommate, but Nurse Nora was adamant that I must.

"We need you in the room, Doc when Mr. Sine Pedibus arrives."

I hurried back with Nurse Nora but, before we could get to Mr. Iratus's room, we saw Mr. Sine Pedibus being wheeled down the hall.

"Hold," I motioned to the orderly. "Let me wheel him in."

Mr. Iratus was lying on his bed when I wheeled Mr. Sine Pedibus in. The first to see us was Mrs. Iratus, who jumped out of her recliner and, for some reason, stood at attention with face quivering with apprehension.

Mr. Iratus, sat up, took one angry look at us, and queried with a sharp tone, "What the heck is going on here?"

"Mr. Iratus." I said with a firm voice. "Allow me to introduce you to your roommate, Mr. Sine Pedibus."

"I want no sudden roommates," he barked. "The bed belongs to my wife."

Mr. Sine Pedibus's face, unperturbed, glowed with cheer as he stuck out his hand for Mr. Iratus to shake. Sudden confusion erased the angry determination in Mr. Iratus's face. He hesitated against Mr. Sine Pedibus's unwavering smile and outstretched arm, looked to his wife for suggestions, looked back at Mr. Sine Pedibus's ruddy face, shining with gratitude, coughed, dropped his gaze, and shaking Mr. Sine Pedibus's outstretched hand, croaked, "Nice to meet you, Sir."

Nurse Nora and I quietly tiptoed out of the room, leaving the roommates to their solemn moments of acquaintance. Out in the hall, the nurses' eyes were full of questions. We pretended not to notice the hum that droned behind us as we walked away. My heart pounded as I marched, and it pounded with the same intensity as when I climbed the stairs in order to avoid the elevators.

Nurse Nora walked along with me, without saying a word. When we got to my office, she flashed a bewildered look and mumbled, "I don't know why I followed you here! I need to go back to the CLC where I'm needed."

We did not know what dialogues passed between the two roommates, nor did we ask Mrs. Iratus to reveal them to us. But we did know that, day after day, Mr. Iratus became less angry and more polite. Towards the end of his stay, he actually said that he was grateful, grateful to the surgeons who saved his feet, to the nurses who cared for his wounds, to the doctors who managed his case, and to the VA for having provided compassionate tolerance in spite of his belligerent ingratitude.

Mr. Iratus was discharged to a nursing home and from there went to a Vet Home. He and Mr. Sine Pedibus stayed in contact. Each time Mr. Sine Pedibus came to the VA for his prosthetics appointment, he would proudly walk into the CLC, wearing his new legs.

The last time he came, he told us, "I'm going to be a best man."
"What on earth does that mean?" Asked Nurse Nora.
"Mr. Iratus and Mrs. Iratus are getting re-married," he glowed. "He's working now, and they live in a small apartment."
"Where's he working?" Asked Nurse Nora.
"He drives vets to their appointments, waits for them, and then brings them back to their Vet Homes.

150

"And what does his wife do," I asked.

"She's employed as a cook in the Vet Home that he was discharged to from here."

"A cheerful attitude is the sunny side of the moon," I said to Nurse Nora after Mr. Sine Pedibus left. "When you cannot change the world, change your attitude, and the world would change for you."[49]

Mr. Sine Pedibus never realized that he was the one who actually cured Mr. Iratus's mind from anger and gave him back a meaningful life, a life full of service and of love for his fellow Veterans.

*

*"I cried because I had no shoes
Until I met a man who had no feet."*[50]

---

[49] From Hanna Saadah's *OU Medical School commencement address*, May 25, 2019, Lloyd Noble Center, Norman, Oklahoma.

[50] Sa'di (pen name of Muslih-ud-Din, Persian poet (1184-1291)

Epiphany
Oklahoma City VA Hospital, 2019

A 75-year-old gentleman, Allein Solum, rolled into our Geriatric Clinic on a scooter. Robust, friendly, elegant, articulate, and wearing an affable smile, he greeted us with, "Hello. You must be my medical team."

Then, seeing our worried aspects, he added, "Don't worry; my legs are very strong."

With unexpected facility, he got off his scooter, holding the oxygen tube to his nose, walked to the designated chair, and sat down. After he caught his breath from having walked three steps, he adjusted the oxygen prongs over his grey mustache and reiterated, "My legs are very strong; it's my lungs that are weak."

After introducing Mr. Solum to our Geri-PACT providers— Psychologist Madison, Pharmacist Brenda, Social Worker Wilma, and Nurse Marissa—I opened with a general question.

"Mr. Solum, could you please tell us about your concerns?"

"Well, Doc, I am taking 40 medicines for my many diseases, and I'd like to get off some of them, if I could. But, that's not why I'm here."

"Are you not satisfied with the medical care you're getting?"

"Oh, not at all. I have no complaints in that regard."

"Well then, what are the areas you'd like us to help you with?"

"I have many doctors, but somehow I still feel that I don't really have a doctor," he frowned, scratched his head, and lapsed into silence.

I waited for him to resume, but he didn't. I found it hard to believe that he came all this way just to tell us that, although he has many doctors, he still feels that he doesn't really have a personal doctor.

"How come you feel that you don't really have a doctor?" I asked, hoping for some profound answer.

"I can't explain it, Doc. The VA has been very good to me and I'm not complaining about the care I'm getting. Maybe it has something to do with my service history."

A long pensive pause followed after which Mr. Solum sighed and resumed.

"You see, after serving for four years in the Air Force, I spent the rest of my time as an undercover agent. What I saw in Vietnam was nothing compared to what I saw as an undercover agent. For 25 years, I had no idea where I was going to go; it all depended on where the missions took me. I lived a nomad's life, smoking three packs per day, until my lungs gave out. That's when I retired, settled down, and became a regular patient at the multiple VA clinics that I now visit."

Surveying Mr. Solum's chart with his numerous medicines and diseases, I noticed that he was taking three medicines for insomnia. Reexamining his smiling, expectant face, I noted that his eyes were, indeed, tired, red, and swollen.

"Mr. Solum," I began. "Could you please tell us about your sleep."

"I've never slept, Doc. When I was in Vietnam, I didn't sleep. When I became an undercover agent, I didn't sleep. And now, as a sick Veteran, I don't sleep."

"Do you have trouble falling asleep or staying asleep?" I quizzed, trying to understand his life-long sleeplessness.

"I have no trouble falling asleep or staying asleep."

"Well then, what makes you think that you don't sleep?"

"Combat."

"Combat? You mean you do combat in your sleep?"

"Yes, Sir, I do it but don't know that I'm doing it."

"What kind of combat?"

"All kinds of flash backs from my service days," he murmured and twice blinked.

"How about nightmares?"

"Oh, they come together. I do violent combat during my nightmares and have violent nightmares when I'm doing combat. I don't really know which comes first, but I blame them both on my PTSD," he twice blinked again.

I gave him respite time because his emotions were welling up in spite of his efforts to suppress them. Then, after some polite silence, I resumed.

"When you do combat, do you do damage to your bed or bed partner or bedroom?" I asked.

"Oh, Doc. How on earth did you know to ask me this? I've never been asked this question before and I'm ashamed to report that, yes, I've hit several of my bed partners over the years and driven them away."

Another pause followed this confession, and again, Mr. Solum sighed before he resumed.

"When I wake up each morning my bedroom looks like a bulldozer ran through it. I've broken chairs, lamps, and side tables; I've torn bed sheets and pillowcases; I've thrown mattresses onto the floor; and I've even broken bedposts and headboards."

Mr. Solum became emotional after describing his combative, nocturnal behavior. Perhaps, he had never told anyone before. Or perhaps his discomfort arose from the fact that, in his former life as an undercover agent, he was the one who always did the interrogating. I gave him time to get used to this role reversal before I resumed.

"Do the three medicines you're taking for insomnia help you?"

"They don't do a bit of good, but I keep taking them anyway."

"Have you ever heard the term, REM Behavior Disorder?"

"Does it have anything to do with PTSD?"

"Not really, but PTSD can make it worse."

"What's REM Behavior Disorder then?" He asked with gaping eyes.

After explaining the disorder and reassuring him that it does have a treatment, his sleep-deprived eyes awoke and began to glow with excitement.

"You're telling me that after some thirty odd years of restless nights, I might be to be able to sleep again?"

"Yes, Sir," I affirmed.

"Are you sure, Doc, or are you messing with me?"

"I'm sure and I have more good news. This disorder might lead to dementia in some people. However, since you've had it for so long without any mental dysfunction, I doubt that it's going to lead to dementia in your case."

*

In a note to Mr. Solum's primary care provider, I suggested that the three insomnia medicines be tapered, stopped, and replaced with a titrated dose of Clonazepam. Handing a copy to Mr. Solum, I wished him well, expecting that he would at least utter a *thank-you*. He didn't. To the team's surprise, he got back on his scooter, adjusted his oxygen tube, and looking forlorn, drove away, avoiding our cheering eyes.

"Perhaps, you scared him when you mentioned dementia," suggested the nurse. "He's 75, you know, and I'm sure he has some friends who are already demented."

I caught up with him at the elevators, where it would have been improper to start a new conversation. I rode down with him to the ground floor, and, when we reached a space where we could talk, I said, "Mr. Solum. Would you please share with me what caused your sudden change of mood?"

He paused, avoiding my gaze and then, looking me straight in the eyes, he explained.

"I know you meant well, Doc, and I'm sure that I'm [sic] gonna sleep better on your suggested medicine, but you broke my heart when you wished me well and didn't ask me to return for a follow-up appointment."

"But, Mr. Solum," I defended. "Ours is a consultation-only clinic. We're supposed to send all patients back to their primary care providers with a written list of suggestions, which I did hand you before you left."

"That won't do, Doc," he answered with a moist voice. "It may do for others, but it won't do for me. Everywhere I go, I see new faces and new providers, and they're all good. But I always feel profoundly alone and abandoned when I leave. That's why I came to your clinic, hoping to make it my medical home. Instead, you sent me away just like all the others had. I feel abandoned again, Doc, and no amount of good sleep is going to fix this feeling."

Mr. Solum had tears in his eyes and so did I. Our modern era's medical fragmentation has caused patients to feel medically homeless. Our clinic was a good example of how sub-specialization and fragmentation have transmuted human beings into diseases. Aphorisms from the Father of Medicine, Sir William Osler, flashed on my mental screen:

It is more important to know what kind of patient has the disease than what kind of disease the patient has.

The good physician treats the disease; the great physician treats the patient who has the disease.[51]

I broke the rules, asked Mr. Solum to return in a month, and gave him a standing monthly appointment. Driving away, he thrice looked back to see if I was still standing where our conversation had taken place, as if my standing there reassured him that he would be seeing me—and not my replacement—each time he returned for his monthly appointment.

In fact, long after Mr. Solum was out of view, I remained standing in our conversation spot, afraid to move for fear that if he were to see me walk away, he would interpret my departure as abandonment.

*

When Mr. Solum returned in a month, he arrived one hour ahead of time. I happened to be passing through the hall when I saw him on his scooter, talking to another Veteran. I stopped, and intruding on their conversation, I teased, "You're early."

"No, Doc. You're the one who's early," he teased back.

"The team and I will be seeing you in one hour," I smiled.

"I have a lot to tell you," he grinned.

---

[51] Sir William Osler (1849-1919) doctor, professor, author, teacher, humanitarian, and researcher.

When we walked in as a team, Mr. Solum had already gotten off his scooter and seated himself on the designated chair. We did not have to introduce ourselves; he surprised us all when he called our names, one after one, and thanked us for not reassigning him to another group. Then, after the team providers finished asking their questions—the pharmacist, about his medicines, the psychologist, about his mood, the social worker, about his house, and the nurse, about his falls—I began with the most pressing question on my mind.

"How's your sleep, Mr. Solum?"

"I'm sleeping like a baby," he smiled.

"You no longer do combat with your bedroom furniture?"

"That Clonazepam is amazing stuff, Doc. Most nights I only need one tablet to sleep peacefully all night long."

"Are you off the three other medicines, which you were taking for insomnia?"

"Yes, and I'm sleeping better than I've slept in years."

Mr. Solum's eyes looked refreshed, his face seemed younger, his aspect was more cheerful, and he acted less fatigued. Good sleep must have rejuvenated him, I thought, feeling a bit smug about my amazing achievement. Indeed, everyone seemed impressed by Mr. Solum's peaceful sleep, everyone, that is, except Mr. Solum. Something else was on his mind, flickering behind his eyes like a distant flame, a flame that held a secret within its folds.

"Now that your sleep has been normalized, do you have any other concerns that we need to work on today?" I asked, hoping to rekindle the conversation.

"Doc. My military life is full of stories that you don't need to hear. In fact, my whole life is full of stories that no one needs to hear."

"But your stories are important because they help us understand you better. Since you'll be returning for monthly appointments, it would be prudent to make good use of our time together."

Silence shrouded the room for an awkward stretch; none of the team providers had further questions to ask; and I was not willing to venture into a sensitive conversation about which I knew nothing. As we waited, Mr. Solum's face slowly lost its ruddy cheerfulness and took on a gray, pensive mask. For a while, he nodded as if he were listening to instructions from some otherworldly source. Then, with a parched mouth, he began.

"My mother put me up for adoption when I was six months old. She was pregnant and couldn't afford to raise two children. I was adopted by a loving, Catholic family and had the best childhood anyone could ask for. Still, I lived haunted by the idea that my mother had abandoned me, which made me feel profoundly alone, especially when I was with people who had been raised by their biological mothers.

"After high school, I majored in philosophy and history. When the Vietnam conflict escalated, I joined the Air Force. My feelings of abandonment and loneliness left me whenever I was on a dangerous mission. Danger relieved me and became my best therapy. After I served four years in the Air Force, I was recruited to work for the government as an undercover agent, and I loved every moment of it because I was always in danger."

Here, Mr. Solum paused and tried to swallow his saliva only to find that he had none. Our nurse handed him a bottle of water.

"What about your spiritual life?" Asked our psychologist.

"Oh, I've tried so many churches, Catholic, Baptist, Orthodox, etc. but never found inner peace in any of them. One day, I was led by my research to the Jewish faith. I went to a synagogue, and as soon as I walked in, a divine peace settled over me, like a religious epiphany. At that very moment I knew that I had found my creed. I've been going to synagogue every Sabbath ever since."

"Have you ever tried to find your birth mother?" Asked our social worker.

"She died when I was ten; that's what my stepsister told me," he mumbled with a subdued tone.

"What else did your stepsister tell you?" I whispered with an equally hushed tone.

"Well," he paused and hesitated. "She was the one who also told me that when my mother gave me up for adoption, her only request was that I be adopted by a Jewish family because she, my mother, was herself a Jew. However, against her deliberate instructions, I was adopted and raised by a Catholic family and was never told that my mother was Jewish until long after I had returned from Vietnam. Only then, when I was told the whole truth, did I understand why I found my peace in the synagogue, found it long before I knew that I was a Jew."

Hearing that, we all froze in the solemn silence of the moment.

"Perhaps, that's why you have abandonment issues," probed our psychologist, cracking the somber eggshell.

Mr. Solum gazed at the floor for the longest time. Then, without lifting his eyes to look at the psychologist, he murmured, as if speaking to himself, "I've known for a very long time that I have a strong, abandonment phobia. I just can't help it. It's part of my makeup."

*

I walked with Mr. Solum to the elevator and waited until the door opened. There, in front of an elevator full of people, I said, "See you next month, Sir."

"See you next month, Doc," he glowed, with eyes full of peace.

The Powers of Love
Oklahoma City VA Hospital, 2019

"I can't talk with all them women in the room," he blushed. "I'm sorry, Doc," he frowned.

I gulped, surveying the disconcerted faces of our psychologist, nurse, social worker, and pharmacist, wondering how to politely ask my Geri-PACT providers to leave us alone for a moment.

As if afraid to awaken his dormant emotions, the psychologist stood up, nodded to the three other feminine faces gazing at her, and tiptoed out of the room. When the door closed behind all four women, Mr. Crassus sighed, and the frowning blush faded from his face.

"I'm sorry, Doc," he reiterated, "but I just couldn't expose my soul to all them women."
"None of us is sorry, Sir," I reassured, hoping to assuage his angst.

*

Mr. Crassus, maneuvered his scooter as close to the designated, oversized chair as space allowed, examined the chair's large dimensions with circumspect eyes, and declared, "I'm way too big for this chair. I've not been able to sit in any kind of chair for years."
"Don't worry. I can examine you on your scooter," I reassured.
"There's not much to examine, Doc. My heart and lungs are fine. I don't smoke or drink. I don't have diabetes or cholesterol or high blood pressure. The only thing wrong with me [sic] is my knees."

"How long have you been on a scooter?" I asked while wondering why he was reticent to discuss his knees with the four women in the room.

"I've been living on my scooter for the past two years, Doc. Before that, I could walk short distances. Now, it's scooter to bed, scooter to bathroom, and scooter to car."

"What happened, Sir?" I asked, still wondering why he wanted the women out of the room.

*

Mr. Crassus dripped silent tears while telling me his story. After 22 years in the Marines, his football knees retired him, but he was too young then for surgery. Slowly, because he could walk less and less, he gained more and more weight, surrendering his Marine figure, over time, to overwhelming obesity.

"I used to be a tall, handsome, muscular, ladies' man, Doc. Then, as if all of a sudden, I became too old and too fat to even have knee surgery. In 30 years, I transitioned from jogging to scooting, moved from athletic to obese, and aged from attractive to repulsive."

*

At 71, Mr. Crassus weighed 388 pounds and was scooter bound. His belly poured forward like a swollen lip, covering his pelvis and thighs. He could no longer clean himself and had to use a special-order bathtub to maintain his independence. He had had many girlfriends but never married, had no children, and lived alone in a house with a ramp and specially built, wide doors.

"Unless you help me get new knees, I'm doomed to drown in my fat, Doc," he proclaimed with a supplicating voice. "If I could walk again, I might start losing weight. I have no life now and no woman will have me. I love women and I'd love to have a girlfriend again. It has been so long since I've been able to have sex that I've almost forgotten what it felt like to have women in my arms."

"Is that why you became uncomfortable with four women in the room?"

"If you were my size, Doc, would you not have felt embarrassed, telling four women, staring at you, that you've not had sex or seen your genitals for more than a decade?"

*

Mr. Crassus made his point with raw, graphic eloquence. In my long, medical life, I had never heard this kind of truth expressed so forcefully, so painfully, and so three-dimensionally. Time had diminished him by enlarging him, trapping him inside a massive body, rendering him precarious emotionally and infirm physically. This once virile, gregarious, attractive, sensual man had ungracefully aged, becoming dulled by pain, pounds, and poverty of soul. What he wanted from me was to help him get new knees because he thought that, with a pair of new knees, he could lose enough weight to become eligible again. I did not have the heart to tell him that with the best of efforts, which include bariatric surgery, one cannot expect to lose more than 25% of one's body weight after five years. If he were to lose from 388 to 291 pounds, he would still be morbidly obese at 76, not to mention the age-related decay, muscle wasting, and frailty, which inexorably accelerate as years accumulate.

"Mr. Crassus. I don't think that you're operable," I said with a subdued, sympathetic tone.

"That's what they always tell me, but I don't see why. They need to operate on my knees, not on my belly. Give me back my knees and I can do the rest."

"How much did you weigh when you retired from the Marines?"

"188 pounds."

"That means you are 200 pounds overweight."

"So what? Give me new knees and I can easily lose that weight."

"But how could I convince the orthopedists to operate on you when you're such a high surgical risk?"

"The worst thing that can happen is that I would die. So what? I'm already dead anyway. I've nothing to lose if they put me to sleep and I never wake up."

"Mr. Crassus," I gasped. "Are you contemplating suicide?"

"No, Doc. I want to live again. I want to chase women again. I want to have girlfriends again. I want to go to sleep with women in my arms again. I have plenty of money, but I can't use it. Do you call this living?"

*

Mr. Crassus exposed his bare heart to me. To him life was women. To live again he needed to have women again. If he couldn't have women, then life was not worth living. Throughout his long, detailed discourse, he always referred to women in the plural. He never used the singular form and never used the word intimacy or relationship. He used the word sexy when he meant beautiful and the word love when he meant lust. He was a true philogynist, through and through.

"Mr. Crassus. Have you ever fallen in love?" I asked, deliberately, because he never evinced love when he was telling me his life story.

"I loved them all, Doc, every one of them."

"But, Mr. Crassus, have you ever fallen in love with one woman to the point that no other woman on earth, no matter how lovely or beautiful, could take her place?"

"I loved them all, as I said, but I couldn't take any one of them too seriously.   Attraction came and attraction left. Nothing really lasted long enough to make a life out of it."

"I'd like to call the team's women back," I suggested. "From here on we are going to talk about your knees and not about women, agreed?"

"Whatever you say, Doc. I'm in your hands and your team is my last hope."

*

I walked out and went to our team's office, not knowing how to apologize. What Mr. Crassus had told me in confidence was not to be revealed. But I still had to make an excuse for him, even when the team knew that I was making an excuse. I just needed something warm to break the ice of rejection, which my female team must have suffered.

I walked into the team's office to find four, pensive, feminine faces working their magic on their computers. They must have been annoyed with me for not forcing the issue that we are one, united team and not five, separate individuals. I cleared my throat twice yet none of them took notice or looked my way. Finally, I fractured the still life with, "Mr. Crassus apologized for not being able to reveal his intimate feelings about women to four, highly educated women. He begs your forgiveness, begs you to return, and hopes that you will be able to help him with his quest."

Our psychologist sneered, and, without lifting her head from the computer, declared, "One of you is not telling the truth."

"You are correct," I confessed.

"Well, who is it?" Asked our social worker.

"It's privileged information," I smiled.

"He's taking too much Tylenol and Motrin," observed the pharmacist with a surprised voice. "When I called him yesterday to ask about doses, he told me that he took Tylenol and Motrin by the fistfuls when he needed pain relief, and that he did not bother counting how many pills he took per day."

"Let's go see what's going on in his mind," encouraged the nurse as she rose from her chair. "Obviously, he has issues, and we shouldn't take his rejection of women personally."

*

Back in the room, our psychologist asked Mr. Crassus enough questions to determine that he was mentally competent. The social worker determined that his home environment was safe. The pharmacist determined that he was overdosing on Tylenol and Motrin. And the nurse reminded us that if his surgery were to be considered lifesaving, it could not be refused. Hearing that, Mr. Crassus jumped at the idea and proclaimed that his surgery would, indeed, be lifesaving because it would re-ambulate him and help him lose weight. I nodded and promised that I would emphasize to the orthopedists that bilateral knee replacements in his case would, indeed, be lifesaving.

Our encounter ended up on a keynote of hope. Mr. Crassus thanked all four women and apologized again for not sharing some of his personal details with them. Then, before leaving, he pulled a picture out of his wallet and passed it around. It showed him still lithe and handsome at the time he was honorably discharged from the Marines.

"See what a hunk I was thirty years ago?" He giggled with pride. "I'll need your help, ladies, to get me back to what I used to be."

*

When Mr. Crassus returned for his appointment in a month, his eyes were full of expectation.

"Well, Doc. When do they plan to do my lifesaving, knee-replacement surgery? I've done my homework. They usually do one knee at a time, starting with the worst knee. Then after full recovery, they do the second one."

"Mr. Crassus. I tried my best to convince the orthopedic surgeons to operate, but they declined because of your weight. They calculated that your post-operative mortality risk would be close to 65%, which is prohibitive. I even called the Chief of Orthopedics and defended your plea for the lifesaving surgery. He said surgery would be tantamount to euthanasia because if you were to survive the operation, you wouldn't survive the post-operative rehabilitation process."

"I'm dying anyway, Doc. So, why should it matter if I die of surgery instead of morbid obesity? At least with surgery, I stand a 35% chance of surviving. With the way my morbid obesity is gaining on me, I'm 100% doomed."

"We all understand your plea, Sir, but the decision is not ours to make," I apologized.

"Well, since y'all can't help me, I'd better go on home, take a bunch of pills, and end my own suffering with my own hands."

"Is this a suicidal threat with a suicidal plan?" Asked the psychologist with a firm voice.

"Yes, Ma'am. Indeed, it is," affirmed Mr. Crassus. "You've left me no other choice."

"In that case, we can't let you go home, Sir," instructed the psychologist.

"You can't do that. I'm a free man and no one can stop me from going home."

"We have our rules, Sir. We'll have to admit you to 8-East and treat your suicidal depression before you can return home."

Mr. Crassus became irate when he realized that he was no longer free to leave and that he was going to be admitted to the Psych Ward instead. While the psychologist called the VA police, I called the admitting psychiatrist who came down right away and read Mr. Crassus the rules...

*

I visited Mr. Crassus daily and watched his slow recovery. When it was time to discharge him, his psychiatrist and I agreed that sending him directly home from the Psych Ward would not be a safe transition. Admitting him to our Community Living Center (CLC) for a few weeks of rehab would be the preferable choice. Mr. Crassus did not decline our offer, especially when I told him that I was the CLC attending for that month.

After the CLC nurses admitted Mr. Crassus, the head nurse informed me that, because of his size, he could not possibly participate in the group physical therapy sessions, and that I had to make special arrangements with Norma, the head of the PT Department. When she pronounced the name Norma, a smirk escaped from her serious lips.

"Why did you say Norma with a smirk?" I asked, bemused.

"He'll soon find out," she smirked again.

*

Norma was a 63-year-old, lithe, petite, no-nonsense widow. In the Physical Therapy Department, she was known as *The General* because she did not allow her patients to make excuses. She pushed them to the limits, got the best out of them regardless of their disability, gave them tough love instead of sympathy, and insisted on maximum independence with minimum assistance. Her disabled Veterans at first left her department angry because she refused to enable them, but later on, they became grateful because she revived the strong soldier, taking refuge behind disability.

When Mr. Crassus scooted down to physical therapy for his first session, Norma met him at the door with a smile that belied her resolve.

"Why don't you park your scooter there and walk back here to my station," she commanded.

"Oh no, you don't understand, Ma'am. My knees are too bad to walk that far," he smiled.

"Nonsense," she smiled back. "If you're not an amputee, you can walk."

"But you don't understand, Ma'am. I've been scooting for over ten years."

"Nonsense," she reiterated. "Get off your scooter and grab that walker."

"But, Ma'am..."

"Don't but-Ma'am-me, soldier. Just do what I say. Come on. Get up. Up. Yes. Yes. Here we go. Now, hold on to that walker. Come on. Take your first step. Good. One more step. Good. Keep going. Come on..."

Standing side by side, Mr. Crassus looked like Goliath and Norma like little David. This proverbial scene was not lost on anyone. The entire department, with all its physical therapists and patients, stopped what they were doing and watched what was transpiring between Norma and Mr. Crassus with gaping, incredulous eyes.

*

The next morning, when I made rounds on Mr. Crassus, he greeted me with, "Did you intentionally choose *The General* for me?"

"Yes," I confessed with a smirk.

"I don't think I can handle her, Doc. I've never met a woman that harsh. I'd like to change therapists."

"She made you walk longer than you've walked in ten years."

"Yes, but it hurt like hell, and you're not giving me enough Tylenol and Motrin to cope with that kind of pain."

"Do you mean we're not giving you fistfuls of Tylenol and Motrin?"

"Well, for a man my size, two tablets four times a day don't do it."

"Mr. Crassus, as long as you are with us, you'll have to abide with what we think is best and safest for you."

*

Our VA dieticians put Mr. Crassus on a strict diet, intended to make him lose two pounds per week. Norma added ten steps for each pound he lost. He protested vehemently but obeyed because, deep inside, he knew that he was wrong, and she was right. When we reviewed his case at our monthly meeting, he had lost nine pounds and was walking 200 steps a day. He was also making voluntary trips to the physical therapy department to chat with Norma. When we informed him that we usually discharge our CLC patients after one month he became disconcerted.

"Why can't I stay longer? I feel the best I've felt in years," he protested.

"We're trying to help you become independent, not enable you to become dependent," I replied. "Sooner or later, you'll have to learn to be your own physical therapist."

"You mean that I won't be allowed to visit the Physical Therapy Department after I'm discharged?"

"If you don't mind the drive, we can arrange for you to have a weekly PT appointment."

"But that won't be enough. To maintain my progress, I'll need to have daily PT visits."

"Let me see what I can do about that," I appeased.

"While you're thinking about this issue, may I have a half-day pass, please? There's something I need to buy, something that no one else can buy for me."

"This would be a good thing," I encouraged. "It would prepare you for regaining your independence."

*

Near the end of the second month, I saw Mr. Crassus in the hall walking with his walker.

"You don't seem to be in pain anymore," I remarked.

"Two Tylenol and two Motrin four times a day keep my knees lubricated. It makes no sense, but the more I walk, the less pain I seem to have. I'm hardly using my scooter," he declared with pride.

"Well then, you should have no trouble going home next week."

"Oh, no. Please, Doc. Don't discharge me that soon. Give me one more month, please," he pleaded.

For a brief moment I thought I saw tears shimmer in his eyes. I was dumbfounded because I could not understand his strong, resurgent feelings of attachment. This was the man who wanted to go home to commit suicide by taking a fistful of pills, who was angry because we had him admitted to the Psych Ward, angry because he couldn't have bariatric or knee surgery, angry because he couldn't regain his hunk figure and be a ladies' man again, and angry because Norma had forced him to walk instead of ride his scooter.

As he and I stood in the hall, trying to find our words, I could see discomfort crawling over his face, the discomfort of having something to say but being unable to verbalize it.

"Would you like to walk with me to the cafeteria to share a cup of coffee?" I invited, knowing that the cafeteria, being no-man's land, would replace our therapeutic relationship with a friendlier one.

"I'd love it, Doc, but you'll have to put up with my slow pace," he smiled, turned around, and walked toward the door.

*

We found a quiet, corner table with benches on each side, for he was still far too large to sit in a regular chair. I told him how proud we were of his progress and of his resolve to become independent. "But, I'm unable to reconcile your resolve to become independent with your resistance to discharge," I probed.

"I can reconcile the two," he sighed, as if inhaling back the words he had just spoken.

"Are you afraid?" I guessed.

"Yes," he sighed again.

"Afraid of failing after you return home?"

"Not really."

"What are you afraid of, then?"

"Afraid of leaving."

"Of leaving the VA?"

"No, Doc. You don't understand and I am having a real hard time telling you."

After a long, gasping pause, Mr. Crassus tilted his bulk to one side, put his hand into his pant pocket, retrieved a small, blue-velvet case, and placed it on the table with a thud.

"Is this a ring?" I asked with astonished voice.

Without answering, he carefully opened the case and turned it toward me.

"It's a diamond ring," I chortled.

"I couldn't get myself to propose. I've had ample opportunities, but I always seem to cower at the last moment."

"Is it one of the CLC nurses?" I giggled, admiring the ring.

"You know, Doc, I've never proposed to any of the many women I've dated. But here I am, wanting to and afraid to propose to a woman I've never dated. Life does make fun of us, doesn't it?"

"Are you in love, Mr. Crassus?"

"For the first time in my life, Doc, yes. I had no idea what love was until now."

"You mean to tell me that you've never fallen in love before."

"I've fallen in lust but never in love and that's why I don't know how to handle it. All I have in me, now, is love. Love without lust. It seems so odd to love without lust when I had spent most of my adult life lusting without loving and dating without proposing."

"Does she share your feelings?"

"I think she does, but I don't know for sure. What woman would want a man as huge as I am?"

"What does she call you?"

"She calls me Tiny."

"Oh, how lovely. And what do you call her?"
"I call her Davidene."
"Is that her real name?"

Mr. Crassus giggled at my ignorance and his eyes gleamed with the excitement of a secret about to be revealed.

"I call her Davidene because we look like David and Goliath when we stand together. I've been vanquished by the most petite woman in the VA Hospital, Doc."
"Norma?" I gasped.
"Yes," he nodded with flaming cheeks.

*

Mr. Crassus stayed with us at the CLC for three full months. On his last day, the chaplain married Norma and him in the hospital chapel after which the CLC nurses gave him a going-away party. Speeches were made and tears surprised the eyes.

For Mr. Crassus, it was the crowning triumph of love over lust and life over form.

For Norma, it was love's triumph over a Sisyphean challenge, because as Greek mythology has it, Sisyphus, notorious as the most cunning knave on earth, was punished to an eternity of rolling a boulder uphill then watching it roll back down again and again.

And for us it was a great lesson, a reminder that the mighty powers of love can always help a sinking soul, no matter how deep its ocean.

Unsaid
Oklahoma City VA Hospital, 2019

"You have a patient that doesn't talk," announced our Geri-PACT nurse. "I asked him my questions and all he did was smile back at me. His wife was the one who did all the talking."

"What are his complaints?" I asked, readying my pencil and paper.

"He had none."

"How many medicines is he taking?"

"None."

"None at his age? Are you sure?"

"None, I'm certain."

"So, why's he here then?"

"I don't know. Something feels strange. You'll see what I mean when you go in."

Armed with this terse information, I walked into the examination room and introduced my Geri-PACT providers to Mr. and Mrs. Illudendam. The couple held on to their neutral faces and did not react when we shook hands. The air, heavy with inaudible words, was neither hostile nor friendly, but it did impart a feeling of strangeness as the nurse had predicted. I surmised, before I broke their wordless suspense, that it was going to take more than words to deliver the truth out of the womb of this couple.

"Mr. Illudendam," I began. "Would you share with us, your Geri-PACT providers, the health concerns that brought you here?"

Mr. Illudendam answered with a smile.

"Mrs. Illudendam?" I redirected the question with my eyes.

"Oh, he's fine," she declared. "He just [*sic*] don't like to talk."

176

"But he must have some health issues otherwise he wouldn't have come to our problem-solving clinic," I suggested with a knowing smile.

"Not really, Doc. Like I said, he's fine."

At this point, our astute psychologist entered our dead-end conversation with a loud interrogation directed at Mr. Illudendam.

"Sir," she shouted. "Are you having trouble with words?"

"No," he replied, astonishing us all with his first word.

"Do you have any complaints?"

"No," he smiled.

"Do you know why you're here?"

"Yes." He nodded.

"Why are you here, Mr. Illudendam?"

"Her," he said, slanting his gaze toward his wife.

At this point, our social worker took the rudder, directing the conversation to Mrs. Illudendam.

"Ma'am. Do you live with your husband at home?"

"Oh, yes. We have a lovely home."

"How long have you been married?"

"Three years. He's my fifth husband and he's the best one so far," she affirmed clasping Mr. Illudendam's hand.

Mr. Illudendam smiled with silent content. His chart indicated that he was 83 and we all assumed, observing his taciturn behavior, that he was either demented, or deaf, or both. Mrs. Illudendam must have noticed our providers' equivocating eyes because she quickly added, "I'm twenty years younger, as you can see, but I didn't marry him for his money. Having worked all my life and having had four divorces, I have enough money of my own."

"You must take good care of him, then, because he seems very clean and very happy," chimed our nurse.

"Oh, no. You got it wrong, dear. He's the one who takes good care of me. He just [*sic*] don't say much but we get along just fine."

We were all at a loss for words because the reality we were observing made little sense to our experienced eyes. Patients come to us with many complaints and numerous medications, hoping that we would simplify their care and reduce their medication burden. Mr. Illudendam had no complaints and was not taking any medications, which presented a most unusual situation. Our pharmacist, who usually examines the patients' medications, was the first to excuse herself. "Sir," she said as she stood up. "Since you're not taking any medicines, may I be excused?"

"Yes, of course," said Mrs. Illudendam with a pale smile.

Our social worker, seeing that Mrs. Illudendam was not offended by the pharmacist's premature departure, excused herself with similar words, leaving our nurse and psychologist feeling somewhat abandoned. In spite of these two unexpected exits, neutral expressions never left the faces of Mr. and Mrs. Illudendam. They sat perfectly content and remained utterly silent.

I coughed and cleared my throat. The nurse, seeing that there was naught for her to do, stole out of the room with a shy blush. Our astute psychologist smiled at me and pointed her eyes at the door. I got up, opened the door, and saw her out.

"They need you alone," she whispered as she exited.

I went back to my seat, trying very hard to look as if I really knew what I was doing.

The neutral facial expressions never changed as both Mr. and Mrs. Illudendam gazed at the silent emptiness before them. But, in spite of what had happened and did not happen, the lingering strangeness, which I had sensed earlier, slowly dissipated. Unexpectedly, in an eerie sort of way, things began to feel more and more comfortable as the three of us shared the silence of knowing and of not knowing.

"Are you happy together or are you having problems," I probed, addressing them both.

"Happiest three years of my life," affirmed Mrs. Illudendam.

"How about you, Mr. Illudendam. Are you happy with your wife?" I asked with a shouting voice.

"Happy." He blushed, looking at her with amorous eyes.

"So, what's wrong then?" I asked Mrs. Illudendam.

"Nothing is wrong," she snapped. "He was lonely but not unhappy. I was the unhappy one until I met him. He literally saved my life," she declared, as a sudden tear dropped from her eye.

To meet her unexpected tear, I changed my expression from inquisitive concern to harking empathy and did not probe any further for fear that my questions might dry up her tears. Another unwiped tear rolled down her cheek all the way to her chin. "I don't know why I'm telling you this," she began, having told me nothing yet. "Even he," she said, glancing at Mr. Illudendam, "doesn't know. Nobody really knows." She sniffled and tissued her nose.

Mr. Illudendam smiled and nodded when he saw her wipe her nose.

"He's too deaf to hear normal conversation," she intoned. "He just smiles because he loves me. He's a good man. God led me to him. I was working at a café when he came in for coffee and a donut. He was so quiet and looked so alone, I couldn't help but love him. We don't need to talk much, he and I. We have a good life with very few words."

Mrs. Illudendam took off her eyeglasses, pulled a tissue from her purse, wiped her eyes, and blew her nose. "I was five when my father slipped his hand up my dress," she began with slow, deliberate, and labored words, "and he kept on doing it. I told my mother when I was eight. He denied it and kept on doing it," she sobbed, "and then wanted me to do more and more things to him. Whenever I refused, he slapped me. My mother worked all night. He wouldn't feed me until I did what he wanted." She let out a stuttering sigh. "I told my mother over and over. He denied it again and again. My mother called me crazy and told me to do as my father says because girls should obey their fathers."

Mrs. Illudendam's words trembled and hesitated as they fell off her dry lips. I handed her a bottle of water. Mr. Illudendam smiled, approvingly.

"He [*sic*] don't hear nothing but he's a good husband," she re-affirmed. "Anyway, I don't want him to know." She sniffled with a bitter, quivering smile and repeatedly tapped Mr. Illudendam's hand.

"When I was twelve, my father raped me." She heaved, letting out a wolf's howl. "He kept on raping me until I dropped out of school and left home. I found out that I couldn't survive without men. They'd let me live with them if I would have sex whenever they wanted. I hopped from one abuser to another, working nights and days, and giving them half of my income for rent. I felt like a reverse prostitute because I was the one paying the men I lived with to have sex with me. They all beat me—beat me even when I was pregnant. One of them married me after he almost beat me to death because he must have felt guilty. There was never any love between us."

Mr. Illudendam smiled again from his remote, soundless world.

"I don't know why I'm telling you all this. My baby died at childbirth. I divorced and remarried, divorced and remarried, again and again, hoping to find a life, a home, and a love. All the men I married just wanted sex. That's all they wanted from me. If I spoke, they told me to shut up. If I didn't fake an orgasm, they slapped me. All four husbands beat the dickens out of me. Only this one man has been kind to me." She lovingly taped Mr. Illudendam's hand again. "He has never touched me and never put his hand up my dress. He's never even seen me naked. We just hold hands. I've never known a kind man until he came along."

Mrs. Illudendam wiped off her torrent of tears while her husband smiled. She sighed while her husband smiled. She sobbed while her husband smiled. Then, as if she had finally discharged all 55 years of abuse, she fell into silence and fixed her gaze at nothing, at a horizon that never glimmered, at an infinity that never existed.

"Since Mr. Illudendam needs no help from me because you're taking such good care of him, how may I help You, Ma'am?" I whispered, handing her a new box of tissue.
"You've already helped me more than you'll ever know," she almost smiled.
"But I didn't do anything."
"Oh, yes. You did everything."
"Everything?"
"Yah. You sat alone with me, alone without your team. You allowed me to grieve. You listened while I talked. You didn't interrupt me. You were not in a hurry to leave me. For fifty-five years I've carried this festering abscess in my heart, and you've helped me drain it in fifty-five minutes." She gulped as she checked the time on her watch.

"Do you really feel relieved?" I asked with incredulous eyes.
"I even feel reborn."

"Is that why you came?"

"Yes. I'm not a Veteran, but I was the one who wanted this 90-minute appointment. It told me that the VA providers give their patients the time they need. No provider has ever spent more than five minutes with me. You may not know this, Doc, but a 90-minute appointment is something unheard of in the outside world."

Mr. Illudendam smiled and looked at his wife with pride, perhaps because he could see that, for some remote reason, she looked like she was finally breathing better.

"Since you have no VA chart, Ma'am, what would you like me to write on your husband's chart?" I teased with a smile of relief.

"Just write that you've helped Mr. Illudendam's wife take better care of her Veteran husband."

Holding hands, Mr. and Mrs. Illudendam glowed as they ambled away. I watched them hold on to one another like a huddle of nestlings, like a heaven-heaved couple that had just been dropped down from a love nest, ever so carefully, ever so dolefully, and ever so hopefully.

The Shoulder Man Tells[52]
Oklahoma City VA Hospital, 2019

"Injustice is normal when dealt from up to down, and nobody dares protest," began Mr. Épaule with clenched teeth.

"Was it injustice that got your shoulder infected?" I asked, hoping that he would not think I'm making fun of him.

"I'm not sure, but I have an idea it did," he retorted.

"Would you mind sharing your idea with my students?"

"What kind of students?"

"They're fourth-year medical students."

"What does that mean?"

"It means that they're going to become doctors in just a few months."

"Good." He smiled and the frowns faded from his face. "Maybe they'll learn something."

Mr. Épaule was an intravenous drug abuser who presented to the VA Hospital with an infected left shoulder and a left arm abscess, both of which grew the resistant bug, MRSA.[53] Since IV drug abusers frequently seed their joints with infection, and since they use their right hands to inject into their left-arm veins, I thought that he would be a challenging teaching case to present to the students. The first lesson I wanted them to learn had to do with making a diagnosis by simply asking questions and doing a physical examination, rather than by ordering expensive and often useless tests, which seems to be medicine's modern *modus operandi*. The second lesson had to do with doubting one's first diagnosis before believing it because first diagnoses are more often wrong than right and putting great faith in our diagnostic abilities can be dangerous. It was kind of Mr. Épaule, despite his manifest disillusionment, to accept being the morning's teaching case.

---

[52] Submitted, 2019, *Journal of the Oklahoma State Medical Association.*

[53] Methicillin Resistant *Staphylococcus aureus.*

Standing around Mr. Épaule's bed, I introduced my six students and asked them to begin taking the medical history by asking one question per student, for as many rounds as it takes, until the diagnosis becomes clear.

"What were you admitted for?" Began James.

"My left shoulder and arm got infected. They lanced my arm abscess and are giving me IV antibiotics."

"Are you better?" Asked Lora.

"Oh, yes. I have no fever anymore, but I still can't move my shoulder."

After a few rounds of questions, the students had formulated their diagnosis. His shoulder and arm must have become infected from a dirty needle, which he must have used a few days earlier.

"Did you ask him when was the last time he injected?" I challenged.

The students froze with embarrassment while Mr. Épaule smiled with knowing eyes.

"When was the last time you injected?" Asked Heather.

"I've been drug free for two years and I'm attending my meetings twice a week."

"Did you fall, scratch, puncture, or injure your arm?" Asked Linda.

"No, Ma'am," replied Mr. Épaule.

"Did you have a cat, dog, or insect bite?" Asked Mathew.

"No, Sir."

Silence loomed as no more questions buzzed in the students' minds. Mr. Épaule had deflated their collective interrogations with his negative replies. Having found no explanation or cause for his mysterious shoulder infection, they stood around and fidgeted. To break the stalemate, I quoted an aphorism from Dr. William Osler. *"Listen to your patient. He's telling you the diagnosis."*

It was Thomas who took the initiative and asked Mr. Épaule, "What do you think caused your infection, Sir?"

"I'm no doctor but I suspect that my urine had something to do with it," said Mr. Épaule with a blush.

"Your urine? How do you mean, Sir? Shoulders and urine have little to do with each other," countered Thomas.

"Like I said, I'm no doctor, but that's what I think." Having said that, Mr. Épaule blushed again.

"In that case, could you please tell us how did your urine infect your shoulder?" Asked James.

"Like I said, I'm no doctor, but I have a feeling it had something to do with it. You see, ten days before, I came to the VA Emergency Room because I couldn't pee. Four nurses tried to put a catheter in me, and they failed, causing me a lot of pain. When I started to bleed, they sent me up to urology where three different nurses tried but none of them could get the catheter in. When I told them that I was about to explode, they called the urologist who used a steel rod to dilate me and get the catheter in. A lot of urine came out and I felt relieved. They gave me one orange antibiotic tablet and sent me home with my catheter."

A silent pause of relief ensued as the students ruminated over the new information. Clearly more questions had to be asked before they could put the case together and make a unifying diagnosis. I did not prompt them, but they could tell from my expression that more interrogation was needed.

"Did you have any trouble with the new catheter?" Asked Lora.

"No. It worked fine but some pus started to come around it by the third day. I went back to the ER and they gave me a cleansing solution, which cleared the pus."

"When did your shoulder begin to hurt?" Asked Heather.

"About ten days later, and so I went back to the ER and they gave me Motrin. The pain got worse and so I went back the next day and they added Tylenol to the Motrin. The pain continued to get worse and so I went back for the third day and this time they gave me Lortabs."

"Were you running any fever?" Asked Linda.

"I started to run a fever when my shoulder and arm swelled, about two weeks after I went home with the catheter. That's when they took me seriously, lanced my arm abscess, and admitted me."

There was a sigh of relief when the students realized that Mr. Épaule's story did, indeed, tie his urine to his shoulder. But, seeing that no further questions were festering, I challenged them with, "I know you think you've found the link, but have you?"

After some eye-roamings with still no questions, I challenged again. "How can we be certain that Mr. Épaule's urine contaminated his shoulder? What if there is another explanation? Have you tried to disprove your diagnosis by asking more questions or are you just gullible and believe only what you think and see?"

"Mr. Épaule," asked Mathew. "Can you think of any other reason for your shoulder infection? Did you have a skin abscess that you squeezed with your fingers, which could have seeded your shoulder with MRSA?"

"Nope. I was living a clean, normal life."

"Am I allowed to go chart digging?" Asked Thomas.

"Chart digging for what?" I responded with raised eyebrows.

"I want to find out if the urine culture that was done at the time when the catheter was first inserted grew the same MRSA that later invaded Mr. Épaule's shoulder."

"And how could you tell if it was the same MRSA?"

"If both bugs were sensitive to the same antibiotics, we could assume that they were one and the same."

While Thomas searched Mr. Épaule's electronic record, we huddled around him with silent, expectant eyes. When we saw that the urine and shoulder MRSA had identical antibiotic sensitivities, we all gazed at Mr. Épaule with closed lips and silent faces. When Mathew explained to Mr. Épaule that his guess was right, and that his urine did in fact infect his shoulder, a smug smile rose into Mr. Épaule's face.

Walking away with my student team, I asked what were the five important lessons that Mr. Thomas had taught us. I received many answers, all of which were half right, but the ones that I was looking for were never uttered. The students were surprised when, finally, I handed these five, time-tested concepts to them.

"1. You can make most diagnoses just by talking and examining your patients. 2. Tests are better used to confirm a diagnosis than to aimlessly search for one. 3. Always doubt your diagnoses until you can finally confirm them. 4. Always give a prophylactic antibiotic before, not after, a traumatic procedure. If Mr. Épaule had been given a prophylactic antibiotic before he was traumatized, not after, he might not have become infected. 5. All of us make mistakes, but not all of us have the capacity to learn from them."

After four weeks of intravenous antibiotics, Mr. Épaule left the VA Hospital with a slightly painful shoulder. I did inform him that had he been given a prophylactic antibiotic before the catheter-with-rod was inserted, he might not have become infected, and that had his shoulder pain been investigated instead of treated with pain pills, the infection could have been intercepted at its inception, which could have saved his shoulder from permanent damage.

Knowing that mistakes were made still bothered Mr. Épaule, but he was not angry when he left.

"Do you still think that *'Injustice is normal when dealt from up to down, and [that] nobody dares protest,'* which was the first thing you said to me when I first met you?"
"Not anymore, Doc. You found the mistakes, you owned up to them, you fixed them, and you taught the young doctors how not to repeat them, and that makes me proud. I've always used the VA Hospital for my medical care, and I do not plan to change."

*

*Justice is the first virtue of social institutions,
as truth is of systems of thought.*[54]

---

[54] John Rawls (1921-2002) American moral and political philosopher.

The Trap[55]
Oklahoma City VA Hospital, 2019

"I love her but she's driving me crazy," whispered Deanne. "We have to do something, Doc," she sniffled. "As I said, I love her to death, but I can't take it anymore."

Having said that, Mrs. Verrückt's niece covered her flustered face with farm-roughened hands and sobbed bitter tears.

I waited for her sobbing to stop and so did Mrs. Verrückt, who sat, detached and unconcerned.

"Tell me more," I invited, after the sobbing ceased.

"She joined the Air Force at 18. She retired from Tinker[56] last year. All her life she's been in the Air Force, and now she's a 78-year-old angry Vet."

Mrs. Verrückt frowned and nodded as one who does not understand English. Her 78-year-old face, plowed by 60 years of service, wore the crowded furrows of time with nonchalant dignity. Her navy-blue, worn-out suit was that of a working woman who had always arrived before time, left after time, and never missed a day's work. This high-browed Veteran woman, more at ease with combat than with retirement, sat alone, erect, aquiline, gazing at us as if we were too far away to matter.

The Geri-PACT examination room, which held the psychologist, social worker, pharmacist, nurse, and me must have seemed like a distant horizon to Mrs. Verrückt's eagle eyes.

---

[55] Pre-published, *Journal of the Oklahoma State Medical Association*, July 2019.

[56] Tinker Air Force Base in Midwest City, Oklahoma.

"As I said, she has spent all her life with people and now she's alone," emphasized her niece. "I manage a farm nearby and come to see her on most days, but I can't be with her all the time."

"How about children?" I asked.

"She never married and was always happy at work and at home. Now that she's alone, she's always angry—angry with me, angry with herself, and angry with the world."

"What medicines does she take?"

Deanne pulled a small, brown-paper bag from her purse and, handing it to me, whispered as if not wanting her aunt to hear, "She only takes three medicines—two for memory and one for depression."

"Are they doing her any good?" I quizzed.

"They're poisoning me," barked Mrs. Verrückt, startling us all.

"Her doctor gave them to her and now wants to increase the antidepressant dose because she's not feeling any better and because her memory continues to decline."

"I'm not depressed," barked Mrs. Verrückt. **"I just need people. I've never been alone before."**

Silence took over that conversation for a while. Her niece, in exasperation, dropped her gaze to the floor. The psychologist scribbled something on her clipboard and then, with a soft, kindly voice, inquired.

"Mrs. Verrückt. What day is today?"
"Sunday. "
"What month is this month?"
"Easter."
"What year is this year?"
"Pearl Harbor."
"Who is our President?"
"Roosevelt."

"If you had a hundred dollars and gave the five of us seven dollars each, how many dollars would you be left with?"
"Thirty-five."

The niece let out a long, stuttering sigh and was about to say something but held her breath because Mrs. Verrückt took one angry look at her and commanded, "**Don't you cross me, girl. I know what I'm saying. You weren't even born when they bombed Pearl Harbor.**"

Mrs. Verrückt's brain, angry at her present and dwelling in her past, was impenetrable to medical interventions. The key to her peace was her niece, who was far too busy with farm work to provide the support her aunt needed and deserved.

"Would she accept to go to a nursing home?" Whispered the social worker. "She could make friends there and would feel less alone."
"**I'm not going to** [*sic*] **no nursing home,**" barked Mrs. Verrückt, glaring at the social worker. "**Y'all need to leave me alone.**"
"Would you come live with me?" Begged the niece.
"**I have my own home and it's paid for.**"
"You could help me take care of the farm animals."
"**I don't do animals; I do airplanes.**"

*

We huddled as a team and brainstormed, hoping to find a solution for our aunt-niece, dueling stalemate. When, after a half-hour of deliberation, we could not come up with a sensible plan, we resolved to defer the matter to the psychiatrist. Back in the examination room with blank, baffled faces, we suggested to the niece that seeing a psychiatrist was our sole suggestion.

"**I'd rather die than see a psychiatrist,**" barked Mrs. Verrückt, "**and I'd rather take poison than take these medicines,**" she declared, pointing to the small brown-paper bag. Then, as if her verbal ultimatum was not enough, she got up, took the bag from her niece's hand, and threw it in the trash.

"Mrs. Verrückt," I pleaded. "You cannot suddenly stop these medicines because you could suffer from severe withdrawals."

"**I can stop them, and no one can stop me. I'm not taking them anymore. They're poisoning me; I know it.**"

"Mrs. Verrückt," I pleaded again. "Would you allow me to help you stop them? I can show you how to taper them, one at a time, and that would be much safer than stopping them abruptly."

Mrs. Verrückt's eyes peered at me with skepticism, but her silence gave me the license I needed. I smiled, picked up the bag from the trash, pulled out the three medicines, and labeled the bottles, # 1, # 2, and # 3. Then, I wrote the tapering instructions on a separate sheet of paper, and slowly read the details to Mrs. Verrückt and her niece.

"It will take three weeks to finish the taper. Just follow the instructions and you will not suffer from withdrawal."

"**Three weeks?**" Barked Mrs. Verrückt.

"If you stop them suddenly, you will have serious withdrawals, and they will admit you to the Psych Ward," I warned.

"**They can't admit me against my wishes,**" she declared, slamming the desk with her palm.

"Yes, they can, if you become delirious and lose the capacity to make decisions," I retaliated with a calm but firm voice.

"**Delirious?**" She screamed.

"Delirium caused by drug withdrawals can be very dangerous and could end in a psychiatric admission," I reaffirmed.

The threat of admission helped Mrs. Verrückt make up her mind to taper rather than abruptly stop her medicines. The niece, on the other hand, was afraid that her aunt might become more difficult to manage without the medicines.

"What do I do if she gets worse?" She asked, holding the tapering instructions in her hand.
"You call me," I whispered and scribbled my cellphone number on the instruction sheet.

When they left, Mrs. Verrückt was still angry; Deanne was still unsure that we, as Geri-PACT providers, were worth the time and effort it took to bring her aunt to us; and our Geri-PACT providers were doubtful that we had made the right decisions for this distressed pair.

*

After Mrs. Verrückt and her niece left us, the team, heavy laden with worries, huddled behind closed doors. What if she deteriorates? What if she becomes suicidal? What if she has guns? What if she decompensates and becomes delirious? What if she drives off and has an accident? What if she wanders away and is unable to find her way back home? Too many what-ifs fluttered about the room, busying our tired minds with vexing questions.

Our psychologist instructed us that living in the past, when one has no future, is a natural ego defense that helps our elderly cope with the realities of aging. Whereas the young temper difficulties by imagining a better future, the elderly do not have that refuge because their futures are fraught with decline and decay. Living in the past was Mrs. Verrückt's way of coping with her sudden loneliness, marginalization, and irrelevance, which accompanied her retirement.

Like burning coals, the team's collective uncertainties smoldered under the ashes of day-to-day business, awaiting the return of Mrs. Verrückt for her one-month appointment. Every no-call day was a good day because it meant that Deanne and Mrs. Verrückt were not in crisis.

More worry was added toward the end of the month when our psychologist informed us that patients who stop their medications don't usually show up for their appointments.

*

Mrs. Verrückt and her niece did show up on time for their one-month Geri-PACT appointment. Something about that odd, anachronistic couple was different, though. They were giggling instead of arguing; the tired face of Deanne appeared refreshed; and the furrowed face of Mrs. Verrückt was smoothed with smug smiles.

With the team assembled in the examination room, I asked Mrs. Verrückt if she was feeling better.
"Better?" she exclaimed with raised eyebrows. "I'm not better. I'm back to my normal self and I feel mighty fine."

The psychologist's eyes gaped at hearing this witty response. Immediately, without warning, she asked, "Mrs. Verrückt, what day is today?"
"Wednesday."
"What month is this month?"
"March."
"What year is this year?"

"2019."
"Who is our President?"
"Trump."

The niece smiled with smug satisfaction and waited, as if she knew that the psychologist would soon have more to say.

"One more question, Mrs. Verrückt," added the psychologist. "If you had a hundred dollars and gave the five of us seven dollars each, how many dollars would you be left with?"

Pointing at us, one at a time, Mrs. Verrückt, with elegant ease, replied, "93, 86, 79, 72, and 65 dollars."

After the astonishment had died down, the psychologist probed again.

"What do you think brought about this complete recovery, Mrs. Verrückt?"
"I stopped taking my three poisons."
"What poisons, Mrs. Verrückt?"
"The two pills for memory and the one pill for depression."

Our psychologist put down her clipboard, as if to indicate that she had no further questions.

"Did you stop your pills abruptly or one at a time, as per my written instructions?" I quizzed.
"I would have stopped them suddenly, but Deanne moved in with me and made sure I followed your instructions."

Here, Deanne's face shone with the excitement of having something to tell.

"Each morning, we leave her house together and tend to the farm animals all day long. Then, after having dinner at my house, we go back to her house for TV and sleep," declared Deanne with unsuppressed pride.

Mrs. Verrückt's face gleamed with satisfaction when I asked, "Mrs. Verrückt, what do you do on Sundays."

"We go to church in the morning, have lunch at Jim's Café, and in the afternoon, we go back to the farm and tend the animals. You see, Doc, unlike us humans, animals don't observe Sundays."

*

Mrs. Verrückt and Deanne left without making a return appointment, leaving our team with more ambiguities and questions than answers. What was it that metamorphosed Mrs. Verrückt from an agitated, demented, Veteran woman to a normal, happy farm girl? Was it the meaningful life that her niece now shares with her? Was it the stopping of her medicines that she thought were poisoning her? Or could it have been both?

Arguments for and against both ideas circulated as we huddled, trying to understand what had transpired. I went back to my initial notes and, in retrospect, it became clear to me that Mrs. Verrückt was not demented when she first presented. She was just angry, agitated, confused, and a bit delirious.

On further discussion, it became clear to the entire team that Mrs. Verrückt had declined enough after retiring to a lonely life that she became delirious. Her agitated delirium worsened when she was treated for dementia and depression, two conditions that she did not have. It is well known that treating delirium in the elderly involves recognizing and treating its primary cause, which in Mrs. Verrückt's case, was isolation. Treating delirium with medications, instead of treating its primary cause, makes delirium invariably worse. Mrs. Verrückt was, indeed, a victim of this iatrogenic[57] error.

Delirium can masquerade as dementia and depression, and it often coexists with both. That none of us could make the correct diagnosis was humbling. Perhaps, we should be paying more attention to what our patients say, even when what they say sounds a bit bizarre.

This proverbial adage by Sir William Osler needs to be tattooed on our medical brains. "Listen to your patient," he emphasized. "He's telling you the diagnosis."

*

Many of our demented, geriatric patients are trapped inside a triangle whose sides are these three medicines—two for dementia and one for depression. These medicines may help when first started, but their salutary effects become negligible as dementia progresses whereas their adverse effects become more pronounced with age. Stopping them when their times run out, even though it would be the correct thing to do, is resisted by the patients' families and by their physicians, resisted not because of reason but because of fear. This socio-iatrogenic[58] trap—of continuing to do harm with polypharmacy[59] rather than taking a chance at doing good by stopping suspect medicines—is our tacit shame.

*

---

[57] Caused by the doctor.

[58] Caused by all the healing profession providers.

[59] Using medicines that are not needed, which could be causing adverse effects and providing no benefits.

"One of the first duties of the physician is to educate the masses not to take medicine."[60]

---

[60] Sir William Osler (1849-1919) father of modern medicine.

Not a Good Idea[61]
Oklahoma City VA Hospital, 2019

"Not a good idea," cautioned Head-Nurse Shadida, when she saw five medical students and me about to enter room 403. "Mr. Habitus, our Desert Storm hero, has enough to deal with as it is. I don't think he's ready for student visitors."

The students' eyes froze in their sockets after Head-Nurse Shadida's admonition. As if what she said was not enough to discourage their learning curiosities, she followed it with a rhetorical question.

"Would any of you guys be happy to receive six strangers if you were sick, blind, paraplegic, had a large pressure ulcer on your butt, and were a divorced father raising three boys in a one-bedroom apartment?"

The students fidgeted and landed their roaming eyes on me, hoping that I would have the answer. Smiling at Nurse Shadida's severe face, I quietly explained that, on morning rounds, I had asked Mr. Habitus if he minded medical students and he told me that he would be happy to receive them.

"They are changing his dressing. Could you perhaps come later?"

"I would like them to see Mr. Habitus's pressure ulcer," I countered.

"You can do what you want, of course, but I still think it's not a good idea. We must treat our heroes with respect."

"Let me ask him again before we all go in," I appeased.

"You're the doctor," she roared, turned around, and marched away.

---

[61] Pre-published, *Journal of the Oklahoma State Medical Association*, October 19.

I poked my head into Mr. Habitus's room as the wound therapists were turning him on his side. The pressure ulcer was large, deep, and relatively clean, thanks to the diverting colostomy, which was done specifically to keep his bowel movements from soiling his sacral wound. I walked around the bed to the other side and, facing him, asked, "Mr. Habitus, I have the five medical students I told you about and I would like them to see your pressure ulcer. Do you mind?"

"Not at all, Doctor. I'm a good teaching case. But, let me take a look at their faces before they take a look at my butt," he giggled.

"Fair enough," I giggled back.

*

I introduced my students to Mr. Habitus and, with the help of the wound therapists, had them take a good look at his large, deep-to-the-bone, decubitus ulcer. A sad awe quivered in their eyes as they watched the wound therapists probe the deep ulcer and change Mr. Habitus's dressing.

"It's good he can't feel [*sic*] nothin," announced one of the wound therapists, addressing the medical students.

"We have to pre-medicate many of our wound patients because cleaning an open wound can be extremely painful," added the other.

"I'm in no pain," chimed in Mr. Habitus. "No pain, no gain, don't apply to me," he giggled.

*

After the dressing change, with Mr. Habitus lying comfortably on his back, I asked the students to interview him. I wanted them to discover what had happened to Mr. Habitus's eyes and legs by asking open-ended questions.

"Mr. Habitus," began student A. "Could you please tell us what happened to your eyes?"

"It's a long story, Son, but knowing how busy you must be, trying to learn all you can in a short time, I'll be brief. I was working in construction and it was cold. My eyes began to hurt, and my vision started to dim. This went on for a few days. Finally, my boss took me to the closest hospital, which was about a hundred miles away. They told me that I had glaucoma, but I went blind in spite of their treatments. Two weeks later, they sent me to a specialist who told me that I did not have glaucoma. He said that I had a rare disease called *Neuromyelitis Optica*[62] and that it was too late to treat me. When I asked him why, he said that the vision-saving treatment uses large doses of IV cortisone and that it had to be given early, when my problem first began, for it to be effective."

"So, what happened next?" Asked student B.

"My eyes retired me and, soon after, my wife divorced me, leaving me with three little boys to raise," he grinned.

Silence dropped like a gray veil over the students' faces. I waited for student C to ask the third question, but she could not because of held-back tears. I gave her time until she comported her emotions and then motioned for her to go ahead.

"Mr. Habitus," she began with a moist voice. Would you please tell us what happened to your legs?"

"The same thing."

"What same thing, Sir?"

"That same *Neuromyelitis Optica*. It gave me ten years after killing my eyes before it returned to kill my spinal cord. My upper back hurt for three days and, by the time I realized that my legs were going, it was again too late to save them. I

---

[62] An autoimmune disease that attacks the eyes and spinal cord but not at the same time.

did not respond to the high-dose IV cortisone, which was started only ten days after my symptoms began. If it had hit a bit lower, I would have been able to sit without support. But, because it hit my chest cord, I now need help to sit and external support to maintain my sitting posture," he smiled, as if happy to have taught the students a valuable, spinal-cord-injury lesson.

"But my arms still work," he appeased with a grin, "and I'm grateful that I can still feed myself and shake hands with my visitors." Saying that, he extended his right hand to student C, hoping to make her comfortable for he could sense her anguish.

She rushed to his side, held his hand with both of hers, and burst into tears. Handing her a tissue with his left hand, he reassured her with a kind voice, "I'm very happy to meet you, Doctor."

Student D asked Mr. Habitus about his Foley catheter. Mr. Habitus explained that he gets urine infections often, which he manages by taking antibiotics at home. However, this time, he became septic, and that is why he had to be admitted.

"I'm on IV antibiotics and my fever is down," he smiled. "It was a close call because my blood pressure dropped too low and that's why they kept me in the ICU for three days," he grinned. "I end up in the ICU about once a year because of sepsis but they always manage to save me," he giggled. "This last sepsis scared me, though, because it came too close to my son's high school graduation."

"When's your son's graduation? Asked student E.
"In one month."
"And who's taking care of your boys now?"
"Their mother and stepfather. They're sleeping on the floor now because it's a one-bedroom apartment, but as soon

as I'm discharged, they'll come back home with me," he replied, glowing with joy.

Silence hovered at this awkward point, leaving certain questions unasked. It was Mr. Habitus who feigned a cough and probed, "I know you have other questions on your minds, Doctors. Don't be embarrassed. I'm happy to tell."

"Mr. Habitus. Did you finish high school?" Asked student A.
"I wish I had, Son, but I left in 10th grade because I had to work."

"Mr. Habitus. How do you get around?" Asked student B.
"I have a wheelchair and my oldest son is my eyes. He helps me take care of the house and drives his brothers to school. Without him, I'd be in a nursing home and my kids would be homeless. I was so lucky because I didn't become paralyzed until after he could drive. And my older brother, who was the one who drove the kids to school and did our shopping for us, had a stroke one week after my son got his driver's license. How lucky is that? Now my son is his driver too. I have so much to be thankful for."

"Mr. Habitus. What's your goal?" Asked student C.
"To attend my son's graduation."
"What will he do after graduation?"
"He's going to college to become a physical therapist."

"Mr. Habitus. How do you spend your time when your kids are in school?" Asked student D.
"I learned to read Braille. I love to read and I'm grateful for my ears because they let me listen to music."
"What do you like to read?"
"My Bible, novels, history, biography, and poetry."
"What is your favorite poem?"

"*Invictus* by William Ernest Henley [63] , who had tuberculosis of his leg bones, had one leg amputated at a young age, had multiple surgeries on his other leg, and lived his entire life infirm with tuberculosis. This same poem also kept Nelson Mandala inspired during his 27-year incarceration. '*I am the master of my fate, I am the captain of my soul'* is how that poem ends," he recited with indomitable joy.

"Mr. Habitus. Who's your hero?" I asked, seeing that the students were ready for a break.

"Helen Keller," he answered without hesitation. "She's the one who helped me overcome infirmity by insisting on joy."

*

Huddling in the hall, Head-Nurse Shadida, surveying our faces with reproachful eyes, couldn't help saying, "It wasn't a good idea, was it?"

"It was an amazing experience," replied student C, "and he's an amazing man."

"Incredible…, indomitable…, inspiring…, heroic…," affirmed one student after the other in support.

Stunned by comments she had not expected, Head-Nurse Shadida's face donned an ashen expression. Unable to believe that her Desert Storm hero was unoffended by our visit, she shook her head with discontent and retorted, "I still think it wasn't a good idea."

"Why not?" I asked.

"Because it's disrespectful."

"Why is it disrespectful?" I asked again.

---

[63] William Ernest Henley (1849-1903) British poet.

"Because if I were sick, blind, paraplegic, with a deep-decubitus ulcer, a Foley catheter, and a colostomy, I wouldn't want five medical students glaring at me."

"But he seemed happy to see us," countered student C.

"He acts happy, Dear, but it's fake," she [sic] matronized, mumbling as she marched away, "No one can be happy having what he has."

*

Back in the students' room, yet still in the moment's momentum, I asked, "Have you ever heard of William Ernest Henley?"

I was answered with blank looks and negative nods.

"Has anyone of you read *Treasure Island* by Robert Louis Stevenson?"

They had all read it in high school.

"Do you remember Long John Silver?"

They all did.

"What were Long John Silver's important attributes?"
"His wooden leg," said student D.
"His forceful personality," said student E.
"Oh. Now I see," gasped student C, as if she had just had an epiphany.

"Robert Luis Stevenson actually based the character of Long John Silver on the indomitable personality of William Ernest Henley because they had become friends during the time when Henley spent three years in an Edinburgh hospital, trying to save his second leg from amputation."
"Was he able to save it?" Asked student C.

"After multiple surgeries and toe amputations performed by the famous Edinburgh surgeon, Joseph Lister, he was able to keep his leg but spent the rest of his life with a maimed foot. It was during these horrific three years in the Edinburgh hospital that Henley wrote his famous poem, *Invictus,* Latin for unconquerable, which has become an icon of human resilience."

I had hardly finished my historical explication before student C pulled-up the poem on her cell phone and showed it to me.

"Is that it?" She asked with excitement.
"Yes. Why don't you read it to us?" I suggested.

With a, moist, quivering voice, student C recited...

*

It matters not how straight the gate
How charged with punishments the scroll
I am the master of my fate
I am the captain of my soul. [64]

---

[64] William Ernest Henley (1849-1903) British poet, author of the poem *Invictus*.

Is it what it is, Sargent Aureum?[65]
Oklahoma City VA Hospital, 2020

"You have a doozy," whispered nurse Linda.

"Why are you whispering?"

"Because, because, because I don't know why," she whispered again, hiding her frown behind a giggle.

When I entered the examination room, Mr. Aureum was sitting in his wheelchair as if he were two conjoined individuals, one calm and the other, agitated. His head was bobbing and his right arm was quaking, but the rest of him sat still and detached. I introduced myself and extended my right hand. It was the wrong thing to do because his thrashing right arm, attempting a handshake, flailed and waved like an inflatable tube, aimlessly flapping in the wind. Reflexively, I hid my right arm behind my back and extended my left. He smiled and shook my left hand with a firm grip. Suddenly, his shaking parts fell still as if his smile had calmed the whirlwinds that were jerking his head and right arm.

"I'm glad you saw them when they were happening," he began. "Nobody believes me when I tell them that the shakes come and go. One of my buddies said that I needed an exorcist."

"How long have you had them?" I asked.

"They started suddenly on April 5, 2019."

"You remember the exact date?"

"How can I forget it? I went to bed feeling normal on Thursday, April 4, and woke up on Friday, April 5, with my whole body jerking out of control."

"Your whole body?"

[65] Submitted, May 2020, to the *Journal of the Oklahoma State Medical Association*.

"Yes Doc. My entire body jerked all day long. I called in sick and stayed in bed because lying down calmed the shakes."

"And what happened next?"

"I woke up fine on Saturday morning, as if nothing had happened. I felt just as well on Sunday and so I decided that I was well enough to go back to work."

At this point, Mr. Aureum's wife intruded on the conversation with, "I told him not to go back to work, but he went anyway. He worked for half a day and was back home shaking like a leaf and shuffling his feet like he was drunk."

"I started falling because I couldn't control my legs and because I felt very dizzy," added Mr. Aureum. "So far, I have fallen 20 times."

Mr. Aureum's story slowly scrolled into my incredulous ears. Over time, his body shakes settled into his head and right arm. His head bobbing affected his speech, making it slurry. His dizziness worsened and he had trouble walking. His gait became slow, shuffled, uncertain, and he often fell because he tripped on his feet. He even managed to fall when using his walker. Seven months after the shakes began, he became wheelchair dependent.

What was most peculiar was that his shakes were intermittent. He had some good days when he felt normal enough to consider going back to work as a palliative care nurse. But, as his disease progressed, his good days diminished, and his bad days prevailed.

I consulted neurology because his shakes became uncontrollably violent. Neurology did a thorough workup and suspected limbic encephalitis because his sodium was low. He was admitted and treated with 1000 mg of intravenous cortisone per day for five days. He improved for one week and then relapsed. I consulted neurology again and this time they treated him for seizures and gave him muscle relaxants. He did not respond and his disease continued to progress. I consulted a neurologist who specialized in movement disorders. He was puzzled and offered no treatment because he could not make a diagnosis. "This is certainly not Parkinson's disease," he affirmed. "I'm fellowship trained in movement disorders, but I've never seen anything like that before."

About 8 months after his disease had started, Mr. Aureum, his wife, and I were left feeling desperate and did not know where else to turn. It was at that time—when my mental sky was tenebrous with clouds of despair—that lightning sparked.

"Mr. Aureum," I began, and then paused as if fearing to tread any further.

"What is it Doc? You seem discombobulated."

"Well, we know that you don't have Parkinson's disease because Parkinson's disease is not intermittent, does not begin abruptly on April 5, and does not behave the way your movement disorder is behaving. All three neurologists and I agree that you do not have Parkinson's disease."

"So, what are you trying to say, Doc?"

"I am asking, if you would be willing, against expert medical opinions, to permit a brief, therapeutic trial with the anti-Parkinsonian medicine, Carbidopa/L-Dopa, better known as Sinemet?"

"At this stage, Doc, I'm willing to try anything. I have nothing to lose because I feel that this movement disorder is slowly feeding on my brain. I'm already half the man I used to be," he grumbled.

There was a long pause during which Mr. and Mrs. Aureum exchanged knowing glances. Then, before Mr. Aureum could share what else was on his mind, Mrs. Aureum interjected with a lugubrious explanation.

"Doc. We are both nurses and have seen what Parkinson's disease does to its victims and have also seen the many side effects of Sinemet that seem to get worse and worse as the disease progresses. Are you sure that this therapeutic trial is not going to end up causing more harm than good?"

As my mind churned, trying to formulate a buttered answer for Mrs. Aureum, Mr. Aureum reaffirmed his decision with, "I'm willing to take poison if you think it might help me."

"Richard!" screamed Mrs. Aureum with a tearful voice. "Let's at least talk it over before you consent. You saw what that medicine did to my daddy. What if it does the same to you?"

A long, pensive pause followed before Mr. Aureum handed me the explanation.

"My wife's father died of Parkinson's disease and she thinks that the medicine actually prolonged and intensified his suffering. It helped his tremors and gait, but it caused nausea, blurry vision, dry mouth, drowsiness, and severe weight loss because it killed his appetite."

"And don't forget that it also gave him dementia and lewd behavior. He grabbed at women, young and old, until we couldn't take him anywhere because he always managed to embarrass us," whimpered Mrs. Aureum. "I couldn't stand for you to end up like him."

"I want to take it, Doc," croaked Mr. Aureum. "It's the only choice that will give me a chance. I can tell that this disease, if it remains unchecked, will ultimately kill me like it killed her dad." Then, looking at his wife, he added, "It wasn't the medicine that killed your dad, dear; it was the Parkinson's disease that did it."

"But you don't have Parkinson's disease," she retorted. "Why take a medicine that could possibly harm you when you don't know for sure that it can help you?"

"I want to take it," said Mr. Aureum with dry, angry lips. "I've done made up my mind. Let's not waste any more of the doctor's time."

Noting that Mrs. Aureum was choosing resignation and Mr. Aureum was choosing hope, words of William James from his book, *Varieties of Religious Experience,* flashed on my mind. *"No fact in human nature is more characteristic than its willingness to live on a chance. The existence of the chance makes the difference between a life of which the keynote is resignation and a life of which the keynote is hope."*

*

I began Mr. Aureum's therapeutic trial with one tablet of Sinemet containing *Carbidopa 25mg/L-Dopa 100mg.* His head bobbing and his right arm jerking stopped but relapsed after a few days. I raised the dose to one tablet twice daily and he responded but again relapsed. The same thing happened when I raised the dose to three tablets a day. But when I raised the dose to four tablets a day, his trembling ceased and his gait improved, but his dizziness remained unchanged.

When Mr. Aureum returned for his three-month appointment, his wife did not come with him. He drove his car to the VA Hospital and came into the clinic using his walker.

"I'm not normal, Doc, but I sure feel a whole lot better," he smiled. "My shakes only reappear if I am late in taking my pills. I'm not falling anymore but I'm still afraid to walk without my walker."

"We have a preposterous situation, Mr. Aureum," I said, scratching my head.

"Preposterous? I'm not sure what that means."

"It means that we have stumbled on the treatment ahead of the diagnosis. In medicine, we first diagnose and then we treat, but in your case, we have done the reverse. The word *preposterous* comes from Latin and literally means that what's *behind* came ahead of what's in *front*.

Hearing that, Mr. Aureum sat down and dropped his head. Then, after an anguished pause, he said, "In that case, I've done my own preposterous research and have made my own preposterous diagnosis."

"You made the diagnosis when three neurologists couldn't?" I teased with a smile, trying to ease his anguish.

"They were all good neurologists, Doc, but none of them had ever been to Vietnam."

When he pronounced the work *Vietnam*, Mr. Aureum's entire body jerked as if electrocuted.

"Vietnam?" I challenged. "That war happened more than half a century ago. I don't get the connection."

"The connection is Agent Orange, Doc," murmured Mr. Aureum with a quivering frown that turned his face ashen-gray. "Exposure to Agent Orange is known to cause Parkinson's disease years later," he explained with a resigned face.

"But you don't have Parkinson's disease," I countered.

"I hate to disagree, Doc," he sighed. "I've been talking to my Vietnam buddies and doing my own preposterous research. Many of us who have survived the Agent Orange bath of July 15, 1967, are now suffering from the same thing."

After his agonizing confession, Mr. Aureum looked exhausted as if the heft of his few words were more than his heart could endure. I sat down, half believing what I had just heard. I knew nothing about Agent Orange, let alone about the Agent Orange bath. What follows is what Sargent Aureum, with belabored difficulty, shared with me:

"I joined the Air Force when I had just turned 18 and became a flightline crew chief and aircraft mechanic. At 20, I was sent to Vietnam and stationed in Danang, where the most intense Agent Orange spraying was taking place. On July 15, 1967, when [sic] me and my buddies were guarding the airport runway, we were attacked with 122 mm rockets and mortar rounds. The two aircrafts on the runway were hit and burst into flames because they were loaded with explosives and with Agent Orange. The ammunition dump, in which a large number of Agent Orange barrels were hidden, was also hit and exploded. Soon, the entire sky was on fire and we all choked on the smoke and the Agent Orange clouds. My lungs began to burn with such intensity that I passed out. Most of our unit choked on the hot smoke. It was a miracle that only a few died.

"When I came back home, I was angry but did not understand why. I drank excessively, smoked excessively, married and divorced three women, could not keep a job because of my temper, and made many a plan to kill myself. However, about 20 years ago, my pastor told me that I was suffering because I had lost the capacity to love and to give. His comment pierced my heart like a bullet because I knew that it was true. I prayed about it and decided to turn my life around. I went to nursing school, became a palliative care nurse, and married my present wife who is and continues to be the love of my life.

"However, Vietnam has never left my mind since that Agent Orange bath. I still attend all my PTSD counseling sessions and they help me feel halfway normal but giving of myself to my dying patients and loving my wife with my new-found heart are what keep me sane.

"The Dioxin, which is a contaminant in Agent Orange, gets into our brains, settles in the *Subtantia Nigra*, stays there for years destroying nerves, and ends up causing Parkinson's disease. The VA compensates those who were exposed to Agent Orange and later develop Parkinson's disease because Parkinson's disease is now considered a service-connected condition. I may not have Parkinson's disease, but I now know that I have an Agent Orange movement disorder, which is sometimes called atypical Parkinson's disease."

When Sargent Aureum finished his story, his face was contorted with the memories of his fifty-three-year-old Agent Orange bath. I could see his gaping eyes, frozen in July 15 of 1967, re-living the horrific inferno of that ominous day.

My ignorance shamed me. I had failed to ask him about his military experience when he first came, and like most PTSD survivors, he was reticent to talk about it. I resolved to spend whatever time it would take to learn all about the late effects of Agent Orange because I did not want to miss yet another diagnosis in yet another suffering survivor.

But one question continued to nag at my mind, a thorny question that I was reticent to ask.

"Sargent Aureum," I pled. "Why didn't you tell me about your Agent Orange experience when you first came?"

Sargent Aureum's lips quivered, his eyes blinked, and his face twisted as if he had just chewed a bitter pill.

'I shouldn't have asked,' I thought, as I watched him stand up, hold on to his walker, give me a polite nod, and amble away toward the door, toward a future marred by an undying past, an unsinkable past that bobs like an iceberg out of life's deep-dark sea.

Some words remained unsaid, however, lingered in the air, hovered like floating droplets coughed into the examination room's suffocating space.

At the door, Mr. Aureum stopped, turned around, looked into my dumbfounded face, and whispered, "I did not tell you, Doc, because I was afraid that talking about my fire bath of 1967 would have made me relive the entire experience again."

*

Ye smug-faced crowds with kindling eye
Who cheer when soldier lads march by
Sneak home and pray you'll never know
The hell where youth and laughter go.

Siegfried Sassoon (1886-1967)

Pilot Error[66]
Oklahoma City Mercy Hospital, 1977

"Any consults?" asked Tavşan, my teen-aged daughter, as I walked in after my fifth day as an infectious disease consultant at Mercy Hospital in Oklahoma City.

"None," I grumbled, half kissing her cheek.

"They're about to show the first flight of the Space Shuttle, Enterprise," she said excitedly. "Let's watch it together?"

"I have work to do, Darling."

"What work? You've just ended your first week with no consults."

"I need to address the announcement cards. It's the first time Mercy Hospital has an infectious disease consultant on its staff."

"Oh, here it is."

"Here's what?"

"The Enterprise," she giggled.

"Friday, August 12, 1977 is a memorable day for America," announced Walter Cronkite on the CBS Evening News.

Having qualified in infectious diseases, I had spent that entire week arranging my office and waiting for phone calls, which never came. Returning home that Friday evening, empty handed, doubled my medical debt and halved my confidence. Worrisome thoughts assailed me as I busied myself addressing the announcement cards. Alone, Tavşan watched the Enterprise take off atop a Boeing 747 on its first, free atmospheric flight.

When the phone rang later that night, I heard Tavşan say, "Yes, it is. Yes. Sure, let me get him for you."

---

[66] Pre-published, *Journal of the Oklahoma State Medical Association*, November 2019.

Her footsteps hurried. I stopped addressing and turned around. When she appeared at my door, her lips glimmered with a smile as three words leapt out together from her excited throat.

"It's the hospital."

I steadied my voice. My pounding chest heaved a deep, expectant sigh. I picked up the receiver. It was nine o'clock.

"Hello, this is Dr. Hawi."

"Hi, Doc." rang an alacritous voice. "This is Frances, the charge nurse on 3A. Dr. Lapins needs you to see Mr. Lepores in 307. He has pneumonia and is not responding to antibiotics."

"What's he on?"

"He was started on I.V. cefazolin three days ago, and erythromycin was added yesterday."

"How old is he?"

"Fifty-two."

"Is he very ill?"

"He's on oxygen but seems stable."

"What does he do?"

"He's a...."

Tavşan listened attentively as Nurse Frances answered my incessant questions. When I stood up to leave, she snuggled her arms around my neck and chortled, "This is the consult you've been waiting for all week long, Daddy."

"I don't know when I'll be back, Dear, but you need to be in bed by ten."

On my way to the hospital, I ruminated over Nurse Frances's details. He works as a commercial pilot for Pan Am, which means that he could have acquired his pneumonia anywhere on earth. My head spun with myriad, far-fetched possibilities, which I had studied and restudied during my preparation for the Infectious Disease Board.

Before going up to his room, I reviewed the chest x-rays. The pneumonia was bilateral, patchy, and involved mainly the lower lobes. At the microbiology laboratory, his blood cultures were still negative. When I arrived at the floor, Nurse Frances was waiting for me with the chart in her hand. She was white-haired, fleshy, grandmotherly, and wore an affable smile.

"You must be Dr. Hawi, the infectious disease detective," she quipped, handing me the chart. "Thank you for coming at such a late hour."

I thanked her with a somber bow and sat down with the chart. Besides the high white count and high fever, his chart details were not helpful.

"You know he flew B-52s in Vietnam," she volunteered, as I handed back the chart.
"That further complicates matters," I sighed.
"But that was several years ago?"
"Some bacteria can lie dormant for years," I replied, with authority.

When I knocked at room 307's door, it was close to ten. Mr. Lepores was sitting in a chair, looking flushed and uncomfortable. He was tall, gray-headed, and wore a pencil mustache that was conspicuously darker than the rest of his hair.

"Hello. I'm Dr. Hawi, the infectious disease specialist."
"It's awful nice of you to come see me this late, Doc," he gasped, and shook my hand. "Excuse me for not standing."
I sat on the bed and, after exchanging a few polite snippets of conversation, I asked, "Can you tell me how it all began?"

218

"I flew in from Philadelphia two weeks ago and was doing some needed work around the house when I felt the first chill."

"When was that?"

"Last Monday."

"Had you flown outside the Continental US during the past month?"

"Not even during the past year, Doc."

For an entire hour I interrogated him. "Have you been in contact with parrots, rats, old barns, attics, ticks, mosquitoes, excrement, sewage, water towers, etc.? Have you been hunting, fishing, camping, hiking, rafting, spelunking, etcetera?"

By the time eleven o'clock struck, we were both exhausted and frustrated, having uncovered no clues. I examined him. He was hot, his breaths and heart were rapid, and his lung bases were moist with crackles. His cough was dry, and I could not get him to expectorate any sputum. Sputum microscopy was one of my fortes, and without it I felt disarmed.

"Do you have any idea what I have, Doc.?" he asked, sensing my frustration.

"Not yet, but I know that I need to change your antibiotics."

"Good. That already makes me feel better. I'm not allergic to anything.

I left Mr. Lepores's room with a heavy heart. Nurse Frances, who was signing off her shift, looked at me with tired eyes and handed me his chart. I wrote my consultation note, discontinued his antibiotics, ordered intravenous doxycycline, and handed the chart back.

"Why doxycycline?" she quizzed.

"It's good for unusual pneumonias."

"So, is that your diagnosis? Unusual pneumonia?"

"It's my working diagnosis until I can come up with a better one."

At home, I found Tavşan waiting for me. My tired, disillusioned expression promptly wiped off her smile. She said, "Goodnight," and retired to her room.

After a restless night, I spent Saturday morning going through my pneumonia files, hoping for an epiphany. By noon, I had half made up my mind to bronchoscope Mr. Lepores if he had not improved on doxycycline. Bronchial lavage could prove helpful and is not as risky as a lung biopsy.

At lunch, seeing my tired face, Tavşan asked no questions. As we ate in silence, the phone rang, startling us both. It was Nurse Frances again.

"Dr. Hawi. Mr. Lepores just spiked a temperature of 105."

Driving to the hospital, I wondered if he were having a Herxheimer[67] reaction to the doxycycline: *"It could be a good sign or else he's getting worse,"* I thought. *"There is no pulmonologist on the hospital staff, which means that I would have to be the one to intubate him and place him on the respirator."*

I raced up to the third floor and rushed to Nurse Frances who, with troubled eyes, handed me the fever chart.

"He seems to have gotten worse since you stopped his antibiotics and started the doxycycline. His blood gases remain about the same but take a look at these vital signs..."

"It could be a Herxheimer reaction to all the bacteria being killed by the doxycycline," I explained. "Sometimes, patients seem worse when they're actually getting better."

---

[67] High fever occurs when a large number of bacteria are quickly killed by the right antibiotic.

I was still panting from having raced up the stairs when, together, we walked into room 307. Mr. Lepores lay quietly in bed, flushed, and listless.

"Mr. Lepores. Are you feeling worse?" I asked, as I sat by his side.
"Yes, Doc, I think I've gotten worse since you changed my antibiotics."

I re-examined him. His heart rate was as high as his fever, 105, and he was breathing 30 times a minute. I doubled his oxygen and, seeing that it hardly made a difference, decided to move him to the Intensive Care Unit.

"Mr. Lepores. I think we can take better care of you in the intensive care unit."
"Oh, no, please," he suddenly screamed, as if awakened from a nightmare. "No ICU for me," he pleaded. "It brings back memories from Nam. I've lost many a buddy in Nam's ICUs."

Seeing the dread in his eyes, I quickly reassured him by saying that we can take care of him equally well in his room, and that the respiratory therapists can bring in the needed equipment and set it up by his bedside. I said all this without knowing if that kind of arrangement was even possible. Then, noting Nurse Frances's disapproving look, I motioned for her to follow me out. At the door, a lean, attractive blonde in her twenties, wearing a white T-shirt and black denim pants, burst in and, with big, blue eyes, surveyed the scene.

"Hi, I'm his daughter, Bonny. How's he doing?"
"Hi, Bonny," greeted Nurse Frances. "This is Dr. Hawi, our infectious disease specialist."

We shook hands, and then I apprised her of her father's condition, making sure that Mr. Lepores heard every word. She became perturbed, gazed at her flushed, panting father, then looked me straight in the eye and reprimanded, "You mean to tell me that after six days in the hospital y'all still don't know what kind of pneumonia he's got?"

"I'm afraid not," I murmured, avoiding her gaze.

"So, what's next?"

"I am leaning toward looking down his lungs with a scope."

"So why don't you?"

"It's not an easy thing to do on someone who is already air-hungry."

"But, if you wait, he'll get [sic] airhungrier, won't he?" She snapped.

I paused, knowing that she was right in concept but wrong in his case. In fact, I was procrastinating because I doubted that bronchial washings would hand me a prompt diagnosis. What I really needed was a lung biopsy but getting it would be much riskier although more definitive. By the time I was ready to share these thoughts with her, tears were dripping from her cheeks, her lips were livid with worry, and her hands clenched her little black purse as if her entire life was stashed inside of it. Nurse Frances, trying to help me out of that awkward moment by paraphrasing what I had said earlier about the Herxheimer reaction, unwittingly heightened Bonny's anxiety with, "Sometimes, things have to get worse before they get better."

Appearing defeated, Bonny reached into her purse, pulled out a white tissue, and commenced to nervously blot her tears. Then, as if the white fluff reminded her of something important, she looked askance at her dad and asked, "Did he tell you about the rabbit?"

"Rabbit? What rabbit?" I jumped with unconcealed excitement.

"Oh, honey, I never touched that poor thing," came Mr. Lepores's protestation from across the room.

"But, Daddy," she screamed. "It could be a clue. Why don't you tell the doctor what happened and let him decide?"

I walked back to Mr. Lepores's bedside and pleaded, "Please, do tell us about the rabbit."

He repositioned himself, glared disapprovingly at his daughter, and related the story with a hoarse, embarrassed tone:

"I was on my riding mower in some tall grass. All of a sudden, the blades caught a white rabbit and scattered it all around me. It was too late to stop and so I kept on mowing, but never touched anything."

"Mr. Lepores," I teased. "Do you think a healthy rabbit would let you mow it down?"

"I guess not," he agreed. "I reckon it must have been sick or dead."

"What does that mean, Doc.?" asked Bonny, seeing the relief on my face.

"It means that your dad has rabbit fever, or tularemia pneumonia, which he acquired by inhaling the infected droplets of the scattered rabbit carcass."

"Does this mean that now you know what to do?"

Before I could respond, Nurse Frances handed me the chart on which I added the stat Gentamycin order.

When I arrived home that evening, I found Tavşan in the living room, excitedly watching the first landing of the Enterprise...

"And that's the way it is on Saturday, August 13, 1977," came Walter Cronkite's departing catchphrase. Indeed, that day was memorable for both America and for me.

Mr. Lungblood[68]
Oklahoma City Mercy Hospital, 1992

"Doctor," whispered my nurse after a shy knock on the exam room door. "Mrs. Mirabelle Morganson wants to talk to you. When I told her, you were with a patient, she began sobbing and mumbling in French."

"Go ahead, doctor. It must be urgent," said Mr. Marshall, lying half naked on the exam table.

I thanked him and scurried to the phone.

"Mrs. Morganson?"
"Oh, Doctor. He has much lung blood."
"You mean he's coughing blood?"
"Oh, yes, Doctor, many lung blood."
"Call 911 and take him to the ER."
"He only *viseet* your office."
"Bring him in then."
"He *forbeed* me to drive."
"Call a taxi."
"He *inseest* he drive."

*

Mr. Morganson waved off the receptionist, marched straight into my office, sat down, and began.

"I asked Chatte to stay in the car. At sixteen, after the Nazi occupation, she joined the French Resistance. She has been easily alarmable since then and overreacts to everything. As you can see, I'm fine."

"But, she said you coughed blood."

---

[68] Pre-published, *The Bulletin*, Oklahoma County Medical Society, May-June 2018.

"I did, but ever since I survived the Normandy landing, I've stopped worrying. Having seen so much death and having lived for fifty more years with a survivor's guilt, there is no room in my soul for worry," he smiled.

*

Mr. Morganson's physical examination was normal and so was his lab, however, his chest x-ray showed an angry, fuzzy, baseball tumor in the left lung. I gave him the available options at the time: bronchoscopy, fine needle aspiration, mediastinoscopy, or early surgery.

"No, thank you," he answered with a knowing smile.
"But we can't let a highly suspicious lung tumor go untreated."
"Perhaps the Doctor can't, but I can."
"What on earth do you plan to do then?"
"I'll smoke for one more month and then you can repeat my x-ray."
"But, that's not very wise, Sir. A lot can happen in a month."
"Indeed, Doctor, a lot can happen even in an instant. But those who haven't been to war don't realize it."
"But we're no longer at war."
"Life is always at war, Doctor, but I am ready for peace, if you know what I mean."

*

A month later, the tumor had grown, and his cough had worsened, but he still felt fine and refused further investigation or intervention.
"Mr. Morganson let's not taunt fate," I admonished.

"It's fate that taunts us," he giggled, "and we're but fate's puppets."

"Your lung cancer may still be curable if you would allow intervention."

"You don't know that, Doctor. You're just presuming."

"And you're just delaying," I reparteed.

"Well then, let me continue to delay and you may continue to presume."

"Is that going to be your strategy from now on?"

" 'Men are the sport of circumstances when, the circumstances seem the sport of men,' said Lord Byron in Don Juan."

"I had no idea you were a literary man."

"After I lost my friends at Normandy, I befriended the dead poets who have helped me find a peaceful oasis in the midst of life's interminable wars."

*

Two months later, he had lost weight, looked pale and frail, but he still came alone to the office wearing a remarkably cheerful aspect.

"Mr. Morganson, is your cough keeping you awake at night?"

"It's getting worse, I admit, but it bothers Chatte more than it bothers me."

"Would you like something for it?"

"What kind of something?"

"For your kind of cough, opioids work best."

"But opioids are addicting."

"We don't worry about addiction at this stage of the game."

"What stage of the game is that, Doctor?"

226

"Your presumed, terminal-lung-cancer stage," I muttered.

A shy gleam shone from his tired eyes. He fondled the cigarette pack in his shirt pocket and after a moment's reflection, quoted:

" 'Cowards die many times before their deaths. The valiant never taste of death but once. Of all the wonders that I yet have heard, It seems to me most strange that men should fear, Seeing that death, a necessary end, Will come when it will come.'[69]

Do you recognize the quote, Doctor?"
"No, but I do understand what you're trying to tell me."
"The quote is from Shakespeare's Julius Caesar, uttered by Caesar before he went to the Senate where he was butchered."
"Do you long to die, Mr. Morganson? Being a military man, I thought you would prefer to fight rather than surrender."
"I am fighting, Doctor, but I'm fighting for peace, not for war. 'Each man bears Death within himself, just as a fruit enfolds a stone,' said Rilke.[70] I prefer death with dignity to death with iatrogenic infirmity[71]. And to answer your earlier question, yes, I would take opioids for my cough at this stage of the game."

The pen froze in my hand. I worried that if I were to prescribe opioids, he would take an overdose and not show up for his next month's appointment. He smiled when he discerned my hesitation and demurred.

"Perhaps, we should try a non-opioid first?"

---

[69] *Julius Caesar*, a play by William Shakespeare.

[70] Rainer Maria Rilke (1875-1926) German poet.

[71] Damaging effects caused by well-intended treatments.

*

Three months later, Mr. Morganson limped into my office, looking like a relic of his former self, and his smile no longer hid his suffering. He moved with caution because of bone pain but his mind was still sharp and intimidating. What quotes from his dead-poet friends is he planning to use against me today, I wondered?

"Mr. Morganson, how do you feel?" I asked with a cliché tone.

"Chatte tells me that I look horrible, but I actually feel fine."

"How's she handling your illness?"

"With stubborn denial. That's how she survived imprisonment by the Nazi's. The more they tortured her and the more they ..." he paused to swallow a tear, "the more she convinced herself that they were temporary, and she was permanent. And she was right. When we rescued her with the rest of the prisoners, she came out cheering: 'I knew it, I knew it. They were temporary and I'm permanent.' "

"Why do you call her Chatte? Isn't that a female cat in French?"

"Because that was her underground name when she worked with the French Resistance. They dubbed her Chatte because she was fast and furtive like a cat."

"And how are your dead-poet friends doing?"

"They keep me company and never stop teaching me. Lately, I have developed a fascination for Epictetus."

"I've never heard of Epictetus. What did he teach you?"

"He was one of the stoics who taught me that I'm being returned."

"Returned? What does that mean."

"Epictetus said: *'Never say of anything, I have lost it, but I have returned it. Is your child dead? It is returned. Is your*

228

wife dead? She is returned.'[72] Therefore, I'm just being returned, Doctor. That thought has brought me great peace."

"What's to happen to your wife after you are returned?"

"Her sister has come to live with us for the while and, after I am returned, they will both return to France; excuse the pun. I've taken care of everything and she'll want for nothing, if you know what I mean."

"But, have you discussed your dying with her?"

"Oh, no," he croaked with a deep, hoarse voice. "She likes to think that I'm also permanent and I'm not about to shatter that salutary delusion for her. Her sister and I, however, have had sober discussions. All will be well when I'm gone."

Awkward silence droned as I composed my last burning question.

"Mr. Morganson. Why did you refuse treatment when I first saw you? We had a chance, then."

"Doctor. Would you have accepted chemotherapy, radiation therapy, lung surgery, and all the painful indignities that were surely to follow if you had had an angry, fuzzy, baseball tumor in your lung?"

I gulped my answer, and then gave him 30 tablets of an opioid for his bone pain.

*

One month later, his wife called and said that he was asking for me. I found him in bed, feeble, hardly able to move, but still smiling.

---

[72] Epictetus (AD 50-120), Greco-Roman philosopher.

"Would you like me to call hospice?"

"Oh, no, they will make me take opioids."

"Hospice will only make sure you have a good end and they can do it without opioids."

"But I am already having a good end without opioids."

He reached for the bottle, which I had given him earlier, and said, "Count them, Doctor. I haven't taken any."

"But why? Would you rather hurt?"

"Yes."

"But why?"

"Because I wish to remain alert during my return so that I may experience all the joyful feelings of my last voyage. I'm where I need to be, and I'm going where I need to go. Just wish me *bon voyage*."

*

Mr. Morganson went smiling into death. He asked that the following Ghalib quote be engraved on his tombstone:

"*Ghalib, I think we have caught sight of the road to death now. Death is the string that binds together the scattered beads of the universe.*[73]"

---

[73] Ghalib, Mirza Assadullah Khan, (1797-1869), Urdu poet.

Arachnida[74]
Oklahoma City, 1993

It took millennia before myth bowed its head to science, but it was a modest bow, not an obsequious kowtow. And whereas science mustered bigger muscles and fought harder, myth grew wider wings and flew farther. The two-hundred-and-fifty-thousand-year-old conflict between earth-bound science and imagination-winged myth is set to persist as long as *Homo sapiens* continue to exist. My story is about one tiny battle in this quarter-million-year, internecine[75], *Homo-sapiens* war.

I have often reflected on the many meanings of this stanza from Rudyard Kipling's *"IF"*:

> *If you can dream and not make dreams your master*
> *If you can think and not make thoughts your aim*
> *If you can meet with triumph and disaster*
> *And treat those two imposters just the same.*[76]

At length, I have come to understand that Kipling's two imposters, *dream* and *thought*, were, indeed, nothing other than science and myth. And as a physician with half a century of experience, I have learned, like Kipling, to *"treat those two imposters just the same."*

Throughout my career, I have witnessed Thomas Henry Huxley's phenomenon—*"The great tragedy of science, the slaying of a beautiful hypothesis by an ugly fact"*[77]—repeat its scenes upon the stage of time, and I have come to realize that Galileo Galilei's aphorism—*"In questions of science, the*

---

[74] Pre-published, *The Bulletin*, Oklahoma County Medical Society, September-October 2017.

[75] Destructive to both sides in a conflict.

[76] Rudyard Kipling, British Poet (1865-1936), *IF* is his most famous poem.

[77] Thomas Henry Huxley (1825-1895), British biologist.

authority of a thousand is not worth the humble reasoning of a single individual[78]—is indeed true, as my little story with a long, wagging tail will soon evince.

For many years, a rural Oklahoma physician treated spider bites with electric current and published his results in the Journal of the Oklahoma State Medical Association. Nevertheless, his discoveries were not taken seriously by the medical community, especially after he was debunked by a laboratory study, published in the same journal.

This was the state of affairs when I saw my first spider bite, which I treated with cortisone plus antibiotics with poor results. After several similar failures and realizing that there was no evidence-based treatment for spider bites, I telephoned the rural doctor and asked his help.

"Hello, Doctor. I am an Oklahoma City infectious disease internist interested in learning how to treat spider bites with electric current? I have read your articles and I suspect that what you are doing works far better than what the rest of us are doing."

A long pause.

"Doctor. Did I call you at a bad time?"
"Oh, no, not at all."

Another long pause.

"I regret inconveniencing you, Sir. Should I, perhaps, call you later."
"No. This is a good time. I just can't believe that a city colleague wants me to teach him my rural technique."
"Am I the first to call, Sir?"
"I've been doing this for over ten years now and, yes, you are the first to call."

---

[78] Galileo Galilei (1564-1642), Italian astronomer, physicist, polymath.

"When would you like me to come for my first lesson?"

"I can teach you all you need to know by phone. You'll need a stun gun and electric wires. The rest is easy, but make sure not to use a new battery. Find a used one, which is near the end of its life, otherwise, your patients would not tolerate the current. And, most important, learn to use it on yourself first before you use it on your patients. This is a must; otherwise you will not be able to empathize with what they must endure. Keep your shocks short and always direct the current across the center of the bite to the opposite side of the body part. Most of the poison is in the middle and the current inactivates it when it passes through it. After the center blanches, inactivate the rest of the red swollen bite and do not stop until all the erythema[79] is blanched. That's when you know that you have inactivated all the poison..."

He talked for about thirty minutes while I took notes. When we were finished, and I had asked all my questions, he wished me well and we parted, never to dialogue again. The following weekend, I bought the stun gun and wires, connected a white wire to the positive electrode, a red wire to the negative electrode, blunted the wire ends, and then treated my thighs to several short bursts of current. With each squeeze of the stun gun trigger, the current traveled through my thighs causing the muscles to twitch. I practiced until I mastered the technique of short, brisk bursts.

It did not take long before I saw my first spider bite on the arm of a young Boy Scout, brought in by his mother. I explained the electric treatment and they decided to try it. I followed my instructor's instructions, using millisecond electric bursts, until all the erythema had blanched. I still remember the mother's gaping eyes, brimming with controlled fear, each time her son's arm jerked. In calm contrast, the lad seemed rather amused. When, the next day, they returned for follow-

---

[79] Skin redness.

up, their eyes glowed with relief. The improvement had been dramatic, and we were all stunned. Excuse the pun.

As my success continued, the word spread, and it became common for me to see one or two spider bites a month. I recall with joy that I never had to send any of my arachnid-bitten sufferers to the plastic surgeon because they all made uneventful recoveries. However, it never occurred to me that this referral process could, one day, be reversed.

The case that reversed the roles was that of a man in his thirties with multiple, purulent[80], spider bites on his abdomen. He had gone to the plastic surgeon for help, but the plastic surgeon refused to skin graft him as long as his wounds were draining. He referred him to me to clear his infection. However, at the microscope, I was surprised at the abject absence of bacteria in the gram-stained smears, which caused me to suspect that the drainage and erythema were the result of arachnid toxins. After discussing the options with the patient and his wife, I called the plastic surgeon and presented my case.

"You want to do what?" he chortled.
"I want to pass electric current through his abdominal wall to inactivate the toxin."
"You're crazy. This theory was debunked by laboratory studies. Electricity does not inactivate the toxin. Just give him the right antibiotic and send him back for skin grafts when he clears."
"There is no right antibiotic. In fact, before he saw you, he had been given several courses to no avail."
"I have always thought of you as a man of science. Whatever happened to change you?"
"Bad outcomes. Steroids and antibiotics don't work. Electricity does."

---

[80] Draining pus.

The conversation ended with him telling me that he did not believe this nonsense. I discussed our conflict with the patient and his wife. They told me that after three weeks they were desperate for results and both opted for the stun gun. For three consecutive days, I treated his draining bites with electric shock until all the erythema blanched. When he returned in a week, the drainage had dried. At three weeks, his abdominal skin peeled and fell off like horny flakes. At four weeks, when he saw the plastic surgeon, he was told that he no longer needed skin grafting. I did not call the plastic surgeon; nor did he call me. We buried our conflict in the proverbial cemetery of cold silence.

Time passed and oblivion set its sail and left our shores. Occasionally, we would find one another at a hospital meeting and talk about football and the weather. It was more than a year later that I was awakened by a phone call at 3 a.m. It was the plastic surgeon.

"Spider bite, spider bite, spider bite," he kept repeating.
"What spider bite?"
"My spider bite. It looks horrible."
"Where is it?"
"It's down there."
"Down there?"
"You'll have to see it to believe it."
"Aren't you heading to the ER?"
"Oh, no. With a bite down there, I'm not going anywhere except to your office."
"And what would you like me to do?"
"I'd like you to zap me just like you zapped that man with the draining abdominal bites."

We met at the office at 4 a.m. A week later he sent me ten T-bone steaks with a thank you note.

"How dangerous it is to be certain that we know," he wrote, "and how much safer it is to be certain that we do not know. Having parachuted 35 times over Vietnam, you would think that I could never forget that lesson, but I sure did." Then, paraphrasing from *The Rock* by T. S. Eliot, he added, "Where is the knowledge we have lost in information; where is the wisdom we have lost in knowledge; and where is the life we have lost in living."[81]

As I filed the letter into his chart, the shortest poem that Robert Frost had ever written danced before my eyes. It may indeed be Frost's most poignant poem, and the poem that brings a smile to my face every time I am confronted with sound knowledge that is considered unscientific.

"We dance round in a ring and suppose,
But the secret sits in the middle and knows."[82]

---

[81] T. S. Eliot (1888-1965), American Poet.

[82] Robert Frost (1874-1963), American Poet.

Anticlimax
Oklahoma City, 1996

During her annual exams at my office, Wilhelmina Moorhead and I climbed together up the ladder of her fifties, sixties, and seventies but, in spite of our long-term relationship, she never delved into intimate conversations until Cecil, a WWII Veteran and her husband of 50 years, died after a protracted battle with rectal cancer.

She seemed confused when I hugged her after the funeral, a confusion that mixed salty tears with quivering smiles and contracted her face into remorseful frowns. Her speech, as fragmented as her breath, came out in disconnected gasps.

"I devoted my entire life to him yet still I feel that I didn't do enough because he always seemed sad. He fought so hard to live but was so happy to die. I feel that something was missing between us, something essential, something untouchable. But I have an appointment with you next month, and we can talk about it," she whimpered. "Thank you, for coming."

*

When a month later I walked into the exam room, I was struck by the dark clouds that shrouded Wilhelmina's face, angry clouds that were not present at the time of Cecil's funeral.

"Wilhelmina, are you sick?" I gasped.
"Yes, I'm sick Doctor, sick of life because life sucks."
Slowly, solemnly, I sat down, held her fisted hand, and inquired, "Is it the children?"

"No, they're fine," she muttered, "and they'll be fine as long as I don't tell them."

"Tell them what, Dear?"

"Tell them that their father lived a lifelong lie with me."

*

While Wilhelmina Moorhead told me her story, she cried acid tears, harsh tears that left red tracks on her cheeks. Going through her husband's *things*, she discovered that he had been unfaithful to her throughout their marriage. He had a lover before they married with whom he continued to have an affair for several years. After *him*, other lovers came and left Cecil's double life until he developed rectal cancer.

She thought he was a perfect husband and father but never understood why they only had sex just to have children. For fifty years she would reach for him and he would turn his back to her. For fifty years she felt rejected as a woman until the day she discovered that he preferred men. That was when she understood, and that was when anger set her soul on fire.

"I knew he loved me," she sobbed, "and I loved him with all my heart, loved him more than my own children, more than I loved myself. But now, I want to un-love him because he betrayed me, because I can't confront him, because I can't scream my anger in his face, but, most of all, I'm angry at myself because I was too naive to suspect the obvious."

*

I don't recall how I assuaged Wilhelmina Moorhead's pain, but I think I did it by listening. She fumed for a long time and the catharsis from expressing herself must have diffused her anger because we hugged at the end, and she managed a faint smile before she left.

*

It was Antiphon of Rhamnus[83] who taught us that, by talking about their problems, people sometimes get better.

*

Several months later, Wilhelmina Moorhead came in for no particular health issue, looking spry and replenished. Her shroud of dark clouds was replaced by clear blue skies, and there was a peculiar freshness in her expression and a pink hint of elegance in her attire.

"Wilhelmina, I am happy to see you looking well."

"I turn seventy-five in one week," she smiled, "but that's not why I'm here."

"Well, tell me then, tell me," I quipped.

"I'm getting married on my birthday and Henry wants me to have a thorough checkup before."

"Henry?"

"Henry Wilburn. He's wonderful and we're in love. He calls me Queen Wilhelmina of the Netherlands and calls himself Duke Henry Mecklenburg, the husband the queen married at age 21. Did you know that Queen Wilhelmina reigned for 58 years, longer than any Dutch monarch? As you can guess, Henry is a history buff and you're seeing him tomorrow for **his** thorough checkup."

Joie de vivre had triumphed over dark disillusionment, I surmised, as I escorted Wilhelmina out after her exam. Living a

---

[83] Greek, Athenian orator, politician (480-411 BC).

second adolescence—surging with new excitement like a blossomed almond tree, noisy with bird gossip—she never mentioned Cecil or the children during her visit. Living a sunny spring after a long, bleak winter, she had no space in her soul for past realities.

*

The next day, Mr. Henry Wilburn charmed the office. Handsome, tall, smartly dressed, and gregarious, he made friends with everyone in the waiting room and announced that he was getting married in a week. He had no health issues, took only one medicine, was five years older than Wilhelmina, and had been widowed for three years. In jest, I addressed him as Duke Henry Mecklenburg, which made him scintillate with embarrassment.

"I feel wonderful, Doctor, but I've not had a checkup since my wife died. We saw so many doctors while she struggled with melanoma and that's why I took a three-year-long medical respite."

"How long have you been on cortisone?" I asked, when I saw his pill bottle.

"I've been on 10 mg/day for more than twenty years, Doc."

"Twenty years on 10 mg a day?" I gasped.

"It's the only thing that has ever worked for my asthma. My doctor tried to stop it on several occasions, but each time he reduced the dose, the asthma would return with a vengeance. By the way, my dear doctor retired last month, and I'll be needing refills soon."

"Have you ever been checked for osteoporosis?"

"I have it, Doctor, but I feel too good to be taking treatments that have so many side effects. Besides, my dentist is against it."

*

I tried to help Mr. Henry Wilburn understand the dangers of long-term cortisone, but his naive nonchalance defied scientific evidence. His gut feelings were his guiding star; his confidence in his own knowledge was his unsinkable ship; and his logical argument, that cortisone had always helped instead of harmed, was all he needed to extrapolate that it never would.

"Mr. Wilburn," I asked. "Have you ever died?"
"No," he giggled.
"Does that mean that you never will? For the same reason, if you've never had a fracture from osteoporosis, does that mean that you never will?"

He smirked with discomfort, the discomfort of realizing that his logic was warped, and retaliated by telling me that I worried too much for my own good. Then, when I handed him his cortisone-taper schedule and offered him safer inhalers, he said, "I like you, Doc, and I respect your opinion, but I can't taper. I'll just have to find me another doctor."

*

I was invited to the wedding but declined because it would have made Duke Henry uncomfortable. Enlightenment provokes existential pain when it confronts false beliefs, I surmised. The human brain, despite modern advances, remains vulnerable to magical thinking, superstitious notions, and gut solutions. Twenty years of cortisone and Henry's brain remained impenetrable to modern scientific evidence. *"What we think is obvious is so far beyond our comprehension,"* said

Ghalib, the great Urdu poet. *"We are still dreaming even when we dream we are awake."*[84]

*

Two years passed before I heard from the Wilburns again. It was Wilhelmina who called to make Henry's appointment. Her voice trembled with urgency and she asked that we see him immediately. "I'll have to drive him," she told the receptionist.

I saw him after hours the very same day. That once handsome, tall, smartly dressed, gregarious man stumbled into the office, stooped to half his height, salivating in a towel, with head below shoulders, and eyes facing his feet. Wilhelmina led him by the arm into the examination room, helped him sit down, and said, "Just wait for me, darling. Don't move because you'll fall."

"What happened?" I whispered, when we were alone in the hall.

"His back collapsed," she whispered back. "About a year ago, he started falling, shaking, drooling, complaining of backache, and would stoop to ease the pain. It didn't take long before he was so stooped that he couldn't straighten up. I took him to the back doctor who did x-rays and told us that his vertebral bodies had collapsed because of osteoporosis. He then referred us to a neurologist who diagnosed him with rapidly progressive Parkinson's Disease plus Parkinsonian Dementia. He has lost so much weight because he's short of breath and cannot eat. When I try to feed him while on his back, he aspirates and has a hard time coughing it up because

---

[84] Ghalib, Mirza Assadullah Khan (1797-1869) Urdu poet.

of his contracted chest. It's much easier for him to spit out his saliva than to swallow it and that's why he carries a towel."

"How are you coping with all this?" I ventured.

"Not well, Doctor. I'm exhausted and I don't think I can take care of him any longer."

"You may have to put him in a skilled nursing facility because he's going to need total care," I cautiously suggested.

"He half knows that when he has a clear day, and I'm sure ready for it."

"Is he a Veteran?"

"Yes. He was one of the pilots who dropped Agent Orange on Vietnam, and his neurologist thinks there's a connection between Agent Orange and his Parkinson's Disease and perhaps his asthma."

"The Veterans Hospital takes excellent care of disabled Veterans," I reassured. "I believe it's best to take him there."

*

A year later, Wilhelmina looked well when she came for her appointment. She told me that Henry was admitted to the Veterans Hospital, placed in their Palliative Care Unit, and a few weeks later died a peaceful death on hospice.

There was no grief in her animated eyes, perhaps because she'd been unburdened after prolonged exhaustion or perhaps because Henry never betrayed her. To fall in love again after Cecil's lifelong betrayal must have required great courage and blind faith.

*

"I miss him, though," she moaned. "He made me laugh and we had a fun year together before he got sick."

"How are the children and grandchildren doing?"

"We go to the same church and I cook lunch for them every Sunday."

"Do you feel lonesome during the week?"

"I'm fine by day but I feel terribly alone at night."

"You must hate sleeping alone."

"Indeed, Doctor. You've hit the nail on the head. I've slept alone all the years I was married to Cecil. Even though we were in the same bed, we slept miles apart in intimacy," she stuttered, and her words quivered as they left her lips.

*

A sallow smirk glinted on Wilhelmina's lips after this doleful declaration. She paused in thought as though she were trying to come to terms with her extemporaneous, half-century-long confession.

Reticent to rub the sore, I held my tongue and waited. Fifty years of lost intimacy, of imprisoned lightning, of touch starvation, and of disconsolate discontent were all thundering inside her heaving chest. The stalemate of silence grew between us until it became bitterly brittle. She sighed and almost spoke. I took the hint and cracked her shell.

*

"I take it then, that unlike Cecil, Henry valued intimacy."

"We always slept naked," she blurted out, bit her lip, and blushed. We cuddled and fondled all night long. It was so much better than sex."

"Better?" I smiled.

"Oh, yes, Doctor. At our age, intimacy is far better than sex."

"How so?" I asked, intrigued.

"Sex is born of desire and with it dies. Intimacy is born of love and with it lives. Henry and I could cuddle and fondle as long and as often as we wanted," she blushed again.

"I'm thrilled to hear that," I affirmed, hoping to temper her discomfort.

"I never felt unwanted or discarded with Henry. We were insatiable for one another."

She paused and looked intently at my face. I smiled approvingly and waited.

"With Cecil, the anticlimax, which was ice-cold and humiliating, left me vacant and livid. I'm sorry to say so, Doctor, but it left me feeling like a discarded, dirty rag."

She paused again and let out a deep sigh while she composed her last thought. Then, with bright, flickering eyes she proudly proclaimed, "With my Duke, there was never distance, dispassion, rejection, indignity, or anticlimax."

*

These violent delights have violent ends
And in their triumph die, like fire and powder,
Which as they kiss, consume...
Therefore, love moderately. Long love doth so.
Too swift arrives as tardy as too slow.[85]

---

[85] Friar Lawrence, *Romeo and Juliet*, a play by William Shakespeare.

Under the Covers
Oklahoma City, 1998

"Genevieve, what a musical name," I smiled. "Were your forefathers French?"

"Oh, no, Doctor," she half laughed. "My father was born in St. Genevieve, Missouri, and named me, his first born, after his town. He was so fond of that little French town and told us repeatedly that St. Genevieve, the Patron Saint of Paris—who saved Paris from Attila the Hun in the fifth century—is also his little town's patron saint because she protected it from the Great Flood of 1785."

"Was that really true?"

"Of course not," she laughed. "The town had to be moved from its initial location on the flood-plain. But fathers do embellish when they tell stories to their little girls," she giggled excitedly as if tickled by that memory.

*

This happy conversation took place many years ago when Genevieve Lorem came in as a new patient. She was in her fifties, elegant, articulate, lithe, brimming with quips, and full of laughter.

"How may I help you, Mrs. Lorem?" I began.

"It's a bit embarrassing, Doctor," she blushed with chin quivering and eyes at the edge of tears, "but I've gotten too dry and my dear husband hates it."

"Do you want hormones?"

"No, they cause cancer."

"Have you tried lubricants?"

"My husband hates them too. Oh, I can't believe I'm telling you all this," she sniffled and gracefully dabbed her nose with a silk handkerchief.

"Well, how about hormone creams? They don't cause cancer."

"Richard abhors all creams. Oh, how embarrassing," she whispered.

"Do you have anything particular in mind?" I whispered back, as if sharing her intimate secret.

"After you examine me, I wish you would talk to Richard. He's been coming to you for several years now and would listen to what you say."

"What would you like me to tell him?" I asked, trying to hide my discomfort.

"I don't know, Doctor. Check his hormones; they have to be abnormal. Try to insinuate that I'm too old and too dry to have sex every night," she blushed again.

"Every night?" I gasped.

"He wants it every night, Doctor, every night, every darn night. To him it's love and to me it's agony. We started at nineteen and he has never stopped," she whimpered. "Don't get me wrong, Doctor. He's a very good man and I love him dearly, but..." she wiped off a tear with her long, manicured fingers and did not finish her sentence.

*

I could not help Mrs. Lorem and I did not dare broach the topic with Mr. Lorem, who was a reserved man, leaving the matter for time to untangle. *"O time, thou must untangle this, not I, It is too hard a knot for me to untie,"*[86] said Shakespeare, and that four-hundred-year-old quotation was all I needed to support my inaction.

Nevertheless, they both continued to come for their annual examinations, but instead of coming together, as was

---

[86] *Twelfth Night*, a play by William Shakespeare.

their habit, they started coming separately. The years ambled and times tumbled, but Mrs. Lorem's chief complaint remained the same. And as the years grew, so grew the shedding of her quiet tears, which she wiped off most elegantly, holding her silken handkerchief with long, manicured fingers.

In her sixties, Mrs. Lorem began to lose her figure to menopausal girth, which rendered her rotund and buxom but, in spite of the menace of years, she managed to maintain an elegant, cheerful aspect.

In her seventies, she began to look tired and elegance started to migrate away. Her intriguing expressions became replaced by a cliché-wondering look; her liquid, graceful body movements gave way to un-choreographed automatisms; and her aristocratic demeanor faded into a resigned, charmless comport. She sighed more than she laughed, muttered more than she quipped, and her primal cheerfulness slowly stooped under the heft of marital years.

*

"He's wearing me out, Doctor. He doesn't know how to show love except under the covers. We hardly hold hands anymore, but each night he holds me with his powerful arms and only lets go when he falls asleep. If sex could kill, I should have died 20,075 times."

"How on earth did you arrive at that strange figure?"

"We married at 19 and now I'm 74. Do the math, Doctor. Multiply 365 x 55 and you'll get 20,075 times. Can you believe that?"

"This is most unusual," I confessed, half believing her numerical exaggeration.

"It's true, Doctor. I'm not exaggerating," she insisted, having discerned my skepticism.

" 'You never really understand a person until you consider things from his point of view—until you climb into his skin and walk around in it,'[87] said Harper Lee. I wonder what mind set, what life view, what existential ethos possesses your husband to make him behave the way he does?"

" 'Sarah couldn't get pregnant till she was 90,'[88] he keeps saying. What a pathetic excuse. I think he's a sex maniac."

"Perhaps he really believes that you can still bring forth an Isaac into his Abraham world."

"No, Doctor. He's not possessed by such lofty beliefs. He's just a sex maniac and I hate him for it. It was fun when we were young, but at our age, it's sick. Sick, sick, and more sick—there's no other name for it," she sobbed, almost convulsing. "But I love him and suffer every night because I don't have the heart to reject him."

For the first time since I began seeing Mrs. Lorem, anger gushed from her eyes, puckering her once beautiful face. Her tears fumed down her red-hot cheeks and fell, un-wiped, onto her lap. Her gnarled, un-manicured fingers no longer reached to blot her salty tears with a silken handkerchief. Instead, when she was through crying, she nonchalantly wiped her cheeks with her bare palms.

*

A few months later Mr. Lorem came in for his annual examination, looking well. Strong, tall, muscular, handsome, and cheerful—his fit form belied his age. At 75 he was in remarkable shape and had no complaints. However, on rectal exam, I found a hard, prostate nodule the size of a pecan. His chart review indicated that his prostate examination was

[87] *To Kill A Mockingbird*, a novel by Harper Lee (1926-2016).
[88] *Genesis* 21:2

normal the year before. While rehearsing my thoughts about this fast-growing prostate tumor, I washed and rewashed my hands, not noticing that he was eyeing my nervous moves.

"So, what's wrong, Doc?" He asked with a firm, assertive voice.

"We have a new problem," I sighed, rearranging my face.

"It's my prostate, isn't it?"

"Yes," I confessed. "You have developed a big mass since your last exam."

"You mean a big cancer?"

"We'll need a biopsy to prove that it is malignant."

"And what do we do after we prove that it's malignant?"

"You'll have a workup to define the extent of the disease and then you'll be offered treatment options."

"Like surgery, or proton therapy, or castration?"

"You and your urologist will have to decide on the best treatment."

"Two of my friends have been through that, Doc, and they both became impotent," he frowned, unable to hide his dark thoughts.

"Let's start with the biopsy and go from there," I appeased.

"I respect you, Doc, but I'm having none of that treatment stuff."

"What do you plan to do?" I beckoned.

"I plan to go home to my wife. I'm not letting such treatment stuff get between us. I'm a Veteran who has dodged the bullets in two wars, Doc. I believe this third one is gonna get the retired Veteran."

*

Mr. Lorem did not schedule a return visit and Mrs. Lorem called and cancelled her annual appointment, leaving me mired in noir wonderings. But forgetfulness, the merciful balsam of bitter memories, slowly faded Mr. and Mrs. Lorem's dilemmas out of my mind.

It took three years before Mrs. Lorem, at seventy-seven, resurfaced on the appointment book, resurrecting my angst. I was eager to ask some questions, but I was also afraid of the answers. It took me a while to calm my heart. Then, after a deep stuttering sigh, I walked into the exam room.

"Mrs. Lorem, it's so good to see you again," I began.

"I've aged doctor. Don't tell me that you haven't noticed; I can see it in your eyes."

"I've also aged, as you can see. It's the natural order of things."

"But you have aged well, and I haven't," she added and fell silent.

It was painful to see how fast she had decayed and what little gleam remained in her barren, expressionless face— a face once brimful with seasons. Rather than meeting her weather-beaten gaze, I busied myself with looking at her chart, hoping that she would be the one to fling open the conversation door. She did not. Instead, with unaware gaze, she stared at her feet.

"Mrs. Lorem," I began, not knowing where to begin. "How is Mr. Lorem?"

With eyes still tethered to her feet, she muttered, "He died a year ago. He suffered horribly. He refused treatment. I was so upset with him that I neglected my own health, cancelled my appointment with you, and haven't seen a doctor since. I know I've aged ten years in the past three."

"I'm so sorry about his and your suffering. I did not believe him when he told me *'I'm having none of that treatment stuff.'* "

"He knew what he wanted, and he was determined to get it," she added without elaborating."

"And how are you coping, Mrs. Lorem?"

"I'm a seventy-seven-year-old shadow, looking for a form," she blurted. He was my entire life and I did not realize it. Now that he's gone, I have no life. I'm just a shadow of my former self."

"But, surely, you still have many meaningful things to live for."

"Like what, Doctor? I have no children, no living relatives, and no passions because all my passions have died with him. I'm just a shadow, Doctor, just an angry, hungry shadow."

"What are you hungry for, Mrs. Lorem?"

"I'm hungry for him, for his touch, his arms, his inseminating communion, his insatiable desire for my body and soul. I was the temple at whose alter he worshiped nightly. I bitterly regret my nagging complaints about his carnal passions. I was too stupid to realize that these extraordinary passions were indeed my main life force," she sobbed.

"Relish the memory of your 57 years together and live in it, Mrs. Lorem. How many women can say their husbands made love with them every night for 57 years?"

"You know he tried to make love with me one week before he died, but he couldn't because of his horrific bone aches. That was the only time I heard him cry."

"These were telling tears. They said with a few drops what volumes of words could not have said."

"You know that I still cry every night; I cry at the time when he used to reach for me."

"But you are still a loving woman, a woman capable of so much giving because you have received so much."

"No Doctor. I used to be a loving woman. Now I am shadow of a life whose glory I could not appreciate until it flew away."

*

Mrs. Lorem and I hugged before she left. "You know, it feels so good to be hugged by a kind man again," was the last thing she said to me.

*

A few months later, Genevieve Lorem's picture appeared in the obituaries, young, beautiful, elegant, vibrant, with a smile as wide as the horizon. I did not try to find out how she died because I knew. She died of starvation— starvation for love, starvation for a man's amorous arms, for a man's insatiable desire, for a man's adoring heart, and for a man's nightly worship at the altar of her soul.

*

Time does not bring relief: you all have lied
Who told me time would ease me of my pain!
I miss him in the weeping of the rain;
I want him at the shrinking of the tide;[89]

---

[89] *Time Does Not Bring Relief*, Edna St. Vincent Millay (1892-1950) American poet.

Olga Young[90]
Oklahoma City, 2004

"He called me ancient, my ornery grandson," she spewed. "I can't hide my anger. I'm honest and refuse to pretend. I hate that little devil."

"Is he the one who was a slow learner?" I asked, suppressing a smile.

"Slow to learn manners but fast to learn mischief," she retorted, shaking her head with discontent.

"How are you feeling, otherwise?" I inquired, hoping to redirect the conversation toward her health checkup.

"Oh, I feel fine, I suppose, except for the daily aggravations I have to put up with. This wicked kid knows how to rile me up. The nerve to call me ancient! He would have been homeless if I hadn't adopted him from my alcoholic daughter. My daughter is the one who's ancient; when they see us together, people think she's **my mother**."

With a miffed move, Olga crossed her lean, lithe legs and pulled her skirt a few inches above her knees. She then fluffed her hair with brisk, backhand strokes as tiny beads of sweat crowded her rouge lips.

I gave her time to simmer down before delving into the medical history. Then, when I was through with the examination and she was through with her exposé, she stared me straight in the eyes and affirmed, "I told you I was fine. I only have one problem, Ryan. The devil must have tempted me to adopt him. His mother drank all through her pregnancy and used all kinds of drugs. I knew he couldn't be normal, but I still went ahead and adopted him. That good deed is going to bring my ruin."

---

[90] Pre-published, *The Bulletin*, Oklahoma County Medical Society, November-December 2018.

Tears dripped down Olga's cheeks. She felt trapped by pains, the pains of immutable realities. Divorced, teaching high school English, working as a real estate agent during weekends and summers, raising a motherless-disturbed boy, and seeing her beauty crawl into relentless wrinkles, robbed her of the joy of living. Instead of sailing with the warm winds of age, whose tides bring her closer to shore, she insisted on sailing with the livid winds of youth whose ebbs pulled her deeper into the sea.

"I was beautiful once," she lamented, "but now I'm a whining wreck. I used to be a head-turner and men would stop to stare at me. Now they look through me as if I do not exist. Besides, what man would want a woman who is rearing a disruptive child? I'm destined to live alone and die alone."

*

Olga did not give me time to tell her that she had a large, left breast mass. Two years earlier, when she was sixty-one, she had breast augmentation, which she thought would make her more attractive. She had to work hard to pay for that surgery, and now she has to work hard to pay for Ryan, who is fourteen and has expensive school and scout activities. Still, I had to reveal to her the ominous truth, and there was not an easy way to do it.

"Olga. Let's step into my office for a chat," was the best I could come up with at the time.

"That sounds serious, Doc," she retorted as she cautiously sank into the chair facing my desk and gazed at me with worried eyes.

"There's a mass in your left breast, dear," I began. "It may be benign," I lied, "but I can't needle it because I may puncture the implant. I'll have to send you to a breast surgeon."

"That's one more problem I did not need," she sighed, and her face, like a wet rag, dropped into her lap.

"I'm sorry, Olga, but it's unwise to procrastinate."

"Do you know how much I paid for these?" she said, flaunting a buxom posture. "They cost a fortune, and now you're sending me to a surgeon to deflate them?"

"I don't know what the surgeon will do. It may not entail removing the implant," I lied again.

"And, who'll take care of Ryan if something should happen to me?" She whimpered.

"Nothing is going to happen to you, dear. We'll walk this rough road together, one step at a time."

*

Olga had a cycle of chemotherapy after mastectomy, followed by another breast augmentation but her breasts no longer matched, which bothered her more than the fact that she had had cancer. But at sixty-five, Ryan was sixteen, and they both had matured because of that tragedy. She no longer seemed discontented with her lot in life, and Ryan was more appreciative of her sacrifices.

"I can't believe Ryan's transformation," she exclaimed. "He has become kind, caring, protective, and supportive. Maybe my breast cancer made him realize that I was his lifeline."

"How are his grades?"

"He's always had a four-point average. On top of that, he's publishing poems in the school magazine and wants to become a Marine."

"And how's your daughter doing?"

"She's the same and has little to do with Ryan or me."

"Does he ask about her?"

"No, but he writes poems about her. He calls her My Heavenly Mother."

"What does he call you?"

"He just calls me Mother."

*

When Ryan joined the Marines, Olga was sixty-seven. When he graduated from Medical school, Olga was seventy-seven. When he finished his family medicine residency, Olga was eighty. When he and his wife had their first child, Olga was eighty-three. When she came in for her checkup, she brought me pictures of her granddaughter.

"Isn't she adorable?" She asked with gleeful eyes.

"She is and I hope she'll grow up to be as beautiful as her grandmother."

"I was beautiful once, but age took it all away."

"We were all beautiful once, and yet, every age still has its own beauty."

"No, Doctor. There is less beauty with age. Let's be honest. We decay as we grow old. Look at me now. I used to spend hours beautifying at the mirror and now I hate looking at myself. I sometimes wonder who's this old hag looking back at me. Age is painful and demeaning, Doctor, and there's nothing we can do about it."

"When did you start feeling that way?"

"When I turned eighty. There is black magic in that number. I feel like a salmon that left home, roamed the oceans, and is now climbing back upstream to where she was born, climbing up the years towards home, towards disintegration, towards death."

"Surely, you can find a more positive way of viewing age."

"Positive, Doctor? What's positive about it?"

"The eighty-three years you have lived that no one can ever take away. Ryan, whom you reared, who surprised you by becoming a disciplined Marine, a family physician, a good husband, a good father, and the one who brought joy to your home after years of toil and trouble."

"To tell you the truth, Doc, I never thought that Ryan would amount to anything. My cancer and the Marines did make a real man out of my rebellious, impolite grandson."

"Ryan's baby girl is now your ambassador to the future. What she becomes may bring more joy to many more generations. The possibilities of aging are endless. We are the base from which the future is launched. Without age, there can be no future. And without future, there can be no age. The past, present, and future are what we really are, dear."

Silence hissed as Olga reluctantly reconsidered her negative views of age. Seeing the defiant disbelief in her cynical eyes, I inquired, "Have you read T. S. Eliot's *Four Quartets*?"

"You're asking an English teacher if she has read T. S. Eliot? I love his symbolism and metaphysical dimensions. But, why do you ask?"

"Because he addresses your anti-aging attitude:

'Go, said the bird, for the leaves were full of children,
Hidden excitedly, containing laughter.
Go, go, go, said the bird: humankind
Cannot bear very much reality.
Time past and time future
What might have been and what has been
Point to one end, which is always present.' "[91]

---

[91] T. S. Eliot (1888-1965) major American poet, author of the poem *Four Quartets*.

"I know the verse, she nodded un-approvingly, but it has never touched me because I'm a realist, Doctor, and you're not."

"Well then, since you're a realist, let me share with you this private story and see what you think of the girl. A patient of mine had a trust fund from her extremely wealthy father, which gave her $2,000 a month, starting from the day she graduated from high school until she finished college, six years later. When the trust ended, her father refused to give her more, which made her angry. She became estranged from him, refused to share her children with him, and complained bitterly about his loveless parsimony to family and friends. Now, my dear realist, what do you think of this girl's attitude?"

Olga thought a while before she answered. Then, with frowns quivering all about her face, she said, "I think she's being ungrateful instead of thankful for a gift she did not have to work for—a gift that she obviously did not deserve."

"Well then, my dear realist, instead of complaining about age, why don't you turn back and thank God for it, because he has given you eighty-three years that you did not deserve, eighty-three years that you did not have to work for?

" 'What is your greatest failing, you ask? False accounting. You put too high a value on what you have given, too low a value on what you have received,' said Seneca."[92]

Olga did not reply. She twitched a smile, gave me a hug, and left. A week later, I received this note in the mail.

*

---

[92] Seneca, Lucius Annaeus (4 B.C-65 AD) Roman philosopher.

My Dear Doctor,

     Our last, life-changing meeting left me with so much to ponder. Perhaps, regretfully, I've had the wrong attitude for most of my life. Perhaps, a change of attitude from thankless to grateful and from morose to cheerful is, indeed, our best antidote against age and adversity. This antidote, so cynically expressed in Lord Byron's Don Juan, perhaps should become the ethos of old age.

> *Nevertheless, I hope it is no crime*
> *To laugh at all things, for I wish to know*
> *What, after all, are all things but a show.*[93]

     With that in mind, I shall from now on endeavor to laugh more and complain less. Emerging from my old age of servitude into my new age of gratitude, here is a little limerick, which I have composed especially for you.

*

> *First you crawl, then you walk*
> *In a while you start to talk*
> *After that you start to stoop*
> *Getting old is pigeon poop.*

With lots of laughs,

    Olga

---

[93] Lord George Gordon Byron (1788-1824) British poet, author of the poem, *Don Juan*.

Back from Hospice[94]
Oklahoma City, 2009

"We had a great sex life, Doc."
"Had?"
"Last week, they put Earl on hospice."

Eldina's tears shivered on her cheeks. With long, smooth fingers, she reached for a tissue and sighed, "We've had sixty great years. I'm just not ready to give him up."

"Tell me what happened? I had no idea he was that sick."

"When at his last physical you diagnosed prostate cancer and sent him to the urologist, his bone scan showed metastasis. They put him on Lupron, and he's been getting worse ever since."

"Getting worse? He had no symptoms when I referred him."

"You should see him now. You won't recognize him. His entire body aches. He has headaches. His eyes are failing. He's lost a lot of weight and is getting weaker by the day. Last night, he tried to turn in bed to..." she sighed. "He tried to..." she cried. "He tried to reach for me and couldn't..." she sobbed. "We had a great sex life until they put him on Lupron."

"Is he still on Lupron?"

"He took his last shot three months ago. 'No more Lupron,' said the urologist. But he continues to fail, and the hospice nurses keep trying to give him pain pills, which he refuses because they make him feel worse."

Eldina and Elmer were high school sweethearts, sixty-two years ago, and were both eighteen when they got married. Tall, handsome, beautiful, and beaming with joy, they always came together for their annual examinations. Eldina, an accomplished pianist and piano teacher, year after year, in the privacy of the exam room, would always extol their wonderful sex life:

"We started having sex when we were sixteen, Doc, and we haven't stopped, and don't intend to."

Elmer, on the other hand, a combat pilot who turned commercial after Vietnam, was too shy to mention their sex life.

Throughout retirement, Eldina played the organ at church and Elmer taught Sunday school. Now, with all their personal and social activities suspended by illness, depression cried silent tears from behind Eldina's downcast eyes.

After her exam, as I embraced Eldina, she whispered into my ear, "Would you please see him?"

I looked into her supplicant eyes and asked, "As a friend?"

"No, as his doctor," she retorted, with reproachful firmness.

"Is he not happy with his hospice physician?"

"Dr. Maroon is very nice, but he doesn't give us hope."

"I don't think he's supposed to," I protested, "because that would be giving you false hope."

"What's he supposed to do then?"

"He's supposed to help Elmer die peacefully, with dignity, and without pain."

Eldina blanched when I said that, and her gaze fell down onto the exam room floor. While I stood there, aloft, alone, afar, suspended between the silent jaws of reality and the saving kiss of hope, her fallen gaze rose up again until it met mine. And then, with feathers in her voice, she asked the proverbial question:

"Do you believe in miracles, Doctor?"

"Miracles? Yes, of course," I gasped. "Medical miracles happen every day," I acquiesced, not suspecting that I was being setup.

"In that case, come and see him, please. You've been our doctor and our friend for over thirty years, and we believe you can help."

In response, I smiled and tried to hide my inadequacy, but she saw through my veil of pretense and answered the question, which I dared not ask.

"We don't expect you to perform a miracle," she reassured. "God will do that for us, but it has to come through you. Elmer and I prayed about it last night and he was the one who told me that you are the only one who can give us hope. He said that after he tried and tried to reach for me and couldn't."

I swayed and buckled under the mighty weight of responsibility. Mr. and Mrs. Rettung wanted me to perform a medical miracle on a dying man, a man that I had not seen for a year, a man who is on hospice. I'll just visit him as a friend, I thought, trying to appease my angst. That will help them both and ease the dying process. As I pondered my next move, with Eldina's expectant eyes fixated on mine, my nurse knocked on the door, poked her head into our silent stalemate, and announced, "Your next patient is ready."

Late that evening, after the usual phone calls and paperwork, I drove to the Rettung's home. Elmer greeted me with a faint smile and a feeble voice, "It's good to see you, Doc."

While Eldina stood like a statue in the middle of the room, I sat on Elmer's bed, held his hand, and listened:

Slowly, among gasps and groans, he told me his one-year saga. After his last physical exam, after I told him that he had a large prostate nodule, and after Dr. Stone, the urologist, told him that he had bony metastasis, he agreed to take Lupron. It was after the fourth shot that he began to ache in the hips and shoulders. Weakness followed and he had trouble getting out of bed or standing up from a sitting position. He lost his appetite, lost lots of weight, and had trouble ambulating. Then the headaches came, and with them his vision began to fail. Scans showed widespread metastasis to his big bones and to his skull. Dr. Stone consulted Dr. Malin, the oncologist, and Dr. Ojo, the ophthalmologist. They offered him aggressive chemotherapy but knowing that it could make him feel even worse, he refused. That was when they all agreed on hospice.

When he finished his story, Eldina, still standing like a statue in the middle of the room, chimed in with, "So, what do you think, Doc?"

Instead of answering her question, I palpated Elmer's temporal arteries. They were tender, and so were his shoulder and hip muscles. It was then, after I had made up my mind that Elmer was suffering from *polymyalgia rheumatica* with *cranial arteritis*[95]—a condition not infrequently associated with cancer—that I began interrogating him:

"Have you had any recent blood work?"
"Not for three months," answered Eldina.
"Has anyone ever given you cortisone?"
"No," answered Eldina.
"Well, in that case..."

*

---

[95] Autoimmune inflammation of brain arteries and hip and shoulder muscles, with causes strokes, blindness, and severe weakness.

Two weeks later, Elmer, walking bright and tall, came in for his appointment.

"Where's Eldina?" I quizzed.

"She's in Missouri, babysitting the grandkids."

"You look well," I added with a smile.

"That cortisone is a miracle, Doc. It didn't take but a few days before my strength began to return and my other aches to go away."

"How's your vision?"

"It's back to normal."

"And how's your appetite?"

"I'm gaining back my weight."

Elmer, after some resistance to my insistence, started taking his Lupron injections again, which thrilled Dr. Stone. A few months later, Elmer and Eldina decided to move to Missouri to be closer to their children and grandchildren.

What a miracle of life, what inveterate inseparableness, and what indomitable love, I thought as I handed them their charts, hugged them both, and bid them farewell. Of course, we promised to stay in touch, but we never did. We lost contact after they left, but they never left my mind. Year after year, their image would flash on my mental screen, as a most beautiful couple who defied age with love.

Four years after they had left Oklahoma for Missouri, I received a beautifully addressed letter from Eldina. At first, I was afraid to open it because I was fearful of what it might hold within its folds. It lay on my desk for two days before I summoned enough courage to violate its sanctity.

*

Dear Dr., Hawi

Elmer died in his sleep last month, and he never needed hospice. He was eighty-four, and just as sassy and handsome as when he was sixteen. We had four good years in Missouri, rich with love and family. And although his cancer weakened him, he continued to reach for me at night until the very end.

All his Sunday-school students came to the funeral. I played the organ, and the church choir sounded heavenly. We had been married for 66 years. Oh, how I miss him in my bones.

When, five years ago, you told us that medical miracles happen every day, you gave us hope, and then God did the rest.

Nevertheless, we were greatly disturbed when Medicare refused to pay for your lifesaving house call because doctors are not supposed to provide lifesaving treatments for patients dying on hospice.

May the Lord continue to perform his medical miracles through the hands of our good doctors.

With love,

Eldina Rettung

Hundred Years per Hour[96]
Oklahoma City, 2015

It was an unhurried, sunless Sunday. Having retired, with 45 medical years now off my shoulders, I reveled in my oblivion. *"In the practical use of our intellect, forgetting is as important as remembering,"*[97] said William James. Still in half sleep, my eyes gaped at an early telephone ring. I had forgotten that I was a doctor, forgotten that these early phone calls were frequent fragments of my once-alarmed life.

"Hello," I answered with half-awake voice.
"Doctor. This is Norma. I hope I didn't wake you up."
"Doctor? I'm not in practice anymore."
"It's my dad, Doc. He wants you to come..."
"You know I'm retired, I yawned, still shrouded in oblivion.
"You're still his friend, right?"
"Right," I rattled; my voice hoarse with remorse.
"Well, my dad wants you to come to his birthday this afternoon..."

That afternoon, I drove to Mulhall, not for a house call, but for a home visit. I had taken care of Mr. Siècle for 45 years. He was the first to walk in when I started my practice—tall, handsome, blithe with wit, and full of war stories. Today, my one-century-old Veteran friend wants me at his double-jubilee. What an honor, I thought, as I drove. I had never attended anyone's hundredth birthday before. My mother died this year, just six months shy of that mark. I had planned to haul the entire family to Lebanon for her birthday. Well, on her behalf, I shall celebrate it with Mr. Siècle instead.

---

[96] Pre-published, *The Bulletin*, Oklahoma County Medical Society, January-February 2017.

[97] William James (1843-1910) American philosopher.

The house brimmed with red cheeks and glittering eyes. Children, grandchildren, great-grandchildren, great-great-grandchildren, and so many other weather-beaten relatives, stormed around Mr. Siècle, hardly listening to his century-enfeebled voice. When he saw me, his eyes lit up, and he raised his hand as if to calm the storm. The crowd parted; the seat next to him was vacated; I sat and held his hand. Quietly, the gaggle of gratulants moved away, leaving us to talk.

"Doc," he smiled. "It sure happened fast."
"What happened fast?" I smiled back.
"The decay."
"You mean, the hundred years?"
"That too, but the decay is what really bothers me."
"You mean..." and I gazed at his swollen feet, his legs, parted to accommodate the bulging diaper, his gnarled, blue toes, and his sprawling, convoluted toenails. He must have noticed my inspecting eyes because he interrupted me with: "I used to wear sexy briefs; now I wear diapers."

I was overtaken by his poignant remark. It took me a few moments before I found an intelligent response.

"But your mind is sharp," I consoled.
"There's the rub, Doc. It would have been easier if my mind had left, and my body had stayed. With a sane body, I could have maintained some measure of independence. A sane mind doesn't do much good for a broken body."
"A sane mind gives you joy, doesn't it?"
"No, Doc. You got it wrong this time. My sane mind gives me agony. I have lost my wife, some of my children and grandchildren, all of my friends, and most of what I have loved."
"Oh, come now. You still have much to love."
"I can't listen to music because of my hearing. I can't watch a ballgame because of my sight. I can't read. I can't travel. I can't go to the bathroom. I can't bathe. I can't even

leave my house. Food don't taste good. A glass of wine wipes me out for three days. My body embarrasses me every chance it gets."

"But you have your great family to love and cherish," I reminded.

"They don't come around much anymore, except on occasions. They have their lives to live, you know. No one wants to hang out with a broken, old man."

"*The great thing about getting older is that you don't lose all the other ages you've been,*"[98] I countered, quoting Madeleine L'Engle.

He nodded, his eyes filled up with dry tears, and he patted my hand.

I looked at the room, full of giggling voices and wine-crimsoned cheeks, loitering, chatting, oblivious of Mr. Siècle and me. Words from Robert Frost's *Home Burial* intruded on my pondering pause:

> *No, from the time when one is sick, to death,*
> *One is alone and dies more alone.*
> *Friends make pretense of following to the*
> > *grave,*
> *But before one is in it, their minds are turned*
> *And making the best of their way back to life*
> *And living people, and things they understand.*[99]

"Mr. Siècle." I ventured. "Surely some things must still bring you joy."

"You reckon?" He quizzed with a wry, drooping smile.

"Well, you've seen so much over so long a time, and you've lived so many good lives. That must bring you joy."

---

[98] Madeleine L'Engle (1918-2007) American activist and author.

[99] Robert Frost (1874-1963) American poet, author of poem, *Home Burial.*

"It's like a train ride, Doc, speeding at one hundred years per hour. From your window, you see things pass, and as soon as they pass, you forget them. That's where I am now, and that's why I wanted you to come."

"It was my honor to come, Mr. Siècle."

"Honors aside, I know that you've retired, but I still need your help."

"I am happy to do what I can," I hesitantly replied.

"I need you to help me get off the train at the next stop."

"Oh, Mr. Siècle. You know I can't do that."

"Oh, yes you can. Everything in me hurts, Doc. Just give me some pills and I'll do the rest..."

As I gazed into the crowded room, I recalled Simone de Beauvoir's adage: *"It is old age, rather than death, that is to be contrasted with life. Old age is life's parody, whereas death transforms life into a destiny: in a way it preserves it by giving it the absolute dimension. Death does away with time."*[100]

Mr. Siècle wants me to help him get off the hundred-years-per-hour train, I thought, as I watched him drool, but I am not capable of euthanasia. Indeed, Oscar Wilde rightly observed, *"The tragedy of aging is not that one is old, but that one is young."*[101] Mr. Siècle is asking me with his young mind to help him dispatch his old, broken body, and I am unable to do it.

When I stood up to take my leave, Mr. Siècle smiled and whispered, "If you live to be my age, you'll ask your doctor to do the same thing for you, and he will do it, because by then euthanasia would be legal. So, for the love of God, Doc, won't you change your mind?"

"Let me think upon it," I appeased.

---

[100] Simone de Beauvoir *(1908-1986)* French existential writer and partner of John Paul Sartre.
[101] Oscar Wilde (1854-1900) Irish playwright.

"Well, don't think too long," he giggled. "I may not be around, if you take your sweet time." Then after a short pause, he asked, "What was that quote again?"

"The great thing about getting older is that you don't lose all the other ages you've been," I repeated.

"Thanks Doc. I love the way you think."

I left Mr. Siècle's home with the weight of my 45 medical years on my shoulders. Indeed, Johann Wolfgang von Goethe was right when he observed that, *"Age takes hold of us by surprise."*[102]

As I drove back home, I found myself speeding, speeding unaware, speeding without knowing why. Frightened, I slowed down and gazed into the life-graying winter along the road. That must be how it feels to ride on a hundred-year-per-hour train, I thought, and was most relieved to get out of my car when I arrived home.

A week later, Mr. Siècle's daughter called to thank me. "Whatever you did, Doc, must have helped him feel better."

"But I didn't do anything," I protested.

"After you left, he took one bite from his birthday cake and then refused to put anything else in his mouth. We tried, but he wouldn't even drink water. He kept rejecting us by saying, *'No one can take away all the ages I've been.'* Last night, he asked us to put his uniform on. He died this morning, in his sleep."

"He was able to get off the train without my help," I murmured.

"What train?"

"The hundred-year-per-hour train. That was how your dad represented his life to me. His old body made him forget

---

[102] Johann Wolfgang von Goethe (1749-1832) German writer, author of the play, *Foust.*

the one hundred wonderful years he had lived, the one hundred good years that not even death can take away."

"He died happy, Doc. Died with a smile on his face."

"It was a good death, then."

"Yes, praise the Lord, it was."

Terra Firma[103]
North Carolina, 2015

"Regretfully, throughout all your high-school years, I have only taught you Newtonian physics. Today, in our last class of your last year, I'm going to broach the concept of metaphysics, that life dimension, which eludes our five senses but, nevertheless, rules our minds.

"Who are we, anyway? Are we only physical beings, or do we also possess ultra-physical dimensions? Are we merely physical facts, or are we also beliefs that masquerade as facts? Are we not but our beliefs? And are not our beliefs but our dearly held superstitions?"

These two excerpts—of Mr. Michael's goodbye lecture, which he delivered to our graduating class of the American Evangelical School in Tripoli, Lebanon, on June 21, 1963—still cling, like drowning arms around my neck.

Mr. Michael traveled with me throughout college, medical school, residency, fellowship, marriage, children, career, aging, and retirement for he was the one teacher who challenged me to dare think for myself. He loved to quote Immanuel Kant's aphorism: *"Sapere Aude—dare to know, have the courage to use your own understanding—that is the enlightenment's motto."*[104]

"A wise man," he would say, *"tries to prove himself wrong whereas a common man tries to prove himself right. Don't fall in love with your own ideas merely because you were the ones who conceived them. Spend time collecting evidence to disprove your own points of view and learn as much as you can from those who disagree with you because those who agree with you, teach you nothing."*

---

[103] Pre-published, *The Bulletin*, Oklahoma County Medical Society, January-February 2018.

[104] Immanuel Kant (1724-1804) German philosopher.

*

Fifty years after graduation, we held a high school class reunion in North Carolina, because most of us had been [*sic*] refugeed by the Lebanese Civil War. Mr. Michael, at ninety-two, came from Los Angeles with his eighty-five-year-old American wife—who had been a career Army nurse—and with his Lebanese cane, which he had whittled out of an olive branch from a piece of land he had inherited from his father. Mr. Michael, my classmates, and I filled in the gaps across half a century of absence, told stories, laughed, lamented, comported ourselves with the abject abandon of children and, after three frolicsome days, returned back to our sundry lives feeling enriched and rejuvenated.

It was two years after that expatriate reunion that I received the tremulous call:

"Doctor, this is Mr. Michael's wife, Marybeth. He's very sick and is asking for you."

"What's going on?" I gasped.

"He's sick with so many things and may not be around very long."

"Is he not happy with his doctors?"

"Oh, no, we have wonderful doctors. When I ask him why he is insisting on seeing you, he tells me that it's personal."

"May I talk to him, please?"

"He has been restless, perturbed, and not himself for about a year now. He hardly speaks and keeps babbling that he needs to see you. His doctors think he's delusional but, as his nurse and wife, I know better. He's distressed about something and won't tell me why because, having spent my lifelong nursing career inside Army bases, he thinks that I wouldn't understand."

The Friday after that call, I flew to L.A. His eyes lit up when I walked in and he said, "Thank you for coming. I have inconvenienced you with a great hardship, but I had no one else I could turn to but you."

His wife seemed stunned by his sudden clarity and terse eloquence. I sat by his bed and held his extended hand. He looked at his wife and kindly asked, "How about some coffee, Dear?"

"I'll take my time," she replied with a knowing smile, and left the room.

I looked into his eyes, brimming with excitement, and smiled back to hide my own surprise. He got out of bed, marched steadily to his desk, sat down, opened a drawer, pulled out an envelope, and handed it to me.

Standing before him, as I had done for so many years as an obedient student, I took the sealed envelope and waited.

"Please sit down," he motioned. "When I fled Lebanon thirty-five years ago, I owned a large piece of land near our hometown, Kahloon, which I had inherited from my father. When, after many years, we realized that we were never going back, Marybeth convinced me to sell the land, and with the money, buy a piece of property here. I resisted, but after I ran out of excuses, I reluctantly sold the land about a year ago and I have been miserable ever since."

"To whom did you sell it, Sir?"

"To my youngest brother, who is eighty now. I'm fourteen years his senior and too old to make that trans-Atlantic, trans-Mediterranean trip again. When I went back a year ago to complete the sale, I realized that I was no longer fit for travel."

I looked at the envelope in my hand and politely waited for him to tell me what to do.

"I have felt naked ever since that sale, like a homeless man, wandering aimlessly without his clothes. I don't want to die homeless and naked. I want to don my own clothes before I am returned home, for I wish to be interred in Lebanon."

"I'm going to Lebanon next month to see my mother, who is almost 100 years old," I volunteered.

"I knew that you go back every year for her birthday. You told me so during the class reunion. That's why I wanted to see you. I've talked to my brother and he's willing to sell me back the land for the same price. In this envelope is a Power of Attorney for you to act on my behalf, and a cashier's check made out to my brother. My hometown is only a ten-minute drive from yours. Here's his telephone number and I have already given him yours."

*

Flying back to Oklahoma, I contemplated the plight of [sic] refugeed immigrants like us, immigrants who arrive at foreign shores with their suitcases but leave their hearts and earth-bound roots in their homelands. And buried with their hearts and roots they also leave their dreams of returning home. Indeed, wars do continue to devastate long after they end:

Because I have two hearts
Because I straddle oceans
Because I am both banks of life
The froth, the currents in between
The dissonant emotions
I see beyond the mighty walls of time
Beyond the eyes, the made-up lips, and faces
Beyond the borrowed sentiments and faint laces
Because I have two hearts,
My soul is vagabond
It camps in many places.[105]

---

[105] Poem, *A Letter from Beirut*, from *Familiar Faces*, a poetry book by Hanna Saadah.

*

In Lebanon, after I completed the land transaction, I called Mr. Michael to congratulate him. With a moist, raspy voice, he thanked me and asked when I would be back.

"I'll be back in Oklahoma in a week, and I'll mail you the title deed as soon as I arrive."

"That will put my heart at ease," he sighed. "Did you walk the land before you bought it back for me?"

"No, I'm afraid not, Sir."

"Oh, but you must. It's beautiful, full of olive trees, grape vines, almond trees, and smells of my father's long-lasting labors. Please walk it and take pictures. That would bring me great joy."

"I will, Sir," I promised.

*

Back in Oklahoma, I mailed Mr. Michael the title deed, some photographs of his land, and a short poem, which I had penned many years earlier, when I realized that, because of the Lebanese Civil War, I too would not be able to return home. When he received the registered envelope, he called, and we chatted. His voice chimed with birdsong and his words rippled like springs.

"I am finally at peace and have regained my *joie de vivre*," he chortled. "I know that I will never see my land again, but I have it tucked underneath my pillow, with the pictures and your poem. I feel safe again, and content that my life cycle has been completed. My fears of dying without my land, fears that had haunted me for an entire year, have dissipated. Indeed, we are our beliefs, and our beliefs are not but our dearly held superstitions."

Mr. Michael went smiling into death and was buried in his Lebanese hometown, Kahloon. In his will, he left the piece of land to his Veteran wife with instructions never to sell it. In Mrs. Michael's will, since they had no children, the land was to be returned to his brother after her death.

*

Familiar faces
I have lived and loved and reasoned
Traveled wide till open-eyed and
* seasoned*
Now, after scorching years and tears
And merciless, erosive fears
I have come to understand
That home is always love and land
That love alone is homeless and
Land alone is loveless and
Home is always love and land.

Familiar faces
Let us not pretend
Though life may decimate and send
Our unsuspecting souls across
Uncharted times and unfamiliar places
Wherever we are loved, we end.[106]

---

[106] Poem, *Familiar Faces* from *Familiar Faces*, my third poetry book.

Silhouettes[107]
Oklahoma City, 2015

Whispers are shy kisses, I thought, as I watched the octogenarian couple snail on the dance floor, few steps behind the music, balancing one another with amorous caution, and clinging with frail arms that defied gravity. Their cheeks glowed with hushed joy, their lips gleamed with sunset smiles, and their eyes beamed like nightlights from behind their swooning eyelids.

Remote from the tenebrous ambiance of the restaurant's dance floor, my wife and I sat in an alcove while I watched geriatric love cling to life with defiant disregard of years and circumstance. And when the music leaped from tango to rock, and youth quaked the floor with jarring gyrations, their movement maintained its measured grace, echoing the siren tunes of their inner harmony, unaware of the surrounding bedlam.

"What are you looking at?" Snapped my wife, a bit perturbed at my taciturn inattention.

"I'm watching that elderly couple dance."

"You must find them more interesting than me," she reproached, half-seriously.

"Observe their buoyant reverie, their sublime emotional dimension, their defiant passion, and their cherished solitude as if they're here but not here, and with us but not with us."

"You and I were like that when we first met and fell in love," she lamented.

"We are still like that, Darling, but only when alone."

"Are you too embarrassed to show intimacy in public places?" she challenged.

---

[107] Pre-published, *The Bulletin*, Oklahoma County Medical Society, July-August 2018.

"A public display of emotion, after so many years of marriage, would seem unbecoming."

"Are you suggesting that we wait till our eighties to behave like them?" she smiled.

"We have what they have, Darling, but ours is no longer new, which is why it must remain private. They are in the spring of love and we, in its autumn. Their orchards are full of blossoms and ours, of ripe fruit."

"Do you know them?"

"The man was a patient."

"How about the woman?"

"I know of her, but this is the first time I see her."

"Are you going to tell me their story?"

"It would be a HIPAA[108] violation."

"Tell it without names or records, Doctor," she snapped. "I can only see their silhouettes from here and would not recognize them if I were to see them again."

*

The man, a retired Army Captain turned realtor, let's call him Adam, was married to a heavy-smoking, diabetic lady, let's call her Eve, who ignored medical advice, did not take her insulin as prescribed, and continued to smoke with nonchalant disregard of consequences. Adam complained about her every time he visited my office, but I was never able to influence Eve to take better care of her health. As they grew older, Adam became more depressed while Eve lost more weight and her lungs failed. Her visits to my office became more frequent and more cumbersome because of frailty, failure to thrive, and emphysema. But, in spite of failing health, two heart attacks, one stroke, several pneumonias, a foot amputation, and

---

[108] Health Insurance Portability and Accountability Act of 1996, which is a US legislation that sets data privacy and security provisions for safeguarding medical information.

oxygen dependence, she managed to survive and laughed in my face each time I urged her to stop smoking. "I turn my oxygen off when I light up," was her favorite comeback.

Adam became a fulltime caregiver and had to delegate his business responsibilities to their two daughters because he could no longer leave Eve alone. He and I commiserated about Eve's decline and I had to augment his antidepressant to keep him functional.

*

Two months before I retired, he called me at three in the morning, sobbing.

"Eve has just died," he cried. "She woke me up choking, clasped her chest, rolled her eyes, and turned blue. I did not try to resuscitate her because she did not wish to be resuscitated."
"Are you alone with her?"
"Yes, but our daughters are on their way and so is the police."

*

At the funeral, Adam was inconsolable. Instead of relief, he felt guilt for not having loved Eve enough during her final years.

"She was too much, Doctor, and drained my love and my patience. We were high school sweethearts. Oh, you should have seen her when she was young and beautiful. I was the most envied groom of my generation."

*

After the funeral, I did not see Adam for several months, but when he came for his annual exam, he told me that he was back to work and that his daughters were staying on because he did not feel as capable and energetic at eighty-five as he did at seventy-five. He also mentioned that he had a love interest, a widow who had been their family friend since high school days.

"We have been dating for a few weeks now, and my daughters are appalled, but I don't care because I am happiest when I'm with her and I feel profoundly alone without her."

"Do your daughters spend much time with you?"

"We're only together at the business. Since I've started dating Helen, they seldom come home anymore."

"Are you planning to marry her?"

"I would love to, but she's against it. She believes that if we could keep our independence and not share children, we would be able to keep our relationship pure and free of interference. *'Children will harm our rare and precious love, whether they approve or not,'* she insists. Like me, she had a hard marriage and her children do not approve of us."

*

Reviewing Adam's chart, after this heart-to-heart conversation, I noticed that he was not taking his mental-health medications.

"Why did you stop your antidepressants?" I asked, surprised.

"Because I no longer needed them."

"When did you realize that?"

"After my first date with Helen. I flew home like a bird, free to sing, free to live, and free to love. Love must revive youth because I feel young again. Are you happy for us, Doctor, or do you think that we're just old and silly?"

"On the contrary, I'm awed and overjoyed. Don't let anyone take away the happiness you two have resurrected in each other. Life is short, happiness is even shorter, and resurrection is rare. You have been blessed with a second life. Live it to the fullest with God's blessings and remember this quatrain from Rupert Brooke:

> " 'Now that we've done our best and worst, and parted,
> I would fill my mind with thoughts that will not rend.
> (Oh heart, I do not dare go empty hearted)
> I'll think of Love in books, Love without end;' "[109]

*

On the way home, having told my wife the story of Adam and Eve, and of Adam and Helen, she said nothing for a long while and then abruptly asked.

"If I die before you do, could you fall in love again?"

"I would hope so," I replied without hesitation.

"Not me. I'd rather live alone and die alone."

"Please do not say that, Darling. Do not make promises you should not keep. Romance, which is love laced with desire—the desire to unite bodies, souls, days, nights, and lives—is one of the few meaningful passions that can rejuvenate old age. Saying no to that kind of love is a betrayal of life, not a betrayal of your deceased husband. Romance will help us die while feeling new instead of old. All the other loves of family and friends cannot do that for us. Dying while feeling aged prevents us from celebrating the ends of our lives, whereas dying while feeling youthful helps us die with joy in our hearts, that sublime joy of having found romance again."

"This has been too much for one evening," she sighed as she wiped off a tear. "I don't want to talk about old age and

---

[109] *The Busy Heart*, a sonnet by Rupert Brooke (1887-1915) British poet.

death anymore. Let's just hold hands and be quiet until we get home."

*

At home, in bed, with the lights off, and still holding hands, my wife whispered, "What are you thinking?"

"I'm thinking of what Gibran said about love in *The Prophet*. I've never really understood that one line until tonight."

"What line? What did he say?"

"He said, '*When you love you should not say, God is in my heart, but rather, I am in the heart of God.*' "[110]

"And what did he mean by that?"

"He meant that to know God we must love, because Love is what delivers us unto God."

---

[110] *On Love* from *The Prophet* by Gibran Khalil Gibran (1883-1931) Lebanese American writer.

Soas[111]
Raleigh, NC, 2017

Coincidence,
She wears green shadows intertwined with dreams
Lurks unforeseen, in silence plots and schemes
At times, she hurries matters to profound extremes
Delights in rolling fortunes in reverse
Coincidence
She sways the universe.[112]

The Tripoli Boys School or TBS—an American missionary institution founded in 1873—did not shut down during the Lebanese Civil War of 1975-1995. However, many of its graduates and teachers, who had immigrated to the USA because of that internecine[113] conflict, held a high-school reunion in Raleigh, NC in 2017. The oldest expatriate at that gathering had graduated from TBS in 1955, eight years before I did. It was during that East-West mélange (for most of the graduates had American wives by then) that I met Sami Mansour.

Peering at my nametag, he extended a welcoming hand and said, "My friends call me Soas."

I was bemused because that was not the name on his tag. Delighted at my intrigue, he added, "I am Sami Mansour, Emeritus Professor of Middle Eastern studies at NYU. I graduated in 1959, four years ahead of you."

Forging an uncertain smile, I replied, "I don't remember you," and after a polite pause, inquired, "So why do you call yourself Soas?"

---

[111] Pre-published: *Al Jadid*, Vol 21, No. 73 October 2017.

[112] From *Familiar Faces*, a poetry book by Hanna Saadah, from the poem, *Familiar Faces*.

[113] Bloody and damaging to both feuding sides.

"I changed my name after I excavated my origins," he smirked.

"Excavated? That's a very deep word," I grinned.

"There's an Irish pub across the street," he pointed. "Let us spend this afternoon's lull intelligently."

"Intelligently?" I repeated with raised eyebrows.

" *'To be able to fill leisure intelligently is the last product of civilization,'* said Bertrand Russell."[114]

Walking to the bar with this meddlesome intellectual who calls himself Soas and seems to know more about me than I know about him, I adopted a listener's strategy.

"What would you guys like to drink?" Asked the lean, alacritous[115] waitress.

"I'll have a Manhattan," he blurted.

"And I'll have a Guinness."

"It doesn't travel well, you know."

"What doesn't travel well?"

"Guinness beer. It only tastes good in Ireland."

Irked, I held on to my polite silence and nodded unintelligibly. He smiled as if he could read my thoughts then roamed his eyes around the room. Soon, the lithe, little waitress returned, laid the drinks before us, and undulated away. I sipped, waiting for him to begin.

"Your family's history was part of my PhD thesis," he announced.

"I did not realize we were that important," I retorted.

"Your family's history may not be important to you, but it is to me, and I spent two years of my career researching its era and its century."

"I don't quite understand."

[114] Bertrand Russell (1872-1970) British philosopher.

[115] Cheerful and eager to serve.

"Your mother delivered me in 1942."

"I hear this kind of remark everywhere I go. She was, for a long time, the only woman gynecologist in Tripoli."

"But I was a special case."

"She began her private practice in 1942. Were you her first case, perhaps?"

"I don't think so."

"So, what was it that made you so special then?"

"My mother needed a hysterectomy because she had very heavy menstruations and was anemic. Your mother had just finished her residency and was assisting the general surgeon on the case. When they opened her abdomen and found out that she was pregnant, the general surgeon walked out to ask my father if he should remove the uterus or close her up and let her carry to term. My father told the surgeon that they already had six children and could not afford one more. When the surgeon went back into the operating room, he was surprised to see that your mother had already closed up the abdomen. He became angry and sent her out to tell my father. My father was furious and told her that when the child is born, he was going to give it to her. Your mother answered that she would be delighted to adopt me."

"So, you're my adopted brother?"

"In an unconventional way, yes."

"Why is it, then, that I've never heard of you?"

"Because that was the agreement. My parents were poor and could not afford a seventh child. Your mother paid for all my expenses and education. She visited us monthly to pay her dues, and when I graduated from high school, she paid for my airplane ticket to New York and gave me $3000 to get started. Besides me, the only ones who knew of the arrangement were my parents and your father. When your mother died last year, I traveled from New York to attend her funeral and I shook your hand while you stood in the condolences line. You were wearing a gray suit and a black bowtie."

I was stunned. No wonder he knew more about me than I knew about him. But family stories are neither short nor simple. He had more to tell and I knew it. I gulped my Guinness while he sipped his Manhattan.

Silence droned.

"After four years of college, I was drafted into the Army and spent two years in Vietnam, which is how I gained my American Citizenship. For my PhD thesis, I returned to Beirut to research your family's era, and the century that held its pedigree. I wanted to know the origins of your mother, her distant ancestry, and what set of coincidences collaborated to bring forth my life-saving lady doctor. I visited her often to ask questions, spent time looking in the birth-and-death records of the churches in Beirut and talked to many old people from that era. It took a year, but when I finished, a deep sense of peace settled over me. I sent your mother a copy, but she returned it to me with a note reminding me that, as long as she lived, no one must know. Well, one year after her death, I could not hold the secret any longer. That is why I came to this reunion. I came to give you a copy of my thesis, which I completed in 1968. The larger part of it is not about your family, but rather about the history of that era, which included the Ottoman Empire's rule, the First World War, the French Mandate's rule, the Second World War, and the Lebanese Independence. But the real reason I chose to study that era was your family's history."

Back at the hotel, Soas handed me his thesis and we parted. The next morning, at the breakfast gathering, he sat next to me and we talked. I had spent the night reading his manuscript, learning much about my mother, her parents, her grandparents, and that entire century, which held my family's history in its lap.

*

The following is an abridged rendition of his story without the century's significant historical details.

It turns out that my grandmother was born in Beirut. Her mother, Jamileh—born in 1842, one hundred years before Sami Mansour (Soas) was born—was a strong, bright, and very beautiful woman. She first married a ship captain, but before she could bear him any children, he was shipwrecked in a storm off the Lebanese shores and drowned. She waited two years before she married Mubarak, who was an erudite mathematician. The fruit of that marriage was Malakeh, my grandmother-to-be, born in 1875.

Until the age of ten, Malakeh was educated at the school where her father taught. When the first Russian Missionary School in Beirut opened its gates in 1887 under the leadership of the Chief Russian Superintendent, Maria Alexandrovna Chirkasova, her father enrolled Malakeh in the new school because, at age twelve, she had already mastered all that the school he taught at could teach her. After graduating at age 17, she taught in all five Russian missionary schools in Beirut and, despite her young age, was revered because she was a gifted educator. In 1902, at the age of 27, Maria Alexandrovna Chirkasova appointed Malakeh as principal of the Russian Missionary School in Amioun, the hometown our family hails from.

Let us leave Malakeh for now and go to my grandfather, Hanna. He was born in Amioun in 1884 and his mother died at childbirth. At the age of two months, he was blinded by trachoma. His sister raised him and when it was time for him to go to school, the Amioun schools rejected him because he was blind. His friends managed to smuggle him into their classes and hide him underneath their desks. After school, he studied at their homes by listening to them read their lessons. One day, an encyclopedic Arabic tome, Bahth Al-Matalib by Bishop Germanus Farhat, was given to one of his friends who, over a year's time, read it page by page to Hanna. He must have had a genius memory because by the time they finished reading the tome, he had mastered the Arabic language and began to earn his living by teaching it. Demand for this precocious, adolescent teacher grew. He gave private lessons, taught in several schools, was revered by his students, and became renowned as grammarian, poet, orator, and educator. His students were his readers and scribes, and the churches and mosques of the region were his homes, for he was a religious man. In just a few years, this blind, self-taught, young man acquired significant wealth and opened his own, private school in Amioun.

Malakeh, as the new principal of the Amioun Russian Missionary School, went to Hanna whenever she needed help with complex Arabic grammar issues, especially those pertaining to classical poetry. With time, her visits became more frequent and their relationship grew beyond the boundaries of scholarship. When Hanna sent her a passionate love poem, she felt frightened and asked her superintendent, Maria Alexandrovna Chirkasova, to reassign her. It so happened that the Russian Missionary School in Bainu, a town in the region of Akkar, was in need of a principal at the time, and that was where Malakeh was sent. But her reassignment did not discourage Hanna who sent her one passionate poem after another until she surrendered to her feelings, came back to Amioun, and married him in 1905 when she was 30 and he was 21. Her Beirut family protested vehemently because she was a highly schooled woman and Hanna was but a young, unschooled, blind man.

Together—after the Turks in 1914 closed the Russian missionary schools in Lebanon and Palestine because the

*Russians and Ottomans were on opposite sides of the war—
they started their own school, which lasted until Hanna was
commissioned by the bishop to teach Arabic at the Orthodox
Parochial School in Tripoli. In 1916, after eleven years of
marriage, Malakeh at 41 and Hanna at 32 had their first and
only child, Mai, who was to become my mother.*

*During those years between the two World Wars,
women were merely educated in primary schools and did not
go to college. Their life functions were to marry, bear children,
and raise families. Contrary to custom, Hanna wanted your
mother-to-be, Mai, to study medicine, an unrealistic goal.
Nevertheless, she did. After finishing high school in Tripoli, she
went to Beirut where she studied medicine, graduating at the
top of her class in 1940—one of the first Lebanese women to
earn an M.D. from the American University of Beirut. After a
two-year residency in obstetrics and gynecology, she returned
to Tripoli in 1942 where she launched her private practice
career. That was the same year she intercepted the planned
hysterectomy of Sami Mansour's mother.*

*

After breakfast, Sami Mansour and I exchanged a
tearful goodbye and promised to stay in touch. When he was
about to get into his taxi, I asked him my final question.

"You haven't told me why your friends call you Soas.
The name is neither Arabic nor English."
"It's an acronym."
"An acronym for what?"
"*Son of A Storm.*"
"What storm?"
"The storm that drowned the ship's captain, your great
grandmother's first husband, allowing her to marry Mubarak,
the mathematician, who fathered your grandmother. The

series of coincidental events that brought about my birth go
back to the beginning of creation, but I could only study the
last century, which began in 1842 when your great
grandmother Jamileh was born and ended in 1942 when I was
born."

*

My grandfather died eleven years before I was born.
My grandmother died when I was ten. My father died when I
was 41 and my mother, when I was 70. I was 71 years old
when I learned that I had an older brother and that I too, was
the son of a storm.

Bobcat Over Friedberg[116]
Leiden, Holland, 2018

Just like our brains are made of synapses, our universe is made of connections. Just like our bodies are vitalized with arteries, the world is vitalized with highways. And just like our childhoods permeate our souls, our histories permeate our cultures. Indeed, coincidence is our law, imagination, our freedom, and memory, our story with which we wrestle with death.

My family, scattered in three continents, uses cyberspace for its *autostradas*. From the Netherlands, my son called, "Dad, you're coming to my graduation, right? It's in two weeks and I haven't heard from you."
"I'm too old for transatlantic flights, Son. The longest distance I travel now is from home to the VA Hospital. I'm an old doc taking care of old vets."
"Seriously, Dad. I've worked 8 years for this PhD. I need my family to share in my joy."

Of course, my wife and I debated, considered the expense and risk, reflected on the hardships of making two, back-to-back, transatlantic trips at our age, and flew to Leiden, anyway, to partake of Nicholas's joy. It was after that ceremony, which took place among Gothic arches in a medieval edifice banking canal waters that a blonde, blue-eyed student, speaking with a heavy German accent, approached my wife and me with an extended hand.

"I'm Ingrid and you are the doctor from Oklahoma."
"*Ing-is-beautiful*, that's the meaning of your name."
"Not many know that *Ing* was a Germanic god and *rid* meant beautiful."

[116] Pre-published, *Journal of the Oklahoma State Medical Association*, November 2019.

"Have you been to Oklahoma?" Asked Judy, my wife.

"No, but I want to visit Ada after I graduate."

"Why Ada? Do you have relatives there?"

"No and yes. No blood relatives. Yes, life relatives."

"Perhaps we should sit down, then, and order coffee," I suggested, seeing that a meaningful conversation was about to un-scroll. The reception hall was alive with shining faces, fancy hairdos, high-pitched voices, frantic movements, hugs, screams, and huddled-photo poses. My son, noticing us, came rushing to our table with arms spread as wide as the horizon.

"Ingrid," he squealed, wrapping her with his long, folding arms. "You've already met my dad and Judy. Oh, I so wanted to be the one to introduce you."

"We're just about to have an Ada discussion," she declared.

"Well, I've never been to Ada, but my Dad and Judy have."

"A lot of our patients came from Ada," added Judy.

"Oh. Oh my God," gasped Ingrid. "You know folks from Ada. Oh, my God. Tell me about them. Tell me all you know. I've never met anyone from Oklahoma except your son and he knew nothing about Ada. That's why I prayed you'd come to his graduation. I've been waiting a long time for this moment."

Ingrid's face quivered with emotion as she exclaimed, pantomimed, and babbled. I looked to Nicholas for an explanation, but his eyes were blank. She must not have shared her Ada connection with him, probably because he had never been to and knew nothing about Ada.

After Ingrid's emotional fireworks subsided, we all waited for her to begin telling, but she did not. Instead, she reached for a tissue from her purse and wiped off a silent tear. The mood slowly transitioned from exuberant to silent, and none of us dared crack Ingrid's reverie. Quietly, like a silken

294

shawl, sliding off the back of a chair, Ingrid excused herself and slipped away, holding a tissue to her nose.

"What went wrong?" Asked Judy.

"Nothing," replied Nicholas as he got up and took off after Ingrid.

"I don't like the suspense," sighed Judy.

"You don't like it because you don't understand it, dear," I reassured.

"Do you?" She challenged.

"No, but she'll return with Nicholas when she's ready to talk."

*

It was the next day at breakfast that Nicholas told us that Ingrid would love to have lunch with us. He would make the reservation and we would meet them at 1 p.m. at the Indian restaurant, which is close to the church.

"She's very sensitive and very spiritual," he warned us. "Every detail in her life carries a unique meaning, which she internalizes with gratitude. I wish I could be like her and find profound meanings in everything."

"How did you meet her?" I asked, intrigued.

"I didn't. She found me."

"Well, tell us more," whispered Judy, as if all ears were upon us. "You're making me curious."

"I was studying in the Library when she appeared and asked if I was Nicholas from Oklahoma. Before I knew it, I had told her all about the school I attended, the friends I had, the churches, the winds, the tornadoes, and the flat, sparsely-forested landscapes."

"Are you two dating?" Asked Judy.

"She was the one to first ask me for a date. That did not surprise me as much as when she told me that she had waited all her life to date a man from Oklahoma. When I asked her why, she just said that it was a spiritual yearning."

"Well, are you two dating or not?" Inquired Judy with a firmer voice.

"We're just good friends and we go out in groups. Neither of us could find romance in the other."

*

We found Ingrid and Nicholas waiting for us at the restaurant. They had chosen a remote table in a quiet corner. We exchanged pleasantries as we ordered, sampled, and sipped tea. Then, without introduction, Ingrid said, "If I get emotional, forgive me and allow me time to recover. I got emotional last night when I was about to tell you my story."

"Go ahead, Ingrid," encouraged Nicholas, holding her hand.

"My grandmother, Dagmar, was 25 years old in 1945 when the war ended. She lived with her family in Friedberg, a small town then. Her father was the town's pastor and her mother, a seamstress. The town held a strategic position on the River Wetter and was protected by 1500 German soldiers and SS officers. Colonel Danz, commander of the city garrison, was a very strong supporter of Hitler and was instructed by Hitler to resist until the last man. The town's people did not really know that Germany was losing the war because all they heard on their radios was Nazi propaganda. It was on the 29th day of March 1945—when the American tanks surrounded the town—that my story began."

Ingrid sighed and took an emotional break before she resumed. The rest of us huddled in silence.

"A German officer, taking a walk outside the town, was captured by Major Walter Smith, commander of the 69th Armor Division, which had surrounded Friedberg. Major Smith sat the captured German officer on the hood of his Jeep, took him for a ride to show him that American tanks had already surrounded Friedberg, handed him a white flag, and drove him to the center of Friedberg, passing through several check points.

"Alone, this Major Smith met with the German officer in charge, Captain Straub, told him that the town was surrounded, and that if he would not surrender, they would reduce the town to rubble. Captain Straub, who obviously knew that the war was almost over, was happy to surrender in order to spare Friedberg from annihilation."

Here, Ingrid took another break and ordered more tea. There was much more to tell because she was getting more emotional as her story unfolded.

"After Captain Straub agreed to surrender, Colonel Danz showed up. He was furious and announced that he and his garrison were going to fight to the last man because these were the *Führer's orders.* At that moment of contested surrender, Dagmar, my twenty-five-year-old grandmother, was in the process of hoisting a white flag onto the Rapunzel Castle. When Colonel Danz saw her, he aimed his gun at her and threatened to shoot her if she did not drop the flag. Grandmother Dagmar froze with the white flag in her hand and Colonel Danz's gun aimed at her chest. It was the most frightening moment of her life; she later told my mother."

With shaking hands, Ingrid attempted to lift the cup of tea to her mouth but couldn't steady it, spilling tea on her lap. Nicholas handed her his napkin, which she used to wipe off her tears. When she regained her composure, she resumed.

"Major Smith, standing alone, surrounded by German soldiers, pointed his handgun at Colonel Danz's head and told him, 'If you shoot this girl, I will blow your head off.' The colonel looked to his soldiers for support but none of them reached for his gun. It was then that Major Smith asked the colonel if he really cared about the 15,000 Friedberg inhabitants that he was protecting. When the colonel said 'Yes, of course I do,' Major Smith told him, 'No, you really don't because if you resist, we're going to wipe the entire town off the face of the earth with you, your garrison, and all the inhabitants you're protecting. Captain Straub can testify to our massive tank force surrounding your town because I took one of his officers for a ride before bringing him back here."

The colonel looked at Captain Straub's bowed head and lowered his gun. Everyone clapped when my grandmother hoisted the white flag on the Rapunzel Castle."

Unaware, we all clapped with excitement when the tension broke and a smile smoothed the contorted face of Ingrid. There was more to come, of course, but the climax had been crowned with a brave victory engineered by a lone American Major. Nicholas, the most impatient among us, urged Ingrid to go on.

"After the surrender, Grandmother Dagmar baked a cake for Major Smith and thanked him on behalf of the town. Friedberg's men, women, and children cued to shake Major Smith's hand. However, the Major could not share in their planned celebrations because he had orders to go liberate the Buchenwald Concentration Camp. At the camp, he found starving inmates, many of whom died when the Americans fed them. Helmutz, one of the inmates who had survived the feedings, later came to Friedberg, established a haberdashery shop, and did business with Grandmother Dagmar's mother, the town's busy seamstress. In time, he befriended the family and later on married Grandmother Dagmar when she was 30, thus becoming my grandfather."

Here, Ingrid smiled, sighed, paused, and then continued.

"Helmutz and Dagmar took a long time to conceive because starvation had affected Helmutz's fertility. The doctors were sure that my grandmother was fine and fertile, but when they checked my grandfather's sperms, they were low in number and slow in motility. Nevertheless, after five years of trying, Grandmother Dagmar got pregnant and delivered a baby girl, Emilia, who was to become my mother."

We were all intrigued by Ingrid's story but could not tie it to her present emotional state. We could tell that an explanation was forthcoming, which helped us rein in our impatience. Ingrid, enjoying the fact that we had become enthralled, resumed.

"Emilia, my mother, grew up in Friedberg and married my father, Fredric when she was twenty-five. They tried and tried to have a child but could not. After spending a lot of money on doctors, who told them that they were both fertile, they gave up and stopped seeking medical help. They had been married for fifteen years when the municipality of Friedberg decided to celebrate the 50th anniversary of the city, which had escaped annihilation in 1945. To my mother's astonishment, the city invited Major Walter Smith of the 69th Armor Division to be the guest of honor and erected a monument commemorating his brave saga. The monument, a triptych, which still stands today, reads: *On the knife's edge—The 29th of March 1945—Friedberg saved from destruction.*' "

At that point we all decided that we needed a break. We left the restaurant, walked along the canal for a while, and settled in a café that overlooked the water tower. It was there that Ingrid finished telling her story.

"You can imagine my mother's excitement when she heard the news because she had heard so much about Major Smith from her mother and knew that, were it not for him, her mother would have been shot by Colonel Danz, and her father would have died of starvation in the Buchenwald Concentration Camp. She became involved in the preparations, volunteered much of her time and money, and chronicled Major Smith's story in the local newspaper to remind the Baby Boomers that, were it not for Major Smith, none of them would have been born. When Major Smith arrived, she was shocked to see an old man instead of a young, brave commander, for he was 76 by then. Nevertheless, his visit was the brightest star in her galaxy."

Here, Ingrid began to bite her lips, chewing them as if she were trying to burst them when, in fact, she was not even aware of what she was doing. The closer she came to the denouement, the slower and more deliberate became her words as if she were savoring that atavistic era with such relish that she did not want it to end. But we are all storytellers at heart, and once we start telling we cannot stop until we finish. Indeed, after a moment's quietude, Ingrid did resume.

"A short time after Major Smith left Friedberg, my mother, at the age of 41, found out that she was pregnant. She called me a Major-Smith miracle when I was born and gave me the middle name of Wunder, which means miracle in German. When Major Smith died in 2008, at the age of 89, my mother cried acid tears and became inconsolable. I was barely twelve then, but I remember how she used to visit his monument and leave flowers as if it were his grave."

Ingrid took another deep breath and was silent for a final pause before she continued.

"As you must have surmised by now, Major Walter Smith grew up in Ada, Oklahoma, and that's why we're huddled here tonight. Were it not for him, my family would have been annihilated and I wouldn't have been born."

We watched Ingrid go limp after her long catharsis, as if she had run a marathon, as if she had found her lost saint, as if she had emerged from the depth of darkness into the laughs of light. When I told her that I was Major Smith's doctor, she exploded in tears and begged me to describe him. When I told her that he was indomitable, that he had tamed a bobcat in his youth, and that he was locally known as Walter "Bobcat" Smith, she giggled with delight. When I told her that even in his eighties, Major Smith was still stocky, strong, sincere, courteous, confident, had the voice of a commander, and eyes that glowed with the fire within, she smiled happy tears because old age had failed to damage Friedberg's hero.

"I'm saving my money," she announced as we walked back to our hotel. "It will take me a year to save enough to buy a ticket."

"What ticket?" I asked.

"My ticket to Oklahoma," she replied, surprising us all. "I want to visit Ada and lay a wreath on Major Walter Smith's grave. I promised my mother, when she was on her deathbed, that I would do so. As soon as she heard my promise, she smiled, closed her eyes, and died."

*

Veterans do not die
They live in the hearts of those they saved
In the hearts of all of us.

The Hith[117]

I do not trust my mind
It tortures and it teases
And wanders where it pleases
Leaving me behind;
I do not trust my mind.[118]

"I'm a fallen man," was how Mr. Cor greeted me when I first entered his room, white gowned with bowtie and stethoscope around my neck.

"I'm Dr. Hawi, the ward attending," I smiled, shook his cracked, weather beaten hand, and crouched on a chair next to his bed.

"How old are you, Doc?" He asked, peering at me with curious eyes.

"Seventy-three."

"You're thirteen years older than I am but you look younger," he smiled, patting his swollen abdomen as if it were a little pregnancy.

"On earth, we're all siblings," I reassured.

"This," rubbing his abdomen, "is what has aged me. When it gets to hurting, there's no stopping the vomiting and the pain. Admission after admission, they tell me that I have pancreatitis and that I need to stop drinking or else it will kill me."

"Have you ever stopped, Sir?"

"I've spent the last ten years stopping and starting," he smiled. "I can feel my life flickering away like a candle flame about to run out of wax. As I said, I'm a fallen man, Doc. Everything that defies gravity must ultimately fall back down to earth," he philosophized, "and I'm sure heading that way," he emphasized with remorseful voice.

---

[117] Pre-published, *The Bulletin*, Oklahoma County Medical Society, January-February 2020.

[118] From *Loving Of A Different Kind*, a poem from the 1987 poetry book, *Loves And Lamentations Of A Life Watcher*, by Hanna Saadah.

*

On daily rounds, Mr. Cor and I stitched up a friendship quilt. Visit by visit, his life story un-scrolled while I crouched on the chair next to his bed. He began his life as a young poet, writing about the tired and heavy-laden. One day, he witnessed a homeless man being dragged by the police and that very night, he heard the Lord's call, *"Come to me, all you who are weary and burdened, and I will give you rest."*[119]

From that point on, he dedicated his life to the Lord, went to seminary, became an ordained minister, used his poetic gifts from the pulpit, and was most revered by his congregation. His wife and three boys were the crown he wore as he summoned the weary-and-burdened to the Lord. Until he turned fifty, Mr. Cor was a paragon of virtue, living a selfless life as husband, father, and pastor.

*

"One Sunday, while preaching the Lord's Word, I saw a woman walk in, hesitate, then furtively take a hind corner seat. She was lean, middle-aged, and fast of pace. Intrigued by her aspect, veiled with meek, mystifying melancholy, my eyes visited her eyes whenever I addressed her side of the pews. When the service ended and I stood to shake hands with the departing worshipers, she glanced at me with affectionate eyes then vanished into the exiting crowd.

"That night, her visage visited my dreams, just like that homeless man's image visited me when I first heard the Lord's call. All week long, like a white-winged reverie, she flew in and out of my awareness. I could not interpret her to my mind, but I could to my heart. I prayed every time I washed my hands that she would come to next Sunday's

---

[119] Bible Verse, Matthew 11:28-30.

services. You can see from my cracked hands that I'm a handwasher, Doc. I wash each time I touch anything that might be soiled. I bet I wash fifty times a day and that was how many times I prayed that she come to my next Sunday service.

"That next Sunday, I searched and searched for her to the point of distraction. My sermon suffered from unintended hesitations and ineloquent pauses, while in vain my eyes roamed the pews. Disappointment grayed my heart as I stood in line, shaking hands and exchanging pleasantries with God's worshipers.

"Then, as if she had intentionally held the end of the line, she suddenly appeared with an extended arm. As we shook hands, I wanted to say something, anything, but my words, trapped in my throat, could not utter a whisper. Instead of words, all I could do was hold her hand with both of mine and quiver a fateful smile.

"She thanked me with the vast silence of her eyes then scurried away with gazelle steps, which pranced across the floor till out the door. I noted that her hands and face were far older than her lithe figure, which was so gracefully proportioned like that of a young Aspen tree.

"At home, my dear wife kept asking me, 'What's wrong, Dear?' I couldn't tell her that I was hit in the heart by a force that I could not resist, a force stronger than gravity. I found myself telling her, 'You know that I love you and that's all that should matter.'

"Week after week, the woman would come and wait at the end of the line. We would shake hands and, when propriety permitted, exchange smiling whispers and soft, eye-to-eye glances.

"I couldn't control my mind. It tortured, teased, and wandered where it pleased, dragging me behind. One day, my good wife told me that I was fading away, that I was distancing myself, and that I was no longer with her when I was with her. I could not tell her that I was hit in the heart by a force that I could not resist. I started to make excuses for my absentmindedness, but I could tell that she knew that I was lying. We grew apart, became roommates instead of soulmates, and we both had to pretend just to keep going. Each time I washed my hands, which is about fifty times a day, I prayed to the Lord to release me from this hit in the heart, but my prayers were never answered.

"One Sunday, I asked the woman to join our Bible study group. She said she would think about it. The next week, I asked her again and she accepted. Over time, we nurtured a courtship whose fierce feelings quietly grew out of our control. That was when we both realized that our platonic entanglement should not go any further, but, despite that realization, we kept on meeting at all church functions.

"One Wednesday, she came late for Bible study, appearing hurried and overwhelmed. With all seats in the circle taken, I got up and offered her my seat. She hesitated and remained standing. I left the room and returned with a chair, which I positioned next to mine. She seemed relieved after she sat, and thanked me by patting my hand, a gesture that alerted the eyes of the room.

"The following Sunday, she avoided me and left as soon as the service ended. It was then that my heartache told me that I had lost her. My heart also ached for my wife who asked me questions that I couldn't truthfully answer. We began to sleep in separate beds, and I started drinking just to get the woman out of my mind. Alcohol worked as long as I drank, but as soon as I would stop, her visage would return to torture me.

"My drinking got much worse after we divorced. I could choose to be inebriated and at peace or sober and tortured. Of course, I always ended up choosing peace over torture.

"I was let go from my ministry and I have been struggling with alcohol ever since. Nevertheless, every Sunday, I attend the services just to gaze at her, but her eyes continue to avoid me. I am a doomed man, doomed to douse her repeating apparition with alcohol, and doomed to surrender my life to unforgiving gravity."

*

When, after many agonizing days, Mr. Cor finished telling me his story, he seemed relieved, which surprised both him and me. It was like draining an abscess, an abscess that had been festering for ten years, an abscess that no one knew about because Mr. Cor, being a man of the Lord, was too ashamed to reveal.

"Mr. Cor," I began, holding his cracked, weather-beaten hand. "I have an explanation that is going to shock you. What you thought was a-hit-in-the-heart was in fact an out-of-control obsession. Obsessions are not reasonable, but they are treatable. Would you allow us to treat you?"

"You mean to tell me that I'm not a fallen man?" he asked with a scorched, stuttering voice.

"I think you are a strong man who has managed to survive a malignant obsession without falling."

"I think what you mean to say, Doc, is that I have managed to survive a hith. Do you know what a hith is?"

"No, I don't, but I would love for you to tell me."

"A hith is an acronym I made up for _h_it _i_n _t_he _h_eart. A hith is inescapable. It can topple anyone, no matter how strong. It is deadlier than bullets and more painful than physical torture."

"No, Mr. Cor," I countered. "Your hith is merely a malignant obsession and obsessions, like compulsions, are treatable."

*

Under good psychiatric care, cognitive therapy, and high-dose escitalopram, Mr. Cor's hith obsession and frequent handwashing came under control. At three months, he was reemployed by another church and began an addiction ministry, which prospered under his pastorship. After one year of sobership, he was reunited with his wife. He is currently writing a book about his saga, explaining that a hith is just another medically treatable obsession and cautioning believers that emotions may delude the purest of hearts and subdue the strongest of souls.

*

Ask my heart sometimes about your arrow
shot from a loose bow.
It would not have hurt so much
if it had actually gone through.[120]

---

[120] Ghalib, Mirza Assadullah Khan (1797-1869).

The Golden Tooth[121]
Lebanon, 1951

"I was married in 1882, when I was fourteen, to a man who was forty-four," began my grandmother, when I asked her why she had a little bald spot in the middle of her head. I was five years old in 1951 when I asked my grandmother that question.

"Four years before we married, your future grandfather, Nicholas, had returned to *Amioun* [our Lebanese mountain town] after spending twenty years in America and serving four years in the American Army. He built a grand stone house and started looking for a wife. He was modern and could read and write both Arabic and English. I hid behind the wall when he came to visit us because I was unschooled, simple, and poor. Smallpox was in the air then, and he told my father that to protect me from coming down with smallpox, he would have to brand me in the middle of my head with a hot coin, a trick he had learned from gypsies who used to pass through Amioun when he was growing up. He was modern, you see, and knew things no one else knew. He knew about the smallpox vaccine because he was vaccinated when he served in the American Army. But the ruling Turks would only give the smallpox vaccine to their soldiers, never to us people.

"During his third visit to our home, my father called me, saying my suitor had brought me a gift of sugar. In 1882, under Turkish rule, people were starving in *Amioun* and no one had sugar. When I ran in, screaming with excitement, my father held me tight to his chest, and your future grandfather, Nicholas, branded me in the middle of my head with an American coin, which he had heated on hot coals.

"As soon as my father let go of me, I ran away with my tears and hid among the olive trees. My mother came looking

---

[121] Pre-published, *The Bulletin,* Oklahoma County Medical Society, July-August 2017.

for me, put oil on my burn, and told me that Nicholas branded me because he wanted to protect my beauty from becoming disfigured by smallpox. She also brought me a sandwich of olive oil and sugar, which I ate when I stopped sobbing. I had never tasted sugar before.

"Still I was so angry at him that I hid each time he came to visit. My mother pleaded with me to marry him, but I was stubborn. Finally, my father asked me on Easter Sunday, when we were at church, what it would take for me to accept Nicholas's hand in marriage. I said that I wanted a golden tooth. At that time, no woman in *Amioun* had a golden tooth, and I wanted to be the first. 'But your teeth are fine,' protested my father. I countered by saying that I do not want new clothes; I just want a golden tooth that shone each time I smiled.

"And so, it was. My father, my fiancé, and I took an all-day carriage trip to *Tripoli*. It was my first trip and by the time we arrived, I was exhausted because the carriage ride had made me sick and I vomited all the way from *Amioun* to *Tripoli*. We spent the night in an inn and visited the dentist the next day. He had to order the gold from a jeweler and shape it to fit my right upper incisor. On the third day, I had my golden tooth and we headed back home. Again, I vomited all the way back, but it was worth it because I was the only woman in *Amioun* who had a golden tooth.

"A month later, I married Nicholas, who was as old as my father; they had grown up together and were good friends. I smiled all the way down the aisle for all to see my golden tooth. When I became pregnant with my first child, Nicholas was ordained as the town's priest and my name changed to *Khouryeh* [the priest's wife]. I bore him eight children; your father was my seventh, and he was four years old when your grandfather, Nicholas, died at eighty-four. He returned from working the land one afternoon, asked me to lay down his mattress and call all the children, for we slept on the floor then and rolled up the mattresses and stowed them in the closet by day. With all of us around him, he recited the Lord's Prayer, smiled, closed his eyes, and died. Life is a long story, Dear, but telling it takes such a short time."

*

That night, I lay awake pondering my grandmother's life. The one question nagging on my mind—the question I did not have time to ask because we had to return home to *Tripoli*—had to wait till Easter Sunday. After church, lunch, and coffee, when the big stone house quieted down, allowing me time for private talk, I asked my question.

"Grandma," I began, for she was eighty-three and edentulous [122] by then. "What happened to your golden tooth?"

A sad gleam shone from her eyes and a faint smile quivered on her weather worn lips as she paused for a sigh of recall and then began. "Your grandfather left me with eight children and no income except for what I could eke from our olive trees and vineyards. He was tall, strong, and could work the land. I was small and frail and could not do the needed labor. My three older boys had immigrated to Argentina and the two boys at hand did their best to fill their father's shoes. But, under French rule, things were just as bad as under Turkish rule. My health deteriorated and I lost all my teeth except for my golden tooth. When your father could not make enough money to pay for his tuition, I resolved to sell my golden tooth, but I was not going to ride the car to *Tripoli* because of the horrible carsickness I would have to endure.

"There was no dentist in *Amioun*, but there was a man who could pull teeth with little pain. I went to him and he agreed to pull my golden tooth for five kilos of olives. He sat me on a chair, tied a thin string to my tooth, passed the string

---

[122] Lacking teeth.

under the chair, up over the door, and tied it to the five kilos of olives, which I had brought him in a basket. He then put a bamboo rod between my jaws to prevent me from biting, and had his wife hold my head tight against her chest. Then, from behind the door, he raised the basket, with the five kilos of olives in it, and dropped it to the floor. My tooth flew out of my mouth, down under the chair, up over the door, and out to where he was standing. It was so sudden that I felt no pain. His wife handed me a roll of cloth and asked me to bite on it to stop the bleeding.

"When I walked out with the cloth in my mouth, I found the man screaming, chasing after the cat who had gotten hold of the tooth and was running away with it. The cat disappeared and so did my golden tooth, and with it your father's tuition. The man felt so bad that he gave me back my five kilos of olives.

"When your father found out, he cried angry tears because I had concealed my scheme from him. He wrote a letter to his three older brothers in Argentina and told them the golden-tooth story. A few weeks later, a letter arrived with enough Argentinian pesos in it to pay for your father's tuition. The pesos kept coming, month after month, until your father finished medical school. Now, he's the one who takes care of us all. Sometimes, what seems like a loss is in fact a gain."

*

My grandmother's stories have formed and formatted me, giving me global dimensions and making me a proud citizen of the world. What a frail, illiterate, head-branded, golden-toothed widow taught me was that the real world-wide-web connects humanity not with electrons but rather with love, labor, and opportunity.

I will never forget her eyes, full of history, and her scalp, stamped with an 1876 twenty-cent coin, a rare collectors' item that left an indelible mark on our lives. My grandmother died in 1972, clear minded, in her own bed, at the age of one hundred and four—on the very same mattress that her husband, an American Veteran who had returned to become the town's priest, died fifty-one years earlier.

My grandmother never came down with smallpox, and we found the 1876 twenty-cent coin wrapped with my grandfather's wedding ring in a yellowed handkerchief stashed inside a small wooden box.

We never found her golden tooth.

*

Timeline:

1838 – My grandfather, Nicholas, was born in Amioun, Lebanon.

1858 – My grandfather immigrated to America when he was 20 years old.

1868 – My grandmother, Ramza, was born in Amioun, Lebanon.

1878 – My grandfather returned from America at the age of 40 years.

1882 – He married my grandmother who was 14 when he was 44 years old.

1918 – My father, Abdallah, was born in Amioun, when my grandmother was 50 years old.

1920 – My grandfather died at age 84 when my grandmother was 54 years old.

1946 – I was born in Amioun, Lebanon.

1951 – The story began in 1951 when I was 5 and my grandmother was 83 years old.

1971 – I immigrated to America after finishing my medical studies at the American University of Beirut, the same university from which my father graduated in 1944.

1972 – My grandmother died at the age of 104 years.

A Schizoid Interview[123]
Lebanon, 1970

"I am accustomed to sleep and in my dreams to imagine the same things that lunatics imagine when awake."[124]

In 1970, as fourth-year medical students at the American University of Beirut, we spent time in *Al-Asfouriyeh*, the psychiatric hospital in Lebanon, which catered to schizophrenics. Professor Vesanus, our revered, American World War II Veteran, who had witnessed firsthand what war does to human sanity, gave us our introductory lecture.

He described the psychiatric interview as a fateful, frightful flight through dark, mental clouds, and admonished us to be especially kind to the mentally ill.

"Had you not been baby boomers, and had you been unfortunate to experience war like the rest of my generation, you could have acquired similar mental illnesses that could have haunted you for the rest of your lives," he stressed.

"Do not challenge an irrational mind with reason," he instructed. "To understand how a sick mind thinks, you must be compassionate, vicarious, attentive, and humble. Like us, the mentally ill reason correctly, but arrive at incorrect conclusions because they reason from the wrong precepts."

After that seminal lecture, which took place many years before the Post Traumatic Stress Disorder was named or recognized, Professor Vesanus began assigning us patients.

---

[123] Pre-published, *The Bulletin*, Oklahoma County Medical Society, May-June 2017.

[124] Rene Descartes (1596-1650), French existential philosopher.

"Why don't you start by interviewing Professor Matooh," he said, pointing his finger at me. "He's a war refugee who had lost his entire family in Poland."

"Professor Matooh?" I gasped. "Professor Matooh, our physics professor?"

"Yes," replied Dr. Vesanus with calm fortitude.

I was surprised at his selection. Asking me, the student, to interview my esteemed physics professor struck me as a violation of establishment mores. I almost protested, but not wishing to affront yet another esteemed professor, I lowered my gaze and whispered, "I heard that he was on sick leave. I had no idea that he was…"

"A paranoid schizophrenic," interjected Professor Vesanus, finishing my sentence.

Perspiring with apprehension, I sat behind my assigned desk in my solitary room and waited for the smartest man I knew to be brought before me. Steps shuffled along the long, dark corridor. An orderly knocked and entered, holding Professor Matooh by the arm. I stood at attention. The orderly eased the professor into the chair facing my desk. Then, pointing to the little bell at my side said, "Ring when you're ready for me to take him back."

Professor Matooh slumped into his chair and ignored my extended hand.

"Good morning, Professor Matooh," I intoned, pulling back my unrequited hand.

Silence.

"You taught me physics a few years ago, Sir."

Silence.

"You taught me well, Sir, and I am but one of your many grateful students."

Hearing that, his eyes gleamed and he straightened up his slumped posture.

"As a former student who visited your office on many occasions, Sir, I feel odd sitting in your place now."

He smiled, rose from his chair, and commanded, "Let's exchange places, then."

I stood up and offered him my seat behind the large desk. After sitting in it, he took immediate command of the situation, as if he were in his own office, and motioned for me to sit in the interviewee's seat. Then, with a vibrant voice, he asked his usual, introductory question: "What's on your mind, bright young man?"

Professor Vesanus's words: *"Do not challenge an irrational mind with reason,"* saved the moment. With pen in hand, ready to take notes, I formulated my first question.

"How are you feeling, Sir?"

"The Universe has no feelings," he answered with mathematical certainty.

"Why not, Sir?"

"Because the Universe is unconcerned."

"Is the Universe God?"

"No. It's an extension of God."

"So where is God, then."

"You're looking at Him."

I gulped. He smiled with smug satisfaction and waited for me to resume.

"May I ask you, Sir, the question that has forever eluded humanity?"

"You may."

"How did the Universe come into being?"

"About thirteen and a half billion years ago, I birthed it."

"Birthed it? What caused you to do that, Sir?"

"I felt a strong urge to write down my thoughts."

"Is the Universe your written thoughts?"

"Indeed, it is, and the more I write, the more it has to expand to accommodate my excogitations. The Universe is my thirteen-and-a-half-billion-year diary."

I was enthralled by Professor Matooh's simple sincerity, explaining the unexplainable with nonchalant ease. More questions stirred, vying to be heard:

"And after birthing this magnificent Universe, what else did you do, Sir."

"After birth, I laid down my laws of physics and set the Universe in motion."

"Do your laws of spatial physics apply to us, *Homo sapiens*?"

"Not only they apply to you, they also apply to all the living creatures on Planet Earth, and on the many other planets that support other lives."

"You mean there is life elsewhere in the Universe?" I gasped.

"Only paranoid *Homo sapiens*—and all *Homo sapiens* are paranoid—make an issue out of life. Life is everywhere. Every atom is alive with electrons. Every light wave is alive with photons. Every star is alive with fire. Every planet is alive with rotation. All of space is alive with my brain waves."

Here, Professor Matooh took in a deep sigh and peered at me with penetrating vision, as if he were eavesdropping on my unvoiced thoughts. With his eyes piercing me, I couldn't think of my next question, but I knew that I needed to find a good one for the interview to continue. Then, remembering that the Universe was his living diary, I formulated my grand question.

"And how about our own writings, Sir? I mean us, paranoid *Homo sapiens*. Are our writings extensions of your thoughts and of your diary?"

Professor Matooh sighed with exasperation before he replied:

"Before *Homo sapiens* wrote, nature penned its chronicles with fossils, the silent, venerable hieroglyphics of life. But earth's history came into awareness only after *Homo sapiens* began writing it, just about 5500 years ago. As an ephemeral millisecond, tossed into a thirteen-and-a-half-billion-year-old Universe, how insignificant, how lost, how miniscule, how divisive are your writings compared to mine?"

"Divisive?" I protested.

"Divisive indeed. Writing divides people into languages, religions, nations, parties, factions, clubs, and armies. Writing is the epitome of awareness, and awareness is the root of all evils."

Here, Professor Matooh shifted in his seat, and as if I had suddenly opened his floodgates, continued.

"Planet Earth was formed only four and a half billion years ago. Single life cells appeared three and a half billion years ago. Organisms appeared five hundred and seventy million years ago. And last to appear, a meager quarter-of-a-million years ago, were *Homo sapiens*."

"So, why did your thoughts formulate the *Homo sapiens* to evolve so late?"

"I wanted an aware life to appreciate my work, because unaware life cannot."

"Are we the only aware life in the Universe?"

"No. There were others, but because they are so much older, they have already lost their awareness."

"Are you pleased with our awareness, Sir?"

"No. Your awareness of life has traded peace for animosity. Unaware life, which is the unwritten life, is at peace. Aware life, which is the written life, is at war."

"And what can we do about that, Sir?"

"Nothing. Only when you get close to extinction will you realize that your awareness is your curse. Only then, when your curse is spent, will you blossom back into humble equanimity."

"Has that happened to other aware worlds, Sir?"

"That has happened to all the older, aware worlds. Without exception, they all got close to extinction before they rose again. When they rose from their own ashes, they forged newer, better, humbler, less aware, and less chronicled worlds. Your world is the newest and, therefore, is the most aware. It has not had time to blossom into the humble equanimity of unawareness. It will, though, but only after it reaches near extinction."

One more question nagged at my mind. A question I was afraid to ask because I knew how he would answer it.

"Sir. Since we must evolve from awareness to unawareness before we can blossom into humble equanimity, should I conclude that the unaware life forms are, indeed, the more developed forms?"

"Indeed, they are. Which is better for Planet Earth, *Homo sapiens* or trees? Which does more good for this young planet, its unaware life forms or its paranoid *Homo sapiens*? Which is the only life form that harms Planet Earth? Is it not the *Homo sapiens*?"

"Are you saying that, because of their awareness, *Homo sapiens* are the most primitive and the most destructive life forms on this planet?"

"Think in reverse-evolution and the answer will become clear. Awareness is counter-natural and, therefore, is both self-destructive and planet-destructive. Unawareness is pro-natural, which is why unaware life forms are far more successful than *Homo sapiens,* and why *Homo sapiens* need to evolve toward humble unawareness in order to survive."

"So, are you saying that what to us seems primitive is actually advanced, and what seems advanced is actually primitive?"

Professor Matooh smiled, nodded a smug *indeed*, rang the bell, and commanded, "Next please."

I collected my notes, rose from my seat, bowed a *thank-you*, and walked out.

*

In the long-dark corridor, the orderly and I exchanged knowing glances as we passed each other.

*

When I reported to Professor Vesanus, he asked, "Did you learn anything?"

"I learned that the Universe views us as misfits."

"The Universe is indifferent," he countered. "What did you really learn from interviewing Professor Matooh?"

"I learned, I learned, I don't really know what I learned."

"I hope you have learned that to know and to understand ourselves—first, we must understand others, and second, we must not take ourselves too seriously."

Beirut's Myriad Eyes[125]
Beirut, Lebanon, 1986

"Your father needs you," shuddered my mother's voice across two seas and 6761 miles.

I could hear the tears in her eyes. "What is it? What happened?" I gasped.

"They operated, thinking it was his gallbladder. It was not."

"Mother. What are you saying? What did they find?"

"Cancer in his pancreas. He's turning yellow. They just opened and closed. Told us nothing can be done."

*

Gaping eyes, crying eyes, laughing eyes, searching eyes, blind eyes, bloody eyes, black eyes, eyes that see through steel, and the eyes of the many-eyed Greek giant, *Argus Panoptes,* were all waiting for me in Beirut when I landed in Damascus.

"Where in America do you live?" asked the Syrian customs officer.

"In Oklahoma."

"I see you're a doctor. Why don't you return to serve your country?"

"Because there's a Civil War."

"So why are you returning now?"

"Because my father is sick."

"Be careful, Doctor. Lebanon is a dangerous place and you might not be able to get out with its port and airport closed."

---

[125] Pre-published, *AL JADID* Vol. 22 No. 75 December 2018.

*

The Syrian taxi driver who drove me to the Lebanese border, refused to take me into Lebanon. "Try these other taxis," he pointed.

Dragging my suitcase, I asked the line of taxi drivers, one by one, but they all declined with knowing eyes. It was a cold night, rendered arid by the desert wind.

Standing alone in the bleak night, I prayed and waited for a Lebanese taxi. The flights out of Damascus leave at 4 a.m. and the traveling Lebanese usually arrive at the Syrian border near midnight. There was no shelter, no bathroom, and no café in sight.

Close to midnight, I saw a pair of cat eyes flickering in the distance. It was a Lebanese taxi with a family of five in it. As soon as they went into the customs office, I approached the driver.

"Are you taking them all the way to the Damascus airport?" I asked with shivering lips.
"Yes," he answered, lit a cigarette, and blew the smoke into my tired eyes.
"When will you be back?"
"As soon as I drop them off."
"How long will that be?"
"About three hours."
"I'll wait for you if you would take me to Beirut."
"It'll be fifty dollars."
"That's fine. Is there a restroom around?"
"Just go on the side of the road. The desert has no eyes."

*

On the way to Beirut, we passed through more checkpoints than road signs. My American passport was never enough; I had to show my Lebanese passport, which stated that I was a doctor, not a good thing to declare at checkpoints. In exchange for letting me pass, I had to answer medical questions and prescribe detailed treatments.

Just before sunrise, my father's home in Beirut lay hidden in darkness except my father's lone, bedroom light. My mother opened the door, held me to her chest, and sobbed hot tears from her sleepless eyes.

"He's in terrible pain and vomits everything we give him and everything we don't give him."
"What does that mean, Mother?"
"He even vomits his own saliva. Nothing is going through."
"He must be totally obstructed, then."
"You're the doctor. Come see for yourself."

*

In the silent room, my father lay pale, frail, and listless. His eyes lit up like fog lights when he saw me, but he could hardly move. An intravenous line hung, dripping into his vein.

"The pain is horrible, it nauseates me, I can't sleep," he whispered, holding my hand.
"How about morphine?"
"There's no morphine in Beirut. Pharmacies are afraid to keep it because the addicted fighters break in and kill to get it."
"How about the American University Hospital?"
"They have very little left and only give it to their post-operative patients."

At sunrise, the *athan* from the surrounding minarets wafted into the sick room, calling the faithful to prayer with *allahu akbar... hayyu alassalat...* The Prophet's land, Arabia, with its vast expanses of silent, spreading sands was the angelic larynx wherefrom issued these siren tunes. My father closed his Christian eyes and whispered, "Listen. Only God can make such heavenly music. It pacifies my soul and dulls the pain. Tennyson was right when he said:

> '*Music that [sic] gentlier on the spirit lies,*
> *Than tired eyelids upon tired eyes.*' " [126]

I felt the pancreatic cancer and distended gallbladder when I examined his abdomen. His eyes were yellow and his mouth, dry. Pain surged with the slightest movement or cough. "We have to divert your bile by connecting your gallbladder to your intestines," I informed him. "This will help your pain and prolong your life."

"How do we do that?" He quizzed with closed eyes.

"With surgery."

"But I just had surgery. Why didn't they do that when they opened me?"

"Perhaps because the surgeons were too overwhelmed with the critically wounded."

"You mean they didn't want to waste time on an old, dying man?" He asked with a knowing smile.

"I can take you back with me to America."

"We'll have to fly out of Damascus. The road is long and full of potholes. There are no ambulances. Every ditch would hurt. The trip would kill me."

"I'll give you morphine before you get into the car and as needed during the journey."

"But, you forgot, there is no morphine in Beirut. They only gave me one shot after surgery and that was all they could spare."

---

[126] Alfred Lord Tennyson (1809-1892), British Poet.

*

The morning ambled in. The newspaper, *Al-Nahar*, was delivered and I read the headlines to my father who was too feeble to sit or read. Visitors came. Street noises grew louder. Cars honked. Vendors screamed their wares into the air. I knew that I had to find a way. I took off to the American University Hospital. The pharmacist, Najeeb Nadir, was my friend during medical school days.

"What are you doing here?" He gasped when he saw me.

"I'm back for a visit."

"Are you mad? We're all trying to leave and you're back for a visit? Beirut is schizophrenic, split into two sides, and they spend their days and nights shooting at each other. The hospital is full of casualties. We're out of antibiotics. The wounded are dying of infection. Get out of this hell."

"My father is sick."

"I know. I was here when he had his surgery."

"I need some morphine so I can transport him to the States."

"Morphine? I can't give you morphine. We hardly have enough for our surgical patients."

"I can't transport him without morphine. He needs urgent surgery."

Najeeb's eyes roamed as if thinking, as if searching, as if scouting for informants. He opened a side door and smuggled me in.

"There's a big man, Abu Jawad, who stands at the corner of Bliss and Jeanne d'Ark. He has a newspaper stand and sells drugs on the side. Tell him I sent you."

"Does he sell morphine?"

"I doubt it, but if there's any morphine in Beirut, he can get it."

*

Abu Jawad, six-foot-six and 300 pounds, stood like a colossus, wearing a wry smile beneath his bushy, black mustache. His circumspect eyes scanned me as I approached, stopped, and feigned interest in his newspapers and magazines.

"Do you have the *Daily Star*?" I asked after I browsed a bit.

"It comes in the afternoon because they have to translate the morning papers."

"Do you know Najeeb Nadir?" I asked after another browsing pause.

"No. Who's he?"

"He's the pharmacist at the American University Hospital."

"Are you looking to buy something?" He asked, roaming his eyes in all directions.

"I'm a doctor. My father is sick. I need to transport him to America. He's in terrible pain. I can't transport him without morphine."

"What kind of doctor are you?"

"I'm a headache doctor."

"What's your father's name?"

"Let's keep names out of this. He's political. That is all I am allowed to say."

"What's your name?"

"Call me Hakeem. I can't tell you my real name because you'll know who my father is."

"How many tablets do you need?"

"He can't swallow. I need injectable morphine."

"Injectable? Only the other side has injectable morphine. It's too dangerous. I can't go there."

"Can you send someone?"

"No. They'll tear him to pieces."

"Can we bribe someone?"

"Give me time to make calls.   Come back this afternoon."

*

Back home, my father's room was full of well-wishers and he was alive with interaction. My mother complained to me. "I can't keep them out. He needs rest. He does not need visitors."

"No, Mom. Visitors distract him. He has less pain when he's with friends."

"Are you sure?"

"Yes, Mother. He needs his friends more than he needs us now."

*

In the afternoon, I re-visited Abu Jawad.   He was expecting me.

"They have morphine on the other side, but it's not for sale. They need it for their wounded. But, the militia-captain's wife has been sick with a headache for three weeks, a bad headache that no one has been able to break. He told me, when he found out that you're a headache doctor, that if you could break her headache, he would give you ten vials."

"What's his name?"

"No one knows his real name.   His militia name is Ghadab. He was an American Marine before returning here to lead the militia."

"How do I get to him?

"We'll drive you from here to the no-man's line. He'll pick you up in his Jeep, take you in, and bring you back to us."

"What if he kidnaps me?"

"He said that he would hold you for ransom only if you couldn't break his wife's headache."

"How can I be sure that he will bring me back?"

"He's a newlywed. He'll do anything to get his bride back to bed," he smiled.

"Do you trust him?"

"No, but he does keep his word."

"How much will all this cost?"

"We'll charge you $100 to take you to the no-man's line and another $100 to bring you back here. Ghadab does not want money; he just wants his bride back."

"When do we leave?"

"Come back at six. We'll deliver you to the no-man's line by seven and we'll pick you up at eleven. He can only spend three hours with you before he goes on night watch."

*

Back home, I discussed the plan with my father. He told me that it would be insane to go to the other side because, being from a political family, they would never release me.

"Why don't you have him send his wife to us instead. No one will harm her here. Despite the war, women are still revered. When she returns to him headache free, he can then send you the morphine."

"Where would I examine her? I don't have privileges at the American University Hospital."

"You can examine her here. Everyone, including Ghadab, knows that I'm dying and, in our war culture, dying men are deemed trustworthy."

*

At six I told Abu Jawad of our plan and divulged my father's name. He agreed with my father. I then gave him $200 for the two trips that I hoped Ghadab's bride would take in my place and pleaded with him to convince Ghadab that his bride would be safe at my father's home. We agreed that the best time for me and for her would be tomorrow morning. I could start seeing her at nine and she should be ready to leave by noon at the latest.

*

On the way home, I stopped at the pharmacy and begged Najeeb Nadir to give me six needles, two syringes, injectable cortisone, and a local anesthetic. Neither my father nor I slept that night. We talked and dozed off until the *athan* sounded the sunrise call to prayer.

Soon the house filled with guests, coffee, cigarettes, politics, newspapers, and stories about last night's battles between East and West Beirut. I prepared one of the bedrooms for the examination and asked my mother to be my nurse.

Nine o'clock. No young bride. Ten o'clock. No young bride. Eleven o'clock. A car stopped. Two women came out with one wearing dark glasses. I waved at them from the veranda. The driver, Abu Jawad, nodded and winked at me.

We escorted the mother and daughter into the prepared bedroom. I listened to the bride's story. She was not a typical headache sufferer. Her headaches began when she was rear ended by a speeding car three weeks before. Her examination confirmed my suspicion that she was suffering from a whiplash headache. I had her lie face down and gave her a quadruple occipital nerve block. In five minutes, the headache disappeared, and she started to sob, not because of pain, but because of joy. I educated her about what she should and should not do and wrote a detailed procedure report just in case she should need more nerve blocks in the future. She thanked me with a hug and then, from her purse, she produced a package and put it in my hand. My mother and I escorted them to the car. She did not have to use her sunglasses when she walked out. Abu Jawad's eyes glowed from under his bushy eyebrows as he drove off.

*

Back in my father's room, after the last guest had left for lunch, I opened the package. There were ten vials of morphine. The vials were old with brown precipitates in the bottoms. The yellowed, threadbare, paper label on the package read:

Sulfate de morphine 10mg/cc
République française
Algérie, 1962

With twenty-four-year-old-French-Army morphine from the year when colonizing France ceded Algeria back to the Algerians, we were able to transport my father from Beirut to America where the surgeon connected his gallbladder to his intestines. When he returned to Beirut, he was no longer yellow nor in pain. He lived nine more months and died peacefully at home with my mother and sister by his side.

*

As I stood in the condolences line at my father's funeral in our hometown, Amioun, the young bride gave me a hug and whispered in my ear, "I've not had a headache since you gave me the block. I'm also pregnant and my husband thanks you.

Here's his phone number if you should ever need anything from our side."

*

We shall not hate; we love; we shall not hate
We are the noble births of earth and fate.[127]

---

[127] From the poetry book, *Loves and Lamentation of a Life Watcher*, by Hanna Saadah, from the poem, *The Refugee*.

Homo senex[128]
Beirut, 1996

At student gatherings, his name, like the Concorde, would land and take off at supersonic speeds, for he was both feared and revered, not loved but respected, not affable but accessible, not arrogant but humbling, not a good lecturer but captivating, and not affectionate but a mighty healer. We all wanted to be like him but were afraid to become him. And although he never tried to intimidate us with his vast repertoire of knowledge, we could not help but feel intimidated because of the steep cliff between his lighthouse mind and our book-mired brains. That was how we all felt about Dr. Kinglea when we graduated from our medical school nest and flew away to build our own nests in the sundry corners of Earth.

Isn't it preposterous that, whereas distance and time bury memory, death resurrects it? I had forgotten all about Dr. Kinglea until forty years later when I saw his young, handsome photograph hanging above his obituary. That was when my memories welled up like tears and brought him back to life. Why is it that we fondly remember those who had influenced us, mostly when we learn of their deaths?

It was my habit each time I visited my fatherland, Lebanon, to promenade up and down my alma mater campus, which, like an embroidered tapestry, draped the slope from the crown of Beirut down to the Mediterranean Sea. It was during one of those nostalgic visits to the American University of Beirut that I spotted Dr. Kinglea, with his silver-topped cane and silver head, sitting on a solitary bench, gazing at the sea. I approached, and from a reverent distance, greeted.

---

[128] Pre-published, *The Bulletin*, Oklahoma County Medical Society, November-December 2017.

"Good afternoon, Dr. Kinglea."

Awakened from his reverie, he peered at me with gleeful eyes, twice smiled my name, and inquired, "Where have you been all these years?"

"In Oklahoma, Sir."

"Come then, sit next to me, and tell me all about you."

Invitingly, he tapped the bench with his elegant cane, and I obeyed, sitting down with knees locked and arms in lap. After an awkward stretch of quietude, I briefly related my life story. He nodded approvingly as if I were one of his ambassadors to the world. Then, with a sigh of silence, I politely reciprocated.

"And how about you, Sir? Well and content, I hope."

"Well, yes, but content, no."

"How come, Sir?"

" *'No memory of having starred, atones for later disregard, or keeps the end from being hard,'*[129] said your Robert Frost.

"That's doleful, Sir. What happened?"

"After a lifetime of loyalty to this institution, I'm still heartbroken at its disloyalty to me. *'It is the fashion that discarded fathers should have thus little mercy on their flesh,'*[130] said King Lear," he intoned. "Gratitude may be a virtue of individuals but not of institutions."

"I am astonished, Sir. You embodied this institution, and to many of us, you were the institution. Whatever went wrong?"

"Nothing went wrong. I lost my powers to age, as we all do, and when I became powerless, I also became worthless. *'This is the state of man, today he puts forth the tender leaves of hope, tomorrow blossoms and bears his blushing honors thick upon him, the third day comes a frost, a killing frost...and*

---

[129] *Stardom*, a poem by Robert Frost (1874-1963) American poet.

[130] *King Lear*, a play by William Shakespeare.

he falls as I do.'[131] I am naught but a childless widower, aging alone."

With my head bowed under the heft of his words, I sank into an echoing well of reflection and waited.

"I never thought I would quote from *Wolsey's Farewell to his Greatness*, but these lines often seem to find their way into my memory," he resumed after an awkward pause. "Shakespeare gives me solace and I read him often. Now that I dwell in the twilight of my eighties, he's my only remaining friend. But, let us leave our melancholy to wallow alone in the mire of memories, and let us redirect our conversation toward joy. Tell me about the Oklahoma people. Have your patients been as loyal to you as you have been to them?"

"My patients are my family, Sir, but ingratitude that gives birth to lawsuits is ever present in our medical wombs."

"That's one problem we don't have here, but we do have others that are far worse. There are no perfect countries on earth, and no matter where we choose to live, we must live in our times."

"What are your thoughts about early retirement, Sir?" I asked, redirecting the conversation. "I often consider it when bureaucracy becomes unbearably burdensome."

"Ah, *'the law's delay, the insolence of office, and the spurns that patient merit of the unworthy takes,'* "[132] he chided. "You're still too young to resort to retirement as a refuge from bureaucratic ills. Just wait and retirement will come to you one day, as it did me—but you must be prepared otherwise it will diminish you. *'Age takes hold of us by surprise,'*[133] said Goethe. Oh, how smug, how unprepared, and how unaware I was when age surprised me."

---

[131] Wolsey's farewell to his greatness from *Henry VIII*, a play by William Shakespeare.

[132] *To be or not to be* from *Hamlet*, a play by William Shakespeare.

[133] Johann Wolfgang von Goethe (1749-1832) German writer, author of the play *Foust*.

I nodded, but more out of politeness than conviction. He was trying to instruct me, using Hamlet's words, that one must not shy away from struggle but, instead, one must prepare for it. When he sensed my uncertainty, his eyes beamed with tenderness. Then, as if he could hear my thoughts, he added, " *'Who would fardels bear, to grunt and sweat under a weary life, but that the dread of something after death, the undiscovered country from whose bourn no traveler returns, puzzles the will, and makes us rather bear those ills we have than fly to others that we know not of.'* "[134]

"I understand your meaning, Sir, but as I get older, struggle becomes more difficult and surrender, more appealing."

He nodded disapprovingly and took a sudden turn.

"Do you ever think about old age?" He whispered.
"I think about death, Sir."
"But do you think about old age?" He persisted.
"I'm afraid not, Sir. It seems too distant to be real."
"Indeed." He beat the ground with his cane. "Youth is taught about life, about disease, and about death, but never about old age. We grow up thinking that old *Homo sapiens* are a different species, a *Homo senex*[135] perhaps. In medical school, we should be taught more about aging so it will become real to us, and so that we can better prepare for it. Nothing surprises us when we're prepared; it is the surprise that bites."

In a quiet moment of contemplation, I gazed at the sea's whispering waves and at the unsurprised horizon, preparing to cradle the sun.

---

[134] *To be or not to be* from *Hamlet*, a play by William Shakespeare.

[135] *Senex* comes from Latin, meaning *the old man*.

"What's the first thing you see in very old people?" he queried, cracking my reverie.

"Frailty, slowness, loss of form, loss of elegance, loss of beauty, and loss of appeal," I replied.

"And what's the first emotion you experience?"

"Pity, sadness, and at times, revulsion."

"You prove my point. You've not been taught a thing about aging. If you had, you would have better answers because you would view the *Homo senex* differently."

"How do you mean, Sir?"

"Your eyes should be trained to see the very old, when they were young and beautiful, rather than old and pitiful. Go ahead; look at me now and try to see me, as once I was, a young, handsome medical student. Can you do that in your mind's eye? Can you reconstruct the bright young man out of this old relic?"

"It's hard, Sir," I confessed.

"That's why we need to train medical students in the art of reconstruction and re-perception."

"And how do we do that, Sir?"

"When you return to your medical work in Oklahoma, start by having your very old patients bring their wedding pictures to their appointments. Study their young pictures before you study their charts, ask them about their young lives before you inquire about their chronic disorders, address the young person lurking inside of them before you address the old person they evince, and you will quickly discover that very young souls are still frolicking inside their old, frail bodies."

"Has this method ever been tried, Sir?"

"No, but why can't you be the first to try it? *The tragedy of aging is not that one is old, but that one is young,'* said Oscar Wilde."[136]

"Is that really true, Sir?"

---

[136] Oscar Wilde (1854-1900), Irish poet, writer, playwright.

"Indeed. Inside of me lurks a very young man, ready to devour life, but my old body censors it. Oh, how rejuvenated I would feel if I were to be re-perceived as young?"

Then, with brimming eyes, he turned his head away and asked, "Are you familiar with the work of Beauvoir?"

"No, Sir. Who's he?"

"Simone de Beauvoir[137], John Paul Sartre's lifelong companion, wrote decisively about aging, but her work languishes in unread books. She made two discoveries which, if heeded, would brighten the tenebrous [sic] ancienthood of the *Homo senex*."

"What did she discover, Sir?"

"Her first discovery was that we do not experience old age from within but from without, because society sees old age as a shameful secret that is too unseemly to mention. *'Old age is not discovered; it is imposed from the outside,'* she contends."

"Why isn't she recognized for this amazing discovery, Sir?"

"Because she admonishes us to spend more time saving people from old age than we spend saving them from death. Medically, we are trained to fight death, not to fight age, and that's a major flaw."

"What was her second discovery, Sir?"

"That old age, rather than death, is what should be contrasted with life because old age is life's parody whereas death transforms life into a destiny, preserving it by giving it the absolute dimension. *'Death does away with time,'* she contends."

He discoursed profusely about revitalizing old age by bringing its inner youth to the forefront. "We need to re-

---

[137] *The Coming of Age*, Simone de Beauvoir (1908-1986), French philosopher-writer. Simone de Beauvoir and John Paul Sartre are buried together at the Montparnasse Cemetery in Paris.

throne the dethroned King Lear in us and leave the affairs of the state to his younger progeny," he announced, holding his staff erect as if it were a scepter.

When it was time to leave, I offered to walk him home.

"No, thank you," he demurred. "I am awaiting the sunset. That's my way of readying myself for *'the undiscovered country from whose bourn no traveler returns.'*[138] I do not wish to be surprised again."

In flight, on my way back to Oklahoma, the similarity between discarded batteries, which had suffused the world with light, and the very old among us, who had infused the world with life, helped me understand Simone de Beauvoir's view of death as the absolute dimension that grants us our destinies.

*

My chance encounter with Dr. Kinglea forever transformed me. Indeed, Ralph Waldo Emerson was correct when he said:

"The chief event of life is the day in which we have encountered a mind that startled us."[139]

---

[138] *The undiscovered country from whose bourn no traveler returns,* is death, from *Hamlet,* a play by William Shakespeare.

[139] Ralph Waldo Emerson (1803-1882), American writer.

Adieu

Veterans and Elders

Let us not pretend

Though life may decimate and send

Our unsuspecting souls across

Uncharted times and unfamiliar places

Wherever we are loved

We end.

Books by Author
Available on Amazon.com

Poetry

1. **Loves and Lamentations of a Life Watcher (1987)**
2. **Vast Awakenings (1990)**
3. **Familiar Faces (1993)**
4. **Four and a Half Billion Years (2002)**
5. **When You Happened to Me (2016)**

Novels

1. **The Mighty Weight of Love (2005)**
2. **Letters (2008)**
       Pre-published as *Epistole*
3. **Back from Iraq (2010)**
4. **Twenty Lost Years (2015)**
       Pre-published as *The Diary of Aziz Al-Mitfi*

Short Stories

1. **Both Banks of Life - *40 short stories* (2016)**
2. **Veteran and Elder Stories – *38 stories* (2020)**

The End

Made in the USA
Coppell, TX
06 July 2020